GRAYBLOOD
◄COMPASS►

SAMANTHA RAYMER

DRAGONWOLF
PUBLISHING

Copyright © 2024 by Samantha Raymer

All rights reserved.

No part of this book may be reproduced in any form or by any electronic or mechanical means, including information storage and retrieval systems, without written permission from the author, except for the use of brief quotations in a book review.

The events and people of this book are purely fictional figments of the author's imagination. Any similarity to real people, places, or events is entirely coincidental.

Paperback ISBN: 979-8-9875269-0-3

Ebook ISBN: 979-8-9875269-2-7

Hardcover ISBN: 979-8-9875269-1-0

For those with "impossible" dreams.

CONTENTS

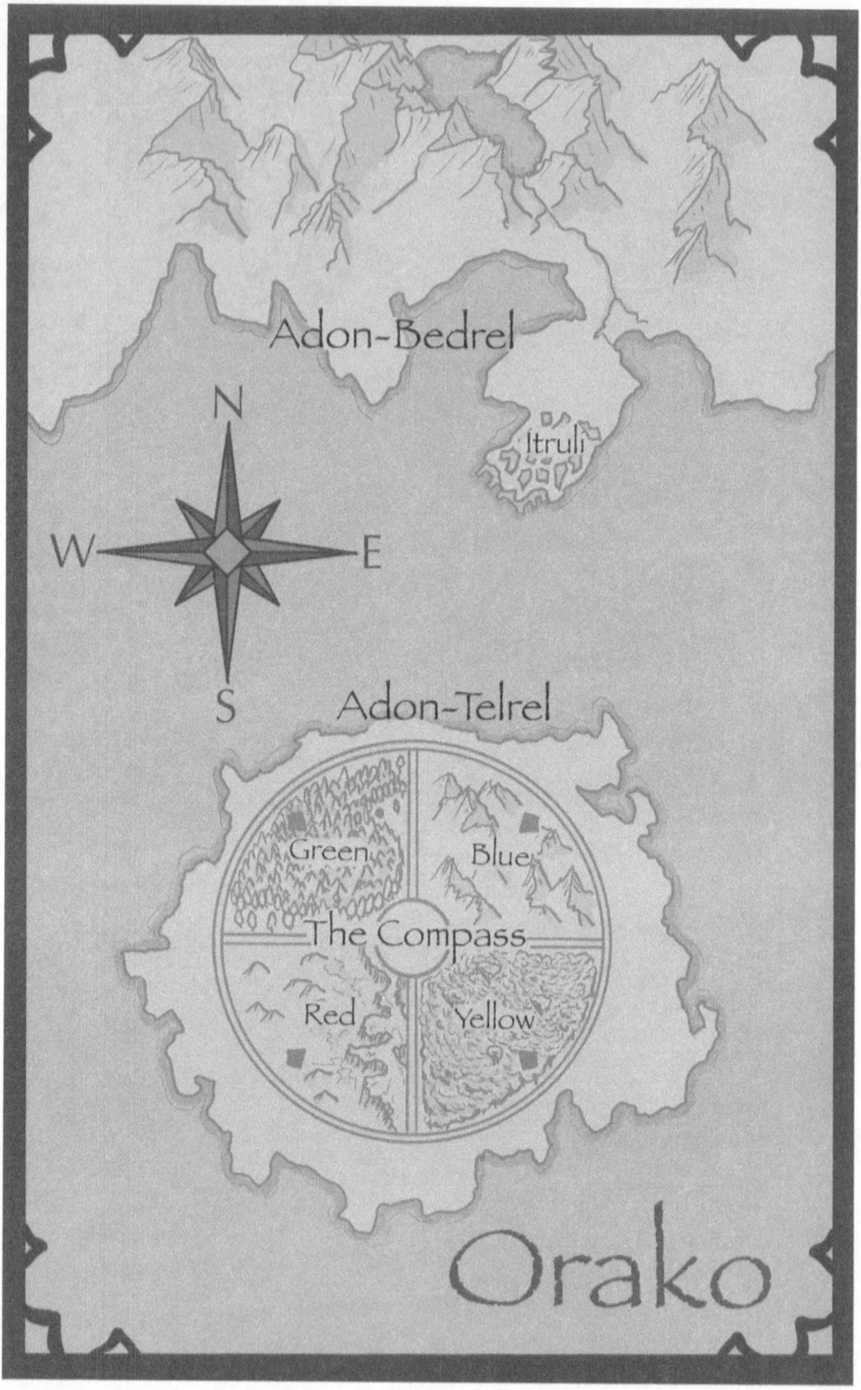

Adon-Bedrel
Itruli
N
W
E
S
Adon-Telrel
Green
Blue
The Compass
Red
Yellow
Orako

Karelth
Akareldia
Ekal
Loric's Home
The Stronghold
The Horizon's Teeth
Aererest
N
W
E
S
Akaidia
Crystal Lake

Above all else, guard your

heart, for everything you

do flows from it.

Proverbs 4:23 NIV

I

RUNE

The exact moment she regained consciousness, Rune didn't know.

What she did know was that she was falling.

Falling very, very fast.

Her eyelids fluttered open, only to be met by suffocating darkness. Wind whipped her cheeks as she plummeted through what seemed to be an endless abyss. She opened her mouth, wanting to scream, to cry out for help to any who might hear her, but her voice was swallowed by the intoxicating silence.

Where was she?

Who was she?

All she knew was her name—and that wherever she was, she didn't belong.

The wind was forcefully sucked from her chest as her body hit the water with a sickening smack, the echo disappearing into the darkness beyond. She sank into the near-black waves, bubbles escaping from her lips as she was pulled down, down into a sea of wet nothingness. The water tugged at her body, consuming her, claiming her as its own. Pain crept into her bones, tearing through her like a rabid animal. Her lungs began to burn, craving the air that was trapped above the surface.

I'm going to die.

The thought slipped into her mind, bright and blinding, gripping her tightly.

I can't die. I don't even remember who I am.

It was the light she saw first, breaking through the still, malevolent waters. Then there was the soft, soundless thud of her body hitting the bottom, the grains of sand shifting beneath her fingers. Something tugged at her consciousness—voices, thoughts, feelings, none of them her own.

I have to get to the light.

Rune righted herself, ignoring the throbbing ache of her lungs. Her toes dug into the dirt, reminding her that she wasn't dead yet. The light flashed steadily in front of her like a beacon, beckoning her closer with each passing moment.

Her lungs heaved as she pushed off the gravelly lakebed, pumping her arms and legs as hard as her screaming muscles could bear. The light seemed to get no nearer, but still, she swam, her body crying out for air. A migraine pierced through her skull, and black spots swam in front of her vision.

I'm not going to make it.

She pumped even harder, thrashing against the current's pull and ignoring everything else around her. Nothing else mattered. Nothing mattered except reaching that light.

Her stomach knotted, and the urge to inhale became unbearable, her lungs crying out in distress. Her vision turned fuzzy, and she felt her consciousness begin to slip away just as she broke the surface of the water.

For a long, blissful moment, she sat there, treading water and gulping in air. After a pause, survival instinct kicked in, and she found herself swimming towards the light once more, her heart thundering in her ears with every stroke. Darkness pushed in around her, clouding her vision, making it impossible to see any farther than a few strokes ahead. Something told her that she was underground, but how she got there, she could only guess.

The darkness thinned, allowing her a glimpse of what appeared to be an island jutting out of the water. Her heart leaped, and she pushed ahead, ordering her aching body to keep going a little longer.

The island was far from large, an insignificant spire of rock breaking the surface of the lake. But any land at all looked extremely appealing at the moment, and it wasn't long before Rune found herself jamming her fingers into the small cracks in the stone while she pulled herself up.

A pale light drifted down from far above, somewhere beyond the dark shadows. Rune examined herself, stunned to discover that she was entirely unscathed. She was clothed in a simple gray tunic and shorts, and her feet were bare. A strand of ash brown hair was plastered to her cheek, and she brushed it back, attempting to tame the soaking mess that seemed determined to cling to her skin.

"You're awake," someone declared suddenly, nearly making Rune stumble over the edge of the island. The voice was thick and heavily accented, reverberating off the cavern and making it difficult to understand some of the words. *"Newcomers like you*

are supposed to be unconscious," it continued, addressing Rune as though speaking to an old friend. *"How unusual—perhaps you could help me."*

Rune pivoted in a circle, her seafoam-colored eyes meeting nothing but darkness. "I can't help you if I don't know who you are."

"I am nothing more than a power source for the great horror you will soon need to face," came the reply, doing nothing to clear away the cloud of confusion enveloping Rune. *"I was imprisoned here by the very same person who now imprisons you."* A pause. *"You shouldn't be here, Rune. So tell me—why are you?"*

Rune scowled, deciding to ignore the fact that this faceless voice had just addressed her by name. "You clearly know more than I do." The words came out sharper than she meant them to, but she didn't take them back. She didn't know who or what she was angry at, but it felt good to be feeling an emotion other than fear.

"Quite the contrary. My knowledge of this place is extremely limited...courtesy of its creator. If I were able to give you any more information, I would."

Information.

What she wouldn't give for information in that moment—especially information about herself.

Every time she tried to push deeper into her mind, to recall something—anything—about her past...she was met with nothing. The memories were *there*—none of them were gone, as she'd first thought. Yet something stood in the way—a barrier, a wall to keep them from reaching the front of her consciousness. Her stomach twisted with frustration, and her throat closed as panic set in.

Was she really stuck here?

Stuck with no recollection of being anywhere else?

Rune shook her head to clear the thoughts away, not ready to face them just yet. "If you aren't going to tell me who I am or how I got here, can you at least show me who I'm speaking with?"

The voice seemed to hesitate. *"If you're certain."*

Almost instantly, a low rumble filled the air, shaking the entire island. The lake began to swirl, dark waves churning violently against the rocks. A massive serpentine head broke the surface of the water, its neon purple eyes gleaming dangerously. Teal scales lined its back, and wavy orange tendrils drifted from its head, matching the similarly colored webbing that flared out from its neck.

Rune's eyes widened, and she took a shaky step away from the creature, her blank mind proving to be extremely unhelpful in the face of such an intimidating sight. Before she could so much as part her lips to form any words, however, six more identical heads emerged from the already churning waters, the seven of them bobbing and weaving around one another in an oddly hypnotic motion.

Her body had no idea what to do with such an encounter, and she froze, her thoughts choking her. She was torn—part of her begging to flee, but the crazier half of her mind wanting to examine the creature.

Just as the panic seemed to be getting the best of her, a thread of sanity slipped through the chaos, wrapping tightly around her consciousness and somehow managing to steady it. She kept her attention trained on the hydra, her mind running through a swift yet effective overlook of its motions. It didn't seem to have any ill intent towards her, and the brief moment of clarity dispelled the haze of blind fear, a technique that felt well-used in her mind.

A habit.

A routine.

Whatever it was, it was working.

The creature lowered its heads towards her, the front one coming so near that Rune could have reached out and touched it if she'd wanted to. She began to regain her nerve, slowly moving around the head, examining it.

"You're the one who's been talking to me?"

The hydra dipped its heads slightly in reply. *"I apologize if I frightened you. I am not used to being seen."*

Before she could respond, a strange glint in the corner of her eye caught her gaze, halting her train of thought. After a moment's examination, she realized that it was coming from a thick metal band wrapped around the creature's neck—around all of its necks. The material was unlike what she somehow knew to be normal silver or iron—it appeared to reflect a nonexistent light, gleaming with an unnatural sheen despite the dim environment. A blue film coated its surface, the color tugging at Rune's memory.

She'd seen that metal before.

And it was driving her insane that she couldn't remember where.

"Do you know anything that might help me? Anything at all?" Rune's voice hitched slightly with the words, making her realize just how terrified she was—and how alone. She knew *nothing*. Nothing about her past, nothing about how she even got into this situation, and nothing about where she would go from here.

The hydra hung its heads. *"As I told you—if I had any more information that could be useful to you, I would tell you. We are in very similar situations, Rune. We are both trapped here, backed into a corner with a terrible purpose looming over our heads. What you are about to face is going to be anything but easy. I'll do what I can to help you from down here, but my powers are severely limited."*

Rune shook her head slowly, taking a step back. *"Down* here? Where are we, anyway?"

"Beneath the arena," the hydra replied simply. *"You must find your way through. Set me free."*

A lump rose in Rune's throat, her stomach knotting itself into a ball. *An arena?* No specific memories returned to her, but she knew what an arena was—the single word making her already dire situation a whole new level of terrifying. "I can't do this, okay? Whatever *this* is, I want no part of it."

"I'm afraid you don't have much of a choice." The hydra's eyes were filled with sadness. *"I have to send you on your way, now, lest the creator realize that there's something different about you. You could be the one to set us all free, you know—there is power in your blood. The kind of power that no one will ever be able to take from you."*

Rune swallowed hard. "I can't use a power I don't even remember having."

The hydra ignored the comment, lowering its front head so that its eyes were level with Rune's. *"You complete the playing field, Rune. The only way out is through. Destroy it. Destroy it all. Then you'll see—then we'll all see."*

Before Rune could form a reply, the light returned again, this time circling around her and causing black spots to dance in the corners of her vision. The world began to blur, and her body refused to respond to any fragment of a command she could muster, her brain feeling like sludge. She didn't know she had fallen until she hit the water, a chilling wetness seeping into her body as unconsciousness overcame her once more.

2

RUNE

Lukewarm water seeped into Rune's skin, gentle waves lapping against her face as she slowly regained consciousness. She sat up with a start, a coughing fit rocking her body as a brief moment of panic gripped her.

Where am I?

She frowned, her mind working through the few memories she'd managed to gather.

The lake.

The hydra.

The warnings.

This must be the arena, Rune realized, blinking a few times as her eyes adjusted. She had awoken in a sizable cavern, with an opening on the far side that allowed beams of early morning light to stream down from the outside. Faintly glowing moss crawled up the walls and ceiling, illuminating the ankle-deep layer of water that completely coated the ground.

A frown crossed Rune's features. *There's no one else here.*

Ripples disrupted the glassy surface of the pond as she

adjusted her position, pulling her knees into her chest and resting her chin on them. Her mind worked through the few memories she had, trying to make sense of the situation.

I woke up, I fell into the lake, I met the hydra, and now I'm—in a cave? A shiver rippled down her spine despite the temperate environment, a feeling of unmistakable loneliness and terror settling deep into her stomach.

She was the prey, backed blindly into a corner with nothing to do except wait for a hunter. *Nothing more than prey...* Rune straightened at the thought, shaking her head vigorously. *I have no memories, no way to know what I'm up against, and no idea how I even got here in the first place—but I have to survive. At least—I have to try.*

Inhaling deeply, she forced herself to stand, examining her soaked figure. Her outfit was almost identical to the one she remembered in the lake, but a few of the elements were new—she now wore a pair of sandals with straps that wound halfway up her shins, and a simple leather belt was fastened around her waist. Upon further examination, she realized that there was actually an unadorned dagger attached to the belt, its hilt fashioned out of a black metal with a silver knob at the end.

At least they didn't leave me unarmed. Rune drew the weapon, examining the perfectly polished blade for a brief moment before sliding it back into its sheath. A faint spark of familiarity in the back of her mind told her that she'd used a knife such as this one before, her muscles knowing exactly what to do with it even if her head didn't.

A hint of a smile toyed with Rune's lips. *If I can fight, I have a chance.* She looked up, examining the open side of the cave. The ground slowly sloped upward, forming a ramp that hopefully led to the surface. It was the only exit, and despite her desire to explore, Rune couldn't help but feel a bit cautious. *I can't possibly be alone. What if someone knows I'm here?*

Only one way to find out, I guess.

With a final glance around at the lichen-covered walls, she began making her way towards the cave entrance, the water displacing beneath her feet with each step. She reached the ramp, holding up one arm to shield her eyes from the sunlight as the other hand covered the hilt of her dagger. A faint aroma of tree sap and damp earth filled her nostrils, the air shifting quickly from the stale, musty cave atmosphere to the fresh, free feeling of the woods.

Thankfully, no one jumped out to attack her when she reached the surface, and she felt her shoulders relax slightly, her arms falling to her side. Rows of massive trees loomed above her, their branches locking together and forming a leafy canopy. Trickles of unaffected sunlight streamed through, joining with the green-tinted rays that forced their way through the roof of foliage. A smile flickered across Rune's features as a gust of playful wind brushed against her skin, tossing her hair around for a moment and disturbing the carpet of spindly grass that coated the ground.

Nothing but trees in all directions. This place certainly doesn't look like an arena—though I suppose I don't exactly have many memories to compare it to.

A sudden rustle nearby shattered her train of thought, and her hand shot to her weapon, instantly alert. The air felt silent —almost too silent, the strange lapse in noise causing her body to go rigid. *I'm not alone.*

She slowly backed away from where she figured the noise to

have come from, positioning herself behind a few particularly thick tree trunks to shield her presence from view. A scream welled up in her throat as a hand shot out from a nearby patch of undergrowth, gripping her arm and dragging her into the foliage.

The only thing that stopped her from lashing out with her dagger was the pair of dark, youthful eyes that stared back at her, not an ounce of hostility in their depths. She paused, allowing herself to examine the newcomer.

The eyes belonged to a boy—one who looked about her age, or maybe just younger. He held a pale finger to his lips, glancing nervously at the dagger in her hand.

Glaring, she sheathed it.

"What do you think you're doing?" she hissed, keeping her voice low.

The boy fidgeted uncomfortably. "Saving your life." He let go of her arm, nodding curtly at the clearing where the cave was located.

For a moment, she didn't see anything—but after a moment, a flash of movement caught her eye, and a lanky teenager stepped out from behind the trees. Rune's blood went cold at the sight of the wickedly curved blade in his hand, her breath catching in her throat. The boy scanned the area, a sense of unmotivated malevolence glinting in his eye.

"Who is that?" The words were barely off her lips before the boy clapped a hand over her mouth, an expression of panic written across his pale features. He shook his head vigorously at her, glancing up nervously. The blood drained from his face suddenly, making Rune's heart skip a beat.

The teenager was looking *right at them.*

"*Don't move*," the boy whispered, his voice nothing more than a breath in her ear. Rune certainly didn't trust him, but the person in the clearing did *not* look friendly, so she decided to take her chances.

The teenager took a few slow steps towards their hiding place, cocking his head slightly as though he knew they were there. He didn't appear to have seen them, but he was certainly about to, and Rune found her fingers twitching towards her dagger once again.

If I leap out now, I can catch him by surprise. She sent a glance sideways at the boy, who was sitting perfectly rigid. *He'd help me—at least, I think he would. Either way, I'm not going to just sit here and wait to be attacked.*

She shifted her weight slightly, moving into a position that would be easy enough to spring out of. Her fingers gripped the hilt of the dagger tightly, ready to draw it at a moment's notice. Beside her, the boy sat perfectly still, his eyes closed and his brow furrowed in concentration. Rune frowned. *What is he doing?*

Suddenly, there was a deafening crash, and it was only by a stroke of luck that Rune managed to keep herself from leaping out of the bush right then and there. The teenager startled just as badly, pivoting in a confused circle. His eyes found something out of Rune's field of vision, and he turned towards it, casting one last glance toward her hiding spot before hurrying off into the trees after it.

The boy let out a breath, craning his neck to make sure that the teen truly was gone before nodding to Rune. "We're clear. That was close."

Rune sat there for a moment, a sense of confusion passing over her. "Why did you help me?"

He shrugged, offering her a smile. "I wasn't about to let you die to some spawn killer. People like him wander around Citadels whenever a new batch shows up, hoping to eliminate the competition or whatever. It's not like it makes much of a difference, but some people are just hungry for violence."

Rune blinked at him, his words sounding like a whole foreign language. She decided to save the small detail questions for later, however, focusing on the ones she deemed to be a bit more pressing. "How many of us are there?"

The boy shrugged. "No one's ever counted. Not so many that you have to worry about people being everywhere, but there's definitely a lot." He reached up, brushing his slightly unruly auburn hair to the side. "I—" he hesitated. "I'm Nyk, by the way."

"Rune. I'm Rune." Saying her name out loud—the only remaining piece of her identity she possessed—it was surreal in a strange, haunting way. She really didn't know *anything* about who she was—or rather, who she had been. All she knew was her position now.

Starting over.

Nyk cast a nervous glance around at the area, fidgeting uncomfortably. "We should probably move—the farther we are from the Citadel, the less people there will be."

Rune cocked her head at him. "You want me to come with you?"

Realizing his words, he froze, his jaw slightly open as color seeped into his cheeks. "Sorry, I—I mean, if you wanted to. I'm already traveling with someone, and I'm sure she'd let you..." he trailed off, his eyes on Rune's neck.

A frown crossed Rune's features. "What is it?"

Suddenly, his face lit up. His grin only increased Rune's confusion, however, and she reached her hand up tentatively, slightly uncomfortable under his gaze. "Seriously—what?"

He shook his head. "I—I'll explain in a second. Follow me, though—Azalea's *definitely* gonna let you come with us."

Still bewildered but intrigued by his elated tone, Rune tentatively allowed herself to trail behind him as he wound through the trees, all the while keeping his back completely exposed to her. He knew she was armed, and he probably assumed that she didn't trust him—but he seemed to trust her. Her hand flitted to her dagger briefly, but she instantly shut down the thought, horrified that it had even entered her mind.

I'm not going to hurt Nyk.

Not unless he gives me a reason to.

They didn't walk for longer than a few minutes, and finally, Nyk's pace slowed, the trees around them growing closer and closer together. He came to a full stop, pivoting in a circle and scanning the area. "Azalea?"

In response, there was a loud rustling nearby, and Rune was caught off guard by a girl who practically melted out of the trees. Her brief moment of surprise was taken advantage of, and the girl—who Rune assumed to be Azalea—grabbed Nyk's arm, dragging him backward. Azalea then proceeded to reach to her side with her free hand, whipping out a dagger and angling it at Rune's throat. Her voice was ethereal, a mix of unnaturally soothing undertones and a fragile, melodic sound that didn't match the words she spoke at *all*.

"You have three seconds to tell me why I shouldn't kill you right now."

3
RUNE

Before Rune could draw her own dagger, Nyk wrenched his hand free of Azalea's grasp, placing himself between the two girls. "Just—wait, okay? She's not an enemy."

Azalea cocked an eyebrow at Nyk. "*Everyone* is an enemy until proven a friend, Nyk. You know that." Despite only being Rune's height, she looked to be the oldest of the three of them, and her uncannily pale eyes bored into Rune's very being. Rune's fingers twitched towards her dagger, but she kept it sheathed, deciding to trust Nyk's judgment.

Nyk shook his head again, backing up towards Rune. "Azalea, she's purple. I wouldn't have brought her here if she wasn't."

Rune blinked at him. *I mean, I guess I could've gotten bruised sometime during that whole underground lake ordeal... but is that really necessary?* Her lips parted, but no sounds formed on them, her mind stumbling over itself in an attempt to make sense of the random statement.

Azalea seemed to know exactly what Nyk meant, however, her arm falling to her side. A half smile worked its way onto her lips, a slight laugh escaping her. "She's one of us? Does *she* know that?"

Nyk turned to Rune, his face as red as his hair. "Uh—no. I don't think so."

Meeting Rune's eyes, Azalea's face shifted, the hostility fading from her expression. "Apologies if we confused you..."

"Rune," Rune interjected, offering a curt nod. "And it's alright—just *please* explain what's going on. It's bad enough not having any memories outside of this—wherever it is we are." A slight tremor slipped its way into her tone, and she had to choke it back, refusing to let her fear resurface just yet. *Not now. Not until I'm safe.*

Azalea's features twisted into a rueful smile. "This place is an arena—one that's divided into teams. Everyone here has a colored mark on their neck, which is what Nyk meant when he said that you were 'purple.'" She turned slightly to the side, lifting her dark, silky hair to reveal an unnaturally bright purple rectangle etched on the skin below her pointed ear. Rune's fingers went to her own neck, uncomfortably aware that her skin displayed the same design.

"You need to have a complete team to escape this place," Nyk added, his words sparking a sudden ember of hope deep within Rune's stomach.

"You mean there's a way out?"

Nyk and Azalea exchanged a glance. "I mean—no one's ever actually *done* it, not as far as I know," the boy told her slowly. "The last batch only arrived today, though, so I don't think it's been possible until now." He turned to Azalea. "What was it? Something about the Nexus opening?"

"'The playing field has been completed. The Nexus is now accessible,'" Azalea recited. "There was something ridiculous at the end about wishing us luck—luck isn't gonna do us any good in here." She made a face, an abundance of emotions written across her features.

"You complete the playing field," the hydra had said. *"The only way out is through."*

But what does that even mean?

"The Nexus—is that supposed to be the means of escape? Our way out?" Rune glanced from Nyk to Azalea, scanning their expressions.

"I—guess? I mean, it makes sense, right?" Nyk glanced over at Azalea. "We need a complete team to even get there, though."

Rune frowned. "How many are in a complete team?"

"Eight—we think," Azalea replied. "Eight batches, eight people per team—and they're all scattered around the arena. Finding every member of a team that big—and *not* getting at least one of you killed in the process—I'm not sure it's even possible."

A thread of confusion worked its way into Rune's thoughts. Only eight people—yes, it was an arena, but that didn't seem like a whole lot to her. For that to be considered such a challenge, this place must be a whole lot more deadly than her first impressions of it. *Either that, or...* "How big is this place, exactly?"

Azalea looked hesitant. "It's huge. Nyk and I haven't traveled too far from this Citadel, but I know for a fact that the arena stretches far beyond."

Rune thought for a moment. "And it's just you two right now?"

Their gazes locked. "Yeah. It's just us." Nyk's voice was threaded with emotion. "Azalea's saved my life more than once—and I'll always be grateful to her for that." He shuddered, a hint of the raw fear that had been hiding beneath his outward shell of calm peeking through. "This place isn't for the faint of heart. It's brutal, just like the people trapped inside it."

The weight of what was truly happening began to settle on Rune's shoulders, and she closed her eyes a second longer than a blink, willing for the awful sense of gut-wrenching panic that was gripping her to go away.

It didn't.

Trapped inside the arena.

Trapped.

That's what she was.

That's what they were.

"Rune?"

Rune's head snapped up at the sound of Nyk's voice, a hint of red coloring her cheeks. The pressing, suffocating feeling had vanished, at least, chased away by the reminder that she wasn't alone. "Sorry, I—I got a little distracted." A sliver of the raw emotion she was feeling slipped into her words. She looked away, rubbing her temples and mentally begging for the awful, empty sensation in her stomach to subside, to give her even a moment of rest. Despite supposedly being her allies, these people in front of her were still strangers—and she could *not* give them the idea that she was weak.

"Well—I suppose that I should have asked you this earlier." Azalea paused, her uncanny yellow-green eyes flickering across

Rune's tense figure. "Would you *like* to join us, Rune? To travel with me and Nyk?"

Rune stood there for a moment, the only sound being the soft huffs of her breath. It wasn't much of a choice, really—but even so, her reply seemed stuck in her throat, resisting her tongue as she formed it. "Yes. I would."

A faint glimmer of a smile formed on Azalea's lips. "In that case, I welcome you to our little group. Let's just hope you survive long enough for us to get to know each other."

RUNE LAY SILENT UNDER THE BLANKET OF STARS overhead, listening to Nyk's soft, rhythmic breaths a few feet away. She had offered to take the second watch shift, which was why she was out in the middle of the clearing, tendrils of feathery grass gently licking her skin.

It's so quiet. Almost peaceful—which is the last word I would ever expect to describe a place like this. A strange burning of emotion threatened to rise up in the back of Rune's throat, and now that she was alone, she was unable to deter it.

The faint sound of crickets chirping amid the rustling leaves created a soothing atmosphere, thankfully being able to stop the misty sheen over her eyes from turning into tears. *I don't know why this is so hard for me. It's not like I can remember things being different.* Her eyelids fluttered closed, allowing a single tear to trace a trail along her cheek. *But I knew they were.*

More tears spilled over as the thoughts circulated in her

mind, lodging a massive lump into her throat. *I'm stuck here now, fighting for my life—a life I don't even remember living.*

Unable to fight it anymore, Rune let out a breath, allowing the heavy, suffocating feeling to settle over her. This was the new reality for her—the only reality she knew. Her memories were gone, her prior life was gone, and the possibility of safety hadn't even been there in the first place. She swallowed hard. *Things are not going to be easy from here—I doubt they ever were. I have to get out of this place, though. I need to get my memories back.*

A shuddery breath rocked her body.

I need to remember who I am.

Facing her emotions was a strange combination of the easiest thing in the world and a greater challenge than it had been hiding them. An awful wrongness sank into her heart as she replayed the few memories she *did* have—a single day where fourteen years should have been.

They're not gone; they can't be.

I have to get them back.

I have to.

The pure, raw *desire* for her memories made her throat close, the imaginary veil in her mind seeming to thicken with each passing second. That veil...it was like a shroud of darkness, dividing her headspace in two. Her memories—her *identity*—they weren't gone, they were hidden, locked away behind inter-locking folds of shadow.

Rune's fingers curled into a ball, a thread of anger joining with the knot of emotion wedged in her chest. The hydra's words replayed in her mind—a few of them sinking deeper than the others.

"I will have to send you on your way, now, lest the creator realize that there's something different about you."

The creator.

This place was no accident.

Her *being* here was no accident.

The memories weren't gone by chance, they were *stolen.*

Rune gritted her teeth. *But why? Why would anyone choose to strip away someone's identity and leave them in a place where their only option was to kill or be killed?*

It was in that moment, laying there beneath the stars, her cheeks still damp from tears—she made a vow to herself.

I'm getting out of here.

And when I do...I will find whoever built this place and make sure that I am the last person to be put through this.

Time seemed to stall around her, the noise in her mind fading into a distant hum as everything focused around her promise. A smile—a real, genuine smile—broke out on her lips, her thoughts latching onto a realization that sparked a glimmer of hope deep within her.

My memories may be gone, and my identity too—but I know who I am.

I'm a fighter.

The words felt entirely natural to her, so she uttered them softly aloud, inhaling the night air and allowing its faint chill to fill her lungs. "A fighter," she repeated, careful to keep her voice low.

Her eyes found the moon, its foreign yet familiar presence oddly comforting to her. A gentle, soothing silence enveloped her, and for the first time since her arrival, she felt her body relax.

That blissful feeling was short-lived.

A sound split the air, and she sat straight upright, her hand covering her dagger and her spine tingling. Rustling in the bushes nearby indicated that Nyk and Azalea had heard it too... tearing through the treetops and shattering any sense of tranquility that had gathered.

A scream.

4
RUNE

A frigid, bloodcurdling chill spread across Rune's body at the scream, the tranquil silence shattered like a fallen vase. Instantly, Azalea and Nyk were in sight, their eyes reflecting the exact same terror that now coursed through Rune's veins. Rune's knuckles began turning white as she gripped her dagger, her gaze skipping across the patches of darkness between the trees so quickly that she thought she'd go cross-eyed.

"What *was* that?" Nyk whispered, echoing Rune's thoughts. Threads of panic strained his voice, causing it to hitch slightly.

Azalea pressed her lips together—hard—her eyes locked on the treeline. "Only one way to find out."

Nyk shot her a glance. "Going *after* the scream in the woods? Azalea, *are you insane?*"

"Better to get them before they get us." The girl's voice was tight, her rigid posture revealing to Rune how she really felt about the situation.

Rune fidgeted slightly, her heart going a million miles per hour in her chest. *Do not show your fear.* She opened her mouth to speak, to formulate a plan—but her train of thought was shattered as a girl came flying out of the trees.

Well—falling was a better word for it.

The wiry blonde crashed into the ground, rolling about ten feet before coming to a stop and letting out a faint groan. Blood streamed from her split lip as she shakily picked herself up, her intense gray eyes shooting daggers at the darkness.

Rune barely had any time to examine the girl before five other figures emerged from the treeline. A rather tall boy who looked to be about Azalea's age was struggling against four teenagers, but he was losing ground rapidly, casting worried glances over his shoulder at the girl on the ground. A surge of hot anger boiled inside Rune's blood. *They're outnumbered.*

It only took a quick glance at Nyk and Azalea to realize that their thoughts mirrored hers. The hostile teens seemed preoccupied with the tall boy, but Rune knew that they would notice her, Nyk and Azalea at any moment—they weren't exactly hidden.

Before Rune could make a motion to join in on the fight, the blonde girl glanced her way, cocking a grin as they locked eyes. Rune offered a nod, casting a brief sidelong glance at the scuffle. *I'm going to help you.* The girl's smile widened, returning the nod. Streams of scarlet had dried, caking on her skin—but she didn't seem to notice, her cocky expression not once faltering.

Suddenly, there was a shout, and a rush of air blew past Rune's face. One of the teenagers was launched backwards, his brawny body flung into the air like a ragdoll. The tall boy's hand was outstretched, a proud smile decorating his pale features.

Did he do that?

He didn't even touch the guy!

Her question was answered when a second tempest of wind—stronger this time—erupted from his palm, ripples of air spreading outward through the clearing as the tossed boy's comrade was sent flying into a massive tree trunk. This time, however, a returning blast from an auburn-haired girl caused the boy to stumble backwards, the two gales of wind colliding with a powerful rupture of energy.

Not only is everyone here fighting to the death...they also seem to have some kind of special abilities. Rune swallowed hard. *This is not looking good.*

A shout rang out, its source a tall girl with her finger pointed straight at where Rune, Nyk, and Azalea stood. "There's more! Three of them!"

Rune's head snapped up, instantly alert. *No sense in waiting anymore.* In one swift motion, she whipped out her dagger, charging forward into the fight. The auburn haired girl pivoted around, sending a wave of wind daggers towards her, but the tall boy flung out his arm, dispelling the attack.

"Luna, a little help?" The boy's platinum blonde hair was disheveled by a swift counter, forcing him back a few steps before he regained control.

Luna's smile widened, and she spread her arms apart, her fingers curling in slowly as she raised them above her head. To Rune's shock, tongues of flame appeared in the air around her, obeying her methodical motions as she swept her hands in front of her and angled her palms toward the attackers.

A flare of light filled the clearing as a jet of fire zipped towards the brawny teenager Luna's friend had sent flying earlier. Rune barely had time to watch the flames slam into their target, however, before she was rushed from behind by a black haired boy. His dark green eyes bored into Rune as he knocked her to the ground, pressing a knife to her throat.

"Five in one night? Here I thought I was unlucky." A smile spread across his face as she squirmed against his grip, her knife arm pinned at her side.

With a scowl, she stopped struggling for a brief second, catching him by surprise. Taking the opportunity, she balled her free hand into a fist, bringing it down hard on the boy's forearm —right where an old instinct whispered would be a tender nerve. Instantly, his wrist went limp, freeing Rune from the immediate threat of a dagger against her skin and allowing her to wiggle free.

He reacted quicker than she'd hoped he would, however, and a jarring shock rippled down her arm as she swung her weapon up to block his blow. *I'm not dying today.* A grunt escaped her lips as she managed to push him away, scrambling to her feet and creating distance between them. Around her, other fights raged, bursts of flames and rushes of wind colliding forcefully. *Was that lightning?*

She shook her head firmly, keeping her eyes locked on her opponent. *Rune, focus. He's trying to kill you.*

He struck first, lashing out with his knife. Rune ducked to the side, biting back a cry as the cold steel nicked her cheek. Gritting her teeth, she stepped off-axis, dealing a powerful blow to the boy's stomach with the hilt of her dagger. A strangled cough was forced from his chest as he doubled over, the raw fury in his emerald eyes piercing into her like a million needles.

Even though she had an advantage, an invisible force seemed to push her away, buying the boy enough time to regain his footing and charge her again. Her muscles felt unnaturally sluggish as she moved to dodge, allowing his dagger to trace a long line of crimson along her side. The pain screamed for her to stop, but she ignored it, dealing an array of swift counter strikes. Somehow, he managed to block them all, but the unseen force that had been restricting her weakened with each attack.

Is that his ability? That invisible pull—is he causing that? Her eyes narrowed. *Better not take any chances.*

The onslaught of slashes seemed to be keeping him busy enough, breaking his concentration. She let out a grunt of exertion, taking advantage of the brief opening in his defenses and managing to land a powerful hit to his collarbone. Her dagger dug into his shoulder, the pain causing his movements to become slower and much less controlled. Blood from his wound spurted out around the blade, turning her palms into a scarlet mess.

I guess past me did know how to fight. Glad I didn't leave myself defenseless.

A snarl of pain from her attacker drove her forward, and she knocked him to the ground easily, yanking her dagger free of his shoulder and pressing it against his neck. Her knees pushed against his wrists, pinning them to his sides.

Glimmers of agony lingered in his eyes, but he held Rune's gaze, a sickening tempest of fury contorting his angular features. "You little *vacillate*," he spat, his voice strained.

Rune scowled. "I don't think you're in any position to be

insulting me." Her tone was cold—completely merciless, and she had to fight to keep the surprise off her face.

I didn't know I could sound like that.

For the first time, an emotion other than rage flickered across his features. He looked almost—regretful. "If you're expecting me to beg for my life, I won't. I know how this works." A ragged breath forced him to pause, a cough rocking his chest. "We fight. We kill. Or we are killed." Malice seeped back into his tone as he continued, his expression darkening. "Do you have the heart to kill, girl?"

A squirmy feeling of wrongness in Rune's gut caused her to hesitate, but she refused to let her expression change as she leaned closer, her dagger drawing a line of scarlet from his skin. She didn't know this boy, and he didn't know her—but he had stood there, moments before, intent on ending the lives of five people his own age simply because they'd crossed paths. If she let him go, there would be no chance of him showing her the same mercy.

Rune, you have no choice.

Her voice was flat and monotonous as she parted her lips, placing her face so close that her breath brushed his ear. "Why don't you find out?"

No sooner had the words left her mouth than she jerked the dagger sideways, dragging the blade along his throat and killing him with a single motion. Green particles—tiny flickers of viridian light—lifted from his lifeless body for a few long moments before his figure dissolved altogether, his weapons falling to the ground with a dull thump.

Dazed, Rune stood, adrenaline pulsing through her veins.

She'd done it. She'd killed him. *I may not remember much, but I don't think that people are supposed to evaporate when they die…*

Shaking off the morbid images, she forced herself to take a deep breath, calming her racing heart. *It was necessary, Rune. If you can't take a life, you better be ready to lose yours.*

Suddenly, a shout caused her head to snap up, the sound of her name grabbing her attention like a magnet.

"Rune, *watch out!*"

The second Nyk's words registered in her mind, she was pummeled from behind, knocked to the ground by the auburn haired girl. She struggled against the girl's grip, but there was no escaping.

"Your turn." Her heavily accented voice dug into Rune's ears, imprinting itself onto her brain.

No. I can't die. Not like this.

People rushed towards her, but they were too slow. She knew they would be. The girl raised a long, wickedly curved blade above her head, using her wind to keep Rune pinned down as she angled the sword towards her chest. Time seemed to slow in those final, fleeting moments as the true idea of death sank into Rune's mind, flipping a switch in her brain.

I am not. Going. To die.

A powerful, burning energy erupted inside Rune's gut, flooding towards her fingertips. The girl's lips twisted into a cold, unforgiving smile as she thrust the blade down, its tip poised at her victim's heart.

5

RUNE

Light.

Bright, blinding, ethereal light.

It exploded from Rune's body, streaming from her skin and flooding the clearing with a powerful glow. The girl on top of her recoiled in shock, and Rune bucked beneath her grip, crying out as the edge of the sword grazed her rib.

She blinked rapidly, hoping to free herself from the pain. *At least I'm alive. At least I can keep fighting.* A shudder rocked her figure. *Not for much longer, though.*

The light began to dim, pooling itself around Rune as if waiting for something. Her body was drained, but she forced herself to reach out her concentration, tentatively allowing herself to command the versatile element. Despite a twinge of distant familiarity from behind the mental veil, the power felt weird and unnatural to her, its energy not quite matching the beating of her heart.

I don't know why this feels so wrong.

It's my power, after all.

A frown crossed her features. *Isn't it?*

Regardless of the ability's nature, it had just saved her life, and she couldn't let her guard down now.

Recovering from her shock, the auburn-haired girl reeled on Rune, lifting her hands to call down a rush of air—but she was tackled from behind by Luna. A tongue of flame erupted around the two, and when the fire finally died down, only one figure was still standing...the other reduced to crimson particles that drifted off into the night sky. Rune found herself choking down a wave of sickness that threatened to wash over her.

Don't tell me you're losing your nerve.

Around them, the remaining two attackers had opted for retreat, casting fury-filled glances back at the group of battered teenagers as they vanished into the trees. Luna's companion turned to her, his chest heaving. "Should we go after them?"

"I would advise against it," Azalea interjected. "None of us are in much shape to fight."

She wasn't wrong.

Looking around at their group, standing there beaten, bloody, and bruised—there was no way that they could engage in a pursuit. Quick, gasping breaths filled Rune's lungs as the adrenaline that had surged through her veins so prominently began to wear off, exposing her body to the full force of the pain her wounds caused. Though Luna looked like she might, none of them argued with Azalea, an awkward silence settling over them.

Finally, the tall boy—Luna's friend—broke it. "Thanks for your help, by the way."

A hint of a smile spread across Azalea's lips—but her eyes

were still guarded, void of emotion. "I'm not sure you needed it. The two of you are rather powerful."

The boy returned her smile. "The elemental abilities are some of the best weapons for survival in this place. Luna and I've practiced ours enough that we can use them at a moment's notice—but a lot of the people we meet seem to struggle with theirs."

Azalea cocked her head at him. "Interesting." She turned to Nyk without another word, leaving the air feeling oddly empty. *There's a lot she isn't saying.* "You alright?"

He nodded. "I'm good."

Behind him stood Luna, blood caking her skin—both hers and her opponent's, Rune imagined. Luna's uncanny gray eyes locked onto Rune's, holding her gaze for a long moment. The straight-haired blonde was roughly an inch shorter than Rune, with a fragile frame, a youthful, innocent face, and a pair of pointed ears—nothing about her screamed 'intimidating.' Even so, something about the way she stood told Rune everything she needed to know about her true strength.

A frown tugged at the corners of Rune's lips—there was something here that she was missing. Something important. Azalea's words from when they'd first met slipped back into her mind, causing her eyes to travel to Luna's neck. *"Everyone is an enemy until proven a friend."*

There, etched unmistakably on the girl's skin, was a purple rectangle—its surface reflecting the moonlight that illuminated the clearing.

Proven a friend. "You're both purple?"

All eyes turned towards Rune, making her face redden. The two exchanged a glance before nodding, the boy's fingers twitching ever so slightly towards the dagger sheathed at his side.

Azalea met Rune's gaze for only a second, an unsaid message passing between them. She hesitated for a moment before speaking, her words slicing neatly through the heightening tension. "I suppose we have something in common, then."

The boy's shoulders relaxed, and the glimmer of hostility in Luna's eyes disappeared. "In that case—you can call me Ivory." He glanced at Luna. "And this is—"

"Luna," the girl interrupted. "They already know that, though." She shot Ivory a rather pointed glance, but he didn't seem to notice.

"Please, you never were one for formal introductions anyway. I just saved you the trouble."

She rolled her eyes, but didn't argue any further.

"I'm Azalea," Azalea began. "My companions are Nyk—" she nodded at the ginger-haired boy— "and Rune."

Ivory furrowed his brow slightly. "I'm not sure if this is a strange thing to ask, but—what are your elements? From what I've heard, every member of a team has a different one, but I've yet to see that theory to be proven."

Luna made a face. "Where'd you hear that?"

He cast her a sidelong glance. "I actually *talk* to people, not just beat them up with fire. It's a good thing to know, though—it might help us get an actual idea of what we're facing."

"Shadow," Azalea told him simply. She lifted her hand, and to Rune's shock, the lines of darkness along the ground cast by the trees actually began *moving* towards her outstretched palm. With a flick of her wrist, she dismissed the uncanny silhouettes, watching as they slinked back to their original positions. "I haven't been able to find much of a use for it, though."

Ivory nodded. "I have a few ideas. What about you two?"

Nyk glanced at Rune. "I'm—uh—mind, I guess? I mean, I can move stuff without touching it, so..." he trailed off, his face going red. "I used it just yesterday, actually. Threw a giant boulder into a tree to distract a spawn hunter."

An openly judgmental expression overtook Luna's face. "Why didn't you just pummel the guy?"

Nyk's features twisted into a combination of annoyance and indignation. "Rune had only just woken up, and I just didn't want him to kill her before she even knew where she was. I also prefer *not* to instigate a fight against some random buff dude three times my size, thank you very much."

Luna ignored him, her attention latching onto Rune. "You're one of the newbies? Like—*batch eight* level newbie?"

Rune blinked at her, her confusion giving her away.

The blonde chuckled. "Dang. Sorry you had to get involved in such an intense scuffle your first night." She paused for a moment. "Wait a second—it was *you* who did that light thing, wasn't it?"

"Uh—yeah." Despite the fact that she still had no clue how the light had happened or why it felt so disconnected from her, she was undeniably grateful for its presence.

A smirk formed on Luna's lips. "I didn't even figure out that I could burn stuff until like—day five. Pretty cool that you got it down so quick."

Rune could only nod in reply, her head beginning to ache from trying to figure out Luna's rather unique attitude. She seemed to have no fear, no filter, and a blatant unpredictability that made it impossible for Rune to guess her reaction to something—almost exactly like the versatile element she wielded. A true wildcard...one in the form of a spirited teenager with the ability to shoot flames out of her hands.

I wonder how she even ended up here in the first place.

"It's a little strange to have five of the eight on our team standing here in one spot," Ivory remarked, snapping Rune's attention back to reality.

"This means that it wouldn't be too much of a stretch to assume that we can find the other three, right?" Nyk pointed out, glancing from Azalea to Ivory. "I mean—our group just doubled in size within a twelve hour span—that is, if you want to stick with us," he added hastily, glancing at Ivory and Luna.

Luna shrugged. "I don't see why we wouldn't. You think we might stand a chance at getting ourselves out of this place?"

The words seemed to flip a switch among the group, the mood instantly becoming *much* more serious. Escape—that was something that had been described to be far out of reach, a concept that wasn't even worth thinking about. But now, the idea seemed much more tangible to Rune, waves of hope rippling through her and causing a faint fluttery feeling in her stomach.

"Do we even know how? Like, if we *were* to become a complete team...what then?" Rune swallowed the bubbly sensation that had begun to take hold inside of her, refusing to allow it a good grip on her heart. *You can't go placing your expectations on something that might not even be possible.*

Azalea thought for a moment. "Like I said yesterday, the fact that the announcement for batch eight *also* included a hint about somewhere called the Nexus...that has to have something to do with escape. I'd assume that it would be in the middle of the arena, based on its name—though how to get inside, I couldn't tell you."

Luna shrugged. "That sounds super complicated. Let's just focus on finding the others and actually *getting* there, first, 'kay? Knowing how to use the key doesn't do us any good if we don't have it."

Azalea's face shifted slightly. "You—you have a good point. The best idea right *now*, though, would probably be getting out of the open."

Everyone nodded their agreement, and slowly, the group began to move towards the treeline. Azalea and Ivory took the lead, their voices hushed as they conversed. Nyk was right on their tail, but Rune chose to lag behind, a spiderweb of jumbled thoughts claiming her attention.

Suddenly, Luna came up beside her, bumping her arm a bit harder than she really needed to. Before Rune could glare at her, though, she flashed a grin, a strange challenge gleaming in the depths of her eyes.

"Welcome to the game, Rune. Let's find a way out, shall we?"

6

REI

A haze of swirling mist and prismatic fog encompassed Rei, her surroundings shrouded in the abundance of white smoke. A jolt rippled through her as she glanced down, realizing that she couldn't even see what she was standing on.

This is—weird.

The sixteen-year-old blinked a few times in an attempt to clear the faint film of blurriness from her vision, but nothing seemed to work. Vapor covered her completely, wrapping around her body and enveloping her in a cloud of opaque threads. She wasn't *uncomfortable*—not in the most literal use of the word, at least. The temperatures were mild, and she could breathe perfectly fine—though for some strange reason, it felt as though she didn't even need to. There was an undeniable feeling of tension in the air, however, a sensation that sank into Rei's body and filled her with unease.

It's a dream. It has to be. She shut her eyes, opening and closing her fists slowly. *If it is a dream, though—why does it feel so real?*

Her mind went back and forth, back and forth—attempting to puzzle out the situation as she dared a cautious step forward into the fog. The white cloud around her thinned slightly with her movements, and she took that as a sign to keep going. Something tugged at her memory, a picture resurfacing in her mind. She frowned, considering the thought.

This place looks a little like the In-Between. Her frown deepened as she recalled her past experiences with the odd dimension—a world with no form, no structure, and no meaning. It was supposedly a point between the waking world and that of dreams, a bridge between life and death. *We can't come here anymore, though. The link was severed during the battle...*

Only a few months ago, her entire world had been united in a war against a great force of darkness—a force that had ultimately been destroyed by Rei's half sister, Zuri. The final battle had destroyed the connection Rei and Zuri had to the In-Between, rendering them unable to return...at least, so Rei had believed. *Is it possible that the link could have been repaired? If so—then why am I here and not Zuri?*

Unlike how she remembered, she was alone, unarmed, and dressed in a simple grayscale tunic and pants. Her feet were bare, but she felt no pain to walk, almost as though she were standing on a cloud. *I've never had a dream like this before...not even during the war.*

But the war is over.

I'm safe.

Akaidia's safe.

So why does everything feel so wrong?

With each step, the air grew steadily warmer, the fog retreating and solidifying into a vaporous dome-shaped boundary. Flimsy streams of metallic liquid slowly melted out of the mist, drifting through the air like tiny rivers of silver. The material airily floated around the perimeter of the "room," stalling in the air for a few moments before molding itself into a circle of glassy ovals that levitated a few feet off the hazy ground.

Curiosity instantly overcame whatever hesitation had slipped its way into Rei's mind, and she approached the nearest shape, tentatively reaching up and brushing her fingers across the glassy surface. It was cool to her touch, almost like a mirror —molding around her palm as she pressed it deeper into the liquid. The moment she removed her hand, the substance bounced back into place, a ripple of motion spreading all the way to the edge of the object.

Smooth, smoky figures began to form at the edges of the oval, shapes and colors dancing their way across the metallic surface. Rei could do nothing but watch as the mirror began to reflect an image that wasn't there, a memory that she never lived. Unable to tear her eyes away, she kept them focused on the spectrum of smoke, watching as the shapes morphed into a somewhat recognizable scene. A strand of blonde hair slipped from where she'd tucked it behind her ear, but she brushed it away, not once breaking focus.

A faint hum of sounds filled her ears—the rustling of leaves, the harsh cries of wind, the sloshing of waves against a gravel shore—sounds she knew, but that she couldn't feel—the atmosphere of a million different places all at once. She was everywhere, yet she was nowhere—a web of aromas overwhelming her senses as she leaned closer to the mirror.

The images began to magnify with each step she took, the noises fading into a single track that solidified her location in her mind. She leaned closer, a distant instinct egging her on as she pressed her face into the levitating liquid. The second her skin brushed the chilled surface, she became a *part* of the image, standing in a body that was no longer hers.

A brawny man stood idly, watching the sun rise over a mountain range that appeared oddly familiar to Rei. He knew that what lay beyond those mountains was freedom, but also a mysterious world that hadn't been reached in millennia. Two millennia, to be exact. A world that so few even knew to exist, one rumored to be inhabited by a ninth high race... His mind wandered to the weapon he'd left behind, thoughts of worry and regret still lingering in his mind. It absolutely could not fall into the hands of his pursuers. They would think he still had possession of it, of course—and the decoy strapped to his side served as a perfect reinforcement for that assumption. By the time they could even be close enough to kill him, however, the true blade—as well as the power it contained—would be long gone.

Rei gasped for air as she stepped away from the mirror, examining her hands for a long moment just to make sure that they were, in fact, hers. *Who was that man?* She rubbed her temples, trying to dispel the hazy fuzziness that had grown around her thoughts. It was as if she'd truly stepped inside someone else's memories—someone that she had never even met. *Nothing like this has ever happened before—and I've been through some weird stuff.*

The mirror directly to her left began glowing faintly,

catching her attention and breaking her train of thought. Despite the faint pulsing in the back of her head, she moved over to the glassy phenomenon, tentatively stepping forward to immerse herself in its metallic depths.

This time, there was a girl just younger than Rei herself, sprinting all-out across a cracked and barren plain. Inhuman growls and bloodcurdling screeches from behind her sent new threads of terror pounding through her blood, empowering her fatigued muscles to push her forward and as far away from her pursuers as possible. No hope drove her, only an animalian instinct to survive. There was no hope anymore. Whoever had created this place—had put her here—had left her alone, with no memories, no weapons, and no way out.

A shiver rocked Rei's body as she broke free from the mirror's surface. Her heart thundered in her chest, a part of her still convinced that she was being chased across a crimson plateau. To be trapped like that—alone, with no memories, no weapons, and no hope of escape—that was nothing short of cruel. In fact, Rei wasn't even sure that there *was* a word strong enough to describe the feeling. *I really, really hope that these visions aren't real.*

The next mirror over began to glow, leaving her no choice but to subject herself to yet another scene. Her muddled thoughts hummed ominously in the back of her mind as she allowed herself to be consumed by the image, her mind whisked away to the body of another.

A young boy—hardly older than seven—glanced up at his mistress's stony expression with tearful brown eyes. A stream of blood ran from the wide gash on his palm, but she made no effort to help him, staring down at him with nothing but ice in her emerald gaze. Her eyes flickered to the metal cuff on his wrist, which served as the home for the blade causing his pain. The sharpened disc itself lay discarded to the side, and she picked it up, handing it to him without a word. Forcing back his tears and the sickening feeling that welled up inside his stomach, he wiped the blood off onto his already stained tunic, gingerly taking possession of the weapon. Closing his eyes and bracing for the piercing sting that failure brought, he took a deep breath, a whistle forming on his lips.

Gasping, Rei stumbled away from the mirror, clutching at her left palm where the gash had been. The cut itself had hurt, yes, but there was a much deeper wound that ran far beneath the boy's skin—the kind of injury that couldn't be healed. A sense of innate hatred for the woman blossomed inside Rei's stomach, and it took her a few deep breaths to recollect her thoughts.

Suddenly, a new realization surfaced, briefly dispelling the sickening sensation in her gut. These people—these places— Rei recognized none of them. Even the man from her first vision, overlooking the mountain range—that had felt familiar, but not in such a way that she knew where it could be. And that woman...wait. *Were her ears...pointed?*

A new feeling began to spark within her, puzzle pieces connecting inside her mind as she plunged herself into mirror after mirror. One thing was clear—these people weren't in Akaidia. They probably weren't even *from* it. Despite the awful things she had witnessed inside the visions so far, the idea of there actually being somewhere else—a world beyond the borders they'd known for over two thousand years—created an unshakable feeling of bubbly excitement. Her heart pounded as she approached the next vision—she only had two left. The smell of cold, musty stone filled her nostrils, and she leaned forward, pressing herself into the glass.

The man reached up with a trembling hand, feeling the half mask that covered the right side of his face. His visible eye flitted across the poorly lit surroundings, faint slivers of moonlight from the lone window illuminating the vibrant purple iris. Unfamiliar voices clamored in his mind, broadcasting thoughts that weren't his own into the mess his headspace had become. A migraine pounded at his skull, and he stumbled backwards, his vision growing blurry. He didn't realize that he had fallen until he hit the floor, a jarring shock rippling down his spine as one of his guards rushed over to help him. A horrible instinct came over him, and he stared up at the innocent man, trying to warn him, to tell him to run—but his voice refused to work. His own body wouldn't respond to his commands, his hands moving without consent. All he could do was watch—helplessly—as his fingers lowered to his hip, gripping the handle of his blade and slowly releasing it from its sheath.

A scream broke free from Rei's throat as she was hurled out of the memory, her hands trembling uncontrollably. She'd killed before—despite the fact that she was barely sixteen, she'd served as a soldier in battles, watching as countless men and women were forced to the ground for the last time. But this—something taking over your own body, something *other* forcing you to murder an innocent person who was only trying to help you —this was something else entirely. A whole new meaning to the word "monster." Part of her dreaded what she would see as she stood before the final memory, but she couldn't stop now.

Rei leaned forward, falling into the metallic liquid for the last time.

She was back in the body of the first man, only this time, he was traveling within the mountain range instead of gazing upon it. He clenched the small object in his palm, taking comfort in the warmth that spread across his skin. The feeble talisman was his only hope—his last chance at freedom.

The wind ruffled his unkempt blonde hair, a few loose strands passing in front of his vision and reminding him of just how long it had been since he'd had them cut. It was all he could do not to give into the fatigue that plagued his weary muscles, reminding himself of the freedom that awaited him. He held up the object in his hand—a four-pronged obsidian compass with a gleaming purple jewel inlaid in the center. A smile crossed his features.

That freedom began right now.

REI JOLTED UPRIGHT AS THE IMAGE FADED FROM HER mind, her sides heaving. She was back in her bed—though most of the sheets had been kicked to the floor. *So it was a dream after all.* Even so, the memories still burned in her thoughts, words spinning like a cyclone in her headspace.

Memories.

Pictures.

A glimpse into a world beyond mine.

A dangerous world.

A deadly world.

One full of people—and maybe even races, like the pointy eared woman—that we never knew existed.

I could find this world.

Find these people.

Maybe I could help them.

Maybe I could save them.

The moment the words entered her mind, Rei did a double take, shaking her head at her own ideas. *Rei, you idiot. For all you know, they could have died hundreds of years ago—if they ever lived in the first place.*

Even so, something deep inside her whispered otherwise—a voice that she would usually deem to be "insane." This time, however, the voice's murmurings matched up with the faint tug on her heart. The final memory from the dream resurfaced in her mind, the image of the object the man had been holding sticking out to her like a candle flame in a dark cave.

Wait a second...

Rei froze. *I've seen that compass before.*

Wasting no time, she flung her legs over the side of the bed, startling Cedar—her golden wolf companion that had previously been sleeping soundly on a pile of animal skins. Her brown eyes darted every which way as she knelt beside her nightstand, leaning over and fishing underneath her bed for a box she'd slid under there a few weeks before. The rough feel of the wood container against her fingertips sent jolts down her spine as she gripped its side, sliding it out into the open air.

Frantically, she tore away the thin blanket that covered the contents within, removing the unnecessarily thick book and old throwing dagger she had stored on top and setting them gingerly aside. Hesitation slowed her movements as she reached for the final object, half-wrapped in indigo cloth and resting against the bottom of the box.

It was her birthday gift—a four-pronged compass crafted of intricately chiseled obsidian with a gleaming purple gemstone set into the center.

A compass identical to the one the man had been holding.

7

REI

"Rei...why in Akaidia are you knocking on my door at five in the morning?"

Normally, Rei might have apologized, or maybe waited an hour or two more so as not to bother her sinewy mentor—but this time was very, very different. *Besides—he's dressed. I clearly didn't wake him.*

"Can we talk?" She must have looked crazy, appearing at his door out of breath while still wearing the loose indigo tunic and pants she had fallen asleep in. Cedar trotted at her side, obviously as confused as her mentor was.

The urgency in her voice must have convinced him not to ask questions, and he stepped aside, gesturing for Rei to enter his home. Master Faron was far from an intimidating figure—he stood only a few inches taller than Rei, and his build was lean, with not many visible muscles. What he lacked in size, however, he made up for in skill—his swordsmanship was unrivaled by anyone else Rei had ever met, and his wisdom far surpassed it.

Rei slid into the wall-mounted bench, resting her arms on the ebony table. Faron's tone concealed undertones of worry as he took a seat across from her, meeting her gaze with soft brown eyes. "What can I do for you, Rei?"

Rei shook her head. "I had something kinda—weird—happen to me last night, and I wanted to talk to you about it."

Her master frowned. "Weird? Weird how?"

She fidgeted slightly, fishing for words. There really wasn't a way to put it that wouldn't make her sound like she'd lost her mind—then again, Master Faron had seen a fair share of "impossible" things in his lifespan. Despite the face that he only appeared to be in his mid-twenties, he was actually far older...a millennium older, to be exact. His aging had stopped just over a thousand years ago, and he had since spent much of his time alone, gathering knowledge and mastering his craft.

No sense in skirting around it. "I had a dream," she began slowly, keeping her eyes averted from whatever facial expressions he might make. "I know I've been having nightmares and stuff about the war, but this was different. It—it almost looked like the In-Between."

She paused, daring a glance upward. Faron remained quiet, his expression passive. Before he could speak, she mustered up the courage to voice the words that had been stuck in her throat since she awoke—the words that wouldn't leave her, no matter how insane they sounded. "I think there's something else out there. Beyond Akaidia. And my dream—that's what I think it was trying to show me."

Silence.

"You believe...that there's another world...beyond Akaidia?"

Not trusting her voice, Rei nodded.

Master Faron took a deep breath, propping his chin up on his hands and stroking his well-shaped goatee. "Explain it to me, if you don't mind. All of it."

He didn't immediately shoot her down, but she could hear the doubt in his voice...and how was he to know that it wasn't just another nightmare? Shuddering, she forced away the horrifying monster-filled images that swarmed into her mind uninvited at the reminder.

Not the time, Rei.

Hesitating for a moment, Rei slowly began to explain about her dream, starting with how she'd opened her eyes and immediately known something was different. Then the mirrors and the visions they'd shown her, the people, the glimpses of a world that no Akaidian had ever seen. "In one of them, there was even a woman—a woman who I could have sworn had pointed ears," she added, her heartbeat thundering in her chest. "The last vision, though, was the strangest. It was the same man the first mirror showed me, and he was standing in a mountain range... holding up *this*." Rei pulled the obsidian compass out of her pocket, setting it on the table between her and her instructor.

"That compass? You're sure it was the exact same one?"

Rei nodded. "Positive."

Master Faron went silent, and Rei anxiously scanned his narrow features. There was something in his eyes—something that whispered of a secret he held back. A jolt rippled through her. *He knows something.*

Before she could say anything, though, he cut her off.

"Rei...that compass belonged to your father. Your *birth* father."

She froze.

My father.

The very mention of the man sent chills through her blood, completely overhauling her outlook on the situation. She'd never met her biological father...even her mother had refused to tell her much about him besides his name, Tayven. In fact...she hadn't even known of his existence until a few months ago, having spent much of her life in the care of an adoptive family. Recently, the truth had been uncovered, and Rei still didn't like thinking much about it. Her real mother had been married first to her father, but he disappeared into thin air shortly before she was born. When her mother had remarried, her new husband had refused to have anything to do with Rei, and she'd ended up in the care of some close friends.

Bile rose in her throat as the bitter, betrayed feelings she'd bottled up rose to the surface once again, causing her to grit her teeth in anger. This whole situation was completely messed up... a man vanishing from the life of his pregnant wife, then a few months later, that same woman abandoning her newborn daughter to another's care simply because her fiancé told her to. Zuri had been born just over a year later, making their half-sisterhood the only good thing that had come out of the situation.

I feel bad for Zuri, having to deal with them her whole life.

"What do you mean, it belonged to my...to him?" *He doesn't deserve to be called my father. He has to earn that title, and he never did.*

Master Faron noticed her avoiding the word, but he made no comment about it. "Tayven came to me, one day—it was a few months before you were born, I believe. He didn't tell me much, only that I needed to give you that on your sixteenth birthday. No sooner, no later. Then—he was gone."

Sounds about right. "This was a gift from him, then?"

"It was. He never told me why he wanted you to have it... but from the look on his face, that compass must have been extremely important. In fact..." A frown crossed Faron's lips. "A wayfinder, I believe he called it. At the time, I had been understandably confused, considering that it didn't seem to work like a normal compass...but I wonder if it wasn't intended to."

"What do you mean?"

"I mean that perhaps its purpose is beyond what it appears to be. If your theories are correct, and there is, in fact, something beyond the Horizon's Teeth—it wouldn't be too much of a stretch to assume that they could have access to technology we are unfamiliar with. This compass may be the key to something else...though *what,* exactly, I can only guess." He scratched his head, his features twisted into an expression of deep thought.

"It is called a *wayfinder*...that's got to mean something, right?"

Master Faron took a moment to respond. "I suppose. But, Rei—we have absolutely no idea what it does, or how to use it. It would be far too dangerous to just—"

"What if I just went?"

The air went still, and Rei felt her cheeks grow red. She hadn't meant to interrupt her instructor...but the words had been so prominent, so *ready,* that she had simply been unable to hold them back. "What if I just...go?" she repeated, softer this time. "If I took Ember, left everything behind, and just flew as far as I could. There *is* something out there," she pleaded, meeting his eyes. Their gentle, doubt filled depths discouraged

Rei, but she persisted, the urgency in her voice chipping away at his resolve. "I know it's dangerous. I know that no one's ever done it. But I can. I have something they didn't." She held up the wayfinder, her heartbeat thundering in her ears.

This is insane. Absolutely insane. What are you doing, Rei?

The pause was long...gut wrenchingly, heart poundingly long. Every single bone in Rei's body screamed at her to cave, to give into the piercing stare that Faron was sending her way—but she didn't. Couldn't. She wasn't sure what it was, but *something* inside her was certain about this even if her brain was going out of its way to call her crazy. Yes, it could have been just a dream...but what if it wasn't?

What if she was right?

"Rei..." he sighed. "I have no idea what's out there. You would be *entirely* on your own, with no knowledge of what you could be up against. Even if you're wrong, and there isn't a world beyond—which would hold innumerable dangers of its own, mind you—the mountains themselves could easily be home to creatures unlike anything you've ever faced. Are you sure you want to do this?"

No.

"Yes. I'm positive." The moment the words left her lips, Rei realized that she meant them...maybe not with her head, but her heart certainly did. *Forget my brain...since when have I ever listened to it anyway?* "In fact..." she cast a glance at the golden wolf curled up by her feet, chest rising and falling soundly. A smile tugged at her lips. "I'll leave Cedar here. I'll leave everything here...everything except my weapons, my riding gear, and Ember."

Faron frowned. "Why?"

She met his gaze. "So you know I'll come back. Without Cedar, I won't be nearly as reckless...and not bringing anything beyond the essentials would mean that nothing's at risk." *Sort of a lie, but really...I do plan on coming back. I just don't want Cedar in harm's way in case something goes wrong.* "I wish I could leave Ember, too, so he's not in danger...but I do *not* plan on walking."

Master Faron leaned back. "You're really going to do this."

She nodded firmly.

"Then...I guess I have no choice but to let you, do I?"

The walls around them suddenly felt a *whole* lot closer as the realization sunk in. *I'm really doing this. I'm going to cross the border.*

If there even is one...

Faron stood, holding her gaze for a long moment. "I'll meet you in the Arboretum at midday. Be packed for a three day trip, at *maximum*."

Then, wordlessly, he led her to the door.

8

REI

The sharp, piney scent of trees filled Rei's nostrils as she pushed open the door to the Arboretum—the only place in Aererest open to the sky.

Aererest was, first and foremost, a city of dragons...which is why it was always so strange to Rei that the entire civilization had been constructed beneath the mountains of the Horizon's Teeth. Yes, it was amazing for security—no one could attack something they couldn't find. But it also raised a lot of questions...starting with how they had managed to find or create a cavern as large as the one she currently stood in.

The whole city was constructed as a series of tunnels and spacious caves, all of them linking together at the enormous central cavity. It was massive in the most literal meaning of the word, and Rei was convinced that you could fit an entire mountain within it. Fluorescent crystals and an abundance of brilliant lichen could be seen covering every inch of stone, working with the suspended torches and dangling orbs of bioluminescent moss to light up the cave almost as clearly as if it were day.

Hanging bridges and cocoon-like structures suspended from the ceiling created a net of color and vibrance all around, the whole place absolutely teeming with life.

And the dragons...

There were so.

Many.

Dragons.

Polychromatic spectrums of color danced through the cave in the form of scaly wings, their rhythmic beating creating a steady hum of noise. From where Rei stood, at the very top level of the cavern—it was a majestic sight, looking down over the prismatic hues through the glass floor of the Arboretum.

As the name implied, the Arboretum was filled almost entirely with towering trees and interlocking foliage, the atmosphere completed by a lack of ceiling above. Rays of sunlight warmed Rei's skin as she navigated along the crystal paths, a smile crossing her features when she caught a glimpse of lime green scales through the foliage.

At the sight of her, Ember cocked a goofy grin, lumbering over and leaning down to press his nose gently into her outstretched hand. The hulking, nine foot tall dragon had been Rei's companion since he was hardly a hatchling—not even a year ago—and she had grown rather attached to the butterfly-loving creature.

"You're sure about this?" Master Faron stepped out from behind Ember, his expression stony.

Rei stroked Ember's neck to ease the knot of nerves in her chest, the weight of the wayfinder in her satchel giving her the courage to respond. "I am."

Something cold nudged her leg, and she glanced down, a

twinge of sadness setting into her throat when she noticed Cedar. She knelt to the wolf's eye level, gazing into the stunningly green depths—a sign of the powerful cultivation abilities she possessed. "I'll be back soon, okay?"

Cedar whimpered in reply, causing Rei's heart to tighten painfully. "We won't be gone long, and I can't risk you getting hurt."

Another whine, this time pleading.

"No, you can't come with me. I wouldn't forgive myself if something happened to you because of my choice." She reached out her hand, gently stroking the wolf's neck. "Just stay safe for me, okay? I'll see you soon."

She paused for a brief moment, closing her eyes and taking a deep breath. *No turning back now.*

"I promise."

"WHY IS IT GETTING *HOTTER*?" REI MUTTERED AS beads of sweat began condensing on her brow. She'd already removed the thick top layer she wore, as the northern territories tended to be subzero even in the late fall—but it seemed that the long-sleeved tunic and loose pants she wore over a final base layer were becoming too suffocating as well. "We're flying *north. How* is this *possible*?"

Even the landscape had begun to shift—patches of foliage grew through the rocks, scrawny trees poked out from the mountainsides, and some of the plateaus they passed had grass growing around any source of water she could spot. An off feeling in Rei's stomach made her wary as she glanced around, trying to make sense of the phenomenon.

Another drop of sweat somehow found its way into her eye, and she blinked rapidly, muttering under her breath. *I can't handle this anymore. It's off with the second layer, then.*

Gently, she reached forward, nudging Ember's neck to let him know that she was letting go. He slowed his pace, keeping his flight pattern as steady as possible while she wrestled with the outer layer of her clothing. The outfit she had on underneath was arguably one of her favorites...even if she did have to cover it up most of the time.

It was tailored specifically to her riding habits, consisting mostly of a moisture-wicking black sleeve that stretched from her shoulders to just below her knees. The skintight sleeve was partially covered by a well-fitted purple midriff, with the right sleeve extending all the way down and ending in a fingerless glove while her left arm remained bare. A pair of loose-fitted shorts equipped with plenty of pockets completed the look, and Rei had also remembered to bring a few pouch-filled belts, which she strapped on top of everything. Her favorite part, though, were the two slits on both sides of the black under layer, designed to look like dragon claw marks.

She hummed softly to herself as she packed her excess clothing away into one of the satchels attached to Ember's leather saddle, digging her lightweight rider's boots into his side to tell him she was all set. Normally, she preferred to ride bareback, but when making lengthier journeys such as this one, she would put up with the saddle in exchange for its storage capabilities.

Her attention wandered to the peaks around them, her eyes

tracing the intricate cliffsides as Ember swooped past. Many of the mountains were outlandishly tall, rendering it impossible for the dragon to fly above them without endangering himself or his rider. For that reason, they had decided to travel at a much lower altitude, coasting through the imposing valleys. It felt liberating to Rei to be traveling through such uncharted territory—a path so unknown and so feared that all Akaidian children had been taught from birth that it was impossible to pass through.

They told us there was nothing beyond.

They told us that the mountains are the boundary, the uncrossable line.

They said that only a fool would dare to venture past the peaks.

A smile crossed Rei's features.

Now I am that fool.

Suddenly, the satchel at her side began to glow with a hazy, purple light...one so faint, Rei could have sworn she was imagining it. A sharp, tingly sensation set into her stomach, sending jolts all the way along her body. For the first time, she noticed that the sky—and even the air—had changed, fogging with a strange lavender haze. Rei couldn't help but rub her eyes, certain that she was seeing things.

She wasn't.

A faint thread of panic worked its way into the constant needle sensation prickling across her skin, and she reached inside her satchel, pulling out the wayfinder. The gem in the center was glowing now, twice as brightly as she had noticed a moment before. It pulsed with an ethereal purple gleam—a shade much too close to the color that tinted the atmosphere to be a coincidence.

The tingling grew suddenly sharper, and she found herself wincing slightly at the intensity of it. Around them, the air became so hazy that Ember was forced to slow his pace in fear of colliding with the cliffs. Rei fought to keep the fear out of her features, a strange feeling worming its way into her gut and sticking fast.

Was this why they had been told to stay away?

Why the mountains had been ruled as the map's edge?

She shook her head, gripping the wayfinder so tightly that her knuckles turned white. *I'm not like those explorers before. I have something they don't.* She gritted her teeth, relying solely on the determination the dream had sparked within her. *I've come way too far to turn back now.*

Just as the tingling sensation became too much to bear, there was a rush of energy, rebounding through her like a bowstring being released. A brief moment of silence followed, pressure pounding in Rei's ears and forcing in on her from all directions.

Then, with a final, ground-shaking boom, the purple haze faded as a rush of hot air blasted into Rei's face.

Ember stalled, startled, hovering in midair. Rei turned around, breathing heavily as her eyes frantically scanned the mountains behind them for any clues as to what had just happened. All she saw, however, was a strange ripple effect in the air, distorting her perception of the peaks.

It's like an illusion—like the mountains aren't really there.

She inhaled deeply, allowing the fresh, particularly crisp air to fill her lungs. *Something's up with this place. Whatever that was, it definitely wasn't meant to make travel easy.*

She righted herself, preparing to nudge Ember forward—but she froze when she noticed the landscape stretching out before her.

In front of them was a flat land of vast plains, patches of forest, and scattered signs of civilization as far as the eye could see. Her gaze wandered upwards, landing on a cloudless blue sky. Even the temperatures had completely mellowed out, settling for a comfortably neutral feel in the air. She glanced back at where the mountain range had been, questions whirling around in her mind.

A word surfaced in her thoughts, but she forced herself to pause a moment before she allowed it to form into a full idea, unsure whether or not she truly wanted to believe what it was suggesting. *A barrier. That's what it felt like.* Her gaze locked onto the transparent wall of energy, the only trace of its existence being the faint purple sheen across its surface.

But if that truly was a barrier...then there's no way it's here by accident. I was right. There is another world beyond the one we know. Her hand found the spiny ridges on Ember's neck, and she gripped them hard, taking comfort in the dragon's presence. *Not only that...but someone doesn't want our worlds to meet. For whatever reason, we've been separated.*

Forcefully.

Rei's eyes flickered down to the wayfinder. The gem had stopped glowing, leaving it looking like nothing more than an elaborate star. There was no indication that it might have just helped her alter the reality of an entire world. Blinking hard, Rei nudged Ember forward, examining the terrain. She couldn't go back to Aererest, not just yet. There were way too many unanswered questions, starting with the existence of the barrier.

Someone had to have put it there.

Someone wants to keep the people here out of Akaidia...or maybe they just want to keep us in.

But who?

And why?

A SCUFFLING AGAINST THE GROUND CAUSED REI'S eyes to shoot open, the grogginess making her brain sluggish. She had decided to make camp for the night on a secluded outcropping near what seemed to be the edge of the mountain range, and she had already been woken at least twice by unfamiliar noises—but this one wasn't like the others.

Suddenly, her eyes found the noise's source...and panic forced her to react.

Another person.

She wasn't alone.

She scrambled to her feet, but the newcomer was much quicker, rushing her with surprising speed and pinning her to the ground. A grunt escaped her lips as she bucked under his grip, but he was strong, and Rei was forced to let herself fall still as cold steel found her throat.

"Bloody coward," she spat through gritted teeth, her mind analyzing the situation with instinctive speed. *This guy knows what he's doing...there's no way I could get his grip free without him killing me.* "What do you want with me?"

The figure gripped her shoulder so tightly that she winced. "A weapon-bearing stranger attacks you in the night, and yet fear is not your first reaction. How intriguing." He leaned closer, just close enough that she was able to make out the malevolent smile on his narrow features. "Hold on to that fighting spirit, kid. Perhaps you could actually be of use to us."

With those words ringing in her ears, he brought his free hand around, slamming his fist into her temple before she could react. Her body went limp beneath his grasp, her consciousness lost to suffocating darkness.

9

RUNE

arkness.

She was surrounded by it. Seeping into her skin, flowing from her palms, shrouding the landscape in a blanket of shadow.

But who was she?

Where was she?

All she knew was darkness.

That's all she could know.

All there was to know.

The landscape shifted, launching her into what felt like a river. She struggled to stay afloat against the rapids, frigid water digging into her skin like needles. Memories—hers, but not hers—swept by as well, caught in the powerful current and being carried off into the blackness around her. There was no light, but somehow she could see, no sound, but she was nearly deafened by noise.

Occasionally, a more familiar image would rush past her, carried by the tumultuous waters. The images were nothing more than tiny glimmers, glimpses into a past that was familiar to her heart yet alien to her mind. Eventually, she forced herself to relax, her attention trained on the strange visions. As her body fell still, the water seemed to mirror her motion, carrying her along gently through the endless land of darkness.

Suddenly, a particular image floating nearby caught her eye, one glowing much more brightly than the others. She drew nearer, and the light began to shift, forming into a glowing image that hovered above the waves. The pace of the water came to a dead stop, and she found herself being immersed into the image, looking at it from the outside but somehow feeling everything that those portrayed within the light felt.

There was a young girl, sitting in a sea of grass and gazing up at a star-filled sky. Her eyes looked like miniature pieces of sea glass, reflecting the celestial bodies that danced above her. Hope brimmed in every ounce of her being, and her palms tingled with an energy that fought to rise to the surface. An energy that could change everything, if only she let it.

Another girl, embodied with the same energy, sat beside her. Another who could control things that were meant to stay untouched. Neither of them knew yet the part they played in this massive, endless universe, but their fates called out to them from just beyond their reach, a power imbued deep within them announcing its arrival. Two girls, each who held fate itself in the palms of their hands—yet both of them blissfully unaware of the fragile glass foundation their world was built atop.

The very foundation that they were born to shatter.

The image faded, and the river began to move quicker than before, the sleek black surface of the water churning over itself as it crashed against unseen shores. The other images, too, sped up, and she could hardly make out even a glimpse of them as they rushed past her in a wave of color. The darkness thinned slightly, but still, no light from outside shone through, leaving her trapped in a raging rapid of madness and memory.

Just as her arms began to tire, she felt grains of sand shift beneath her feet. A gasp escaped her lips as she grasped onto the only tangible thing her fingers could find—a conveniently placed stone hidden just beneath the surface of the rapids. The river fought to sweep her on, but she continued to resist it, keeping her eyes trained on a single patch of darkness that appeared to be shifting ever so slightly.

Suddenly, a blinding flash of light distracted her, causing her to lose her grip on the stone. A new image consumed her, throwing her forcefully into an entirely alien situation. This memory wasn't like before...there was nothing familiar about it.

Even so, the picture was clear as day.

A seven headed creature, sleeping soundly beneath the churning waves. This wasn't a peaceful sleep, though—the creature's mind longed to be awake, but his body refused to let him be, keeping him docile as enemies infiltrated the island he called home.

Something terrible was about to happen.

Something truly evil.

Something fueled by a darkness unlike what the realms had known for millennia.

This wasn't the first time the darkness had shown its face, however—and as consciousness slipped from his body, he wondered if that darkness had finally returned.

The image faded, and her body was swept up against an unseen shore, her mind still encapsulated by the blurry fragments of light that consumed her vision. The fragments began to move, swirling around one another and becoming a new memory. This time, it was more familiar to her, but it still didn't sit quite right with her consciousness.

A girl her own age, cloaked in a veil of darkness. Her chest heaved with heavy breaths, and she blinked rapidly to clear the sweat from her eyes, glancing out over the barren plain stretched before her. Beyond that plain stood a city, one that was presumably unconquerable. Yet—unknown to many—a dark deity had managed to crawl its way in, silently overthrowing rulers and dominating against all who resisted against it.

A hint of a smile found its way onto her lips. She wouldn't interfere, not yet.

Something told her that it simply wasn't time.

The images kept coming, faster now, hardly allowing Rune a breath. They danced through her mind, rewriting her consciousness into whatever it was they desired.

Cold stone.

Blinding lights.

Streams of smoke.

Blood.

Battles.

Fear.

So much fear.

A scream erupted from her lips, and she writhed against the waves, her mind no longer her own. Thoughts—hundreds, millions of them—tore her down, sweeping through her consciousness and leaving nothing in their wake.

Then, suddenly—silence.

A single, crystal clear memory began forming in her mind,

but it didn't hurt like so many of the others had. It was distant —a faraway fragment of her being, something she knew but had never actually seen. The memory's subject took shape, but this time, she turned, her eyes passing through the panting girl on the shadowed shores.

"Who are you?"

The voice shattered the veil of confusion that had settled over Rune, and she flinched back, startled by the glowing figure. The image leaned towards her, a lavender glow emanating from the teenage girl's body. A pair of ethereal purple eyes stared into Rune's, her voice resounding in Rune's thoughts as the world faded into light.

"Who are you?" she repeated, the words sounding lilted and strange.

Rune.

I'm Rune.

But who are you?

With a jolt, Rune awoke in a cold sweat.

Who are you?

Who are you?

Who are you?

Who—

"I don't know!"

Rune curled into a ball, pressing her fingers to her temples. Normally, she would have been mortified that she just practically shouted something—in the middle of the night, no less—but she was too shaken to care.

That wasn't a normal dream.

It couldn't have been.

She shook her head, a hysterical laugh threatening to break forth from her lips. *Who am I kidding? I don't know what anything normal feels like.*

"Nightmare, huh?"

Luna's remark snapped Rune's attention away from the pounding headache her thoughts were giving her, and she turned, her eyes locking on the blonde's deceivingly innocent gray ones.

"Something like that. Did I wake you?"

"Nah." Luna stood, softly moving over to Rune's side and taking a seat. "I couldn't sleep. You were thrashing pretty hard, though—I'd started debating whether or not to wake you up or something." She cocked her head at Rune. "Must've been a pretty crazy dream. Where'd your mind even get something to have nightmares about, anyway?"

Rune made a face. "The fact that we're stuck in an arena with the possibility of no escape isn't nightmare fuel enough for you?"

Luna shrugged. "I mean—it's not *great*, but it's also the only thing I've got memories of, you know? Hard to miss something you can't remember."

Rune leaned forward, pulling her knees into her chest and resting her chin on them. "I'm not so sure. Some part of my mind *knows* something—even if I don't. The memories aren't gone, I can feel them. I just don't know how to get to where they are."

Luna's brow furrowed. "Can't say I feel the same way. Do you think you're actually dreaming about your own memories, though?"

"I don't know." Rune's eyes wandered up, finding the blanket of stars overhead through the interlocking branches of the trees that surrounded them. "One of them felt like it could have been a memory, but there was other stuff too—stuff I know I've never seen before." She shrugged, leaning back and propping herself up on her hands. "It doesn't matter. Just a dream, anyway."

Was it, though?

Rune shook her head, dislodging the thoughts. *Not your problem right now. You've got bigger issues to deal with than weird nightmares.*

Beside her, the blonde mimicked Rune's movement, resting on the damp grass. Miraculously, the others were still sound asleep, their soft breaths filling the still air. "Hey...Rune?"

"Hm?"

"The memories—or whatever it was you saw—what did they look like?" For the first time since she'd met Luna, the girl's voice seemed to be void of sarcasm.

Rune closed her eyes, tentatively allowing the dream to once again flood her thoughts. This time, however, she held more control, keeping the tempest of questions and voices from infiltrating her headspace. "Well—the dream kinda felt like a river, and the memories were like light—reflections of some past that I don't remember. Not all of them were familiar, but one of them was—one of two girls sitting on a hill." She frowned. "I could sense something different about them, though. A power, a force hidden deep within them."

Within their blood.

Rune froze. *"There is power in your blood. The kind of power that no one will ever be able to take from you."*

The hydra's words to her.

Could one of those girls have been her?

If so, who was the other one?

You're being ridiculous. It was a dream.

Still, she was unable to shake the idea from her mind as Luna turned to look at her, an unreadable emotion taking over her youthful complexion.

"You think that was one of your memories?"

"I doubt it. Always the possibility, though."

They lapsed into silence, the chill in the pre-dawn air feeling like a promise to Rune. Sure, her situation was far from ideal, and the dream had done nothing to help with her feelings of dread. Even so, the idea that escape just *might* be possible lingered in the back of her mind, and she refused to let it go, holding onto it with every ounce of her being.

A bone chilling howl sounded in the distance, but Rune didn't hear it, her body finally relaxing as she drifted off into a fitful sleep.

IO

RUNE

A mouthwatering aroma wafted through the air, toying with Rune's nose before she even opened her eyes.

The dream from the night before still burned vibrantly in the back of her mind, stirring up the mess of thoughts once again. It took all her effort to keep them down, reminding herself of her priorities. *Find a way out of the arena first. Deal with weird nightmares later.* Her gaze found the sun through the leafy canopy overhead, its late morning rays streaming through cracks in the lush ceiling and warming Rune's skin.

"Look who's *finally* awake." Luna's remark shattered the silence, dissolving most of the residual fatigue that lingered over Rune.

"Please, *you* only woke up a few minutes ago," Ivory shot back, his naturally gentle voice not at all matching the look he was shooting his friend.

Luna shrugged, indifferent. "I wasn't last."

Rune sighed, pulling herself to her feet and finding her way over to where the rest of the group sat encircled around a small fire. Nyk was seated on the far side of the makeshift pit they'd dug, rotating an amply sized chunk of meat over the hungry flames.

"You caught something?" Rune gestured to the spit.

Ivory nodded proudly, his silvery blue eyes shining. "A fox. Went out hunting this morning, before the rest of you guys woke up. Not the best tasting meat, I'll admit, but I've certainly had worse."

"It's not like I've got much of anything to compare it to." Her stomach growled, and a faint blush crawled across her cheeks.

Luna chuckled. "It's not *that* bad, just a little tough. Best around here are the birds, but they're so hard to catch it's almost not worth it. Take my advice, though—do *not* try the squirrels. They're horrible." The expression on her face sold her point.

"Hey!" Ivory protested. "We didn't have much of a choice, if you remember. They were *not* as bad as she's telling you," he whispered to Rune, earning him a glare from Luna. "She's just being dramatic."

"Am not!" A burst of fire flared up in front of Ivory, dancing in front of his face harmlessly before dying back down. Ivory didn't flinch, even going so far as to smile slightly. The softness of his pale features only added to the unfazed look, and he reached up, absently brushing a stray strand of platinum blonde hair away from his eyes.

"Come on, Luna. I know you wouldn't actually hurt me." His tone was teasing, but his voice seemed to be naturally gentle, giving the words a strangely soothing air.

Luna raised an eyebrow, a playful glint in her eye. "Don't test me." She did a good job of maintaining the act, putting just the right amount of challenge into her words.

"How long have you guys been traveling together?" Nyk asked, leaning forward and carefully reeling the spit in. The sharp, slightly tangy aroma of the fresh meat only made Rune's stomach more insistent, hunger gnawing at her like a ravenous pack animal.

How long has it been since I've eaten?

"Long as I can remember," Luna replied airily. "Which isn't a whole lot, I guess, but it sure feels like it. I met Ivory right outside the Green Citadel, shortly after I awoke."

"*Green* Citadel?" Rune echoed, too tired of not knowing anything to mask her confusion. She remembered hearing the word 'Citadel' before—Nyk had mentioned it, back when Rune had just woken up. At the time, however, she hadn't thought to ask for an explanation.

"Oh, yeah—sorry, forgot you're a newbie." Luna cocked a grin at the annoyance in Rune's expression. "The arena's divided into four sections—called biomes—and each biome's labeled with a color. We're in the Green Biome right now— Ivory's traveled to Blue before, but I've never been myself. The biomes each have their own citadel, where people wake up after their memories have been wiped."

Rune shuddered. "That's—unsettling."

Luna nodded with a grimace, thanking Nyk as he handed her a sheared slice of meat. "It gets worse. The leylocks are giant energy barriers that separate the biomes. Try to cross from biome to biome without the right leyshard—and they kill you. On the spot."

The blood drained from Rune's face. "You just...die?"

Luna nodded again, but her smile had faded. "Saw it happen once. Not my favorite memory, I'll tell you that."

Rune barely noticed when Nyk offered her a slab of meat, and she thanked him absentmindedly, staring into the dying flames. "I guess that's why it's so hard to get a full team, then. If the arena's divided—and you can't cross between sections without whatever a leyshard is—it's gotta be a challenge to find everyone."

A grim expression had taken over the blonde's face. "This whole place is just one giant death trap. If the people don't get you, the environment will."

Azalea's gaze turned glassy, and Rune realized that she hadn't said a word the whole time. "It's difficult to think about. Even though we don't have memories, I know for a fact that this place—and the horrors it contains—isn't just some *natural occurrence*. Someone *built* this. Put us in here. On purpose." Her voice cracked, shattering whatever fragments of the teasing mood had remained.

Silence fell over the group, and Rune's own thoughts replayed in her head, echoing Azalea's words.

"I have to send you on your way, lest the creator suspect that there's something different about you."

This place is no accident.

My memories aren't just gone.

They were stolen.

Her fists clenched. *I'm gonna get out of here, and I'm gonna get them back.*

Taking a deep breath to calm the anger that had begun to edge her vision, she glanced down at her meat, which was still untouched. She sank her teeth into the food, grimacing as she struggled to tear off a chunk. The taste wasn't terrible, but Luna hadn't been kidding about the rough texture.

Luna chuckled, noticing Rune's struggle. "It takes a sec to get the hang of it. Told you it was hard to chew."

Red flooded into Rune's cheeks. "I never said you were wrong."

Nyk made a face as he took a bite. "Doesn't help that I overcooked it a bit."

Luna shrugged. "I don't mind a well-done chunk from time to time. She opened her fist, allowing a flame to spark and dance along her palm. "A little char coating is always best."

Ivory raised an eyebrow at her. "Can't say I agree."

The blonde shot him a look. "That's because *you* have no taste."

Ivory crossed his arms, leaning back against the tree. Even sitting down, his long, lithe frame practically towered over the rest of them. "I think you're outnumbered on this one, Luna."

Glancing around at the rest of the group's mildly mortified expressions, Luna returned to her meal with a huff, muttering something under her breath. Even so, her eyes gleamed with an underlying playfulness, and Rune got the feeling that teasing didn't bother her in the slightest.

Actually—I don't think anything bothers her.

As she ate, a warm tingling began to seep beneath Rune's skin, each passing moment only increasing the intensity of the feeling. At first, it was barely noticeable—but as the sun rose higher, the feeling amplified, and Rune found herself wincing slightly at the unfamiliar buzzing beneath her skin.

Well—this is new.

Wait...

A memory resurfaced in Rune's mind—the moment a few nights before, when the girl had pinned her down, plunging a knife towards her chest. In that moment, her instincts had taken over, grabbing a hold on whatever energy it could find and forcing it out of her body—resulting in a blinding flash of light that had happened to save her life. That feeling had returned now, but on a much more docile scale, taking the form of a gentle pulsing in her gut instead of the endearing tempest she'd experienced during the fight.

The tingling...is it the light?

Curious, she extended her hand, reaching for the buzzing in her stomach. She inhaled slowly, embracing the sharp scent of smoke and the crisp, prominent aromas of pine sap as the energy responded to her call, filling her with an empowering sense of strength. The breath left her lips as she slowly traced her fingers across the air, focusing on the faint tingle where the sunlight met her skin.

At first, there was nothing—then a gentle trail of golden rays began to bend around her palm, refracting unnaturally on the ground. The power was strange—an alien force, an ability that her body shouldn't possess but somehow did. Even so, her mind was able to mesh seamlessly with the light, allowing her to bend it effortlessly to her will.

"Okay, show off." Luna grinned at her, faint sparks glimmering around her fingertips.

Rune fought the urge to roll her eyes, but a smile threatened to creep across her lips. "You have quite the knack for snide comments."

Luna leaned back, placing her hands behind her head. "I

prefer to state it as a talent for making the ordinary way more interesting."

Rune raised an eyebrow, losing the battle with her smile. "Whatever you say." Closing her fists, she extinguished the glow that had begun to radiate from her skin, snapping the sunrays back to their natural positions.

Nyk grinned at her. "Awesome."

"Yeah, okay, it's pretty cool," Luna admitted, twirling a lone blue flame around her fingertip. "Though I'll stick with my fire, thanks."

Rune couldn't help but let out a laugh, her eyes skipping across the faces of the group.

My friends.

The word startled her for a moment, making her hesitate. *Friends.* Friendship was something she knew she'd had, but of course couldn't remember, leaving a wide, frustratingly familiar gap in her thoughts. *What is a friend?* Emotions flooded through her, but the pictures that went with them remained unseen, shrouded behind the thick curtain of darkness that her mind had become. New memories—Luna laughing, Azalea teasing Nyk, the playful glint in Ivory's eye—they slotted themselves into the emotions, fitting together like two pieces from different puzzles that somehow connected.

Beside her, Azalea shifted suddenly, leaning forward. "What now, though? Where do we start looking?"

It took Rune a moment to realize that she was referring to their remaining teammates—who could be in any of the four biomes.

She's right...how are we supposed to find them?

Luna extinguished her flames, resting her chin on her palm.

"Well—it's not like we've got a map or anything, but we could try the only place that we can actually get to."

Azalea frowned at her. "And where would that be?"

The blonde's lips curled into a smile as she reached into a hidden pocket by her ankle, pulling out a palm-sized disc. Like a compass, there were four points, each labeled with an engraved letter. The points divided the disc into four equal sections, each section framed by the outside of the circle and containing an indented quadrant. The indented pieces had a strange feel to them, making the compass feel as though it were missing parts of itself.

Azalea's jaw fell slightly. "You have a leystone? Where'd you get it?"

Luna's smile widened. "One of our attackers from the other night had one. They didn't notice me, so I decided to borrow it."

Ivory made a face. "Is *that* why they were chasing us?"

"I—that is completely irrelevant. Show them the shard, please?"

Ivory raised an eyebrow, shooting her a 'we'll finish this conversation later' look before he reached into a pocket similar to Luna's, pulling out a thin shard of glass shaped conveniently like the indents on the leystone.

"Ivory's had a blue leyshard ever since I met him," Luna started, running her fingers along the glassy surface of the shard. "But not until now have we had a leystone to match it."

Nyk's eyes traveled from Luna to Ivory, realization dawning on his face. "So that means..."

Luna grinned, holding the leystone out as if presenting a prize to the group. "First stop: the Blue Biome."

II

REI

"**W**ake up."

Rei groaned. The gruff voice above her, the painful bindings around her wrists, and the hard ground she lay on made her want to do anything but that.

The strange figure who'd so rudely surprised her in the middle of the night had been traveling with a dragon of his own, as she had discovered when she'd regained consciousness midway through the flight. Her hands and feet had been tied, however, and with the blindfold around her eyes giving her no way to make a plan, she'd eventually given up and allowed her body to drift back off to sleep. The demanding voice that had decided to interrupt her slumber, however, sounded nothing like her kidnapper. Where his voice had been silky and hypnotic, the new tone was raspy and rough, making it sound as though the man had swallowed a jar of rock dust.

I'm not sure what I was imagining when I thought of a world beyond the Horizon's Teeth, but this definitely wasn't it.

Something cold pressed into Rei's palm, and her eyes shot open as a sharp, raw pain surged through her. She barely managed to choke down the startled cry that had welled up in her throat, refusing to give her captors the satisfaction of thinking they could control her. Warm blood trickled down her hand from the gash he'd drawn with his dagger, but she refused to look at it, keeping her eyes evenly locked on the beady brown ones of this new enemy.

It was late—the sun was already sinking beneath the horizon, the last dying rays of light illuminating the land with a vermilion glow. Despite the sky darkening with each passing second, she had no issue making out the rough features of the man before her. His height was less than impressive, but he made up for it with broad shoulders and a muscular build. His eyes were far too small for his wide face, and an unkempt beard encircled his mouth. Rei frowned as he mussed his wild black hair back, revealing a pair of stubby, *pointed* ears. Even stranger were the shiny, earth colored patches that decorated his face and arms. They looked almost like dragon scales—but that was impossible.

Wasn't it?

"Ay, boss. Kid's awake." His mouth twisted into a gleeful smile.

Out of the corner of her eye, Rei watched as a slender man rose from where he sat by a roaring campfire, making his way over to them.

"I thought I had told you to stop calling me that." Rei straightened at the voice of the man who'd carried her here. "My name is *Evander*, Haric. I expect to be addressed as such."

Haric muttered a spiteful apology as Evander brushed back

his hood, revealing the face of a handsome man who looked to be in his mid twenties. From his sharp blue eyes and wrinkle-free emerald tunic to his neat sand-colored hair and youthful smile, the stark contrast to Haric's appearance only made Rei more curious about her situation.

How did they end up working together? And why?

Evander leaned closer to examine Rei, and she held his gaze evenly, refusing to show any sign of weakness. He, too, had pointed ears—though his were much longer and far more grace-ful-looking than Haric's.

"What an interesting girl," Evander mused. "Not an ounce of fear in her eyes." His gaze traveled to her bleeding palm, which was now throbbing horribly. She bit her lip against the stinging pain, relying on the adrenaline pumping through her blood to keep her reaction somewhat controlled. "Didn't cry out when you cut her, either. She might be the one we've been looking for."

Haric rolled his eyes. "You say that every time. And every time, we get our hopes up, only to have them dashed when 'the one' winds up speared through by a guard."

Evander shot his comrade a dirty look. "There's something different about her."

Haric made a face. "I'll believe it when I see it."

Rei glanced from one man to another, the struggle to keep an indifferent expression on her face becoming a whole lot harder. *Others? Speared through? Guard?* Her thoughts warred against one another in her mind, fighting for no reason other than to cause more chaos. *What do they want with me? And why does Haric think it's going to get me killed?* A cold tremor ran down her spine as the words sank in, the harsh reality they brought becoming yet another reason why she needed to get out of there as soon as possible.

Evander turned back to her, kneeling down so their faces were level. "Alright, kid. Can you fight?"

Rei bristled at being called a kid—he only looked to be about a decade older than she was. Some sensible part of her, however, warned her to hold her tongue. "Why do you want to know?"

His expression shifted, and his hand hovered over the hilt of the dagger at his side. "Answer the question."

Rei scowled. "I'm considered fairly skilled in combat by most standards. If you *really* want to know, though, then you can untie me and we'll have a little test."

Evander's face twisted into a glare, and for a moment, he looked ready to do just that. But Haric stepped forward, shooting him a meaningful look. A half-smile dawned on Rei's lips as he recomposed himself, still glowering pointedly at her.

"That cocky smile of yours won't be there much longer, I can promise you that." Evander's tone was full of malice as he stood, casting her a wary gaze. "We're wasting time. Aiz, grab her."

At a motion of his hand, a man she hadn't noticed melted out of the shadows, grabbing her bound wrists and roughly hauling her to her feet. Evander tilted his head at her, her stomach twisting at the raw malevolence in his smile. "Let me make a few things clear to you. You are here because I want something—something that you are going to get for me. Not far from here is the entrance to an elven stronghold, one with the sole purpose of guarding a very special sword—the one that I will be sending you to steal. You are to enter the stronghold, complete the heist, and return to this encampment by dawn."

Rei raised an eyebrow. "Of all the people you could have targeted for something like this—you picked a teenage girl—and you intend to let her run *free* in some stronghold? Do you realize how ridiculous you sound?" Despite her bold words, her heart raced in her chest, and it was all she could do to swallow the overwhelming fear that threatened to suffocate her. *I am in way over my head here...*

Instead of getting angry, Evander's smile only widened. "I figured that would be your response—which is why I decided to bring along a bit more *leverage* to ensure your cooperation."

The moment the words left his mouth, the blood drained from Rei's face, a million horrible possibilities instantly spiraling inside her mind. Her worst theories were confirmed, however, as two more men stepped into her field of vision— their hands clasped firmly around a thick chain tied to the neck of a bright green dragon.

Rei choked down the anguished cry that welled up in her throat, her lips forming his name but no sound leaving her mouth. Ember was here—he wasn't safe. The situation had just reached a whole new level of dire.

Seeing Rei's expression made Evander's smug grin feel even more like a million daggers plunging into her heart, her emotions surging up within her chest. *I hate this man.*

"A bit more willing to do it now, aren't you?" She refused to respond, but something in her eyes must have given her away. Evander took a step back, reaching for the dagger at his side. "You will be escorted to the stronghold by Zaif, Haric, and myself—and your dragon will be left here with the others. If

you fail to bring me the blade by morning, he *will* be *killed.*
Have I made myself clear?"

Rei nodded numbly, her heart plummeting into her stomach. She didn't resist as the man on her left—Zaif—grabbed her
shoulder roughly, steering her towards the treeline where
Evander had motioned for her to go. He and Haric lagged
behind, but she barely noticed, casting one last glance over her
shoulder at Ember's unconscious form.

Fury rocked her chest, and she took a deep breath, allowing
it to fill her. She needed that anger, that drive. It was so much
better than the fear that had seemed to have become her new
reality.

Just before her vision was obscured by the trees that loomed
over the encampment, she made a promise to herself, whispering the words and believing, for only a moment, that Ember
could hear them.

I'm coming back for you.
I promise.

Even the sunset seemed to hold an ominous
warning, painting the sky shades of scarlet as it vanished
beneath the skyline. An uneasy feeling settled into Rei's
stomach with each step she took, making it practically impossible for her to breathe normally. The heavy weight of Ember's
life—and her own—settled on her shoulders, crushing any last
sliver of her previous attitude.

"Almost in position," Evander muttered, hesitating for a

moment to scan the area before the group emerged out into the open. "It appears that my schedule calculations are correct, and there are no guards patrolling the immediate area." A hint of a smile crossed his lips.

"You don't have to sound like a soldier every time you open your mouth, you know," Haric grunted. "Simple talk is jus' fine for us regular folk."

Evander scowled at him. "Old habits are difficult to break. Do something for a few centuries, and you, too, will find it quite a challenge to stop."

A few CENTURIES? Rei didn't realize that she'd stopped moving until Zaif shoved her roughly from behind, muttering something under his breath. Her mind wandered to Faron and the phenomenon that had kept him from aging over the past millennium—could this be a similar situation? It was possible, but Evander was speaking about it as though it were nothing more than a common occurrence.

Haric shrugged, casting a glance back in Rei's direction. They were all wearing cloaks, which made it difficult to make out individual faces. The men's features were unmistakable, however, even in the darkness. "Not sure what went through your mind with this one, boss. Just because the kid is a bit spirited don't mean she can handle stealing one of the most protected treasures in the realms."

Evander gritted his teeth. "*Don't* call me that. And it isn't your place to doubt my judgment. What do you care, anyway? She isn't your kid."

What a wonderful group. A shiver rippled down her spine, and she swallowed hard, forcing herself to focus on one step at a time. The unfamiliar words in Haric's statement didn't quite sink in, the fog of uncertainty in her mind keeping her from thinking straight.

"Don't you think it was a bit over the top to threaten the dragon's *life*?" Zaif asked, his tone challenging. "Let's be real—there's no way this kid can get the sword. I don't see why we should waste a perfectly good creature like that." Rei bristled, remembering her vow. *Just you wait.*

Haric snorted. "Please, it looks like a runt anyway. What dragon breed you ever seen that's *green*?"

Rei bit her tongue to keep herself from saying anything, knowing it would only get her into a worse situation than she was already in. *You, my friend, just drew a massive target on your own back.*

Evander glared at them. "Quit arguing. We're here."

Rei had to admit: she'd been expecting something a *lot* more intimidating than a cliff wall.

Evander's expression shifted into a scowl when he turned and saw the look on her face. "You can't judge by appearances, I'm afraid." His eyes wandered to the cliffside, a brief note of fear lingering in their depths for barely a moment.

He's afraid of this place?

The man cleared his throat, grabbing Rei's wrists tightly. "Alright—let's just get this over with. The sword is kept in the very center of the stronghold, but that's just about all we know...nobody we've ever sent in has made it out, so I advise you to be the first. Bring us the blade before dawn, and you can go free with your dragon. It's as simple as that. I could care less whether you live or die, but I want that weapon. Understood?"

Rei bit back her terror, using the sharpness of her anger as a way to clear the haze from her mind. *Now is not the time to get overwhelmed.* "If it's so important, why don't you do it yourself?"

Evander leered at her. "Don't ask foolish questions." Drawing his dagger, he sliced neatly through the ropes that bound her wrists, and she watched as the torn pieces fell harmlessly to the ground. She flexed her fingers, eyeing the red welts that the rope had left behind.

"You better not try anything," he hissed, slowly unclipping a second dagger Rei hadn't noticed before from his belt. "Make one move towards any of us, and you'll be dead so fast you won't know what hit you."

Rei eyed him coolly as he hesitantly handed her the weapon, waiting until she'd stashed it in her own belt before taking a step back. She made sure to thread her gaze with just the right amount of malice—enough to let her captors know that it wasn't weakness holding her back from attacking.

"You didn't actually think that we'd send you in unarmed, did you?" Evander spat.

That was exactly what Rei had thought, but she would never admit it to them. A smaller, more rational voice inside her pointed out something that she was desperately trying not to think about: if every previous captive had tried this heist—*armed*—and still failed, then she was in for something far more difficult than she'd previously imagined.

Either that, or the previous captors were horrible fighters.

"I wish you luck, kid." For the first time, Evander's voice didn't sound snarky or enraged. "The death you're going to face inside is not one I'd wish on anyone, even my worst enemy." Wedging his fingertips into an oddly deep gouge in the rock, he wrestled the stone to the side, grinning in satisfaction as the practically invisible door slid away to reveal an uncomfortably dark hallway.

Wonderful, Rei thought ruefully, casting him a wary glance as he stepped away from the cliff face.

"Have fun!" Haric proclaimed in a mock-cheerful tone, his smile revealing a mouthful of chipped, yellowing teeth.

Rei fought the urge to gag, turning back to the entrance. *I've fought in wars. I helped kill a DEMON, for the moon's sake. Dark, creepy hallways are perfectly fine.* Reminding herself of what was at stake, she steeled her nerves, casting her captors one last vengeance-filled glare before taking a step into the stronghold.

TURNS OUT, SILENCE COULD EASILY BE WORSE THAN noise.

Especially if that silence seemed to haunt you, jumping out and terrifying you with every step, creeping out of the darkness and stalking you, and giving you the constant urge to glance over your shoulder even though you knew there wasn't anything there.

Rei had been having that feeling a lot lately, especially since the battle.

But that did *not* mean she was used to it.

Rei took a deep breath, focusing on the heavy sound her feet made when they met the marbled ground. From what she could see, the hallway was very clean and well-kept, judging by the sleek stone walls with obsidian veining and the smooth, blemish-free ceiling that mirrored the floor.

The only problem was the lighting.

Or lack of it, rather.

I can't even imagine working here, Rei grumbled mentally, using the complaints as a distraction from the less-than-comforting atmosphere. *You'd have to be able to see in the dark to not go insane.* With a sigh, she stretched out her hands, her fingers trailing along the walls. *This'll help a bit, at least.*

Ahead, the hallway began to widen, distracting her from her thoughts. She felt the walls pull apart from one another until she couldn't touch both simultaneously, and after a long moment, she decided to lift her right hand and hug the left side.

Rei wasn't sure how long she kept going, one step at a time —but time could play funny tricks on you in a dark hallway that supposedly led to an excruciating death. But it also led to a sword—a sword that could set her and Ember free. Right now, nothing else mattered.

A loud, horrible click shattered the silence, her heart rate doubling in a matter of seconds. She stumbled over something, letting out a startled cry and scrambling to regain her balance.

The floor shifted beneath her feet, causing her heart to crawl to a stop.

The tile she stood on had *lowered* at least an inch into the ground.

She only had a few brief, terrifying moments of realization before an alarm began to sound, echoing through the hallway to announce her arrival.

12

REI

*N**o.**

The alarm blared in her ears, sending a constant reminder that the entire facility was now very aware of her presence. Frantically, she scanned the wall with her fingertips, searching for something, anything to hide her. It was dark, sure—but something told her that the visual impairment wouldn't be much of an issue for her pursuers.

There. Her fingers caught on something that felt different from the rest of the wall—a plate that was a bit smoother than the others, shifting slightly when she applied pressure. Distant footsteps strengthened her resolve, and she spread her arms apart, tracing the perimeter of the odd piece. It stretched all the way from the floor to wherever the ceiling was above her, but only spanned about two feet in width.

Ideal? No. Useful? Maybe. The possibility of the slight shake she'd felt when prodding it being nothing more than a loose screw lingered in the back of her mind, but she refused to listen to it, clinging to the only shred of hope that she could find. Her fingertips found the edges of the panel, which were sunken ever so slightly into the wall.

The footsteps of guards grew steadily closer, sparking a sense of urgency in the back of her mind. She allowed the adrenaline to pump through her, to fuel her. Bracing herself for hardly a moment, she drove her palms into the plate with as much force as she could muster. The plate budged, but refused to give way, and she swallowed her panic before stepping back to give it another go.

Thundering, rhythmic sounds echoed through the halls, the footsteps practically upon her now. Her fingers flitted to her hip, clasping around the hilt of Evander's dagger. It was such a small weapon—but if all else failed, it would be her only chance.

A single dagger in the dark...against hordes of soldiers... she shut down the thought, taking a few steps back and steadying herself. A shaky breath rocked her chest, and her eyes fluttered closed, a single tear carving a trail in the dust that coated her face.

What have I done?

I knew the danger. I knew, and I still went. Her fists clenched. *I thought I could handle it. I thought I was invincible. I was a fool.*

Time seemed to slow as the burning in her chest intensified, the weight of her situation finally settling on her shoulders. *I was right. There is a world beyond the Horizon's Teeth.* Another tear found its way along her cheek, and she made no effort to wipe it away. *If this is the reality of that world, though—I guess it isn't such a bad thing that Akaidia will remain in the dark.*

Swallowing hard, she planted her feet, angling her right shoulder at where she knew the plate to be. It was probably hopeless, yes. She could easily be living her last moments—but even so, something inside her refused to let her give in, a force that had fueled her from the beginning. The very feeling that had brought her here, the idea of just *knowing* that something was out there.

Something that called to her.

I'm not going down without a fight.

I'm not giving up.

I'm not going to die.

She gritted her teeth, hesitating for a brief moment. *This is going to hurt.*

The sounds of footsteps coming terrifyingly close vaporized any doubt that lingered in her mind.

Rei sprang forward, bracing her shoulder to collide with the wall.

But—the wall never came.

Instead, a strange tingling sensation rippled over her skin, as though she were passing through a barrier of gelatinous liquid. Overwhelmed by her momentum, she stumbled forward, tripping over herself and just barely managing to stop her fall before she lost balance.

The sound of footsteps was slightly dulled now—they'd grown *nearer*, sure, but any noise she heard was muffled, as though she were underwater. Bewildered, Rei rose to her feet, pivoting around and reaching out to feel for whatever she'd just inadvertently passed through.

All her palms met was cold, hard stone.

That's impossible.

She felt it again, just to be sure—tracing her fingers all along the smooth slab that was undeniably solid. The space she stood in was roughly two feet wide, matching the loose panel she'd been trying to move. *Glad I'm not claustrophobic, I guess.* Before she could attempt to salvage some fragment of a rational explanation for what had just happened, an unfamiliar voice met her ears, sending a shudder down her spine.

"This is the spot?"

Silence, then the low, ominous grating of metal. *They're armed. Of course.*

"Yes. That's the trigger tile."

More silence followed by muffled shuffling, like the guards were circling in confusion.

"Misfire, maybe?"

"I guess. Old runes can be faulty sometimes—fading of the ink causing a mistranslation, or something like that."

A rustle of clothing.

"Stone's clearly been pressed—ain't no accident. Besides— didn't we switch to a carving system last year?"

"You'd know better than I would. I'm a guard, not an enchanter."

A pause. "An intruder couldn't know about the passages, could they?"

Someone snorted. "No chance. Even if they knew about the runes, no sane person would charge headlong at a solid wall. It'd be far too risky."

A smile crept across Rei's lips. *I suppose that makes me insane, then.*

"Should we check the passages anyway?"

Don't you dare. Rei drew her dagger silently, poising it at the wall.

"Don't bother. Even if there is an intruder, they'll be discovered long before they get so much as a glimpse of the sword."

We'll see about that, won't we. She lingered a moment longer, waiting until their footsteps had faded into the distance before she truly allowed herself to relax. Nothing about her situation was safe—but now she had an exploitable advantage. *I'm in the passages. Guess that makes sense.* She frowned. *Probably means that there are a lot of guards hidden somewhere in these tunnels, though.*

Rei turned around, sliding her dagger back into its sheath and stretching her arms out to feel both sides of the wall. It proved to be a much more convenient way to navigate, and she made quick progress, weaving through twists and turns using only touch to guide her. Miraculously, it was completely silent the whole time, with zero signs of other life anywhere.

There was only one problem.

Which way was the sword?

She kept her attention trained on keeping track of the tunnels, mapping each turn she made and counting every footstep. Her thoughts joined with her heartbeat, forming a steady, thrumming rhythm that spurred her forward. *This is for Ember. For my promise to Cedar. I've got to get that blade.*

I've got to make it out of here alive.

Suddenly, a new sound shattered her train of thought, causing her to freeze.

The brief hesitation saved her life.

A loud clatter alerted her to the presence of another person, and she reacted on instinct, whipping around towards the source of the noise and throwing a blind punch with as much power as she could muster. Miraculously, it landed, finding what she thought to be her opponent's jaw and causing him to grunt as he stumbled backwards. Scrambling away, Rei drew her dagger, holding it out at the darkness while her heart thundered in her ears.

What a great time to not be able to see anything.

A whistle in the air was the only warning she had of the strike, and she swung her dagger up to intercept it. Appreciation for all of Master Faron's rigorous training sank in as metal met metal, her body automatically knowing what to do next.

Quicker than her opponent expected, she ducked to the side, planting a blow directly into where she knew her target's stomach to be. Just as she'd expected, he let out a strangled breath, retreating.

Even though she couldn't see, her instincts drove her forward, remaining senses heightened as she found the man's figure in the darkness and knocked him to the ground. A breathy cry escaped her lips as his blade dug into her side, but she only gritted her teeth, fumbling around until she found his wrists and pinning them with her knees. He squirmed under her weight, and her wound sent tremors of agony rippling through her as she readjusted to keep him incapacitated. Right before he was about to buck her off, her fingers found his throat, and she brought the dagger down without hesitation, her arm fueled by an animal-like desire to survive.

Horrible flashbacks instantly slammed into her as soon as her weapon met flesh, causing her chest to tighten as the memories overtook her mind.

The life leaving the man's eyes as he fell to the ground, scarlet liquid staining the snow. The sick, squirmy feeling that had wormed into her stomach, planting a weed among the flowers she'd fought so hard to cultivate.

Beneath her, the guard's body went limp, and she slowly rose to her feet, clutching the dagger so tightly that her knuckles were probably turning white. The memory simply refused to leave her mind, but she somehow managed to choke it down, her eyes burning. Warm, sticky liquid coated her fingers, a painful reminder of what she'd just done.

That was another time, another place. I am not that girl anymore, she reminded herself, closing her eyes despite the fact that she couldn't see a thing anyway. *I will not be afraid to take the lives of those who intended to take mine.*

Forcing herself to keep her mind on something else, she knelt beside the man's body, searching tentatively for anything that might prove useful. It took her a moment, but she managed to locate his weapon—a blade that seemed to be somewhere between a sword and a dagger. Careful to keep her hands clear of the sharp edges, she fumbled around with the handle, finally fastening it to her belt.

After a moment, her fingers found something she was unable to recognize—a smooth, spherical orb dangling from a thin necklace. Grimacing at the blood on the chain, she lifted it over his head, exploring the odd object. *A key, maybe? Some sort of identification?* There were no bumps or ridges, but the material had a unique texture, hard like a crystal yet warm and leathery to the touch. Curiosity piqued, she raised it to her own neck, debating whether or not to put it on. *Couldn't hurt, I guess.*

The moment the necklace was fastened, light erupted in front of Rei's eyes, causing her to flinch back and cover her face in shock. Slowly, she parted her fingers, realization flooding through her as she lowered her palms. *I can see. I can see everything.*

She rose to her feet, pivoting in a circle and blinking rapidly as her eyes adjusted to the bright environment. Somehow, the orb had dissolved the darkness completely, leaving her standing in a perfectly lit passage. *This must be how the guards are able to see in here,* she mused, examining the polished marble floors and painfully simple gray walls.

A small spark of hope began to flare up inside her with each new observation, a smile tugging on her lips.

Then her gaze found the body of the man she'd killed.

The spark was instantly smothered.

Laying in front of her was a boy—a boy barely older than herself. *Eighteen, maybe? Nineteen?* Her heart ached as she examined his face—a youthful complexion twisted into an eternal expression of agony. Tears burned in her eyes as she crouched beside the boy, guilt settling in her gut. The man she'd killed all those years ago was branded in her thoughts, his face intermingling with the boy's in her mind.

That man had a family somewhere.

So does this boy.

They didn't deserve this.

Then, from somewhere much deeper and darker within her: *They would have done the same to you.*

Her mind flickered to a scene she'd all but forgotten about —when she'd broken down in front of her squadron leader after her first battle. The words of the young woman were still ingrained clearly in Rei's memory, even if her mind had tried to blot it out from the raw fear and grief she'd experienced.

"Look at me, Rei. Whatever you do, do not let the guilt of those deaths be your master. If the roles were reversed—if it was your body lying out there, not theirs—I can assure you that they would be thinking nothing of it. War does horrible things to a person—it strips away their humanity, leaving them no better than animals. Know what matters most. Hold it close, and do not let it go. Out there, on the battlefield—it's all you have."

Rei rose to her feet, blinking back the tears that threatened to break loose and forcing herself to reset her priorities. *Ember's life is at stake here. My life is at stake.* Her hands balled into fists, anger boiling in her blood. *The people who kidnapped me—who blackmailed me into coming in here—they knew this would happen. They thought they were sending a teenager to her death.* A grim expression tainted her face. *Those men deserve nothing but the fate they promised me...I wish more than anything that I could be the one to give it to them.*

Before her mind could trap her again, she turned, taking off down the hallway. Her eyes traced the monotonous gray walls, her pace nearly tripling with the presence of her sight. *Remind me to never take light for granted again.*

The rhythm of her footsteps became like a metronome for her thoughts, keeping them in time with each push forward.

Find the blade.

Make it out.

They thought I'd die.

They thought I'd fail.

A smile crossed her face. *They thought wrong.*

"What *exactly* do you think you're doing?"

Rei's blood ran cold at the guard's voice, her fingers moving to the hilt of her dagger. *Grown man—behind me, somehow.*

Probably from that intersection I just ran past. "Uh...going for a stroll?"

The guard lunged for her, but she was ready, whipping around and crossing her weapons in front of her to block the incoming blow. This man was a much more experienced fighter than her prior opponent, and he broke through her defense with surprising speed, leaving her barely any time to scramble away. The wound in her side that she had been somehow able to ignore since the first fight burned with agony, waves of pain rippling through her body. She gritted her teeth, parrying the flurry of counterattacks and narrowly managing to remain out of harm's way.

Realizing Rei's skill, the man let out a surprisingly loud shout, and Rei had only seconds to react as a second guard seemed to melt out of the wall beside her. *Passages within the passages? Are you kidding me?* She blocked the strike and stumbled backward to create distance between herself and the two men, but not before the newcomer's sword had drawn a long, red gash across her cheek.

The first guard lunged for her once again, his sword hooking around the weapon she'd taken from the boy and sending it clattering across the floor. Panic fueled her movements as she ducked out of the way, frantically racking her brain for options.

I can't win like this. Not when they control the fight.

Deciding on a tactical retreat, she pivoted around, bolting in the first direction she could see that was not blocked by a sinewy man. A chorus of shouts and thunderous footsteps behind her indicated an uncomfortably close pursuit, and adrenaline pulsed through her, propelling her forward.

"She's after the sword!"

Of course I am. It's not like I have much of a choice. After a moment, however, the words sunk in. *Or maybe—could I actually be heading in the right direction?*

The idea was yet another spark to fuel the blaze, pumping her with more energy than her body had ever generated in her life. Air whipped at her face as she rounded a corner, her blood suddenly running cold as she realized that her current path ended in a dead end.

Or...a not-so-dead end. Her eyes honed in on the wall at the limit of the tunnel—two feet wide, solid-looking, and definitely not something anyone would charge at with the intent to crash at full speed.

Yet that was exactly what she planned to do.

Rei clenched her fists, silencing every single survival instinct she had as she careened into the visually impassable surface. A tingling sensation rippled across her skin as she barreled through, emerging into a circular room with at least twenty guards spread out around the perimeter.

All eyes instantly shot towards her—but hers didn't move from the center of the room.

There, embedded firmly into the ground, was an elaborate sword hilt crafted of obsidian.

I found it.

It didn't take long for the moment of shock to wear off, and every guard was instantly upon her, converging on all sides to intercept her before she could reach the sword. Rei was already moving, her attention locked on nothing but her target.

Nothing else matters.

She felt them close in on her, smothering her in a mass of angry stares and outstretched blades.

She didn't know how she would get out.

Didn't know how she'd survive.

But something—a voice deep inside her—whispered that as long as she could get her hands on that weapon, she would be alright.

A guard lunged forward, intending to grab the blade—but he was too slow.

She got there first.

Rei threw herself into the air, her hand outstretched towards the blade. Just as the guards raised their weapons to strike her, her fingers found the smooth obsidian hilt, clasping firmly around the handle as her body met the ground.

In a blinding explosion of purple energy, everyone but Rei was blasted backwards against the wall.

13

REI

Energy.
So.
Much.

Energy.

It surged through her—pulsing through her blood, empowering her limbs, overtaking her completely. Even if she had wanted to pull away, she couldn't—her hand was glued to the sword, fingers clutching the hilt like it was her lifeline.

Truth be told—it was.

She hadn't realized that she'd closed her eyes until she opened them again, the room sharpening into perfect clarity around her. Aches that she knew should have been there weren't, the pain of her wounds stripped from her body entirely. The wounds themselves were still there—bruises covered her skin like freckles, and blood was caked to the numerous gashes she'd acquired.

But she felt nothing.

Slowly, confidently, Rei pulled herself to a standing position, not once breaking contact with the sword. A flash of movement in her peripheral vision warned that the guards were regaining their balance, but despite their obvious intention to take her life, not an ounce of fear was present in her mind. She kept her eyes on the hilt, her body completely trusting the purple energy to keep the guards at bay.

It was a strange feeling—the power was alien, yet it was a part of her. A shard of her very being, lying dormant within her until awoken.

Rei adjusted her position, tightening her one-handed grip on the weapon. Every rational voice left inside her warned that there was no possible way she could break the blade free from the stone it was wedged so deeply inside, but the strength coursing through her whispered otherwise.

A guard standing straight across from her raised his head, eyeing her in amused disdain. "No one can pull that blade, little girl—not even us. I don't know how you got this far—but I'm afraid you've got nowhere left to run."

Rei held his gaze evenly, her eyes swirling with an age old anger that came from somewhere beyond herself. This weapon was so much more than just a sword—so much more than just a piece of sharpened metal.

It held power.

Real power.

"Who said anything about running?"

Flipping her right hand upside down and gripping the hilt firmly, she pooled all her strength into her arm, tugging upward on the blade with everything she had.

At the first sign of force, the stone gave way.

A gasp escaped her lips, breath flooding into her lungs as

the last of the energy was freed from its containment. The purple glow that had been keeping the guards away retreated, accumulating around Rei and encircling her idly, as if waiting for something. A feeling of pure, raw freedom—of *wholeness*—settled into her heart, sticking fast.

This is true power, she realized, pivoting in a circle to examine the room. *True power, like when Zuri commanded the Flame. This is why Evander wanted the sword. This is why he sent me here, why he decided to blackmail who knows how many people to get it.* She glanced down at the weapon in her hand, her eyes tracing the elegantly crafted hilt. *But—I don't think I want to give it to him anymore.*

What if I don't have to?

A smile slowly crossed her lips, and vivid memories of their threats on Ember's life resurfaced in her brain, making her blood boil with rage.

What if I don't have to play his game?

She glanced at the guards, all of whom were gripping their weapons tightly...yet not a single one made a move towards her position. Some had fear in their eyes, some disgust, and some were eyeing her like she wasn't even a mortal being anymore. Rei hesitated for a moment, unsure of what to do next.

You could just kill them all.

Rei did a double take, stunned at the thought. She shut the idea down immediately, shaking her head. *No. It wouldn't accomplish anything.* Her eyes narrowed, Evander's smug expression branded in her mind.

The only blood that will be on my hands is the blood of those who deserve their fate.

These people don't.

Rei raised her head, keeping her expression neutral and her eyes locked on those of the guards. When she spoke, her voice filled the deafening silence of the room, echoing off the corner-less walls. "Which of you can show me the way to the exit?"

Silence.

Rei sighed. "Let me rephrase that. I am going to leave, and you are not going to stop me. I mean you no harm, but I *will* use force if I have to." She turned her attention to the nearest guard, who shrunk away from her gaze. "At least point me in the right direction."

With a trembling hand, he motioned to a wall panel on his left. The whole room had no visible entry—the only point of access was the passages, which Rei had to admit was an extremely impressive security system. *They really went all out to defend this.*

She nodded at him, even going so far as to offer a smile—which resulted in a hilarious look of bewilderment from the man. Facing the panel and crossing her fingers that he hadn't told her to run headlong at a regular wall, she rushed forward, her body phasing seamlessly into the tunnels.

Now I just...go straight?

Silence was her only companion as she followed the passage to wherever it led, her thoughts like a hurricane. Memories, feelings, faces, and the pure, raw aura of power consumed her mind entirely, her body unsure of what to do with everything that had happened.

Don't think about that now.

Don't think about the power.

Don't think about the death.

Remember why you're here.

Remember why this weapon is in your hand in the first place.

Her chest was tight, and her body was crying out at her to stop, but she somehow managed to keep going, one numb step at a time. The walls around her turned to nothing but a blur, her focus locked on the always distant end of the tunnel.

Then, suddenly—something made her stop.

"I must admit, you are the smartest intruder we've ever encountered."

Rei froze, her blood running cold.

"But I'm afraid that we're going to have to put an end to whatever little adventure you think this is."

Slowly, Rei pivoted around, turning her piercing gaze on the guards that seemed to have followed her. Despite the millions of responses on the tip of her tongue, she remained silent, waiting to see what they would do next.

They outnumbered her, but she didn't fear them.

There was no fear anymore.

"Look, *kid.*" A man who looked to be the leader stepped forward, his eyes burning with fury. "I don't know how a *teenager* like yourself even managed to get this far, or how you're holding the sword—but no one has *ever* entered uninvited and left with their life." He scanned her expression, which remained as neutral as she could keep it. "You didn't actually think I'd let you ruin that, did you?"

"No." Her lips twisted into a smile, but her eyes remained stony. *No more games.* "But for your sake, I was certainly hoping so."

With a grunt, the man lunged for her, clearly underestimating just how much strength the sword was giving her. She swung her blade up to effortlessly block his strike, a shower of purple sparks erupting around them as the weapons collided. The other guards closed in on her, but she kept them at bay with relative ease, her muscles fueled and her senses heightened.

Like this, I'm unstoppable.

Her mind flew through calculations in half the time it would normally take her, keeping her always a few steps ahead of her opponents. Despite the numerous opportunities presented, she always refrained from taking the lives of the guards, settling for a less fatal blow instead. *I'm not going to take any more from this place than I already have. They don't deserve to die—not for simply doing their job.*

Her brow furrowed, her pace nearly doubling as new energy flooded through her. *My kidnappers, however—that's another story.*

Ducking another blow, she stepped off-axis, delivering a swift counter-strike to the nearest man's exposed knee. He buckled under the hit, giving her just enough time to disarm him and pin him to the wall. Sharp waves of purple drifted around her, shielding her from the remaining enemies.

"Listen to me," she hissed, holding her sword to the man's throat. "I do not intend to take any of your lives—and I want to leave as badly as you want me to. So, if you would be so kind as to point me to the exit, I'll be on my way."

The man's eyes reflected a burning rage, but his expression was one of defeat. *Probably doesn't feel too great to be bested by a sixteen-year-old, regardless of the weapon I'm using.*

"Alright." The word was nothing but a grunt through gritted teeth, but Rei accepted it, stepping back and lowering her sword to her side.

He stared at her for a long moment, finally turning and

moving a little ways down the hall. Pressing his hand to a part of the wall that looked exactly like the rest, he closed his eyes, murmuring something under his breath. A soft click sounded, and the wall went blurry for a brief moment, fading in and out of vision as though it were a mirage.

"There. I unlocked the exit passage." He stepped aside, refusing to meet Rei's eye as she moved past him. Before she stepped into the tunnel, however, she cast one final glance in his direction.

"Thank you."

A smile flickered across her lips at the raw surprise on the man's face, and she turned her back on the group, breaking into a run down the tunnel. Each step brought her steadily closer to freedom—to Ember—filling her with a whirlwind of emotions.

Anger.

Grief.

Resolve.

Hope.

They all melded together inside her, amplified by the adrenaline and energy that pulsed through her blood. Her strength was dying—she could feel her body aching, even beneath the magical facade the sword seemed to be providing. Even so, her pace didn't slow, her muscles refusing to allow anything between them and freedom.

I'm almost there.

Almost safe.

After what felt like an eternity, the tunnel's limit finally came within sight, appearing as yet another solid wall. Rei pushed harder, any hesitation cleared from her mind. *One more doorway. One last leap.*

With a grunt of exertion, she flung her body at the end of the passage, a tingling sensation traveling across her skin as she phased through—her feet meeting the damp ground beneath a lightening pre-dawn sky.

Rei inhaled deeply, allowing a breath of the morning air to fill her lungs. She was free—she had made it. Her mind flickered to Ember, who was still trapped in the hands of the men who had sent her here. *I'm safe—but it's not over yet.*

Wasting no time, Rei bolted into the woods, tracing the steps she remembered taking the night before. *Has it really only been a few hours?* Her heart moved as quickly as her mind, pumping a strengthened resolve through her veins as she sped through the trees. The sky seemed to be racing her, lightening with every step. A purple haze rimmed her vision, and suddenly she was flying, her feet hardly touching the ground.

A large mahogany tree loomed ahead, the final landmark before she reached the encampment. With a cry of triumph and a spasm of pain from her bleeding side, she broke through into the clearing, turning all heads towards her.

For a long, heart-pounding moment, all was still—Rei standing idly by the trees, her eyes tracing the men who'd kidnapped her, and her captors, who's gazes were locked on the sword in her grip as shock overtook their expressions. She couldn't help but smile at the pure bewilderment—she'd done it. They thought she'd die, but she didn't—she was bloody, injured, exhausted, and full of rage, but she was alive.

Just you wait...I'm not finished yet.

Rei made the first move, stepping forward cooly into the dying moonlight. Out of the corner of her eye, she noticed Ember's head perk up from where he slept, his eyes lighting up with recognition. *I came back for you,* she thought, her stomach churning at the sight of the horrible state he was in. *Always have, and always will.*

"You—you're alive." Evander's words were nothing but a greedy breath.

Rei cocked her head, regarding him icily. "At least *try* not to sound surprised. Now release him." She nodded at Ember.

Evander's expression turned stony. "First, the sword."

"Release him. *Now.*" A few guards flinched away from the raw fury edging her tone, but Evander didn't budge. *Guess he's got more guts than I gave him credit for.*

"The sword. Then the dragon."

Rei took a threatening step forward. "You're playing with my patience. I came for my dragon, and I don't expect a *snake* like you to be able to keep your word. So I'll ask again: release Ember, and I'll give you the blade."

Evander's eyes narrowed. "I'm afraid that's not going to happen." He flicked his hand towards the men nearest Ember, his gaze steely.

At his signal, they closed in, drawing their weapons. For the first time, she realized just how tight the bindings were—the cruel metal clamps latched onto his wings to prevent flight, the chain around his neck, and the similarly styled links attached to his ankles.

That was the last straw.

People had talked about seeing red before—but this wasn't just red. It was raw, violent *hatred.* Purple energy rimmed her vision as rage dulled her senses, the pain and fear in Ember's eyes pushing her forward.

Plan B it is.

"I've played your game," she spat, her tone dripping with so much venom she could hardly recognize her own voice. "Now I'm *done.* If you wanted the sword, you should have stolen it yourself." A cold, wrathful smile spread across her face. "Finders keepers, I'm afraid."

Evander's eyes glittered with greed. "Your mistake, kid." He snapped his fingers, glaring pointedly at the rogues surrounding Ember—Zaif and Haric among them. They raised their blades, and Ember cowered, his snout clamped shut and any natural defenses he had stripped from him.

Watching the men bring their swords down towards the dragon—*her* dragon—something inside Rei snapped.

She lunged towards them, alien power fueling her muscles as she slammed the weapon's tip into the ground. Energy erupted from the earth, a wave of jagged purple spears breaking through the terrain beneath the men and killing them instantly. She had never felt this way before—so strong, so *invincible*—a force that simply could not be stopped, no matter who was against her. The purple energy was like an extension of her body, molding into any form she desired and bending to her commands without resistance. Power and rage melded together in her blood, coursing through her as she reeled on Evander, scarlet liquid streaming down her face.

"I told you to let him go," she growled, pacing slowly towards him. His eyes found the bodies of his dead comrades, dread consuming his features.

"You—you can't do this," he stammered, scrambling back from the bloody teenager practically glowing with pure strength. "The Master—the Eidolon himself—he'll come for you—"

Rei cut him off, flicking her hand to surround him with spikes of deadly purple energy. "Your master, hm?" *So he has a master...someone who probably sent him to get the sword.* "He and I do need to have a little chat sometime." She raised the blade to his chin, pausing a moment before slicing it neatly across his throat. "Why don't you leave him a message for me?"

The feeling of rage ebbed away as his body crumpled to the ground, leaving a cold, empty husk of energy in its wake. Numbly, Rei turned, rushing to Ember's side and cutting him free.

A wave of fatigue suddenly hit her, and the sword slipped from her grasp as she collapsed to the ground, the strength leaving her body as quickly as it had come. A sound reached her ears—footsteps, maybe—but she couldn't move, unable to do anything but lay there as her thoughts dissolved into a mess without rhyme or reason.

The Eidolon will come for me...

But who is he...

Why do I feel...so...tired...

Green scales surrounded her as the footsteps neared, but her body was too far gone to react to anything, the world fading in and out as her consciousness slipped away. Someone leaned over her, dark eyes peering into hers. The last thing she felt was strong, unfamiliar hands gripping her gently, lifting her into the air before everything was lost to darkness.

14
RUNE

"Luna, we've talked about this. You can't set something on fire just because it's in your way."

The glare Luna shot at him could have withered flowers, but Ivory was entirely unfazed. "You're no fun."

With a huff, she clenched her fist, extinguishing the flame that had begun to burn in her palm. Ivory glanced sideways at her, waiting until she rolled her eyes dramatically at him before turning back to the trail. Rune couldn't help but smile at the exchange, reaching out to lightly finger the rough bark of a tree they passed.

They'd only been traveling a few hours, making their way steadily across the thickly wooded terrain of the Green Biome. Thankfully, there had been no sign of any other people, meaning that for a while, Rune had managed to forget the fact that they were still trapped in an arena.

I may not know what it was like outside of this place—if I ever was—but I'd imagine that this comes pretty close.

Late morning sun illuminated the land, adding vibrant hues

to the monochrome natural shades—the amber undertones to the tree trunks, the faint green glow as the light passed through the leaves, the tiny stones mixed in with the soil—Rune inhaled deeply, a breath of earthy aromas filling her lungs. Fragmented golden rays created an ethereal atmosphere, and each time she passed through a beam, faint tingling would rush across her skin.

The light—the strange, unnatural power that she knew she shouldn't possess, yet did—it called to her in a way she was unable to explain, lingering in the back of her mind with each step she took. Curiosity wormed its way into her thoughts, and tentatively, she stretched out her hand, attention locked on the odd sensation she felt each time her skin came into contact with a direct patch of sun.

The tingling intensified the moment she became aware of it, and she inhaled sharply, her concentration shattered. Blinking a few times, she tried again, this time bracing herself for the barrage of pins and needles that instantly greeted her.

It wasn't as bad this time—now that she was ready for it— and she flipped her hand palm side up, focusing everything she had into the single ray that illuminated it. Everything else around her blurred, but her senses were somehow heightened, making her suddenly aware of the tiny, intricate glimmers that drifted all around her. She couldn't see anything, but she could *feel,* the world taking shape within her mind's eye despite the fact that her vision had all but been reduced to nothing.

The light. I can see the light—all of it.

Her smile widened into a grin, and she lifted her hand, watching as the sparks beneath her skin slowly moved outward. A memory surfaced at the motion—the memory of her first night here, when she'd turned her own body into a light source and blinded her attackers. She'd used this very technique then, but she simply hadn't noticed, her instincts kicking in before her mind could truly register what had happened.

Strange.

Rune blinked a few times, the distorted light-vision fading back into regular sight. Her pace had slowed, and she'd fallen behind—the rest of the group was at least ten feet ahead of her, their chatter filling the area.

With a smile, she tilted her head upward, eyes tracing the cloudless sky.

Blue.

Blue like the sky, like the biome we're trying to get to.

Maybe—if only for a moment—I can forget where I am, and what I'm facing.

Maybe even forget the life—or the death—that awaits me.

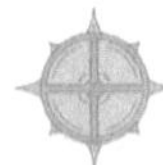

RUNE CURLED INTO A BALL, BURYING HER FACE IN HER knees. That was the third time that night she'd awoken in a cold sweat, plagued by relentless nightmares with meanings buried deep within their horrors. The third time she'd been forced to watch memories that she had never experienced, and even some that she felt like she had—memories that she would have preferred to stay buried deep in the farthest reaches of her mind.

The screams.

The blood.

The *power.*

Different people, different lives—but the power was the same.

It was *always* the same.

Lurking within each dream, calling out to her, whispering in her ear while darkness crept in on her from all sides.

She didn't know what it wanted.

Didn't know why it was here.

But it was.

And for a reason unknown to her—it had decided that it didn't want to leave.

Letting out a breath, she leaned back, resting her head on the makeshift bed she'd formed of nearby moss and gazing up at what she could see of the stars. The feeling of the dreams still lingered in the back of her mind, but the gentle night breeze calmed her, allowing her short, ragged breaths to finally regulate. *I'm alright. I'm alive. They're just dreams, Rune—they can't hurt you.*

Each set of images she'd been hurled into—each memory she'd been forced to experience—they'd all felt terrifyingly real, so much so in some cases that she almost believed it to be a part of her past life. Those dreams were always the strangest—blurry, fractured, and separated, yet entirely clear, images that simply didn't match with the horrible tempest of emotions that always embodied her as she watched them.

She was never harmed, yet her body screamed with pain.

There was no noise, yet her ears rang.

None of it lined up.

None of it made any sense.

Yet—somehow, she knew everything there was to know about it.

Rune sank into the moss, closing her eyes and wishing that the world in her mind would vanish with the gesture as her vision did. Her thoughts were a mess—a twisted, cluttered disaster—and she made no effort to sort them out, knowing that her efforts would be futile.

A groan escaped her lips as she rolled over on her side, holding out her hand and examining it closely. Her fingertips appeared gray in the moonlight, a familiar tingle rippling across her skin—but this time, it was far less intense, barely noticeable. Wrapped around her wrists like bracelets were rows of elaborate patterns—a birthmark crafted of intricate swirls and strange designs, something none of the rest of her friends possessed. The marks were a part of her, as much as her hair or her eyes...unlike the strange purple blotch on her neck.

On all of our necks.

A gust of brisk air sent a wave of rustling through the leaves, causing a chill to ripple down Rune's spine. She pulled her knees in tighter as goose bumps popped up along her arms, a result of the sudden drop in temperature. *I still don't understand the point of this place. Why am I here? Why are any of us here?* The images of her first fight in the arena—the night she'd met Luna and Ivory—resurfaced in her mind, a new observation clicking.

Teenagers.

We're all teenagers.

Nothing more than kids.

A shudder rocked her body, and her stomach tightened, bile rising in her throat as the truth of the words sank in for the first time. *Not only did the creator of this arena strip who knows how many people of their memories, forcing them to fight to the death for no reason at all...he did it to kids.*

Yet again, a word arose in her mind—a word that carried far more weight with it than any of the other thoughts spinning around inside, commanding order out of the cacophony that her headspace had become.

Why?

Of all the hundreds of questions running circles around Rune, it was that one she desired the answer to the most.

She bit her lip, casting a glance upward and rolling over to a more comfortable position. *If I ever want a chance to find out the answer...I'm going to have to fight. Hard.*

Despite the turmoil in her mind, Rune's body was weary, her eyelids growing heavy as she watched the moon crawl slowly across the sky. If she had to guess, there looked to be about two or three hours until dawn—not an exorbitant amount of time, but to her aching muscles, any extra minute of sleep would be a miracle.

Hoping beyond hope that the dreams wouldn't return, she allowed herself to relax, giving in to the sleep that fought to overtake her.

A GHOST OF A FROWN CROSSED THE TEENAGER'S FACE, her odd violet eyes tracing the practice dummies her mentor had arranged in front of her. "That's all?"

Her mentor smirked, crossing his bulky arms over a muscular chest. "Contrary to what you seem to believe, I do happen to have at least some respect for your skills. Which is why..." He clapped his hands, shouting a command in an unfamiliar language. To her delight, the wooden figures shifted in place, letting out a long creak before sluggishly spurring into motion. A rune appeared briefly on their foreheads—the one she had come to know as the 'hard mode' marker.

She didn't think she'd ever get used to the way he could just do that—call out a word and make things that should be impossible happen.

He raised an eyebrow in her direction, nodding at the now animated enemies. "Just because it's three in the morning doesn't mean I'm going to take it easy on you." A grin crossed his lips, though it was difficult to see beneath the well-trimmed black beard. "I will admit, I am feeling a bit generous, though—go on, take the first move."

Without wasting a beat, she charged straight for the nearest enemy, sword braced. The moment her feet touched the ground in front of it, the wooden figure sprang into action, swiping upwards with a dulled metal blade and meeting her weapon as she swung it down. Each of her following strikes was blocked too, but after a few moments, the relentless force of her attacks began to wear on the target. In a disturbingly person-like fashion, fatigue began to set into its nonexistent muscles, allowing her to overpower it. The moment her sword met its neck, the whole dummy went limp, returning to the inanimate wood it had once been.

Her mentor nodded in approval, flicking his wrist once again. She only had moments to react before three more of the practice targets set upon her, a loud clang slicing through the air as steel met steel.

Despite the distant ache of her muscles that began plaguing her as the fight went on, she relished every adrenaline-powered blow, both hers and her opponent's. The training was a welcome distraction from the horrible nightmares that had been haunting her as of recent, vivid images engulfing her mind while she slept. Something about them was different, though, distinguishing them from a normal dream...she couldn't quite put her finger on it, but the feeling was there, always lurking in the back of her mind.

It was almost as if they weren't dreams at all...but memories. Memories that weren't her own.

15

RUNE

Memories.

For what was probably the millionth time, the girl's voice replayed in Rune's mind, running circles in her thoughts despite her numerous attempts to dislodge it. When she'd finally gone to sleep, yet another dream had found her—but this one was different from the blatant nightmares and traumatic imagery.

This one felt...real.

Like Rune had really been standing there, engulfed in that girl's life.

And the feeling—that her dreams were more than dreams, that they might be memories—someone *else's* memories—that girl was feeling it too.

If I keep having dreams about her...does that mean she might be dreaming about me?

Maybe even about my memories...the ones I lost?

She paused.

No.

This is insane.

Rune shook her head vigorously, frustrated by how prominent the odd nightmares had become in her mind. They were by far the least of her concerns at the moment, but for some reason, she just couldn't get them out of her head. The endless whisperings—the voices, the truths that she couldn't tell from the lies, the resounding clamor that had become her reality—she hated it.

Hated all of it.

"Rune?"

Rune jumped, completely lost in her thoughts. Nyk's voice shattered through yet another cycle of winding memory, forcing her back to reality.

A frown twisted his features. "Are you okay?"

"Yeah...sorry. Just a little distracted." She winced as the lie left her lips.

The redheaded boy slowed his pace to walk beside her, glancing around constantly at their surroundings. "It's really peaceful here, isn't it."

Rune nodded. "It's weird. You'd think that for being trapped in an arena, you'd be a bit more on edge, but..." She trailed off, knowing that they both understood the rest.

Nyk hesitated for a moment. "Do you think it'll be like this? When we escape the arena?"

He makes it sound so easy. "Maybe." She paused. "You think there even is a place outside the arena? I mean...what if this is all there is?"

A shudder rocked his body. "I really hope not. There's just...this feeling, you know? That there's something *more*. I can't be the only one, right?"

Rune's eyes traveled up the spindly trunk of a nearby aspen, her mind latching onto his words. "No. You aren't." *I guess I've just been afraid to hope.*

Even though hope really is all I have...

Silence blanketed the group over the next hour of travel, Rune's legs growing weary from the uninterrupted motion. The forest wasn't too much of a bother to navigate through, at least—the temperatures were comfortable, the ground was packed and relatively level, and the undergrowth was mostly manageable. It was just a matter of distance...if she had to guess, they'd covered at least five or six miles since early that morning.

Up ahead, the conversation had somehow found its way to fire, which was undoubtedly Luna's doing.

"Wait...were *you* behind the giant wildfire on the west side a few weeks ago?" Azalea raised an eyebrow at the petite blonde.

Luna kept her eyes ahead, but a sly smile spread across her lips. "I might've had a thing or two to do with it. It was *not* my fault, though," she protested at Azalea's disproving expression.

Ivory let out a snort, earning him a glare from Luna. "It wasn't! *They* started it!"

"*They* didn't set fourteen trees on fire trying to prove a point!" Ivory argued.

"Fifteen," Luna muttered under her breath, grinning when Ivory shot her a pointed glance.

Rune couldn't quite hold in her laughter, relishing the distraction from her thoughts.

Azalea looked just as amused, glancing back and forth between the two. "That's—one way to win an argument, I guess."

Luna turned to Ivory, her face illuminated with triumph. "See? That's *exactly* what *I* told you!"

Ivory made a face. "Whatever you say."

Luna looked tempted to reply, but decided against it, settling for sparking a plume of blue flame and tossing it airily from one hand to the other. A blanket of silence fell over the group, and Rune turned her attention to the trees, a sense of distant comfort settling over her as her mind mapped the terrain.

As they moved, she noticed that the trees were becoming steadily thinner, allowing new rays of light to penetrate the canopy and lighten the area. The patches of undergrowth became fewer and farther between, which allowed them to quicken their pace.

Ivory glanced back, locking eyes with Rune for a moment and offering a brief smile. "We're getting closer."

"To the Leylock?" Rune's eyes scanned over the surrounding terrain once again, but she didn't notice anything out of the ordinary.

"Well—yes," he began, fingers fidgeting with the hilt of the dagger at his side. "But also to our first and only stop before we cross the border."

Just as the words registered in Rune's mind, they broke free of the woodland, leaving them standing in a decently large field bordered by trees. A few teenagers milled about, weaving between questionably constructed huts—not a significant amount of people by any stretch, but much more than Rune had seen in one place so far.

"Where *are* we?"

Luna turned to Rune, a grim smile on her face. "The only

place where someone might actually talk to you before they try to stab you in the back. Welcome to the Outpost, Rune."

The Outpost wasn't exactly *large*, but it didn't need to be—Rune only counted seven or eight people, all of them casting distrustful stares at one another while trading for weapons and materials. Her eyes skipped over the scene, making mental notes of anything that seemed particularly interesting.

A girl who looked to be maybe eighteen with an array of scars lining her face stared down a heavily built male, a scarlet rectangle displayed on her neck.

An underfed boy slinking in the shadows pulled his hood up, concealing a messy head of hair and a vibrant black marking.

A nervous-looking girl who could be barely fifteen clutched a serrated dagger until her knuckles turned white, her long, matte hair covering her neck entirely. A few moments later, she reached up, brushing a few strands behind her ear and revealing a sliver of pearl white against her chocolate-colored skin.

Someone bumped Rune's arm, and she flinched back, her gaze meeting that of a young man, likely a few years her elder. Her hand moved subtly to cover her dagger as she scanned the boy's movements, keeping her eyes locked on his unsettlingly-pale blue ones while noting other details in her peripheral vision.

"Sorry," he muttered in a thickly accented voice, dipping his head at her apologetically. "Wasn't looking where I was going."

His auburn hair was shot through with veins of periwinkle, giving it an effect like an ocean as he ran his hand through it.

Rune dared a glance over to where the rest of her group had begun to make their way farther into the outpost, oblivious to her delay. "Uh—no problem." *I guess he's not going to try to kill me. Maybe he just sees that he's outnumbered or something?*

She kept her hand by her dagger as she turned her back on the stranger, keeping her ears open for any sign of sudden movement towards her. Ahead, her group had come to a stop, standing in a circle and conversing in low voices. Azalea smiled at her as she approached, moving over to make room.

"I think it's best if we split up," Ivory told them, craning his neck to get a look at their surroundings. "We can stick in groups of two or three, meet back here before midday."

Rune's eyes wandered upward, scanning the sky. They'd set out about an hour before dawn, so the sun was still only a quarter of the way up...giving them an ample amount of daylight to work with. "What'll we do, though? Here, I mean?"

"Trade for stuff," Luna replied. "Food, materials, weapons—whatever. I'll stick with Ivory, and you guys can figure out what you want to do."

Azalea turned to Rune, her expression unreadable. "I think Nyk and I will stay together...you're welcome to come with us, if you'd like."

Rune hesitated for a moment, weighing her options. She was still very new to the arena, that was true—but she *could* fight, and a part of her wanted a moment on her own to sort out her thoughts.

"I'll be okay by myself," Rune told her after a pause. "Is there anything in particular you want me to try to find?"

Azalea's eyes went to Rune's side, where her dagger—the only weapon she possessed—was strapped. "A sword, if you want one. You'll have to trade something pretty good for it, though." She reached into a hidden pocket on the underside of her tunic, pulling out a tinted glass vial no larger than her finger. A murky gray liquid sloshed around inside, splashing against the tightly sealed cork at the top as if trying to break free.

Rune gingerly accepted the vial from Azalea, holding it up to her face to examine it closely. "What exactly *is* this?"

"Shadeleaf sap," Azalea explained. "I found a relatively large quantity of shadeleaf a few weeks ago, and brewed up some bottles to have on hand for trading. It's a poison," she added at Rune's questioning expression. "One drop is enough to kill if you can get it into your opponent's bloodstream. I figure that it would be in pretty high demand around here."

Rune glanced warily around at their environment. "Giving a stranger poison doesn't seem like a great idea—especially in a place like this. Are you sure?"

Azalea nodded, unfazed by Rune's arguments. "I've done it before—saved my life, actually. Whoever you trade it to probably has a target in mind already...or maybe they just want to have it for bargaining power. There are ways to avoid fights if you have enough leverage."

Rune shuddered at the morbid thought. "Why wouldn't they just kill me and take it?"

A smirk crossed Azalea's features, an expression she didn't make often. "You'll have to make sure that thought doesn't occur to them. I'll leave it to you to figure out how to do that."

When Rune nodded a hesitant agreement, she turned

around, casting one last glance over her shoulder before catching up with Nyk. "And—Rune? Do *not* touch that lid. I really wasn't kidding about how toxic that stuff is."

Rune watched them head off towards the northern side of the Outpost, part of her screaming to drop the vial and run far, far away from the liquid death it contained. Ignoring the voice, she reached down, tucking it into a satchel Nyk had made for her.

The streets—if they could even be called that—were made of hard packed dirt, covered with splotchy, uneven patches of gravel. Rune scanned her surroundings, absorbing as many details as she could while searching for someone who might be able to offer her the deal she was looking for.

Smells hung in the air, various putrid stenches mingling with the aromas of the forest and the musty scent of people. The huts were all constructed with a jumble of wooden framework, animal skin, large leaves, and dried mud. Many were falling apart in places, but some seemed as though they were built only the day before. Out of the corner of her eye, she noticed a scarred teenage boy, resting in the shade of a makeshift tent. There was an array of weapons scattered around his feet, which seemed promising to Rune, and she found herself making her way over to him, keeping her hand poised over her dagger.

He raised his head as she neared, his expression reflecting a dull boredom. A long, elegant sword rested at his feet, and another was strapped to his back in a tightly-fastened sheath. The blade she could see was forged of a gleaming, durable metal, and the onyx hilt was marbled with veins of ivory for an eye-catching contrast.

"What do you want?" His voice was hoarse and scratchy, as though he were scarred from the inside as well. "My services aren't free, you know."

Rune swallowed her unease, holding his gaze coolly. *Services...is he some kind of assassin, maybe?* "I'm here to make a trade." She took a step closer, making sure he noticed the weapon at her side.

"I doubt you have anything to interest me."

"We'll see about that." She reached her free hand towards the vial at her side, raising it to catch the light. A sly smile spread across his face at the sight of the liquid, a glint of covetous desire sparkling in his eyes.

"What're you asking for it?"

Rune kept her face stony, her lips curled slightly in what she hoped was a confident smile. "The sword." She nodded at the weapon by his feet. "And its sheath."

His smile faded. "This is pure embersteel. I'm no fool."

Rune narrowed her eyes, refusing to let him know that the word held no meaning to her. "Neither am I. The sword and the sheath, or no deal."

His scarred features twisted into a scowl. "I could just kill you, you know. Then I'd have my sword *and* my poison." He eyed the vial hungrily, fingers twitching towards the hilt of his weapon.

Rune instantly whipped out her dagger, stepping close enough to reach out and grab his blade before lowering the point of her weapon and angling it at his throat. "Let's not make this messier than it needs to be. Make the trade, or I'll find someone else who can."

"Fine." He glared at her, but didn't move. "Take them."

Rune crouched down, being sure to keep her dagger between her and the boy as she picked up the sword. Once it was securely in her grasp, she re-sheathed her dagger, keeping her eyes locked on his while setting the vial at his feet.

Casting a glance over her shoulder, she turned away, slinging the sword and its sheath over her shoulder and fastening it with minimal effort. A feeling of success swelled inside her—a very welcome sensation—and she allowed herself to smile as she moved towards the far side of the outpost.

As Rune neared the tree on the eastern edge of the field, she began to notice a dull hum in the air, the vibrations sending jolts of energy down her spine. Her senses heightened, her body instantly alert, and she was suddenly aware of the alien feeling that emanated from somewhere beyond the massive oaks.

The feeling intensified as she took a step back into the forest, driven forward by an empowering sense of curiosity. Energy rippled across her skin, goose bumps forming in its wake.

Then—suddenly—the woods vanished.

She blinked a few times, trying to make sure she wasn't imagining it—but it was as real as the satchel that bumped against her side.

In front of her wasn't a forest.

It was a flat, rocky tundra.

Not a speck of green was visible on the mountains that loomed in the distance, and the land stretching before her was broken up by wide plateaus and steep valleys. Behind her, the trees loomed, but ahead, there was only stone.

And if the sudden change in terrain wasn't strange enough...a massive wall of what appeared to be pure energy drew a boundary right between the two biomes, spanning in all directions as far as Rune could see.

The barrier crackled with electric pulses, a faint blue tint giving it a tangible feel as her gaze followed it up to the sky. *The Leylock—it has to be.*

Somehow, the word seemed to fit perfectly onto the menacing monstrosity that loomed before her.

"Rather intimidating, isn't it?"

Rune's blood ran cold at the voice, and she turned around slowly, her hand going to her dagger. The moment her gaze met his, everything in her froze—her mind struggling to comprehend how this was even possible as she was swallowed by a sickeningly familiar pair of green eyes.

The eyes of the very boy she'd killed only a few days before.

16

REI

"You didn't actually think I'd let you ruin that, did you?"

"Don't bother. Even if there is an intruder, they'll be discovered long before they so much as get a glimpse of the sword."

"The death you're going to face inside is not one I'd wish on anyone, not even my worst enemy."

"You are here because I want something—something you are going to get for me"

"The Master—the Eidolon himself—he'll come for you—"

He'll come for me.

Rei let out a gasp, beads of sweat streaming down her face as a choked scream bubbled up in her throat. Panic gripped her, and frantically, she glanced around, her vision blurred from the adrenaline that coursed through her body.

Kidnapped.

Blackmailed.

The sword.

Ember.

Going unconscious.

Someone grabbing me...

Before she could tear herself out of bed, a figure came out of nowhere, gently grabbing her shoulders and forcing her to lay back on a pile of pillows. The sheets were unruly, as though she'd kicked them around a lot in her sleep.

I probably did.

Her heart raced as she stared at her rescuer—or her captor—hands still shaking from shock.

It was a man—tall, sturdily built, and rather muscular, looking to be in his early thirties. Despite his stony, unreadable expression, his dark eyes held no hostility, and there was no force behind his grip.

"Deep breath. You've been out for a long time."

Rei swallowed her unease at being in the presence of such an odd stranger, wincing as her attempt to sit up straight was met with an aching soreness from what seemed like every muscle in her body. "How long?" Her voice was hoarse—weak from its lack of use.

Still, his expression didn't change. "A week."

A WEEK?

She made no attempt to hide her shock. "And you—have I been here the whole time?"

He nodded. "Your body needed rest." Seeing that she had regained a bit of her composure, he stood, removing his hand from her shoulder. "I'll give you a bit of privacy to think, if you need it. There's a change of clothes on your bedside table." He nodded at the intricately carved wooden nightstand.

"Wait—" Rei's mind flew through hundreds of questions, but one fought to the surface first. "Ember—where's Ember?"

For the first time, a smile crossed his bearded features. "Your dragon is safe and well. I'll let you see him once you've changed—feel free to come find me when you're ready to talk. I'm sure you have a few questions."

Got that right. "You're just—leaving?"

He paused in the doorway, but didn't look back at her. "I'll be in the kitchen—it's down the hall, to the right. Take your time."

With that, he left.

Okay...

Reeling from the interaction, Rei turned her attention to the bedside table, where a clean-smelling outfit was neatly folded and stacked. *Wonder how he had clothes my size.* A funny feeling found its way into her stomach at the thought of a complete stranger—one with such a blunt mannerism, no less—taking care of her as though she were his daughter.

There were two doors to the cozy, sparsely furnished room—one, which the man had left through, and another, which Rei assumed led to a bathroom or changing room of some sort. Grimacing at the jolts that ran up her legs when her feet met the ground, she made her way over to the second door, pushing it open and peeking inside.

Looks promising.

A full-length mirror was mounted on the wall, a table beside it. She set the fresh clothes down on the table, stepping back and taking a good look at her appearance.

The first thing she noticed was that her current outfit was

mostly untouched—though it seemed like the man had trimmed it back in some places to reveal her wounds. The wounds themselves were free from bandages, but it seemed like that could have been a rather recent development, as many of them were almost entirely healed.

He healed me. Rescued me from a random clearing in the forest, brought me to his home—and healed me.

I didn't know that there were people like that out there.

Just as she was reaching down to grab her clothes, a new observation stopped her in her tracks, her breath catching in her chest. Slowly, she turned her eyes back to the mirror—the very eyes that seemed to be the problem.

They weren't brown anymore.

They were violet.

Dark, powerful, unmistakable violet.

Slowly, she backed away from the mirror, her heart hammering in her chest. *No. That's not possible. It's not—*

But...there it was.

A slightly hysterical laugh escaped her lips. *The same purple as that energy from the sword. The energy that I felt imbue me, that I felt pump through my blood.* She froze, the realization hitting her. *Could that energy have done something to my eyes?*

The sword.

I have to find the sword.

She glanced over at the door. *That man probably has it.*

Her eyes wandered down to her current outfit, which was torn, caked with dried blood, and not smelling the greatest. *I appreciate that he didn't undress me...but I really need to change.*

Peeling the old clothing off of her skin, she picked up the

article on top of the clothing pile beside her—a pale violet tunic with mid-length sleeves and gold patterns stitched into the hem. Simple black pants made of a lightweight fabric accompanied it, and upon further examination, she noticed a pair of leather sandals that looked to be about her size resting on the floor.

Using the basin of water on her left, she did her best to tame the matted mess her hair had become, combing it through with her fingers and somewhat managing to pull it back into a decent ponytail. Miraculously, the basin seemed to never lose a single drop of water, and the liquid within stayed completely clear.

Somehow, she was entirely unfazed by the phenomenon—possibly due to the fact that it didn't even make the top ten in "weirdest things Rei has seen since crossing the border."

Satisfied with her appearance, she balled up her old outfit, discarding it in a nearby trash bin. She felt a twinge of sadness as the clothes left her hands—it had been arguably one of her favorites, but there was just no saving it.

Rei, focus. You need answers.

Wasting no time, she slipped through the bathroom door and back into the main bedroom, her mind once again stumbling over the hundreds of questions she had accumulated. She opened the bedroom door, pausing a moment to glance down the wooden hallway before heading to the right, like the man had instructed her.

It didn't take long for her to emerge into the kitchen—a neat, homely space, lit by the natural sunlight that streamed through multiple windows. The man was sitting at a raised countertop, sipping on a drink—tea, maybe—and staring outside at what looked to be the edge of a forest, just a little ways away.

He glanced up as she approached, watching her stalk over to where he sat and place herself directly across from him.

"You found everything alright?"

Rei nodded, swallowing back the sense of urgency and forcing herself to have manners. "I did. Thank you." Her tone softened with the words, the weight of everything he'd done for her finally sinking in.

"I assume you have some questions, then."

For the first time, she noticed the strange lilt to his voice—the words were indecipherable at first, but the syllables seemed to rearrange themselves inside Rei's mind, translating the words.

"Yes."

He glanced up, a hint of surprise on his features. "So you *can* speak Jurorish. Interesting."

She blinked at him. "I...what?"

"The language I just spoke to you was not the natural tongue...yet you understood it perfectly. I suppose it makes sense, though, given that you wielded the Blade...I'm not sure why I'm surprised." He cocked his head slightly. "Or why you are."

Rei flinched backward involuntarily, eyeing the man. *Should I tell him where I'm really from? That I don't know anything about this world?* Hesitation grew within her stomach, and she frantically searched for a way around the topic. "I..."

He raised an eyebrow, cutting her off with only the simple gesture. "Why don't we begin with names, then. I'll make sure to answer all of your questions after."

She nodded. *Questions answered sounds great.* "Rei. I'm Rei."

The faint smile returned to his lips. "You may call me Loric." He leaned back, setting his cup on the slate countertop. "Before we chat...do you need anything to eat?"

Rei frowned, suddenly reminded of just how long she'd been unconscious. Hunger should have weakened every bone in her body, but for some unknown reason...she felt fine. "Surprisingly...no. I'm okay."

He nodded, unsurprised. "That would be the torrelroot, then. I had you drink it while I healed your wounds—it's a special kind of herb that supplies you with nutrients, especially when your body is incapable of providing for itself."

"So...basically...I don't need to eat?"

Loric shook his head. "Not unless you want to. It'll be evening in a few hours, and that would be an ideal time for your body to begin readjusting to solid food. You're going to be a bit weak for a while, which is perfectly normal—I just need you to have some patience."

Rei paused for a moment, doing a double take. A spark of the all too familiar panic welled up inside her even at the simple words, reminding her of everything she'd been through. She swallowed it down, refusing to allow her mind to return to the chaos. "What happened to me, exactly?"

Why are my eyes like this? What did the sword do to me? Why am I here?

Why?

Why?

Why?

Questions surged up within her, but somehow, she kept them controlled, Loric's calm, indifferent attitude helping to keep the horrible mess from bubbling over.

"Why don't you tell me?" Loric eyed her questioningly, a strand of his neatly-styled jet black hair falling in front of his face. He brushed it back, not once breaking eye contact. "I *will* give you the answers you need, Rei, but I would like to know what a teenager like yourself is doing with one of the most powerful weapons in the realms...and why you don't seem to know a single thing about it."

Rei blinked at him, his words hitting her from a thousand different directions at once. *Most powerful weapon in the realms...*

The realms...

This world is bigger than I thought.

Far bigger than Akaidia..

Does this man know about Akaidia?

What will he say if I tell him?

Only one thing was clear about this whole situation: she was in way over her head.

Overwhelmed, Rei found herself unable to do much besides stare blankly, her tongue like a foreign object inside her mouth. *I really don't know anything.* Before, she had been so sure that she wanted to learn more, to explore this new world...but something deep inside her warned her to be careful.

For the first time in her life, she had a question that she actually didn't want the answer to.

"I..." she cleared her throat, shaking her head slowly. "Look —it was a mistake, okay? There were these people—they kidnapped me, and threatened Ember so that I'd steal the sword for them. I don't know why they thought I could do it, but I never really wanted it...I just wanted to get me and my dragon out of there alive." *And revenge. I wanted revenge.* "I'm sorry, but—I have to get home." Panic gripped her suddenly, a realization dawning.

The wayfinder.

"They took something from me. It looked kinda like a compass, made of obsidian and with a purple gem in the middle—"

"You mean this?" Loric reached into his pocket, holding up the object.

A wave of relief washed over Rei. "Yes, that's it. I...I need it to get home."

He glanced down at it. "Interesting. I figured it belonged to the brute I grabbed it off of...didn't realize it was yours." His eyes met hers, their piercing depths boring into her very being. "Do you mind explaining to me just why you need a *wayfinder* to return to your home? There are very few people your age who've even seen one...much less had to use it."

Alarm bells went off in Rei's mind, her posture going rigid. She had no idea if she could trust Loric—she felt like she could, but she wasn't sure.

She wasn't sure of anything anymore.

"Please. Just...let me take Ember home. You can keep the sword—I don't need it." Her tone was threaded with hints of the odd, homesick desperation she was feeling, the sensation gripping her throat and practically choking her.

Loric raised an eyebrow, watching her carefully. "I...I'm sorry, Rei. I can't do that."

She bristled. "No?"

"You really don't know, do you."

Frustration began to build up inside her stomach, her expression hardening. "No, but I would *really* appreciate if you explained. I do not have much patience for people who think they can contain me."

Instead of getting angry, or making a motion towards her... he sighed. "I am not trying to hold you captive, Rei. But I don't think you quite understand what's at stake here."

"No?" A disbelieving chuckle escaped her lips. "Why don't you tell me, then? I'm sure this ought to be good."

I've had enough of this.

"Look—thank you for saving my life. I just...I can't stay here. I...I don't belong in this world."

Her words barely seemed to faze him as he stood, staring her down. She had to admit, maintaining eye contact with someone of such a bulky frame made her stomach churn slightly, but she refused to back down.

"You can't leave, Rei."

"Why not? I thought you said—"

"I am *not* your captor."

"Then give me a reason."

"Rei..."

"Give me a *reason*, Loric!"

"Because *that sword* only bonds to *one person*!"

Silence.

That was the first time in the entire conversation that he'd raised his voice—and it was a terrifying, terrifying experience. Rei stood there, stunned, the words taking a long moment to sink in.

"*One* person," he repeated, having regained his calm. "*Thousands* of people have been waiting for this sword to choose its next wielder. If you leave..."

"Waiting? For...for how long?" Rei somehow found the

courage to speak up, her mind still numb from the shock of hearing Loric shout.

He shook his head, despair plaguing his features. "It's not a simple matter of patience, Rei. For these people—it's a matter of life and death."

17

REI

Chosen.

Rei had been "chosen" before...in many different situations, actually.

For training drills.

For leadership positions amidst her peers.

Even for a place as the co-commander of an entire army.

But this...this brought a whole new meaning to the word.

Her voice shook as she parted her lips to speak, words tripping over themselves in an attempt to break free. She had so many questions—so many answers she wanted—but in that moment, only one mattered.

"Why?"

Why was I chosen?

Why am I here?

Why?

Why?

Loric took a deep breath, leaning back in his chair and examining her. "I don't know."

Don't know.

Don't know.

Don't know.

Rei shook her head, all other things forgotten. "Then tell me something. Anything. You can't just *say that* and then end the conversation."

He pondered for a moment. "Alright. But if I'm going to explain everything, I'm going to need you to return the favor. Agreed?"

She nodded without a second thought, her mind simply so desperate for answers that it was willing to do whatever it took to get them. Her whole life had just turned upside down—things were never going to be the same again, she knew that. Even so, a small, selfish part of her whispered that she could have both—the truth, and the life she'd grown to love.

I'll never be able to just go back to that life.

A shiver rocked her body.

Never. Not if what Loric says is true.

Loric leaned forward, crossing his arms and resting them on the counter. His gaze held hers, a vast array of emotions warring on his features. "You might want to sit down for this."

She shook her head, impatience fueling the gesture. "I need to know, Loric. Please."

The man let out a long breath, swallowing hard as though he were dreading the words he was about to speak. "The sword...that sword is a very ancient weapon, one known as the *Saquis Mal*—or the Phantom Blade. It—" he hesitated. "It contains a great amount of magical energy, a type unique only to it and its bearer. Based on how I saw you in that clearing... I'm sure you already have some experience with this power."

Rei nodded. It did line up with what she'd felt during that night...though many details had faded from her memory. "Why would it choose me, though? If it's so powerful?"

He cocked his head at her. "To be completely honest with you, that's exactly what I am trying to figure out. You understood me when I spoke Jurorish, so I suppose you would be the right race...though even if you were, Casimir's bloodline died out. Unless you'd like to correct me on that."

She blinked at him. *The right race??? I'm human...just like he is. Though...I guess he might be referring to the people with pointy ears? And maybe even Haric, with the dragon scales?* "You're insane."

He raised an eyebrow. "And why's that?"

There it is again—that weird lilt in his voice.

"Well—first of all, you're telling me that I can perfectly understand another language, one that I can't even pronounce the name of. Second, all your claims about me being the 'right race' are completely ridiculous—I'm *human*, just like you. Just like everyone." She shook aside the thoughts of people with pointed ears...that was something to be addressed another time.

Loric barked a laugh. "I don't think they're as ridiculous as you're making them out to be. For starters, that question I just asked you was *not* in the natural tongue—and you not only understood perfectly, but replied to it as well, all without knowing what you were doing." He leaned forward, his eyes holding a strange curiosity in their depths. "Rei, I have never—not once—met someone unfamiliar with the high races. My appearance may be very similar to that of a human's, yes, but I'm not human—and according to the fact that you managed to make a bond with that blade, neither are you."

Rei couldn't do anything but stare. *Has he lost his mind?* "No offense or anything, but I think I know my own species better than some random stranger from a—" she broke off. *From another world.*

"From a..." he prodded quietly.

She shook her head, wrapping her arms around herself. "It doesn't matter. You're insane."

Still, he didn't seem to be offended. "I really don't think so, Rei. Where did you say you were from, anyway?"

She froze. "I didn't."

"I know. But it might be helpful if you did."

Silence. The thing was, he wasn't wrong—but something about admitting the truth terrified Rei. From the moment she'd stepped foot into this new world, she'd been met with nothing but hostility—even by people who might not have been aware of where she'd come from.

"I'm not from here." Her voice was soft, quiet—a whisper, if even that.

Loric frowned. "Not from..." He broke off, his expression shifting. "You can't mean...that wouldn't be possible..."

Rei winced. "Beyond the mountains. That's where I'm from."

Loric eyed her as though she had just sprouted a second head, his calm facade completely gone. "Those mountains are guarded by a magical barrier, Rei. They have been for millennia. No one can get in, no one can get out—that's just how it works. So how..." his gaze flickered down to the wayfinder, which was still firmly in his grasp. Realization dawned on his face. "I see."

Guarded by a magical barrier. I was right. That's why everything felt so strange...

He glanced up, meeting her eyes. "Where did you get this?"

"It was a birthday gift. From Tay—my father." She hated saying the word, but in this case, there was no avoiding it.

"Your father?" Intrigue had seeped into his voice. "What is his name?"

Her lips curled into a frown. "It doesn't matter."

"I won't know that for sure unless you tell me."

Fine. "Tayven."

"Tayven," Loric echoed, the name coming off his tongue as though he were simply testing out its sound. "What does he look like?"

Rei hesitated, surprised by the barrage of questions. "I don't know."

He looked at her as though that were the most ridiculous thing she'd said all day. "You don't know."

"I never met him. He disappeared before I was born."

His expression shifted. "Oh." For the first time since she'd woken up, the brawny man seemed at a loss for words.

Sensing incoming sympathy, Rei quickly added on to her statement. "It's not like it's that big of a deal, anyway. My mother didn't raise me—some of her friends did, and they were great parents. They neglected to mention whose child I *really* was, though..." she trailed off, a familiar prick in her chest burning at the reminder.

"Your mom didn't—"

"Look, it doesn't matter, okay? It's not like you care about my questionable family situation. Could you *please* just explain why any of this affects whatever bond I have with the sword?"

Loric cleared his throat, staring at her with a strange glint in his eye. "For starters, the sword has only been known to bond to one family—the descendants of its creator. That bloodline was ended relatively recently—at least, we thought it was—which is why I was understandably surprised to find that there was a teenage girl swinging it around like she'd been wielding it for decades.

"You see, the level of raw strength you used that night—that was very, very close to the sword's limits. It would take years of rigorous training to get where you were—but based on your reactions so far, you had no idea you were doing it."

Rei shook her head.

"So this is my problem, Rei. I have seen people from other bloodlines bond with the sword for mere *moments*—for a single battle, perhaps, if they got lucky. But their souls simply didn't mesh with it. Yours, however—a girl's from a world that was locked away millennia ago, one who doesn't even know her true parentage—in one night, you not only bonded seamlessly with the sword, but you exerted more energy than some of the most powerful heroes could ever dream of wielding."

I did that? "And you're surprised because I'm not part of this...bloodline?"

He nodded. "They were always the most powerful wielders, and the ones who could hold onto the sword the longest. It was familiar with and trusted them, so it allowed them to command it in its entirety."

"You say that like it's a living creature, one that can think."

"In a way, it can. I'm not saying it's alive—it's an inanimate object, and always will be. But it does have an innate level of understanding about those who bond with it, and based on that understanding, it decides how much power to grant the wielder."

Rei's mind whirled with the information, struggling to digest it all. "And I somehow got...all of it."

"Yes." He cocked his head at her. "I highly doubt you could do it again, though. My guess would be that the adrenaline took over—though you still haven't explained to me how you were in that situation in the first place."

"I told you, they kinda...kidnapped me. I only did it because they threatened Ember."

"The dragon?"

"Yes."

"I see." Loric paused for a moment, frowning slightly. "They forced a girl...to go steal a mythical weapon?"

"That was pretty much my thought process." Rei shrugged, using the gesture to mask the residual fear and fury that still lingered in the back of her mind from the memories.

Loric tilted his head at her. "I'm impressed."

She hesitated, caught off guard by the statement. "With what?"

"Many things. For one, the fact that you managed to break into one of the most secure vaults I know of and leave with as few injuries as you did. And...with your maturity in handling the situation."

Rei shuddered. Memories of that awful night flooded through her mind—the rage she'd felt, the raw fear that had gripped her, the feeling of her knife finding her enemy's throat in complete darkness.

"I wouldn't call it maturity." *I was only trying to survive.*

"Still." His frown deepened. "How old are you, Rei?"

"Sixteen."

"Sixteen..." his eyes glazed over for a moment, and he shook his head, a distant memory lingering in his gaze. "Far too young to bear the burden you've been faced with."

Rei looked away. "I'm used to it."

Loric didn't seem to know what to do with that statement, so he simply cleared his throat, looking anywhere but at her. "I—is there anything else you can tell me about your father?"

Rei bit her lip nervously, the abrupt subject change leaving a gaping hole in the air between them. "Not really. All I know is his name—Tayven—and that he left behind the wayfinder with nothing but the instructions to give it to me when I turned sixteen."

The strange glint in Loric's eye didn't fade as he glanced away, deep in thought. There was something he knew...something about her father. "Here's the thing that troubles me, Rei. There was a man I knew, once—I was just barely an adult at the time, but I still remember him quite clearly. His name was Casimir."

The name instantly rang a bell in Rei's mind, an earlier part of her conversation with Loric resurfacing in her thoughts. "He was part of the bloodline—the one you think I'm somehow connected to." A shiver rippled down her spine as he nodded, setting off a whole new chain reaction of questions and theories.

"The thing is, Rei—Casimir often chose not to go by his first name. Instead, his close friends would call him by his middle name: Tayven."

Rei's eyes widened. *Impossible.*

"Not only that...but just over seventeen years ago, he disappeared." Loric met her gaze. "He was last seen in the town of Ekal—within only a hundred miles of the Barrier Peaks."

Rei froze, every muscle within her deciding unanimously to cease working. Her brain was numb, her body rigid—and no matter how hard she tried to convince herself that it was nothing more than a coincidence, something deep within her rang true at the sound of the words. A phrase formed on her lips—one she feared, dreaded, hated—but the only one that seemed to fit the looming silence that had settled between them.

"Casimir—is my father?"

"It would appear so, yes."

She swallowed hard, taking a few steps backward and leaning on the counter to steady herself. She'd come to this world out of curiosity, but now—her fate was linked to this place, her life bonded to it through the blood of a man she'd never even met. "That's why I could wield the sword."

"You're a direct descendant of the Blade's creators, Rei—the most powerful one I've ever seen. We may never know for certain what happened to him, but if Casimir truly is your father..." he paused, as if searching for the right words. "There is no mistaking it. By blood and by bond—you are the next wielder of the Phantom Blade."

18

REI

Rei's knees buckled, her body slowly shrinking to the wood floor. She didn't care that she was staring blankly into space, or how confused and terrified she had to have looked.

There was a sound of dull scraping as Loric pushed his chair back, rising to his feet. Rei couldn't see him, but she heard him, circling around to where she had curled up in an attempt to block out the revelations that weighed on her.

"Are you alright?" His voice was deep and gentle, a soothing touch amidst the bed of thorns she'd found herself in.

She shook her head, averting her gaze. "I just—I need a minute."

"That's understandable." Instead of returning to his seat, he sat down beside her, near enough to be comforting but also leaving room between them to give her space. "It's a lot, I know. And while we may not be very well acquainted with one another, you *can* trust me with anything you need."

Something in his voice whispered to her of many promises

just like that one, vows to be still and listen when she needed it most. Those promises came from somewhere deep within her—others had said them, but very rarely had she felt true meaning from the words.

"Sorry, I—" she sighed, fighting back the tears that burned in her eyes. "I don't know why this is so hard. It's not like I'm new to having pressure put on me, or being faced with responsibility—"

"You're allowed to be upset." Loric shut down her rant with the statement, saying it with such confidence that in that moment, she believed him.

Tentatively, she raised her gaze, meeting his eyes. There was no judgment in them—nor was there sympathy, which she appreciated. Everything about his expression held a note of calm—the sort of calm you feel when you've already faced the worst that the world can throw at you, so you simply can't find it in you to be bothered. Rei latched onto the feeling, allowing it to fill her as she slowly leaned back against the counter.

There were so many things she wanted to say, but none of them felt right, her tongue refusing to allow the words to form. The question she spoke wasn't one she was thinking, but it somehow summed up all her thoughts, trapping them inside a bubble of confusion and forcing them out of her mind.

"What do I do now?"

Loric leaned back, his eyes tracing the elaborate ceiling patterns above. "Well...you're welcome to stay here."

Rei turned, surprised. "With you?"

He nodded. "To learn. And train. I suppose you don't know much about this world, do you?"

She shook her head slowly, the idea taking shape in her

brain. "What about my friends, though? I told my mentor I wouldn't be gone very long. He's probably worried enough already. I know, I can't go home—" she added as Loric opened his mouth to speak. "But I can't just let them think something's happened to me."

"Rei..." Loric sighed. "I didn't mean that you could never go home. I'll admit, I was a bit shaken as well...an unknown girl appearing in the woods, one who can bond with an extremely powerful weapon yet has no knowledge of it or this world. But now that we've spoken, I see that you are a lot more mature than I gave you credit for...and I do apologize for that."

Rei blinked at him, stunned into silence. *He's admitting what he really thought of me—and apologizing for seeing me that way? Who is this man, anyway?* "I—uh—yeah. I mean..." Red seeped into her cheeks, and she looked away, flustered. "Thank you. For your help."

He nodded, a smile flitting across his rugged features. "Of course. And Rei—there is no need for you to make a decision right now. I realize that there's probably a lot on your mind, and you may want some time to sort through that. So..." Slowly, he rose to his feet, offering her a hand. "Why don't I take you to see your dragon? It might do you good to get a little fresh air."

Rei's face instantly lit up, and she accepted his hand readily, allowing his firm grip to pull her to her feet. "Where is he?"

Loric's smile widened, the infectious gesture spreading to Rei's own lips. "Follow me."

He led her through a sparsely decorated hallway, which, despite the lack of furnishing, somehow still felt rather homey. Most of the rooms they passed had the doors shut, but a few were opened, allowing Rei a brief glimpse into small spaces stacked with books or papers.

Guess he really likes to read.

It didn't take too long before the hallway came to an end, widening into one of the largest rooms Rei had seen so far, with glass serving as the walls for two of the four sides. Wooden support beams that seemed to be simply decorative crisscrossed over the windows, creating a mesmerizing effect. The ceiling was constructed similarly, with angled logs slotted together to form unique patterns. Rows of intricate lanterns hung suspended from the beams, prepared to flood the room with light when the midmorning sun would fade.

"Out here." Loric pushed open a heavy-looking oak door, motioning for Rei to step through first and shutting it behind them. She held up her hand, squinting as her eyes adjusted to the brightness.

My eyes...my purple eyes. She blinked rapidly, debating whether or not to ask about them. In the face of everything she'd just found out—the rapid change in her appearance seemed almost trivial. *It's kinda cool, I guess. Definitely going to take some getting used to, though.*

They traveled along the side of his house, which was relatively large compared to what Rei was used to. Wooden paneling was lined above a two-foot layer of stone bricks, and neatly trimmed vines were slithering up along the walls in some places. The door they'd gone out seemed to have been the back door, as they'd emerged onto a stone patio overlooking the edge of a massive forest.

Ahead, Loric stopped, his head tilted back and his eyes tracing the sky. Rei's gaze followed his, her heart leaping when she noticed a rather familiar form gliding airily through the clouds overhead.

His name built in her throat, but she stayed silent, simply grinning at the blue expanse above them. Ember was surprisingly graceful, twisting around and performing stunts that Rei had never seen him attempt before. *He looks happy, at least.* Her attention wandered to Loric, whose eyes were still locked on her dragon. *Loric took good care of him.*

Up in the sky, Ember angled his wings downward, swooping low for another run of twists and loops. As he passed by, he caught sight of Rei, not seeming to believe it at first. A giggle escaped her lips as he halted midair, pivoting around with his ears perked and tail thrashing. The moment their eyes met, the broadest smile Rei had ever seen from a dragon spread across his lime green snout.

Before she knew it, Ember was hurtling towards her, hitting the ground at a run and careening into Rei, knocking her over. She laughed—really, truly laughed, joy brimming from every muscle in her body—as the dragon piled on top of her, neither of them caring about his hulking size.

"Rei okay! Rei okay!"

She laughed, his chirpy voice ringing in her ear. The ability to understand basic dragon speech was one of her favorite parts about being able to live in Aererest—it also made her wonder if the skill was possible with other animals as well, like how her sister could communicate with her wolf.

"Yes, bud. I'm okay."

Ember finally seemed satisfied with giving her a rather uncomfortable dragon-hug, bouncing up and resting back on his haunches. *"Faron be anger. You be gone much time."*

Rei crawled over a few feet to where Ember sat, leaning back against his body. A sickening feeling took hold of her stomach as she imagined what her mentor must be thinking right now. She'd promised to only be gone for three days—but Loric had said she was unconscious for over a week.

Over a week. Her stomach tightened.

What if he thinks I'm dead?

What if...what if he's told someone?

"I know, bud. I know." He slid his forelegs forward, laying down in the cool grass. Rei buried her face in his neck, relishing the familiar feeling of his scales.

Loric crouched down beside them, watching the girl and her dragon with a soft smile. "You'll be happy to know that he had no issues recovering from whatever harm he suffered. I was a bit worried by the magically unconscious teenager with *several* severe wounds—but Ember's injuries were extremely treatable."

Even the news that Ember was unscarred couldn't ease the growing knot in her stomach, her mind tripping over itself to imagine the hundreds of horrible scenarios that might have taken place.

She choked back the feeling, blinking rapidly to make sure that no tears would spring to her eyes. "I have to get home. Even if it's only temporary."

Sensing the urgency in her tone, Loric let her speak.

"I promised Master Faron I'd be gone for only three days. *Three.* He's got to think I'm hurt, or worse..." She trailed off, her throat closing before she could finish the thought.

Loric's gaze went to the ground. "I—I suppose that might be able to be worked in. It would be difficult—but I understand your desire to set the minds of your loved ones at ease."

She nodded, her tongue unable to form any words. Everything about this place—the nightmarish scenarios she'd found herself in, the revelations she hadn't been expecting, and even a suspected family bond to a weapon that ran far into the very foundation of an alien world—it was overwhelming. Completely, utterly, overwhelming.

Loric, while providing as much support as he could, could do little to lift away the ever-growing burden she'd found herself bearing. He could only provide understanding, hoping that the soft glimmers of light they brought could help to combat the thick shroud of darkness that had settled over her mind.

And the memories...

Threats.

Lies.

Feelings.

Darkness.

Power.

It all swirled together into a giant mass in her brain, plaguing her the moment her thoughts wandered. The feel of Ember's scales beneath her fingertips helped ease them temporarily, but she knew that the moment he left—the moment she was alone—they would return, attacking her from every side and leaving her defenseless and vulnerable against their sting.

He will come for you.

Come for you.

Rei glanced up, a question surfacing as the memory faded. "Loric? Who's the Eidolon?"

Loric's body went rigid. "Where did you hear that name?"

"The man who kidnapped me said it, right before I—I

killed him. He said that the Eidolon, his master, would come for me."

"He *specifically* said that the Eidolon was his master?"

Rei nodded.

Loric let out a breath, a look of nervousness crossing his features—an emotion Rei hadn't seen much from him. "That complicates things, I'm afraid. It means he's after the sword."

"Why...why does it complicate things?"

The brawny man pressed his lips together, looking away. "You see—I was hoping that I could perhaps allow you to journey home, to see your friends and assure them that you are alright before we began training. But it seems that option is no longer available to us." He turned back to her, his eyes filled with a deadly seriousness that sent cold shivers rippling down her spine. "If that man is, in fact, after you—he will stop at *nothing*. While you might be briefly protected within the magical boundaries of your world, he *will* find you—and not only that, but he will find a way to break through your only means of protection for Akaidia."

"And...that would put my friends in danger, too."

"Exactly."

Ember seemed to sense her distress, curling his tail in and resting it on her lap. *"Rei okay?"*

"I will be." She glanced down. "I just—I need to figure this out."

A frown crossed Loric's features. "Who are you talking to?"

Rei's head snapped up, startled. "Oh—" Red flooded into her face. She'd completely forgotten that Loric probably couldn't understand Ember's speech—meaning that she definitely appeared to have lost her mind. "Ember—I—it's really hard to explain."

Loric nodded, looking intrigued but also like he wasn't sure that he wanted to know. "Anyway..." his tone sobered. "You're going to have to make a choice, Rei. I'm sorry."

She choked back tears, looking away. "I know. But I just... ugh. There's no right way to do this, is there."

"There rarely is." The amount of pain packed into those few words was enough to pique Rei's curiosity, but she figured it was better if she didn't ask. Her eyes wandered to Ember's tail, resting across her lap.

Ember's tail...

"Wait, I got it!" Rei sat up quickly, startling both the dragon and the man. "Ember—what if we sent Ember back to my world? With the wayfinder, and a message from me? The Eidolon's after the sword, right? He wouldn't be tracking a dragon."

A pensive look took over Loric's face. "That...could actually work. Though, Rei—it would mean losing your only way home. That wayfinder is the *only* known way to cross that border."

Rei swallowed hard, refusing to allow the tears that burned in the back of her eyes to spill over. "This is the only way to keep everyone I care about safe." She turned to the dragon. "Including you, bud."

Ember pouted. *"Want to stay. Help Rei."*

"You will be helping me. I need you to tell Master Faron where I am, and most importantly, that I'm *safe*." She leaned in, pressing her forehead to his icy scales.

"Will be safe?"

Rei nodded vigorously, refusing to allow any doubt into her tone. "Loric will keep me safe. I promise."

"I will." Loric rose to his feet, gazing down at her softly. "I'll bring you paper and a pen, so you can write a message for Ember to bring with him." He reached into his pocket, pulling out the wayfinder and handing it to Rei. "Take as much time as you need. I'll be inside—come in when you're ready."

Rei did a double take. "Now? He has to leave now?"

Loric paused. "Like I said, take as much time as you need. I recommend letting him go before evening, though."

A choked feeling in Rei's throat refused to allow her to speak, so she simply nodded, watching Loric's figure disappear back into the house.

Thousands of thoughts warred in Rei's mind as she lightly kissed Ember's nose, forcing herself to tear her hands away from his neck for what would be the last time in who knew how long. *I can't believe I'm doing this. I can't believe I'm letting him go—that I'm letting my only way of getting home go...*

Maybe I should stop.

Reconsider.

Try something—no.

There isn't another way.

Her throat closed, a sob building in her chest. *Cedar, Ember, Master Faron—I'm not going to see them for a long time.*

Maybe forever.

She shook her head vigorously, shutting down the idea. *No —I'm going to find them again, someday.*

I have to.

I promised.

Ember watched her as she backed away, offering the bravest smile she could muster. She'd never been fond of goodbyes—and she'd had to say far too many of them in her lifetime.

But this—this wasn't just a goodbye.

It felt like a part of her very being had been severed, and that that part was now resting delicately within the compartment on Ember's saddle.

"Be safe, Ember. Please."

Ember nodded. *"Ember safe. Rei safe. See again, very soon."* Sadness seeped into his smoke-colored eyes. *"Come home. Promise?"*

Her reply was nothing more than a breathy whisper, but he heard it perfectly, clinging to every word. "I promise."

Then he was gone—turning and taking off, pumping his wings to gain altitude as he ascended into the vibrant, sun-painted sky. They had spent the whole afternoon together, soaring over the forest and soaking in the last fleeting moments before the goodbye neither wanted to say. A part of her wanted to scream to him, to cry out, to call him back to her, where he belonged...but she didn't.

She simply stood there, watching as her dragon disappeared on the horizon. In that moment, the only thing she could think about was the piece of her heart that he'd taken with him.

19

RUNE

Rune scrambled away from the boy, her hand instantly shooting to the dagger sheathed at her side. Memories of the fight bombarded her, running circles in her thoughts as her eyes scanned his body language, watching for any sign of aggressive movement.

How is this possible?

I killed him.

He dissolved beneath my grip.

SO HOW IS HE STANDING HERE?

To her complete shock, he met her gaze with a pair of striking emerald eyes, not an ounce of hostility in their depths. Her attention wandered to his neck, where a faint pink line could be seen—the very place where she had drawn the dagger across his skin. He seemed entirely unconcerned, however, shrugging off her silent response to his question.

"Sorry. Didn't mean to startle you."

With that, he turned, skirting around Rune and continuing on his way without a single backwards glance.

What?

Rune could only stand there, stunned, as a literal *walking corpse* made his way towards the leylock...apparently oblivious to his murderer standing behind him. *This isn't possible.*

For a moment, she wondered if it was a mistake—and there was another in the arena who was somehow his mirror image. But as she watched him leave, he turned his head to the side, scanning his surroundings.

Displayed on his neck was a perfect yellow rectangle.

A color she remembered all too well.

Memories washed over her like she was standing beneath a waterfall, and she turned her back on the boy, blinking rapidly. Her hand was still clenched around the hilt of her sheathed blade, as part of her wasn't totally convinced that he wouldn't just whip around and attack her.

But—he didn't.

Dazed, Rune forced herself to move forward, heading back towards the outpost at an accelerated pace. *I have to find the others. If he's here, maybe his teammates are, too...*

The thought spurred her into a run, and she took off towards the far side of the town, scanning for any sign of her friends. It shouldn't have been that difficult to locate them— there were only about nine or ten people in the outpost, after all —but the confused fog in Rune's mind made it difficult to concentrate.

So difficult, in fact, that she barely managed to stop herself from barreling into Azalea.

Rune stumbled back, her cheeks burning as she muttered a hasty apology. Azalea only laughed, her gentle, unconcerned smile loosening a bit of the tension in Rune's body.

"Something wrong? You look like you've seen a ghost."

Rune's eyes wandered towards the leylock, the boy's face still burning in her brain. "I did. At least—I think so."

Azalea cocked her head at her. "Sorry?"

"The—the boy, the one from the other night—that I killed. He's here. He *saw* me. And...he didn't even seem to know who I was." A shiver rippled down her spine.

Azalea thought for a moment, her gaze following Rune's. "Here? That's weird...usually people are sent to a new biome after a reset."

Now it was Rune's turn to be confused. "I...what?"

Guilt instantly blossomed in Azalea's expression. "Oh...I forgot you didn't know."

Rune stared at her. "Now would be a really great time to tell me."

"When you die here...you don't really *stay* dead."

"Isn't that kinda the point of dying, though?"

Azalea looked torn. "You'd think so, but no. If you're killed, you reset—memories wiped, placed into a citadel, the whole ordeal." Her gaze traveled to the ground. "Starting over from the beginning. An endless, bloody cycle."

Horror gripped Rune's heart as the words truly sank in, their meaning resonating in her mind. "Let me get this straight. You can *die*—hundreds, thousands of times—then come face to face with your *murderer*—and you just *wouldn't know*?"

Azalea bit her lip nervously. "Yes...that's pretty much it." She winced at Rune's expression. "It's a lot, I know. I'm sorry for not telling you sooner."

Rune raised her gaze, locking it on Azalea's. "How do you know I'm new, then? That I wasn't just...*waking up*?"

"I mean—there's always the possibility, I guess. *But*—" she interjected before Rune could respond— "The timing of batch eight being announced *so close* to when you met us is just too perfect." She trailed off uncomfortably, casting a glance at Nyk. "I remember telling him about this too—and when I first discovered it. Trust me, you're reacting far better than either of us did."

Familiar footsteps coming up behind them stopped Rune from responding, and she forced a smile onto her face, offering a wave to Luna and Ivory.

"Did you guys see who's here?" Luna cast a glance in Rune's direction as they joined the group.

"You mean the guy Rune killed?" Nyk piped up, making Rune wince.

Luna nodded. "I know about the phenomenon and all, but I still wanted to stab him again, just to make sure he wasn't gonna come after us."

Ivory groaned. "I had to stop her. And trust me, that was *quite* the task." He shot Luna a look so intense that Rune was both surprised and impressed that the blonde barely seemed to notice.

Azalea looked like she agreed with Ivory wholeheartedly. "Trust the reset. It wipes everything."

"No. It doesn't." Nyk's voice was so quiet that, for a moment, his words didn't even register in Rune's mind.

All eyes instantly turned to him.

Azalea furrowed her brow, meeting his eyes. "What do you mean, *it doesn't?*"

Red seeped into Nyk's face, coloring his cheeks the same tone as his hair. "The reset. It doesn't wipe everything. I was too embarrassed to say anything before—it's not really that important, anyway." He reached down, lifting the bottom of his tunic. A collective round of gasps rippled around the group—except for Luna, who looked mildly impressed.

On his side was a long, jagged scar, starting at the bottom of his right rib and stopping a few inches to the right of his spine.

Azalea's gaze flickered from Nyk to the scar. "How do you know you didn't have it before you came to the arena?"

"When I woke up, the wound was still freshly healed," Nyk responded, his eyes on the ground. "In fact—if I agitated it too much, it would start bleeding." His hand went to his side, almost as though he wished he could cover it up.

How awful...

Ivory frowned, cocking his head. "I can't believe I never knew about this before."

Nyk shrugged. "Most people don't notice. Not really something you look for, I guess."

No one really seemed to know what to say to that.

"We..." Azalea's eyes traveled up to the sky, where the sun was nearly at its midway point. "We really need to go. If we plan on getting far over the border, anyway."

An awkward silence ensued as the group made their way towards the far end of the outpost, and for the first time, not a single conversation was made.

FOR ONE THING, NO ONE IN THEIR RIGHT MIND WOULD

be staring straight up at an impenetrable wall of crackling blue energy and think; *let's run right through it.*

Yet...that was exactly what Rune intended to do.

Scattered memories hovered in the corners of Rune's vision as her eyes followed the energy barrier upward, her stomach knotting into a rather uncomfortable ball of nerves. Somehow, the tiny, insignificant object Luna grasped was supposed to allow them safe passage through the monstrous wall of death that loomed before them.

Luna took a step forward, reaching a tentative hand up to the wall as if she were going to touch it. Her fingertips stopped just short of it, the energy crackling threateningly beneath where her palm hovered. She held it there for a long moment, the only sounds in the crisp pre-dawn air being their soft breaths and the dull hum of the Leylock.

Luna broke the silence, speaking in a voice softer than Rune had ever heard from her lips before. "I'll go first." She tilted her head up, taking a step back. "After I'm through, I'll toss the stone to whoever's next."

"That will work—right?" Azalea sounded slightly nervous, eyeing the barrier tentatively.

Luna shrugged, a bit of her more familiar nonchalant air returning to her tone. "Guess we're about to find out."

Azalea turned to Ivory for help, but he just shrugged, not looking concerned in the slightest.

"Her plans usually work," he informed them lightly, his already twitchy eyes flicking back and forth from Luna to the leylock. "*How* they work, however—I couldn't tell you."

He barely managed to duck out of the way as Luna swatted him.

Rune took a step forward, watching closely as Luna stretched her arm out and lightly brushed her hand against the leylock. The humming in the air instantly intensified, and the wall seemed to bend around her fingertips, energy repelled by an invisible shield.

The leystone, Rune realized. The blue glass shard embedded inside the miniature compass began to glow brighter and brighter as Luna stepped deeper into the wall, her skin tinted blue everywhere the barrier touched. It knitted itself shut behind her, bridging the gap created by her form. She pivoted to face them as she emerged on the other side, brandishing the stone cheekily.

"Tickles a bit when you go through," she warned, words slurred as though she were underwater. A broad grin spread across her lips, and she began lightly tossing the leystone from hand to hand. "Who's next?"

The group exchanged glances, all of them slightly hesitant to volunteer.

"Fine, I'll pick. Rune, catch."

Rune barely had time to react as the barrier let out a deafening crackle, and she somehow managed to lift her hand, preventing the leystone Luna had flung through from colliding with her face. She fumbled the compass as it barreled into her hands with a *bit* more force than she thought necessary, miraculously getting possession of it before it hit the ground.

Luna smirked. "Catching is *not* your strong suit, huh?"

Rune scowled. "Not when people fling magic rocks at me through an energy barrier, no."

The blonde cracked a grin. "That's the spirit. You coming or what?"

Taking a deep breath to stuff down the incredibly obnoxious bundle of nerves that insisted on nagging her, Rune approached the leylock, gripping the stone so tightly her knuckles began to turn white. Uncomfortably aware that all eyes were on her, she lifted her free hand, lightly brushing her fingertips across the translucent surface of the barrier.

The energy crackled threateningly, sending waves of electric pulses rippling across Rune's skin. It was one of the strangest materials she'd ever felt—neither hot nor cold, a solid object yet also a liquid that had no form. She quickly decided that it would not be in her best interests to attempt and figure out exactly *how* the barrier was working—her only concern was that it was, and that she now had the ability to cross through it entirely unharmed.

Here goes nothing, I guess.

Balling her hand into a fist, she pushed it forward, allowing it to lead her through as she stepped straight into the massive wall of magic death.

20

RUNE

She was only engulfed by the energy for a few seconds, but it felt like minutes, the raw, unfiltered power lunging at her from all sides only to be stopped by the flimsy shield the leystone provided. A tingling sensation spread across her body, intensifying as she pushed deeper into the leylock.

The wall released a loud crackle as Rune broke free, energy snapping back into place behind her. A ripple effect spread across the leylock as it knitted itself back together, closing the gap that her body had created. A shiver rocked through Rune's body, and she glanced around, her eyes widening as they took in her surroundings.

There was no *possible* way that she had just been standing in a temperate forest only moments before.

The air in Blue was significantly colder than in Green, and Rune wrapped her arms around herself, watching her breath condensate in the air before her. Beneath her feet was nothing but stone—stone was all there was for miles, formations of rock and dramatic changes in elevation that loomed out of endless gravel plains and creating a rather daunting landscape. Everything was entirely barren—not a speck of green in sight. Crystal clear lakes varying immensely in size were scattered about generously, providing a mysterious effect to the horizon.

This isn't natural. It can't be.

She turned to Luna, rubbing her arms vigorously. "You f-forgot to mention how cold it was over here."

Luna looked slightly confused, sparking a flame and twirling it across her fingertips. "I didn't notice. Perks of being the fire wielder, I guess?"

Rune shrugged. "Maybe."

Luna gestured to the leylock, unbothered by the icy gusts that seemed determined to extinguish her flames. "Who's next?"

It didn't take much longer for Nyk, Azalea, and Ivory to make their way across, each of them looking equally as uncomfortable with the sudden temperature drop as Rune felt. Ivory was first to adjust, flexing his fingers and lightly wrapping them around the hilt of his dagger.

"Where are we supposed to go now?" Nyk asked, his voice pinched from the cold.

Ivory squinted into the distance, his pale features making him appear ghostly against the barren landscape. "The only way we can go. Forward."

Azalea turned to him, a slight frown decorating her delicate features. "How many people do you think could be in Blue?"

He shrugged. "From what I can remember, there aren't a lot, especially compared to the other biomes."

A pensive look came over her, and she turned away, scanning the horizon with an odd look in her eye. "We may have underestimated the difficulty of this."

"What, finding our team?" Luna piped up, shooting her a glance. "It can't be that bad, right?"

Azalea shrugged. "I mean, this is way closer than I ever thought I'd get—" her gaze shifted to Rune for a brief moment — "but we still have a ways to go, especially since there are many other groups with the very same goal."

Rune made a face, something not lining up in her mind. "Why *are* we fighting, anyway? If none of us have any memories, and we have to unite to escape...why is everyone so bent on killing the opposing teams?"

"Because it's a race." Nyk's reply was soft, filled with malice. "Only one team can get out of here, so everyone's doing whatever they can to set the other groups back."

A...race?

Rune's blood ran cold. "You forgot to mention that detail."

He looked away. "I forgot you didn't know."

She decided to stay silent—it wasn't like she could blame Nyk for not telling her sooner. The arena was a horrible place, and despite the fact that she'd only been here for a few days, it felt like a lifetime—though that probably had to do with her inability to remember an existence outside of it. Even so, the new revelation shook her in a way that she didn't care to admit, rattling the very hope she clung to so tightly.

What if we fail...if someone else gets there first?

She forced herself to offer Nyk a smile, masking the turmoil within her. "It makes sense, I guess. We'll just have to make sure we get there first."

Luna shot her a grin. "That's the spirit, newbie."

Rune sighed at the nickname. "I just want to get out of here, honestly."

The blonde nodded. "Feel that. We should probably get a move on if we wanna be out of the way before sunset. Here's to hoping that our teammates aren't complete knuckleheads."

TRAVEL THROUGH THE BLUE BIOME WAS A MASSIVE step up in difficulty from the forests of Green. Azalea, thankfully, had been smart enough to trade for thicker and more durable outfits, which provided an ample shield against the chilly climate. Beads of sweat decorated Rune's brow as they slowly made their way up a particularly steep incline, her heaving breaths condensing in front of her like a fog of tangible effort. She wrapped the thick navy tunic she wore tighter around her torso, shoulders trembling as the occasional shiver rocked her body.

Luna, however, seemed almost entirely unaffected by the temperature, and had decided to stay in her previous outfit instead of changing into a warmer set of clothing. Though her breath clouded, just like the rest of the group, there was not so much as a hint of discomfort in her level gaze.

"Seriously, Luna—how are you not freezing right now?" Nyk rubbed his arms violently, shooting her a sidelong glance.

Luna shrugged, closing her fist to snuff out a flame she'd been toying with. "I'd tell you it's the fire, but to be completely honest, I'm not sure." Her words had lost their sarcastic edge, replaced by an underlying fatigue. "I know I *should* be cold—even if I don't really understand what that feels like."

Ivory glanced over, scanning her features. Her eyes were the exact same color as the overcast clouds overhead, appearing like a reflection as she traced the sky with her gaze. "Your cheeks and ears are red, just like ours. Are you sure you shouldn't wear something warmer?" He, too, seemed to be nearly unbothered by the cold, but Rune still noticed his shoulders tremble occasionally.

Maybe he's just more used to it than we are.

Luna thought for a moment, her expression distant. "I don't know how to explain it—but temperature isn't an issue for me." For a brief moment, Rune could have sworn that she heard a hint of raw emotion masked within the girl's voice. "It's one of those things that you just *know,* but don't remember why or how you know it."

She sparked another flame, and Rune watched as her face adjusted, the odd lilt disappearing from her tone. A half-smirk worked its way onto her lips, but it seemed forced—nothing like the natural gestures she was so used to displaying. *Something about this place is bothering her.* "Besides—fire doesn't get cold. Defeats the whole purpose, you know?"

Ivory turned away, his eyes locked on the horizon. "Fire doesn't. But controlling it does not mean that you have become it."

Silence lapsed over the group, and Luna continued to toss the orb of sparks from hand to hand, twirling it about her fingers airily. A strange feeling gnawed at Rune, forcing words to her tongue before her mind could even debate whether or not to say anything.

"Luna—are you okay?"

Luna glanced up, surprised. "I—what?"

"You seem off."

"She's not wrong," Azalea chimed in, stopping and turning to look back at the group.

Luna's gaze shifted to the ground, and she stopped moving the flame, holding it steady above her outstretched hand. Her lips parted, but she hesitated a moment before allowing the words to leave her mouth. "I just—have this feeling, I guess. I can't explain it, and I don't know what's causing it—but it's like an invisible string, pulling at my mind. It's been happening since we got here." Her eyes skipped across the landscape, a tumultuous storm of emotion raging in their depths.

"Familiar, but foreign." Rune spoke up softly, all attention snapping to her. "I know what you mean."

Luna turned to her, puzzled. "No offense, but you've only been here for what—two days?"

"Five," Rune corrected, too distracted with the theories that had begun to surface in her mind to be bothered by the comment. The dreams she'd had, and the feelings that had come with them—they'd been massively different, yet connected by a feeling, an innate sense of distant familiarity.

A home I've never belonged to, or an old friend I've never met.

"It's something you *know*, right? Something you know that you know, but don't know how you know it?"

Luna let out a half-laugh, extinguishing her flame and reaching up to rub her temples. "There were way too many 'knows' in that sentence." She blinked a few times, lowering her hands slowly. "I—I guess that's pretty close. I mean, I'm not one for poetic description or anything, but I think it makes sense."

Rune let out a nervous chuckle, hoping that no one noticed the red blossoming in her cheeks. "I wouldn't exactly call that poetic."

The group had slowly come to a stop, standing in a valley between two fairly shallow inclines. Sheltered partially from the wind by the walls of stone on all sides, Rune found herself relaxing a bit, grateful for the lack of extra chill.

"Could we rest for a bit?" Nyk asked, his face displaying as much fatigue as Rune was feeling. Her legs and feet ached from the constant motions of walking over the past few days, throbbing pains making each step more and more difficult.

Ivory nodded, glancing around. "I don't see why not. We've gotten pretty far already, anyway."

Late afternoon sun illuminated the stone, peeking through scarce gaps in the thick cloud covering overhead. They settled down beneath a rocky outcropping, and Rune leaned back, letting out a breath as she allowed herself to rest against the cliff-side. A few of their group began chatting, but she remained silent, relishing the break from the unrelenting movement of her body.

Beside her, Ivory leaned over to his right, examining a patch of gravel with intense interest. After a moment of this, Rune's curiosity was piqued, and she turned to him with a slight frown.

"Something wrong?"

He sat back, glancing over at her. "I don't know—something doesn't feel right."

Rune moved to his side, and he shifted around so she could see the gravel clearly. His finger hovered over a strange arrangement of rock—nothing out of the ordinary that Rune could tell, but clearly, he had a better idea of what was or wasn't 'natural' for the situation.

"Doesn't that look a bit like a footprint to you?"

She met his gaze. "I'm not sure. I guess it could be."

Ivory nodded, cocking his head at the ground. "I mean, usually, I wouldn't be as suspicious of something like this—but this whole area is weird to me. See those?" He gestured to an array of spike-like formations sticking out of the far side of the valley. "Those can't possibly be naturally occurring. Someone caused them. And that..." He pointed to a section of the rock that almost looked burned, as though someone had come through and blasted it with a concentrated beam of flame. "There was a fight here. Recently."

Rune couldn't do much but stare, her mind going through the observations Ivory had made. They all lined up—perfectly. *He's good. No wonder his hunting skills are so advanced.*

Before she could form a reply, however, something unseen made her body freeze.

The noise was soft, barely audible, but it was just enough to halt the chaos that had begun to consume Rune's mind once again. Ivory heard it second, his body going rigid as he rose to his feet, hand twitching towards his sword. The air seemed to thicken around them, and one by one, the rest of the group realized what was happening, positioning themselves defensively against the possible threat. A dull crackle of energy began to hum beside Rune's ears, strands of hair drifting above her head as if drawn upwards by an invisible force. The ground rumbled beneath their feet—not an earthquake, but enough to set them on edge.

A flash of movement appeared in the corner of Rune's vision, and she whirled around to face it, drawing her dagger and whipping it at the source. There was a clatter as metal collided with stone, and the air itself seemed to hold its breath, the tension so thick Rune could have drawn her sword and cut right through it.

Then, suddenly, a bolt of lightning erupted from a boulder beside them, missing Rune by a hair's breadth and fizzling into energy. Two males that looked a bit older than herself stepped out from behind the massive stone, electricity rippling across the taller one's outstretched palms.

Neither boy spoke, but everything they wanted to say was conveyed clearly by their body language and stoic expressions.

Luna seemed entirely unfazed by the intimidating presences before them, stalking to the front of the group and flashing a cocky grin. "Two on five is a bit ambitious, don't you think?"

The electric hum in the air intensified as the taller boy turned to his companion, an unseen message in his gaze—but his companion couldn't take his eyes off Luna. The ground stopped rumbling as he dared a hesitant step forward, expression laced with pure, raw shock. The taller boy shot him a look, but he didn't flinch, examining Luna as though she was a ghost.

Luna made a face, waves of heat emanating from her clenched fists. "Uh...you good, dude? My face is not *that* interesting, you know."

The boy froze, his expression a confusing mixture of shock, sorrow, and even joy. His mouth opened and closed a few times, as though he were deciding what to say. Finally, he managed to choke out a single word, his voice hitching slightly.

"Luna?"

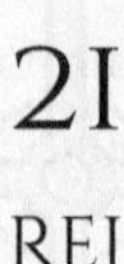

21

REI

"Alright, Rei. How skilled of a fighter would you consider yourself to be?"

Rei thought for a moment, memories weaving through her mind. *Let's see—started training at a young age, was forced into a war at ten for some reason, banished to a forest full of nightmare creatures, participated in a battle against a demon —I'd say I've got a little bit of experience under my belt.* "Pretty good, I think."

Loric's lips curled into a smile. "Let's see it, then."

Rei blinked at him. "Am I...sparring you?"

His smile widened. "If you'd like. Not exactly what I had in mind, though."

She pivoted in a circle, frowning at their surroundings. They were standing in Loric's backyard—a part of it, at least. In the middle of the grass, he'd constructed a patio made of finely-sanded stone slabs, their gritty surface providing decent grip while still being smooth enough that shoes weren't always necessary. The whole training ground was bordered with wooden panels, providing a slight lip on the edge. The most confusing part, however, was the fact that there was no one there but her and Loric—and four or five human-like training targets constructed of wood that were haphazardly scattered about the space.

"Do you want me to beat up on the dummies or something?"

He smirked. "Something like that."

Loric lifted his hand, clenching it tightly and angling it at the targets. To Rei's utter amazement, a glow began to emanate from his fist, and slowly, he allowed his fingers to release, spreading out in an oddly hypnotic motion. A shout rang through the air—its meaning completely unknown to Rei.

"MAITHEI-SHO!"

Loric's voice lingered for a moment, his tone holding a deeper energy than Rei had never heard from anyone before. A low grinding sound from the far side of the training area began to resound through the air, and she could do nothing but watch —dumbfounded—as the targets began to *move*.

He just made a bunch of inanimate objects come to life with two words.

His hand fell back to his side, a look of satisfaction crossing his rough features. The dummies turned to face Rei, their faceless bodies causing a shudder to ripple through her. *I don't know what's worse—the fact that I'm about to spar some living pieces of wood, or that this isn't even the weirdest thing I've seen this week.*

"I take it your world is unfamiliar with runic enchantments?" He sounded so calm...so unconcerned by the previously unmoving battle targets now ambling towards Rei's position.

She nodded. "Yeah...something like that." *He better show me how to do that later.*

A grin crossed his face, though it was difficult to see beneath his beard. "Go on, then. Show me what you got."

The dummies reached into sheaths on their back, each one pulling out a metal sword that probably could have cut them straight through. *This is crazy. Like—actually crazy.* They advanced on her, and she settled into a defensive position, smoothly unsheathing a basic weapon made of lightweight steel. *It's just a fight, Rei. You can do a fight.*

As soon as the lead dummy was within range, it lunged for her with surprising speed, bringing its sword down ruthlessly towards her head. Instinct took over, and she swung her own weapon upward to block the blow, parrying to the side and stepping within her opponent's guard to deliver a counter-attack. Her stab was barely knocked away, giving her just enough time to reposition the blade and deliver a second strike.

With a dull *thud,* her weapon embedded itself firmly into the target's body. The would-be fatal blow caused it to go limp, and she watched as it crumbled to the ground, reduced to the same position from which it had been awakened. She stared blankly for a few moments, watching in awe as the wood seemed to knit over the wound she had dealt, making the surface like new.

Magical training dummies that can put themselves back together. Sounds about right.

"A bit too easy for you, it seems." Loric nodded at her, his expression stony. "*AHD-NOR!*"

A red glyph burned brightly on the foreheads of the four remaining targets, disappearing again too quickly for Rei to get a good look at it. Their stances shifted slightly, weapons angled more accurately towards her current position.

Did he just...up the difficulty?

Can he do that?

Her sandaled feet dug into the ground, and she lowered her body, keeping her center of mass close to the training floor. A bit of the familiar adrenaline that she often felt during sparring matches pumped through her once again, heightening her senses.

This time, the group converged on her as a single unit, spreading out towards the edges of her vision. *Oh no you don't— you can't actually think I'm gonna let you get behind me, do you?*

Before she could question whether or not the targets were even capable of coherent thought, she lunged to the right, choosing the side that seemed to be anticipating her attack the least. A few swift strikes were all she needed to break free from the ominous circle they'd created around her, shattering their formation and forcing them to regroup. *Game on, you walking sticks.*

The 'walking sticks' were able to recover much quicker than Rei had anticipated—but they weren't fast enough. By the time they had assembled into a remotely defensive positioning, she'd already cut one down, her blade aimed for a second.

Fatigue set in as she traded blows with the remaining enemies, occasionally biting back a cry as one of their weapons nicked her skin. The cuts were never deep—likely due to the fact that these were, in fact, *training* targets—but they still stung, especially since she still wasn't entirely recovered from her prior wounds.

Slowly but surely, she managed to decrease the number of

opponents she faced, forced to use nearly every trick she could think of to keep herself from getting stabbed.

Rei doubled over as the last wooden figure collapsed, chest heaving. Her muscles cried out in agony, and her lightweight tunic was soaked in sweat, exhaustion dictating every part of her. "Was that...all?"

Loric cocked a slight smile. "That was the test. Later this afternoon, we will begin your *actual* training."

Is this guy for real?

Before she could reply, he took a step towards her, unsheathing a weapon from behind his back and presenting it in front of him. Her throat tightened slightly, memories—both bad and slightly better—bombarding her from all sides. *The Phantom Blade—the something mal, or whatever he called it.*

"Before you rest, though—I'd like you to try and summon the sword's power, like you did at the stronghold."

Rei closed her fingers around the ebony hilt, its leathery grip like a splash of ice water to her skin. A jolt rippled through her the moment she came into contact with the weapon, a rush of energy passing over her—though it felt significantly weaker than the first time she'd experienced it.

Loric's expression shifted slightly, and she noticed that he was staring at her eyes. "Is—something wrong?"

He shook his head. "Nothing of concern. I simply hadn't seen a wielder's eyes actively change color before. I've heard of it happening, of course, but to see it—it's incredible, really."

My eyes changed color...again? "What color are they?" She blushed a little asking the question—a question that she never thought she'd have to voice.

"Similar to before, but a lighter shade." A chuckle escaped

his lips suddenly, causing her to relax. "Apologies—I'd completely forgotten that you didn't know about this. When you form a bond with the blade, its energy infuses you, making your eyes appear purple. The tone is always brighter when you're in contact with the sword."

"Oh..." Her eyes found the weapon. *So it was the energy. I was right, I guess.*

Curiously, she reached out with her mind, feeling for the tingly hum that the energy had emanated when she'd wielded it for the first time. It didn't respond to her calls, so she tried harder—but still, nothing. Frustration began to set in after a few moments, her lips curling into a frown.

"It's not responding."

Loric nodded, unsurprised. "I figured this would happen. My theory is that the adrenaline you must have been feeling was so intense that the energy was simply drawn to you that night— on an extremely impressive scale, I might add. The factor of the magical buildup within whatever seal kept that sword in place could have played a pivotal role as well—imagine a breached dam of pure power, inhabiting the first vessel it can find all at once."

"So—you're saying it's going to be a lot harder for me, now that things are a bit more normal?" *I can't believe I'm using the word 'normal' to describe this situation...*

He nodded again. "At least, I think so." His eyes flitted upward, where the morning sun was still steadily climbing up towards the halfway point in the sky. "Let's head inside, get you some rest. We'll come back out in a little bit."

REI COLLAPSED BACKWARD ONTO THE RATHER comfortable bed, unable to keep the smile off her lips despite the throbbing aches that plagued her body. Loric had worked her *hard*—it felt good, though, to be able to really *do* something again. Many of his training tactics were extremely different from how Master Faron had taught her—where the gentle combat instructor had broken up sessions with plenty of constructive praise, Loric simply offered nods and suggestions, complimenting her briefly on the rare occasion that she did something exceptionally well. She didn't mind, really—it was a different environment, yes, but she found herself growing to appreciate it by the end of the day.

Maybe I will enjoy it here. She rolled over, her eyes fluttering closed without much resistance. *Is this world my future? This mysterious weapon, these odd people and their impossible abilities, this place that I still know nothing about—is this where I belong?*

Her stomach churned as the memory of Ember's silhouette disappearing into the distance resurfaced in her mind. *But... what if I never get to see Akaidia again?*

Thoughts whirling, she took a deep breath, sinking back against the pillow as she slipped into a tentative state of sleep.

WATER CRASHED AGAINST UNSEEN SHORES, DARKNESS

pressing in on all sides. She was in a cave—she knew that much—but nothing else seemed to be coming to her mind.

It was empty.

Void.

No memories sprang to her as she searched for them, her heart aching for the pieces of her life that were no longer there.

They should have been—but they weren't.

They were gone.

Forever? She didn't know.

All she knew was darkness—darkness in the form of shadows, cast by the cavern around her. Darkness in the form of frigid waves, lapping against her face while she somehow floated on their surface. Darkness in the form of desolation—the raw, empty feeling of her mind where it felt like a hole had been ripped through her.

Consciousness was not hers to claim, not just yet. The world was a fuzzy haze, her thoughts jumbled and her body weak. Only one thing remained in perfect clarity—a thought that plagued her, haunted her, pushed her down and tried to drown her.

Her memories were gone.

Her identity had been stripped from her.

She was lost.

Her eyes fell closed, and she stopped resisting, allowing the shadows to sweep her away.

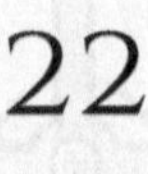

22

REI

oah...Loric seriously likes to read.

Rei stood in the doorway of the massive room that made up most of the second floor, with the only other room being a small closet that was locked as far as she could tell. Bookshelves lined every wall, reaching all the way from the antique wooden flooring to the slanted ceiling above. Iron lanterns hung suspended from the rough oak rafters, the flames inside flooding the room with a soft light.

This place is incredible. A broad smile spread slowly across her lips as she stepped further inside, inhaling the musty scent of books that filled the air. Gaps between the bookshelves provided room for small, rounded windows with crisscrossed frames, allowing gentle sunbeams to illuminate parts of the floor. Wooden panels creaked beneath her weight with each step, her fingers reaching out hesitantly to brush the weathered spines of the shelved books.

The center of the room was occupied by an assortment of

tables, stacks of books piled up to impressive heights and papers scattered sporadically about. More comfortable seating was located near the perimeter of the room, set up beneath the windows or along the far side.

It was late in the afternoon, and Loric had given her a break after their rigorous training sessions that morning, telling her to explore the house as she pleased. So far, she hadn't found too much of interest—a couple abandoned bedrooms, an office, and a room that could have been a workshop of sorts. This library, however, was definitely up her alley.

Rei stopped in front of the nearest shelf, pulling out a rather thick navy volume and squinting at the faded text on the cover. The runes, of course, were unlike the dialect she was used to—yet somehow, she seemed to know their meaning, the scrawls of ink rearranging themselves in her mind to a more understandable word. *An Adventurer's Guide to the Dwarven Clans: Which Ones Should You Avoid?*

That sounds...interesting. With a slight chuckle, she shelved the book, moving a few feet to the left and trailing her fingertips along the spines. *Probably not too useful to me at the moment.* A cloud of dust exploded in her face as she selected a deep emerald title, making her turn away and break into a coughing fit.

Any book that tries to kill me has got to be something good.

She glanced down at the text, which was inscribed in the same language as the previous book. *The High Races of the Iltaran Realms.* A slight smile crossed her lips, and she flipped open the leather cover, brushing away a thin film of dust that had gathered on the yellowed pages. The runes had lost a bit of their color, but most were still legible.

Curiosity piqued, she made her way to one of the few open

spaces on a nearby table, resting the book atop the wood and dragging a chair over. She skimmed through the parchment, pausing to marvel at the hand-drawn diagrams of pointed ears and strange markings. There was even a drawing where vines seemed to be growing out of the woman's head, interwoven into the immaculate braids she displayed. The text at the top read "Gnomes", and Rei found herself examining the page more carefully in case she'd missed an important detail.

Woah... Her smile widened. *They can talk to each other by sending electrical signals through the ground...just like trees.* A twinge of sadness wormed its way into her heart as her mind flashed to Cedar—the wolf had possessed a powerful cultivation ability, meaning that Rei had learned a significant amount about the plants she'd grown. She shook her head to clear the memories, the pain in her chest subsiding after a few long, torturous moments. *This is my world now.* Her throat tightened, but she forced herself to finish the thought. *I'm not going to be leaving it anytime soon. My friends are safe, and it's up to me to make sure that they stay that way.*

With a sigh, she turned to the next page, immersing herself inside the strange new information that each word held. Back in Akaidia, she'd been much more of a stories person than a statistics person, preferring to read about ancient legends and fantastical tales than books stating facts in an agonizing, monotonous way. Here, though, everything felt like a story to her—the likelihood that a human might have a wieldable alignment versus an elf, or the color-changing eyes of a kinetling based on their magical form.

And the alignments...

Rei cast a glance over her shoulder at the bookshelf, wondering if there was a book that might be able to explain the strange energies to her. The alignments were mentioned often, especially when a race's natural magic was brought up on the page. From what she gathered, the mysterious forces were the root of whatever magical abilities that people here could possess, the very foundation that the world was built upon.

I can't believe we never knew about this, back in Akaidia. A frown crossed her features as the meaning of her thought sank deeper into her mind, sparking an idea that she hadn't considered before. *You'd think that after one and a half millennia, one might notice something as prominent as this magic supposed to be.*

Rei continued reading, skimming through the book and pausing whenever she found something of interest. Her attention lingered the longest on the section about humans, a part of her wondering if there was an explanation for the strange bonds that she—and so many others—had forged with an animal. *Could that have something to do with the alignments, too? Even if we don't know it?*

When her eyes found the page on a human's magic, however, she froze, all the blood draining from her face.

Humans possess no natural magic of their own.

Rei's chest tightened, and she read through the rest of the entry, just to make sure. According to whoever had written this, the human race was void of any innate magical ability, like a faerin's shadow form or an aquili's water adaptation. On the other hand, they were mentioned to have a unique ability that other races did not possess, a trait described as "magical capacity."

Her mind was too preoccupied with the fact that there was no mention of animal bonding *anywhere* to question what that might mean.

Maybe the bonding ability is from another race? The one Loric mentioned that I shared blood with—the one my father was? The moment the thought entered her mind, though, something within her shut it down, knowing that it simply couldn't be true. *Even if I was a part of that race, that doesn't mean that the rest of Akaidia is, too.*

Her frown deepened, and she raised her gaze, her distant stare locked on the flickering flame of a lantern overhead. *Loric mentioned that the mountains surrounding Akaidia were guarded by a barrier. Maybe there's more to the story. Maybe whoever put that barrier in place was trying to hide something... like a group of people who somehow possessed abilities that no other race shares...*

"I see you've found the library."

Rei practically jumped out of her skin at the sound of Loric's voice. "I—yeah." Her voice was tight, her mind still reeling from the revelations she'd had—and he noticed.

"Something bothering you?"

The will to shake her head lasted only a second. "A few things, actually."

He nodded, stepping into the room. His brawny frame seemed strangely relaxed as he pulled up a chair beside her, glancing down at the book she was reading. "If you have questions, I don't mind answering them."

Rei hesitated for a moment. "What really happened with Akaidia? With my people?" She met his eyes, a challenge lingering in the depths of her features. "We aren't human, are we."

He didn't even try to deny it. "No."

"What are we, then?"

Loric paused, deep in thought. "It's complicated." He tilted his head at her, examining her carefully. "Could I tell you a story, Rei?"

Rei blinked at him, startled. "A story? What story?"

"A story about a war, one fought long before you were born. A war that I think you'll find to be very informative."

The word 'war' instantly set sirens off in Rei's mind, but she simply nodded, intrigued by his odd reaction. "I—I guess. But what does this have do with Akaidia?"

An odd glint in his eye only heightened her curiosity. "Everything. As a matter of fact—this war is the reason that your world exists."

A war that created a world. She stared at him, her breaths short. *My world.*

"It started just about three thousand years ago, when a small colony of humans was discovered to harbor natural, or biological magic—something no human had ever been born with before. This colony was near an elven settlement, so in the beginning, the abilities were simply labeled as the product of elf-human cross breeding—frowned upon, but not necessarily out of the ordinary.

"Over the years, this population began to grow, however, their powers growing with them. People were discovered to possess a unique type of magic that no other race had ever been recorded wielding—bond magic."

Rei inhaled sharply.

"This magic had never been seen before, and was treated with great hostility from most. In the past, when a new magic had been discovered, the group possessing it would eventually be labeled as their own race, but for some reason, a lot of individuals seemed to reject the idea of this small colony becoming their own nation. The colony, of course, fought back, creating a name for themselves and beginning to separate from the other races. Given time, most of the conflict around their existence died down—but the elves couldn't seem to let it go.

"The kedori—which was the name they chose for themselves—opted for a course of rebellion, creating a settlement in the southern regions of Akareldia. One of the nine realms," he added at Rei's puzzled expression. "I'll explain that to you a bit later. But the important thing to note is that Akareldia is mainly elven inhabited—meaning that the kedori were practically encroaching on enemy territory.

"There were threats of war for many years. In fact, for about three or four centuries, the new race grew, tensions rising with their numbers. The elves grew increasingly more hostile as the kedori began to take up more and more territory—hence growing closer and closer to elven borders.

"One day, a bold group of elven rebels decided that they were fed up with the centuries of failing politics between the races. In a reckless move, they trespassed on kedori land, finding and massacring as many of the people as possible. Naturally, the attempt was met with rage, and despite the fact that the elven government had no part in the rebellion's actions, the kedori responded with the assassination of thirty-seven members of the high council. The remaining twenty-seven members immediately declared war.

"The war lasted for a hundred years, earning it its name: The Centennial War. Both sides suffered heavy casualties, and the kedori race was hunted nearly to extinction. Finally, the last few members remaining surrendered. The elves were torn between wiping out the race and sparing them, a decision that sparked controversy among the high council. Finally, they came to a truce—and decided to banish the remainder of the kedori.

"The Thunder Peaks—now called the Barrier Peaks, but you know them as the Horizon's Teeth—were enchanted with a barrier rune by one of the most powerful jurorian enchanters ever born. The small population of kedori that remained were stripped of all memory of the realms and were relocated to the Akaidian Peninsula within the mountains, forced to create their own lives apart from the rest of the world."

The silence following his words was quite possibly one of the loudest things Rei had ever heard in her life. A shiver rippled down her spine as the weight of the story sank in, settling on her like a massive boulder and crushing her from above.

"So..." she began wearily, pausing for a few moments to process. "Any *other* life-changing and reality-shattering revelations that I should know about?"

A smile crossed Loric's gruff features. "None on that scale, no."

She nodded, unsure what else to do. "Why did it escalate so far?"

Loric's smile faded. "Fear, Rei. The elves feared the kedori, and the kedori responded with nothing but spite." He raised his gaze to hers, steel in his eyes. "Fear is the root of many horrors. Only courage can bring peace."

Rei swallowed hard, blinking rapidly a few times. "Do you think I'd ever be able to set them free?"

He didn't shut her idea down immediately, which she saw as a good sign. "Perhaps. You have plenty to handle before that day comes, though, so I advise you to stay focused."

Loric rose to his feet, wandering over to a nearby shelf and lightly brushing his fingers along the spines. A crimson volume stopped him in his tracks, and he pulled it out, examining it for a moment before turning back to Rei. "Do you enjoy stories, Rei?"

She nodded.

"Then you might want to read this."

The smooth leather of the book felt like paradise as she accepted it from Loric, her eyes tracing the cover. "*Tales of the First Darkness.* Sounds ominous."

He let out a laugh. "It's not nearly as bad as it seems. Those are some of the oldest stories ever told, legends that date back to before the very first written records. I think you might enjoy it —it could help you get a glimpse at the culture of our world, too."

A smile found its way across Rei's lips, and she hefted the book in her hands, fingering the rough parchment. "Are any of the stories real? Or parts of them, anyway?" In her experience, legends had always held a grain of truth.

Loric looked away, but his lips had curled upward beneath his beard. "Some believe them to be."

"Do you?"

He had begun walking across the room towards the hallway, but her words stopped him, his hand lingering on the doorframe.

"I..." His body relaxed a bit, even though he didn't turn around. "Let's just say that if the ancient powers ever returned to our land, I wouldn't find myself too surprised."

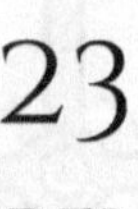

23
REI

W*ham!*

Rei's body slammed into the gravel, and she let out a strangled grunt, the iron taste of blood welling up in her mouth. She laid there for a moment, allowing herself to regain her strength before painstakingly hauling herself to her feet.

"Did you really think it necessary to make them *this* difficult *this* early in the morning?"

Loric shrugged, entirely unfazed. "*You* were the one who begged me to train because you couldn't sleep. Besides, we both know you'd be furious if I ever went easy on you."

Rei snorted, but didn't argue—after all, he wasn't wrong. She returned her attention to the six targets left standing, her fingers tightening around the weapon in her palm. *Alright, Rei. Keep your head on straight, and seriously, try not to get yourself stabbed during a training exercise.*

Her heartbeats thrummed in time to the rhythm her strikes created, each clang of metal and whoosh of air adding to the special drumbeat only she could hear. A cocky grin found its way onto her lips as she pressed back against her enemies, fending them off without exerting too much effort.

I think this might be one of my best runs yet.

Moonlight illuminated the weathered stones of the training arena, reflecting off her steely gaze as she plunged her sword into the final dummy, sending it to the ground. Her sword slipped from her grip, and she sank to the ground with a breathy laugh, wiping the sweat from her forehead and grinning at the sky.

Nightmares had plagued her over the past month, only worsening by the day. They hadn't been normal nightmares, either—they were like the one she'd had all that time ago, a dream about a girl trapped within an endless void of darkness. She'd tried not to dwell on it too much, but it kept resurfacing in her mind, week after week, haunting her regardless of whether she was awake or asleep.

Her smile widened, and she let her body fall limp against the stone, eyes tracing the stars overhead. "Thanks, Loric."

Heavy footfalls indicated that he was now beside her. "Of course. You said you'd been having nightmares?"

She shrugged, not really wanting to mention the fact that she'd been hallucinating the same scene for over a month now— or that the scene almost felt *real*. "Just stuff from my past haunting me, I guess. Nothing too serious." The lie made her wince a little, but Loric didn't seem to take notice.

"If you need to talk, I'm here."

She cast him a grateful glance; something about the way he said those words filled a place in her heart that she'd never even known to be empty. Loric simply smiled at her—a broad, caring smile, the type that she didn't see often from him.

Over the past month, she'd felt herself drawing nearer to Loric, opening up to him in ways that felt different from confiding in anyone else. He wasn't too much of a talker, but he never shied away from sharing information, answering questions about the stories she read or helping her translate a runic language she was unfamiliar with.

I still miss Akaidia...but maybe, just maybe, this place has finally begun to feel like home.

Loric perked up suddenly, a bit of the more familiar slyness returning to his grin. "I'd like you to try the Blade again."

Rei groaned. "Seriously?"

"Seriously." He stared her in the eye, his gaze like steel. "It doesn't matter how much we train, Rei. Your skills in raw combat are quite impressive for your age—but if you come face to face with someone with any sort of magical capability, they *will* have the upper hand over you."

She sighed, pulling herself to her feet and accepting the blade from him. "And you're sure I can't just learn to cast enchantments first, like you do?"

He shook his head. "Those took me decades to learn. We know that your power—when it comes to wielding that sword, at least—will be extremely difficult to match in the field of battle. You just have to—"

"Access it again," Rei finished, frustration seeping into her tone. "But I've been trying for *weeks*—and I still can't get so much as a little glow out of it."

Loric crossed his arms, taking a step back. "Give it time. Although..." His expression shifted slightly, and Rei could practically see the idea forming in his mind. He clapped his hands twice, shouting a command word. One of the dummies she'd defeated earlier sprang to life again, a black glow emitting from the rune on its forehead—a color she'd never seen before. Her fingers tightened around the Blade's hilt, a sense of unease settling over her.

"Loric? What are you doing?"

He didn't respond, offering only a nod of encouragement. Swallowing her nerves, she turned to face the dummy, her knuckles beginning to whiten from the sheer force of her grip.

Something isn't right about this. Loric's never woken just one before—not even when the drill is supposed to be for a duel. Her chest tightened, but she took a deep breath, reminding herself of where her trust was placed.

Loric wouldn't hurt me.

Planting her feet, she held the Blade out in front of her, gritting her teeth and reaching out her mind for the distant hum of energy she *knew* to be there. It didn't respond, but she refused to give up, fighting harder and harder to tap into the sword's power.

By the clans! Listen to me!

In front of her, the enemy began moving, slowly at first, then picking up its pace. A faint black aura around its body only intensified the panic she'd been feeling earlier, and her mind spurred into overdrive, trying frantically to reach for the only thing she knew could help.

All instinct had forsaken her.

Her feet were rooted to the ground.

Her opponent charged her, but all she could do was stand, watch as it leapt into the air and brought its weapon up to strike her down.

This was no ordinary strike—and even though her arms

were already moving to counter, her mind somehow inherently knew that it wouldn't be enough.

The Blade's brittle obsidian surface would shatter on contact, leaving her defenseless.

I need something more.

Time stalled around her, adrenaline flooding through every vein in her body. In that instant, her senses were heightened, creating new links that her mind hadn't even considered to be options before.

More.

Her opponent's sword fell through the air, slicing neatly towards Rei's head. Alone, she couldn't stop it.

Except—she wasn't alone.

Clarity surged into her, overwhelming her entirely as the blades met. A purple glow erupted around them, Rei's body overcome with pure, raw power. It wasn't nearly as intense as before, but the distant tingling was so much more natural now, her mind moving in sync with the force instead of trying to reject it. A cry escaped her lips as she pushed back, streams of energy overwhelming the target.

The sound of splintering wood was the only warning Rei had as the target was obliterated by the energy, its body reduced to nothing but slivers. She was unable to celebrate her victory, however, as a pounding headache had already begun to work its way through her temples, bringing with it a world of darkness that felt all too familiar.

Her body hit the ground, the sword remaining tightly clenched in her grip. A lavender haze consumed her vision, stripping her of her consciousness and leaving her as prey to the shadows.

PURPLE.

All Rei could see was purple.

A glow, a fog, a mist, a cloud—she didn't quite know how to describe the tangible yet ghostlike form of it, drifting through an endless void that she recognized but was unable to name.

Her eyes moved to her side where her fingers were still tightly wrapped around the hilt of the Phantom Blade. *Is this a dream, then? But how did I bring the weapon with me?*

A thought slipped into her mind—it was hers, but not hers, a deep inner instinct that she could neither explain nor identify.

The Blade brought me.

Suddenly, the air seemed to solidify, the purple fog curling inward and enveloping her body. The scene began to shift as a strange feeling settled into her stomach, her eyes locking on something new—and infinitely more terrifying.

There was a silhouette of a man, standing in a room where the moon was the only source of light. He leaned against the windowsill, his features blurred by the darkness. Some part of her knew this man—but how she knew him, she had no idea. He was familiar to her, yet alien...and although they'd never met, she couldn't help but feel a deep connection between them.

The man turned to her, purple meeting purple as their eyes locked. "It's true, then. At long, last, the fabled Phantom Blade has been claimed—though it is not my hand that the weapon rests in."

Rei blinked at him. "I—you can see me?"

"But of course." A bitter laugh escaped his lips. "Why, you're but a child—a child who appears to have no knowledge of the weapon she holds. And to think that I was worried."

Indignation flared through her, but she bit her tongue, deciding to listen to the tiny voice inside her that miraculously managed to keep her sane. His gaze bored into her very being, a jolt of horror rippling down her spine.

Most of his features were shrouded in shadow, but the left half of his face was covered with a thin, faintly glowing mask—a mask inlaid with purple veins and forged of a material that practically cried out for the sword she clutched. A single amethyst was set where his eye should have been, only adding to the unease that had settled into her body.

Who is this man?

"No response." He cocked his head, a twinge of annoyance seeping into his voice. "Looks like you at least have a bit of self-control."

The scene began to blur, purple fog once again rimming the corners of Rei's vision. His figure faded in and out of view, but his words were crystal clear, slithering into her ears and taking a death grip on her heart.

"I'm not sure who you are, where you're from, or how someone like you got your hands on that sword in the first place—but I promise you this: I will find you."

His gaze steeled, his form suddenly becoming crystal clear.

"And the Eidolon always keeps his word."

24

RUNE

Luna's body went rigid, the blood draining from her face at the sound of the boy saying her name. Rune had never seen so much turmoil within her eyes before—a distant familiarity, an inexplicable confusion, and the resulting frustration from the conflict of the two.

"How do you know my name?" Her tone was slow, even, and methodical—completely out of character for the outspoken blonde.

The boy's expression shifted, and he took a step back, sadness and guilt pooling in his gaze. "You don't remember me...do you."

Her features softened ever so slightly, but she still shook her head. All thoughts of battle had left their minds a long time ago—everyone's attention was locked on Luna and this boy, Ivory's especially.

The boy's companion stepped forward, the background hum of electricity waning. "You know them?"

"Just her." The shorter boy nodded at Luna, eyes veiled with a misty sheen.

He dared a few steps closer, making sure to keep his hands away from the weapons at his side. Luna watched him approach, unmoving. She made no attempt to stop him, but there was no eagerness in her expression either, her face a blank mask of the numbness that resulted from feeling too much emotion. Ivory's hand twitched closer to his sword, but he stayed where he was, watching like a hawk would its prey.

The boy looked Luna up and down, his amber-eyed gaze lingering on the flames that still danced across her clenched fist. "You...you really don't remember? Any of it?"

A hint of pained regret crossed Luna's features. "No."

He nodded, closing his eyes for a second longer than a blink. Hesitation held his tongue for him, but he finally seemed to settle on the words he wanted, awkwardly lifting his arm to offer her a handshake. "Ryder. My name is Ryder."

Luna paused, her eyes tracing the deep umber tones of his outstretched hand before tentatively taking it. "Guess it wouldn't be much use if I introduced myself, would it."

Her tone still isn't there—but at least the words sound more like something Luna would say. Rune fidgeted in place, her attention wandering to the other boy, who remained at a careful distance from the rest of them. He watched them quietly, a hint of unease in his expression.

Ivory took a step forward as Ryder backed away, his gaze finding the rest of the group for the first time. "If you don't mind me asking...how do you know Luna?" Ivory's question wasn't innately hostile, but the words were still laced with a protective undertone.

Ryder looked away. "She found me. When I'd first woken up, that is. We agreed to travel together, considering that we were on the same team and all." He paused, his voice trembling slightly. "We were doing really well for quite some time—until a few weeks ago, when we were attacked by a rival group that greatly outnumbered us. I fought as hard as I could...but I couldn't save her." A shudder rocked his body, and he returned his gaze to Luna's. "I knew you'd end up in Green, so that's where I decided to go. Kaleo and I met on the way—" he nodded at the taller boy— "and he agreed to help me look for you."

Kaleo looked extremely uncomfortable with the introduction, but he did take a step closer, eyeing them all with intense suspicion. Rune placed herself in line with Azalea and Nyk, neither of whom had said a word the whole time.

Luna held Ryder's stare cooly, though her eyes reflected just how shaken she was by the whole situation. "You're saying—I died. Like—you watched me die."

Ryder only nodded.

"Huh." Her lips twitched, as though she were trying to force a smile, but her expression didn't change. "That explains all these weird feelings I've been getting, then. Maybe they're my memories—or at least, they were."

Silence fell, none of them really knowing how to respond to her statement. Finally, Azalea spoke up awkwardly, glancing from Kaleo to Ryder.

"You're both purple, then?"

The boys exchanged a glance, but nodded, each turning their head to reveal a rectangle the same shade as the one Rune had seen on her friends' necks. Ryder brushed away a few stray braids out of his face, quickly tying them back into a stubby ponytail. His stocky frame and angular features made up for his lack in height, and patches of amber scales the same shade as his eyes were scattered across his skin like freckles.

Rune couldn't help but notice the immense variety in appearance across the group they'd gathered—how she, Nyk and Ivory didn't have pointed ears like the others, the natural plants growing from Azalea's head, the bracelet-like birthmarks around her own wrists, and even the small outline of a diamond Rune had noticed on the nape of Nyk's neck.

We're all so different.

Kaleo's monolid eyes scanned across the group, lingering for a moment on Rune's. She stared into their vibrant turquoise depths, her mind automatically trying to decode the veil of emotion swirling within. His dark hair was straight, but slightly unkempt, with bangs falling just below his eyebrows and loose strands drifting with the wind. He brushed them aside, expression unreadable. "I have to admit—I've never encountered five of a single team in one spot before."

The sharp edges had disappeared from his tone, leaving behind a voice that was both soft and firm, gentle yet unwavering. He didn't speak at volume, but every syllable was clearly pronounced, projected in such a way that implicated hours of practice.

Strange how I feel like I know these things, and how I can identify them, but I am unable to recall their origin.

"Guess that's seven, now." Luna's words sent a shiver down Rune's spine, the true realization of just how close they were to a complete team finally sinking in. Another thought slipped into her mind moments later, causing her to frown slightly.

"Sorry—I—" She reddened as all eyes turned to her, her voice unfamiliar to the conversation. "I just realized that we never told you our names." A slightly hesitant smile spread across her lips, letting out a breath as the force of the attention lessened. "I'm Rune. Light element."

"Ivory. Air." He spoke curtly, but not unkindly.

Luna shrugged. "I'm not too difficult to figure out." A flame rippled briefly across her palm. Rune could have sworn that Ivory rolled his eyes, but his lips were twitching towards a smile.

Azalea and Nyk introduced themselves as well, the tension in the air thinning slightly now that the conversation had calmed to "normal" levels. Rune found her eyes traveling across the barren stone patterns, making a mental note of any gouges or outcroppings that seemed interesting to her.

This place looks like it's been the location of a lot of fights... She glanced over at the rest of the group, some of whom had begun to engage in uneasy discussions.

"You're all from Green, right?" Rune practically jumped out of her skin at the sound of Kaleo's voice beside her—she hadn't heard him approach.

"Yeah. At least, that's where I woke up—and where I met them."

"So you're the newest."

She looked over her shoulder. "I am. Azalea and Nyk found me first, then we encountered Luna and Ivory soon after."

He cocked his head at her. "Did you just wake up, then? For the first time?"

Rune nodded hesitantly. "As far as I know—which isn't very far, to be fair."

For the first time, a half chuckle escaped his lips. "It's Rune, right?"

She nodded again, unsure why even the simple gesture felt odd in his presence. *He makes me nervous, and I can't for the life of me figure out why.*

"You guys just keep getting lucky, don't you."

All conversation instantly ceased with the sound of the voice, its speaker unseen. Rune's mind instantly latched onto the noise, cycling it through her memories and matching it up to the few she had. The sound was familiar—too familiar, a thickly accented female tone that sent alarms spiraling through her thoughts. With a sickening lurch in her stomach, the face of their utterer slipped into her headspace, only moments before the girl herself stepped out from behind a crevice in the valley.

Auburn hair.

Bands around her wrist, just like mine.

Silver eyes.

Eyes that bored into mine as she swung her blade towards me, the intent to kill obvious on her face.

Luna killed her—but I guess her teammates found her again.

"Seven...what a nice number." A cold smile spread slowly across her lips. "It's time to level the playing field a bit, though." At her cue, five other teenagers gathered behind her—a few of them familiar, many of them not. The one Rune had killed was there—but even when their eyes met, she saw no recognition in his gaze.

Luna was first to recover from the surprise appearance, marching forward without a care in the world. "I'd just love to see you try."

The auburn haired girl narrowed her eyes. "It would be my pleasure."

"Why did we let her do the speech?" One of the boys grumbled, earning him a glare.

"Shut up, Jett."

Jett shrugged, stepping forward and raising his hands above his head. A massive chunk of rock was gouged from the ground in front of him, floating up and levitating above his palms. Ryder answered by clenching his fist, causing a ripple of smaller stones to detach and drift threateningly in the air around him.

Seeing that their opponents had no intention of making the first move, Luna swept her arms upward in an arc, a wave of fire following the gesture as she directed it straight at the enemy. The blast was deflected by a burst of air from the auburn-haired girl, and a shout rang out, three of her allies skirting around her and charging for Rune's group.

We outnumber them, and they know that...but they just don't seem to care.

Rune dug her feet into the ground as they approached, gathering the cloud-covered sunlight from the air around her and pressing it together into a single beam. The attack landed perfectly, diverting their attention for only a few moments— but a few moments was all that was needed. Rune caught a brief glimpse of a yellow rectangle on a beady-eyed boy's neck as he was blown backward by Ivory, letting out a grunt as his body hit the cliff wall.

Both sides fought with no holds barred, but neither was able to gain much ground, continuous blows exchanged but no particularly devastating ones able to land. Rune noticed as the yellow team slowly began to shrink back, pushed against the cave wall as their options dwindled.

Suddenly, Jett froze, his eyes locking on the auburn-haired girl's. Around Rune, her team still fought just as hard, but their opponents suddenly began to let up, their attacks turning to nothing but defensive parries. Alarms blared in her mind, her fists clenching. *Something isn't right.*

She didn't have to wait long to discover what it was.

Jett whipped around, lobbing a massive chunk of stone at the far side of the valley. It landed right in front of a particularly large gap, one that Rune had noticed on her way in but never really thought twice about. A bloodcurdling shriek split the air moments later, the sound stripping all the color from Kaleo and Ryder's faces. The rest of the group, however, only looked confused.

Luna lobbed another wave of fire at their opponents, but the team had all but disappeared, melting back into the stone and retreating. She cursed under her breath, turning back towards the source of the horrible sound. "Bloody cowards."

Rune was unable to peel her eyes away, her heart thundering in her chest. "What...was that?"

Kaleo gripped his sword so hard that his knuckles were turning white, his eyes filled with true fear. "Howlers. A den of them."

Before she could ask for an explanation, the first creature stepped into the light, letting out yet another shriek as it fixed its beady yellow eyes on the group. Rune's blood ran cold, her chest tightening.

We are going to die.

25

RUNE

Calling a howler simply "terrifying" wasn't exactly doing the monster justice.

It had a broad, lumbering body like a bear's, but its head resembled a wolf, with exaggerated features and a long, spindly tail that swung threateningly back and forth. What it had couldn't possibly be called fur—spikes of black and gray hair were spread across its body, matted together to create a visually impenetrable shield. Wickedly serrated claws stuck out from its four feet, and the creature had a rather dramatic under-bite, drool slipping out from behind the row of bloodstained fangs.

A shiver rippled down her spine. *This thing can't be real. It just can't.*

The roar it made in response, however, sounded very, very tangible.

"Maybe we can distract it?" The tremor in Nyk's tone betrayed just how little he himself believed in the idea.

"Once those things have a target, they can't be diverted." Kaleo's voice was grim. "And right now, we're the targets."

Luna eyed the beast cooly, watching as it stalked slowly closer. "It's one on seven. How bad could it be?"

With ironic timing, an array of new howls sounded from the open crevice, and one by one, three more howlers began to reveal themselves.

Ivory shot her a look. "You really had to say it, huh."

Luna responded by sending a burst of flame towards the howlers—which proceeded to do absolutely nothing. She groaned. "Great. They're fireproof."

Ryder scowled. "They're everything-proof. No elemental attack or physical weapon can penetrate that thing's fur."

Rune's heart sank, and judging by her friends' expressions, she wasn't the only one. "How do we beat them, then?"

Kaleo kept his eyes locked on the creatures. "We don't. We divide them."

Ryder met his eyes, an unspoken message passing between the two boys. Kaleo opened his mouth to speak, but that was when the front howler charged, splitting him and Rune off from the rest of the group. Rune whipped out her sword, clutching it in a death grip as the rest of the howlers began forming a circle around them.

"Let's go, before they surround us!" Ryder's shout held no meaning to Rune, but Kaleo seemed to understand perfectly, grabbing Rune's arm before she could react and dragging her away from the rest of the group. She opened her mouth to protest, but stopped when she noticed the look on his face—he had a plan. *I just have to hope that that plan works.*

They scrambled up the side of the valley, Rune's muscles

crying out in pain but being silenced by the rush of adrenaline flooding through her. The rest of her friends had broken off in the opposite direction, leaving the four howlers hesitating on the ground while they each debated their targets. Three of the beasts gave chase to Rune's teammates, leaving only one to come after her and Kaleo—the one that looked to be the leader.

"Follow me. Fast."

Rune didn't argue, breaking into a run behind Kaleo and not daring to glance back. She could hear the breaths of the monster, its shrieks growing nearer and nearer at a terrifying pace. "It's gaining!"

Kaleo cursed, banking right and taking her towards what appeared to be a wide open plateau of stone. The creature followed them effortlessly, Rune's chest tightening with every step. Kaleo was always a few strides ahead of her, not once glancing back.

"Up ahead, you're going to have to jump," he warned, his voice carried by the wind.

"Jump *what*?"

Her answer came before he even opened his mouth—a massive crevice, at least ten feet across. Lungs aching, she pushed forward, her mind analyzing the gap. It would be an uncomfortably far jump...but the creature behind them refused to leave them much of a choice, letting out a horrible roar as if to remind them of its pursuit.

Step.

Step.

Step.

She would have to time her jump just right, or she wouldn't have enough power to make it across. Her fingers balled into fists, the adrenaline pulsing through her overriding the fear that built up in the back of her mind.

I can do this.

Just as she was about to jump, there was a shout followed by a thud, then the realization that Kaleo was no longer in front of her. Instinctively, she whipped around, watching as he scrambled away from the creature with a weapon in his hand.

They locked eyes, but his expression shifted, a shout of warning leaving his lips just before her foot snagged on an unseen rock jutting out from the ground. Time slowed as she lost her balance, her fingers somehow managing to find a lip of stone on the cliffside as she tumbled over the edge. She hung on for dear life, her shoulder screaming in protest as her body swung back and forth.

Her breath resonated in her ears, the achingly terrifying feeling of nothing but an abyss beneath her feet serving as the only thing that kept her grip from slipping. Above, she could hear Kaleo struggling against the monster, her resolve growing with each passing second.

I have to get back up.

I have to help him.

She gritted her teeth, ignoring the throbbing ache that pulsed through her ankle from when she'd tripped. The pain didn't matter, not in that moment. All that mattered was the certain death below her...and her teammate above.

With a grunt, she samanaged to swing her other arm up to the ledge, scrunching her eyes shut and pulling herself up with all the strength she could muster. The stone budged slightly, causing her to cry out in pain as her ankle was slammed against the side of the cliff face.

Come on. Just a little more.

She readjusted her position, steadying her hold on the rock. The sharp stone dug into her fingers, but she ignored it, clawing her way up slowly. Then, suddenly, Kaleo was there, his sturdy arms gripping hers and joining with her efforts to haul her up and safely out of the gap.

"Thank you." Her voice was breathless, tinged with pain.

He nodded, his lips parting to say something in response— but Rune didn't give him the chance, springing forward and tackling him to the ground as the howler lunged towards them. She bit back a cry as her ankle was agitated yet again, her mind telling her to stop but the adrenaline commanding otherwise.

If I stop, we'll both die.

Kaleo scrambled back as the creature regained its footing, pushing her away from him. "We have to split up! Go!"

Rune's body moved before her mind even processed the information, the quick reaction saving her life. The howler charged her, but she dove to the left, catching herself on the rough ground and rolling out of the way as the creature barreled past. Her palm tingled slightly as she righted herself, a faint white rim surrounding her vision.

The light.

Ryder had said that no elemental attack could penetrate the fur. But what if drawing blood wasn't her goal?

Rune kept her eyes locked on the creature's as she gathered the tingly energy from her core and pooled it into her fingertips. A dull buzz in the back of her mind let her know that the power was nearly too much for her to keep contained, which was perfectly fine—control wasn't exactly the objective in a situation like this. Her mind raced, flinging calculations in every direction. A faint glow began to drift around her palms, surrounding them in a white haze.

Kaleo's eyes flickered to her hands, a glint in his eye telling her that he understood her idea. He raised his head, their gazes locking for a brief moment before he silently began creeping across the stone towards her position. The light intensified, and the howler's attention was now entirely set on her, its movements hesitant as though the glow deterred it. Rune mentally pleaded that it wouldn't notice Kaleo flanking it, a crazed, deadly sheen passing over the monster's face.

Hurry, Kaleo. I don't know how much longer I can hold this.

The power thrummed against her skin, pushing as if desperate to escape—but she couldn't let it, not yet. It didn't seem to understand, battling against her to be released.

Please, Kaleo. Please. The sheer amount of control she had to exert began to wear down on her, a burning sensation blossoming in her core.

The Howler let out a low growl, taking a slow, threatening step towards Rune. She stood, rooted to the ground, her throbbing ankle refusing to let her run. She heard Kaleo moving towards her, but she couldn't see him, her eyes fixed only on the tumultuous hatred brewing in the howler's gaze.

In only a moment, the sound of Kaleo's soft footfalls went silent, and she became suddenly aware of his presence beside her. Tense, suffocating silence lingered, lasting for only seconds but feeling like hours. Then, in a rush of motion, the creature let out an earsplitting howl, lunging for her with a terrifying new speed.

Adrenaline flooded through her, sharpening her senses and giving her a new, supercharged clarity. With a cry, she flung her hands towards the creature, her palms overcome by a blinding white light. She was vaguely aware of a strong hand grasping her shoulder, tugging her away as the creature howled in pain and anger. Light stung at her eyes, blinding her, impairing her vision as she stumbled after the figure she knew to be Kaleo, groping around within her chaos-induced mind for some form of reality to grab hold of.

Can't see.

Can't think.

Can't move.

The glow faded, freeing up her vision just long enough for her to see the howler charging them once again.

Can't move.

It's coming.

There was a rush of wind as Kaleo flung himself in front of her, aiming a sleek wooden bow that he'd unhooked from its position on his back directly at the Howler. He didn't flinch as the beast approached, cocking his head slightly and steadying his aim. Rune hated that she could only watch as the beast opened its mouth one last time, prepared to let out a final, triumphant roar as it raised its foreleg to strike.

There was a dull *twang* as Kaleo released the arrow, allowing it to fly directly into the creature's open mouth. The tip wedged itself into the weak, exposed flesh, embedding deep and causing the creature to let out a strangled screech. Rune watched it fall, the spark of life leaving its eyes before its body even hit the ground.

Stunned, Rune fumbled for a handhold, searching for something, anything, to prop herself up on. She didn't need to test it to know that her left leg—the one that had snagged when she fell—was unusable at the moment. Her ankle throbbed horribly, and she stumbled over an unseen obstacle, accidentally putting weight on her injured foot to stabilize herself. A cry of pain instantly erupted from her lips, and she doubled over, barely stopped from hitting the ground by a pair of strong hands grabbing her shoulders.

"Lean on me," Kaleo commanded, his voice steady.

Obediently, Rune relaxed, the adrenaline draining from her blood. She was vaguely aware of being gently lifted to her feet, and allowed Kaleo to sling her arm over his shoulder and support her injured side. A groan escaped her lips as he began to guide her gently forward, and she bit down on her tongue, choking down the pained cries that billowed up in her throat.

"Thank you," Rune mumbled, instantly regretting the unnecessary movement.

Kaleo nodded, shifting slightly under her weight. "I saved your life, you saved mine. Call it even?"

She managed a faint smile. "Deal." Another starburst of agony stabbed through her leg, causing her pace to falter.

Get yourself together.

Minutes felt like hours as Rune limped along, guilt weighing on her for forcing Kaleo to move at such a glacial pace. The initial agony had begun to subside, leaving behind a dull, horrible ache that sent splinters of pain up her leg. Rays of crimson light decorated the sky as they neared a practically invisible opening in a nearby cliffside—the place that Kaleo was taking her, Rune realized.

He helped her through the opening first, a heavy breath rushing through her as she emerged into a cave occupied by the rest of their group. Remorse flickered through her as she watched the worry disappear from her friends' gazes, replaced by the very same relief she now felt. Kaleo gripped her arms firmly, gently helping her to rest against the cave wall.

"She's injured. Hurt her ankle in the fight."

Azalea moved closer, grimacing at Rune's foot. "How much can you move?"

It took a moment for the girl's words to register, and Rune forced herself to swallow the pain. "I can't use the leg. Other than that, I'm alright."

"Can I look at it?"

Rune nodded, grimacing slightly as she readjusted. Azalea inhaled sharply, sending needles like ice rippling down Rune's spine.

"How bad is it?"

"Definitely broken." Azalea leaned back, biting her lip nervously. "It might take a while to heal—I'll have to set it and make a splint, but you won't be able to use that side for at least a few weeks."

Rune's face burned with frustration and embarrassment, fully aware of the stares her friends were sending her way. None of them were accusing—but even so, she felt as though she were letting them down with this kind of a setback. "What do we do now, then?"

Azalea averted her eyes, staring blankly into the distance. "I —don't know."

26
REI

Rei stared up at the sky, the late morning sun gently illuminating the landscape. The air had grown much cooler recently, though she never found herself needing more than a short sleeved tunic and pants during her training sessions. Loric had finally called a break, but despite her aching muscles, she was sprawled on the hard stone and grinning from ear to ear. The thrill of fighting filled her body with strength once again, allowing the dream from the night before to almost fade from her mind.

Almost.

She forced herself to a sitting position, glancing to her right. "Hey, Loric?"

Her mentor turned, his face unreadable.

"Can the sword give you...visions?"

His expression changed instantly, and he began moving towards her, his eyes filled with a strange intensity. "What makes you ask that?"

"Yesterday, when I blacked out during training...I saw something. Then there was a man, one with purple eyes, just like me —and he talked to me." A shiver rippled down her spine. *The Eidolon always keeps his word.* "He called himself the Eidolon."

The blood drained from Loric's face, panic unlike the kind she'd ever seen before from him consuming his features. Her chest tightened, true fear setting in at the sight of her generally calm mentor's reaction. *It can't possibly be that bad...*

"He *spoke* to you?"

She nodded. "He was kinda rude."

Loric looked away, muttering something to himself. "The answer to your question is yes, the sword can give you visions. Usually, it doesn't happen until the wielder has already been bonded to the weapon for a few years...but you seem to be a special case."

A frown crossed her lips. "And the Eidolon?"

That time, he was better at hiding the shift in his expression at the name, but she still noticed. "I don't want you to worry about that, Rei. Just let me know if it happens again, alright?"

She glared. "I'm not an idiot. Those men who kidnapped me—the Eidolon's their boss, right? So to have him just *waltz* into my dream and insult me for literally no reason—oh, and threaten me, just for good measure—I think I have the right to be at least a bit concerned."

"He threatened you?"

"I mean—he said he was going to find me, and it certainly didn't sound like he just wanted to chat."

Loric sighed. "We'll cross that bridge when we come to it. Right now, I want you staying *focused* on your training—and that means no worrying about visions or the rude men that happen to be in them. Understand?"

"Not really."

His hand found her shoulder, gripping firmly—not enough to hurt, but providing just the right amount of pressure to grab her attention. "I'm afraid you're going to have to trust me on this, Rei. I *will* tell you what it means—but now is not the time."

She still hesitated, hating the idea of having to wait for an explanation...but she'd not yet encountered a situation where Loric had led her wrong. "Fine, I'll forget about it. You have to show me how to do that enchantment stuff, though—you know I've been dying to learn it."

Loric shot her a look, but she stared right back, unwavering. *If you're gonna hold back information from me, I'm gonna make sure I at least get something in return. And if you think I'm gonna let this go, you're dead wrong...*

"Alright. What do you know of the runic system?"

She blinked at him. "Well—I know its name, now."

He rubbed his temples with a sigh, but his lips were still twitching into a smile. "I guess we'll have to start with the basics, then."

Finally—I get to learn actual magic. As fun as combat training is, it's not exactly a new experience for me. She frowned as Loric turned, heading towards the house. "Wait—where are you going?"

"Runic casting is not a combat art, Rei. I will be able to teach you best upstairs, where you can practice the designs in a calmer environment."

She didn't argue further, trailing behind him as he led her through the now familiar hallways of his home and upstairs to the library. A smile worked its way across her features as she stepped inside the spacious room, a room that had become extremely special to her throughout the time she'd spent with Loric. Hours upon hours had been spent up here, studying about worlds she'd never heard of and the civilizations that inhabited them. What she'd been having trouble understanding, however, was the magic that seemed to be so prominent in every situation—the forces linking together every race, allowing them to perform exceptional tasks.

Loric took a seat in front of a mahogany table, motioning for her to sit beside him. Setting aside the sporadically placed books that cluttered the space, he rummaged around, locating a few empty pieces of parchment paper and setting them in front of Rei.

"Runic enchantment is one of the few forms of magic that almost any race can perform—although the jurori are the best at it. It involves drawing a specific design onto the surface you wish to alter, then channeling a small fragment of your magic into that design—usually via a key word or phrase."

To demonstrate, he tore off a strip of the paper, pulling out a sharpened writing utensil and quickly sketching a simple design of crisscrossing lines. He leaned closer, murmuring a phrase that Rei didn't recognize. The paper twitched under his hand, slowly levitating upwards as he lifted his palm higher above it, a smile toying with his lips when he noticed the pure awe in Rei's expression.

"Levitation rune. Simple, yet effective." He lowered his hand to the table, the paper following with it. "In this case, I paired it with an extra keyword to make it stay in line with my hand motions. *Haasa.*" The paper fell still.

"Can I try?"

He nodded. "Of course. Copy the design I drew onto your paper."

Loric handed her the charcoal stick, and she lowered it to the parchment, carefully drawing each stroke in the exact same way he had a few moments before. When she sat back to examine her word, she had to admit, it was a bit underwhelming—nothing more than a few lines on a page. *How did he make it look so much cooler?* "Now what?"

"This part's a bit tricky, and I do *not* expect you to get it immediately." He leaned closer, eyeing the drawing. Based on his lack of things he had to say about it, she assumed she'd done a decent job. "It's less about the words, and more about the power that rests behind them. The runic system is fueled by magic, as many things are in this world. If you don't put the proper energy behind it, your enchantment is nothing more than a drawing and a few letters."

Rei frowned down at the parchment. "I have to put magic—into my words?"

"Sort of." He tilted his head sideways, glancing at her for a long moment. "Since you have no prior experience with magic arts, I suppose the best analogy would be the feeling you get when you use the Blade's power. That feeling is not unique to the Blade alone—that energy you wield is magic, at least at its very core. Try focusing on that energy as you're speaking, even though you aren't actually holding the weapon."

"What do I say?"

"*Shumon-la* is the basic command for levitate." His lips curled into a smile as realization dawned on her face. "Your mind translated it for you, didn't it."

She nodded, still confused. "Translated?"

"Runic commands are most often spoken in Jurorish, a language that carries magic quite well. *Shumon-la* is no different."

Her frown deepened. "Why did I hear the actual words, though? When you spoke to me before, it was translated right away—so fast that I didn't even realize you'd changed languages."

He nodded, unsurprised by her question. "All races speak at least two different languages instinctively—their native language, and the natural tongue, which is a universal speech that all intelligent beings are able to understand. My suspicion is that half bloods, like yourself, are able to speak three or more—though interracial children are so rare, there isn't much research to support that theory or show how far the trait can go.

"When I spoke that magic command to you just now, I actually put a small amount of magic behind it, just like I would when casting. Since I didn't direct it at a rune, the magic simply dispelled, but your brain still heard it as an enchantment *before* recognizing the word itself. Later on, you will learn how to separate the natural tongue from the other languages in your mind, therefore hearing the words as they are—but don't worry about that now."

Rei couldn't help but grin. "That's super cool." A memory resurfaced in her thoughts, causing her to do a double-take. "If runic commands are in Jurorish, though, then why can't I understand the ones you use to animate the targets?"

Loric's features were overrun by a half-smile. "You have quite the eye for detail, Rei. That's because the commands I use on a daily basis aren't in Jurorish at all. Most people use it for its ease, but some—the very best of the best—are able to learn a far more difficult dialect. The challenge is well worth it, as enchantments cast under the alternate language's influence can carry far more magical power than the basic forms—but very few are ever able to reach that level."

"Wow," Rei breathed, soaking in the information and holding it tightly. She turned to Loric, all thoughts of the paper forgotten as a new question found its way to the front of her mind—a question that had been weighing on her for quite some time. "Where does all this magic come from, anyway? Some of the books I've read have mentioned the alignments, but I don't understand where the power comes from in the first place. It has to have a source, right?"

"It does have a source." He stood, eyeing her for a moment before stepping away from the table and reaching into his pocket. "It's long past when that I should have shown you this —but no better time than the present, I suppose."

Rei slid the chair away, rising to her feet. "Shown me what?"

He smiled. "It's not really a *what*, Rei. It's a *where*."

Before she could ask any further questions, he pulled his hand out from his pocket, bringing with it a flat, four-pronged star glinting with pale blue energy. The closer she looked, the more she realized that the energy was actually *inside* the stone, an empty husk encasing a foggy orb of airily drifting forces.

"Is that magic?"

"A form of it." He set the stone down between himself and Rei, taking a few steps back and gesturing for her to stand beside him. "That object is an Aligned Energy Storage Vessel, but it's usually just referred to as an alistone. This particular alistone is embodied with arcana, one of the two aligned forces."

"What's the other one?"

"I'll show you." Loric lifted his hand, which, to Rei's amazement, began to glow with a maroon hue. After a moment, the faint aura solidified, forming into a bundle of erratic threads that wove around his fingers. The gesture was so simple, yet so incredible—the way the energy moved, the way it felt, the way it danced around with an innate longing to be free —she couldn't fight the grin that spread across her lips as she turned to her mentor, hundreds of questions bubbling up in her throat.

He chuckled at her expression. "This is glyph, the other half of the aligned spectrum. I'll explain a bit more about the energies and what they do once we get there."

"Get where?"

His smile widened. "You'll see."

She remained silent as he lowered his palm, angling the glyph towards the alistone he'd set on the ground. With a slight flick of his wrist, the energy shot out in a perfect beam, piercing through the stone and mingling with the fog within it.

For a moment, nothing happened—then, the two energies seemed to explode, expanding outwards rapidly and twisting around one another while slowly forming into an elliptical shape. They were a pair, yet they could not touch, a set, but they could not combine—a harmony, a balance, a perfect unity working just the way it was supposed to. Rei watched, dumbfounded, while the perimeter of the energies widened into a circle.

Suddenly, there was a flash of green, and the circle collapsed in on itself, creating a single rift that hovered within the air. Pure, raw power emanated from it, along with strange feelings of disjunction, like a tear cut into the fabric of reality itself. Rei instinctively flinched away from the unnatural mass, every muscle in her body tensing.

"What...what is that?"

"The way to where we're going." He took a step forward, offering his hand to her. "Go on, then. I'll be right behind you."

Rei gaped at him. "You mean go *into* that...thing?"

He nodded, entirely unfazed. "It's perfectly safe."

"Somehow, I doubt that." Even so, she found herself resting her palm in his, gripping tightly. His hand was calloused and rough, but a faint sense of security wrapped itself around her as he wrapped his fingers firmly around her hand.

"It's going to feel a bit weird, but you *cannot* let go of my hand, alright?"

She hesitated, but agreed, deciding to put her trust in Loric. *Alright...let's just walk straight forward into the giant portal of doom, then. Very normal, I'm sure.*

Loric went first, stepping halfway into the gateway before turning back to look at her. Energy bent around his body, emitting a dull crackling sound that slurred his voice slightly. "You ready?"

Not trusting her voice, she nodded, allowing him to gently lead her forward. Her fingers brushed against the odd surface of the rift, and tingles spread across her skin, but there was a noticeable lack of pain. Swallowing her unease and steeling her nerves, she scrunched her eyes tightly shut, pushing herself forward and into the portal before she could talk herself out of it.

Suddenly she was falling, then standing, then floating, then stumbling across a surface that wasn't there—empty space stretched around her in all directions, nothing solid anywhere in sight. Panic gripped her instantly...she had never seen anything quite like this before. It reminded her vaguely of the In-Between—a dimension of infinite white space between the waking world and the one beyond—but the In-Between wasn't full of swirling purple gasses, glittering stars, and waves of energy that twisted and twirled around each other in the endless void she'd somehow found herself inside.

Then she remembered Loric's hand—and suddenly, she could feel him again, pulling her away from the masses of magic. Her feet found an unseen surface, and she turned, her eyes meeting her mentor's. A few waves of maroon energy drifted around him, but he hardly seemed to care. The air around her, however, was noticeably barren.

"Loric...*where are we?*"

Loric only smiled, slowly taking a seat on the invisible platform and gazing out at the sky. Rei sat beside him, unsure of what else to do—although she had to admit, it was seriously unnerving trying to sit down on something you couldn't see.

"I'd like to welcome you to the Apeiron, Rei—the dimension of magic."

27

REI

As far as Rei could tell, the Apeiron simply did not have an end.

The dimension appeared vaguely how she imagined the night sky to be up close, intermingled with vibrant hues only seen during the most beautiful of sunsets or sunrises. Ethereal waves of purples, maroons, yellows, pale blues, and greens drifted across the expanse like massive rivers of magic that led to everywhere and nowhere at the same time. Occasionally, the bright colors would fade into a grayscale mass, emanating a powerful aura that overshadowed their polychromatic counterparts. The black and white rivers spanned between nine massive gatherings of swirling energy, connecting them together in an intricate web.

"This is—this is incredible." Rei's voice was nothing more than an awed breath, and she glanced around wildly, attempting to somehow take it all in. "I don't understand—has this been here, all this time?"

"The Apeiron is an infinite dimension that exists in an alternate reality beneath the nine worlds," Loric explained calmly, a slight sparkle in his eye at the raw amazement on Rei's face. "So yes, it has. This place is the source of all magic, a part of the universe that unites worlds that otherwise never would have met."

He pointed to the nine masses of energy, the only parts of the rift that weren't intermingled with bright and sometimes conflicting color tones. "Those are the realms, Rei—nine completely different universes, all connected by the dimension they share access to. The one we're from is called Akareldia." His finger moved towards the third mass in the row of energies, its form mostly consumed by white hues. "Each realm—just like every living being—possesses a particular alignment, or a side of the magical spectrum that their soul leans towards. That alignment, whether it's strong enough to be wielded or not, connects every living thing, linking them to—and through—the Apeiron."

Rei couldn't help but grin, glancing down at her palms. They seemed so ordinary—so insignificant, surrounded by an indefinite space of pure energy. "That means I have one? An alignment?"

He nodded. "Of course. You're around the age when people begin to figure out how powerful that alignment truly is."

She flexed her fingers a few times, imagining the swirling power that drifted around them bending to her will. "How will I know what mine is?"

"Trust me—it's not exactly easy to miss." A chuckle escaped his lips. "It can be a bit more dramatic depending on whether you're arcanic or glyphic, though. Glyphic triggers are generally much more intense, and arcana tends to reveal itself during times of perfect balance or tranquility. Those circumstances are not set in stone, however—I've heard of some rather outlandish awakenings."

"Huh. So it's gotta be...awakened...before I can use it?"

"It does." Loric leaned back on his hands, gazing up at the sky. "You seem a bit uncomfortable. Something wrong?"

"Just the platform, I guess. It's weird sitting on something I can't see—feels like it'll give out at any second."

Her mentor let out a laugh. "I suppose that would make sense. Here."

He flicked his wrist, a few waves of maroon energy passing over an invisible surface that seemed to stretch all the way around them. The energy formed into a cube, converging at the top before solidifying into a transparent yet visible material.

"Better?"

She rose to her feet, tentatively reaching out a hand and brushing her fingers across the "wall" in front of her. It was cool to her touch, leaving a faint tingling wherever her skin made contact. "Feels like glass."

"It's called a waypoint—a temporary magic 'cube' that forms within the open space of the Apeiron, making it so that we can actually stop within the dimension instead of passing through."

"Will it disappear?"

"When we leave."

"Oh."

He chuckled softly to himself. "Sometimes I forget how little you know of Iltara."

She looked away. "You'd think that after over a month of training with you, I'd at least be familiar with the basics." *Iltara*

—even the name of her own universe was unfamiliar to her. A hint of frustration worked its way into her stomach. "Do you think I'll ever be able to really belong here?"

Loric turned to look at her, intensity swirling in the depths of his dark eyes. "You *do* belong here, Rei. It's your home. Your knowledge of it is irrelevant."

*Home...*tears burned at her eyes, and she choked them back, refusing to allow herself to go down that path. *I left Akaidia behind. This is my world now.* "Do you think I'll ever be able to cross the mountains again? That when I said goodbye—it wasn't really for the last time, was it?" Even after nearly four weeks of training, she still couldn't quite get the thoughts of her previous life out of her mind. No matter what she tried, the memories refused to leave her be, resurfacing in her thoughts every chance they could find.

Loric gently placed his hand on her shoulder, the gesture comforting to her. "I told you, Rei, I'm not going to keep you from your home. Right now, it may be dangerous for you to return, but that won't always be true."

She nodded, forcing herself to believe his words. A soft exhale parted her lips as she let out a breath, her eyes tracing the picturesque sky once again. The Apeiron barely felt real—she wasn't sure it ever would. But...it *was* real. The world beyond her own, the one that she'd seen as nothing more than a fleeting dream—it was real.

And now, she was a part of it.

"Thank you."

Loric cocked his head at her slightly. "For what?"

"For everything. Saving my life, letting me stay with you, training me, bringing me here..." she trailed off, looking away as red blossomed on her face. "I realize that it's probably a bit late to be saying this, but I feel like I should."

He chuckled, rising to his feet slowly and offering her his hand. "It's been a difficult adjustment for you. You're a tough kid."

She cracked a smile, letting him pull her up. "So...you gonna explain what the alignments are, or what?"

Loric raised an eyebrow. "I suppose it's about time you knew. I could have sworn that I've told you already, though."

She shook her head. "Not that I remember."

He nodded slowly, thinking for a moment. "Alright. I will warn you—this is a bit of a complicated topic."

A grin spread across her face. "Tell me *everything*."

REI LAY IN HER BED, WATCHING STREAMS OF moonlight paint odd patterns on her ceiling. Her mind spun with new revelations, memories mingling with information she'd only just uncovered. *I can't believe that all these things really exist.*

The alignments were definitely her favorite topic of conversation, and she'd asked Loric question after question, barely giving him any time to speak before new ideas would pop into her head. Arcana, the force of creativity and order—and glyph, the force of strength and chaos. Perfect opposites that created a perfect balance, serving as the main power source for nine worlds and every single form of magic that had ever been discovered.

A frown crossed her features as the memory of a book she'd read slipped back into her thoughts, piquing her curiosity just enough to make her roll over and pick the volume up off her nightstand. It was the one Loric had given her, a collection of legends and myths from the ancient times. Thanks to its runic enchantment, the lantern at her bedside flicked on with only a slight press of the gemstone at its base, allowing her to see just well enough. She flipped through the pages, searching for the words that had made her do a double-take. Finally, she stumbled across the chapter, her eyes flying over the faded text.

While mere soldiers were forced to their knees by the great darkness, those with magic bound by blood stood tall, an impassable barrier against the all-consuming void. One of these bloodbound had the power to not only resist the darkness, but to combat it, united energy bending to his will and destroying that which existed out of balance.

Rei examined the words more closely, squinting at the parchment. *United energy bending to his will. Could he have controlled both alignments?* Loric had told her that a single person only had the ability to wield one of the aligned forces... never both. Was this story suggesting otherwise?

Her gaze found a section at the bottom of the page, where the legend ended. *The story keeps calling him the Grayblood. Each alignment has a pure form—white for arcana, black for glyph—and those colors together make gray.*

That can't be a coincidence, can it?

She shook her head, closing the book and shutting off her lantern. The flame flickered out, but her mind refused to let her rest, filling her head with thoughts of ancient tales and heroes that may or may not have ever existed. *It's just a story. I'll ask Loric about it tomorrow.*

Her eyes fluttered closed, the words on the page still lingering with her no matter how many times she tried to convince herself to let them go. She wasn't sure what it was about the story that made it stick with her so intensely—she'd always enjoyed tales of great heroes and impossible odds when she was younger, a trait that had never seemed to leave her entirely. A few stories always stayed with her better than the others, however, and this one seemed to have joined the collection.

All these legends—real or not, they represent a whole culture that no one in Akaidia ever even knew about.

What Loric had said to her earlier joined with her thoughts, his voice weaving in and out of her headspace.

This world—this strange, incredible world—do I really belong here?

28

REI

A pair of sea green eyes met Rei the moment she opened her own, the realization that she was dreaming yet again instantly hitting her.

The eyes belonged to a girl about her own age, set into a face framed by locks of ash brown hair as she stared off towards a darkening horizon. She sat outside on a rocky outcropping, her hands folded across her lap and her left foot bandaged in a splint. Rei motioned towards her, but she didn't flinch, her focus trained solely towards where the sun was gradually disappearing in the distance.

Unsure of what else to do, Rei approached hesitantly, the ghost of a word toying with her tongue as she paused at the girl's side. In that moment, a wave of familiarity washed over her, a feeling filling her—one she knew all too well.

I know this girl.

The second the thought surfaced in her mind, the image of the girl shifted, colors melding together into a jumble of recollection. Memories of other nightmares returned to Rei's thoughts, dreams that had felt far too real to be ignored—the very same sensation that haunted her now. And the girl...

I've seen her before. These dreams...she's been in nearly all of them since I found the Blade.

There was no telling exactly why Rei could recognize this person when all her prior nighttime visions had been nothing more than a jumble of feeling and color—but for some strange reason, she knew exactly whose eyes she'd been seeing through all that time.

She stepped in front of the girl, kneeling to her eye level. Rei's body didn't even cast a shadow on the ground, but still, she reached out her hand, watching as it passed right through the girl's shoulder harmlessly.

I'm not really here.

"Who are you?" she whispered, her voice filling the silence with a sound that the green-eyed girl couldn't hear.

There was, of course, no reaction...but the scene itself began to fade in and out of view, replaced by an image unfamiliar to Rei. Instantly, she realized it was a memory—except the memory wasn't her own.

The first few visions came slowly, allowing her ample time to examine them before they faded into a new scene.

Water sloshing against her skin, thoughts returning to her mind as she slowly became aware of her situation. Unseen wind tousling the underground lake's surface, leading her to believe that there might be a way out...but at the moment, any thoughts of escape seemed to be eluding her.

Blinding light illuminating a forest clearing, the scene

completed by a backdrop of stars. The light was hers—refracted from her skin, sourced from her body—and while she was more than grateful for the ability's existence, something deep inside her whispered that it didn't belong.

Her eyes tracing a star-filled sky, her mind fumbling to understand the gravity of where she'd found herself. She was trapped—hopelessly, utterly trapped—fighting for a life that she wasn't entirely sure she'd ever lived.

The images began moving faster now, flickering through Rei's headspace at an ever-increasing pace.

The feeling of her knife bearing down on another's throat, blood painting her skin.

A breeze tickling her face as she extended her hand, brushing the light with her fingertips and allowing its rays to penetrate her skin.

Fear grabbing hold of every bone in her body as she dangled over a seemingly endless abyss, chased by a creature she could no longer see.

Then, with a jolt, the memories dissolved altogether, leaving Rei drifting along in a space of infinite blackness. Shadows pressed in on her, covering her with an invisible veil. A shiver rippled down her spine as she felt herself pass through something of a blanket, emerging into a blurry scene.

Undersaturated colors and bright lighting made it difficult for Rei to understand the details of the images, but the feelings stuck with her all the same, a tingling sensation traveling across her skin as a girl turned to face her.

"Why are you here?"

The voice wasn't the girl's, but it came from the lips of

another very much like her, one so similar that Rei could have sworn that they were one and the same. It took her a moment to realize that this girl wasn't speaking to her—the other partaker of the conversation remained unseen.

The scene began to blur as the girl's lips parted again, her dark green eyes finding a position that made them eerily close to locking on Rei's.

"War comes with a cost." Her gaze steeled. *"The question is, are you willing to pay it?"*

A STRANGLED GRUNT ESCAPED REI'S LIPS AS SHE SAT up quickly, sweat streaming down her face. She reached up, rubbing her temples violently as heaving breaths rocked her chest. That dream had been the worst she'd had so far...not because it was the most violent, or the most terrifying, but because it was the most *real*. For a moment, it had felt like Rei had actually been standing there, right beside the girl—sharing her memories, watching her life.

This feels wrong.

Everything about this feels wrong.

That girl can't be real...she's just a figment of my imagination.

Isn't she?

If that green-eyed girl was real...Rei swallowed hard, forcing herself to play out the idea as a genuine possibility. *There's a lot I don't know about this world. Maybe getting connected to a complete stranger's inner consciousness via dreams is normal here.* She winced the moment the thought entered her mind. *Something tells me that Loric probably would have mentioned something if that were true.*

But what if Loric doesn't know?

What if this is something new?

Something different?

Dangerous?

Rei shook her head vigorously, trying in vain to dislodge the thoughts. *Why can't I just have a normal night's sleep for once?* With a sigh, she swung her legs over the side of the bed. *Fresh air will clear my head.* Her fingers found the Blade, which had been propped against the side of her bed, and she strapped it on over her clothes, not bothering to change into anything more combat-appropriate.

I'm not sure why I'm even bringing this...but it feels like I should.

It wasn't too difficult for her to slip out the back door, stepping into the slightly damp grass. A quick glance overhead told her that she had at least three or four hours until sunrise, giving her plenty of time to amble about and think.

She followed the gravel trail into the forest behind Loric's house, her gaze tracing the trees. The forest had been one of the most comforting places to her throughout her time in Iltara, as it was the closest environment to the heavily wooded surroundings she grew up in. Familiar sounds found her ears, easing a bit of the tension in her headspace and allowing her to finally relax for the first time since waking up.

Moonlight filtered through gaps in the leafy canopy overhead, and she paused, inhaling the earthy scents the wind brought her way. Constellations littered the indigo sky, making for a breathtaking backdrop beyond the towering pines. Moss crawled up nearby trunks, a natural blanket for the rough, flaky surfaces.

Suddenly, a twig snapped nearby, putting Rei instantly on edge. In barely a moment, her sword was in her hand, energy brewing beneath her fingertips. *Relax. It's probably just an animal.*

But...what if it wasn't?

She held her breath, crouching down in an attempt to conceal herself amidst a mess of low-hanging branches. Her heartbeat pounded in her ears, any sense of tranquility she'd somehow managed to grasp vanishing in an instant.

You're being ridiculous, Rei.

That was when the man appeared out of nowhere, tackling her and bringing her to the ground.

Rei screamed—a howl filled with fury and fear—and she struggled against him, kicking out and scratching at his arms like a feral animal. Her senses heightened, and energy surged through her veins, empowering her enough to fling him off and send him flying into a nearby tree.

She whirled around, gripping the sword tightly and calling to the power. The attacker gave her no time to reset, however, regaining his balance quicker than she'd anticipated and lunging for her yet again with a surprising burst of speed. Starbursts of pain rocked her body as she was slammed against a tree trunk, shards of wood digging into her back and forcing a guttural cry from her lips.

In a brief moment, time seemed to slow, and Rei noticed a

hazy aura of maroon surrounding the man's hand. *Magic. He's using magic against me.* She grunted as he swung the butt of his dagger at her neck, aiming for a knockout. Her shoulder throbbed as she twisted her body to block the blow, her mind tracking his movements instinctively.

He's not trying to kill me. He's trying to neutralize me.

A new spike of fear ripped through her.

Trying to capture me.

Her heart rate doubled, and she funneled as much magical energy as she could muster into her legs, pushing the man off her and scrambling back to put distance between them. He let out a heavy breath as he staggered away, and she took the opportunity, frantically reaching out for the same hum that had been there when she'd first drawn the sword.

It responded...but it didn't feel the same.

Vaguely aware of her muscles beginning to fatigue, she decided to retreat, realizing that this man was a whole lot stronger—physically and magically—than she could handle by herself in the middle of the night.

A flat-out run seemed like the best option at the moment, but before she could so much as take a step, a wall of packed earth shot up from the ground in front of her, stopping her in her tracks. She whipped around as a new figure revealed herself, a massive boulder levitating over her short frame.

Great Akaidia—there's two.

In a panic, she backed away from the rock-moving woman as quickly as she possibly could, not realizing that it put her right in the path of the man she'd knocked down before. He was on her before she knew it, but this time, she was a bit more prepared, thoughts focused solely on the sword that had somehow managed to stay firmly clasped in her grip.

It was a struggle to defend against his attempts to knock her unconscious and concentrate enough to build her magic at the same time, but she kept going, the adrenaline that pumped through her granting much-needed resolve.

Not much longer...

His fingers found her throat, her vision blurring as he began to squeeze the consciousness from her body.

Please, not much longer...

A cry erupted from her lips, a last plea as she forced herself to hold on through the pain.

She screamed a single word—not the word that she would have expected to come to her mind in that situation, but it was the only one that felt right, her voice echoing through the trees at an almost impossible volume.

"LORIC!"

The word gave her strength, and she bucked under the man's weight, lessening the strain on her neck for a brief moment.

Just as Rei finally mustered enough power to break herself free, she felt something graze her arm—and all the energy was instantly sucked from her body. It was the kind of wound that she could normally pass off as nothing more than a scratch, but this time, that didn't seem to be an option. A bitter, iron taste welled up in her mouth as her body hit the ground, the metal pressing into her skin and sapping every ounce of magical strength she had left.

No. NO!

She was paralyzed—the magic stripped from her body,

leaving her empty and vulnerable. The sword was ripped from her grasp, and she wanted to fight back—to kick, to scream, to reclaim what was hers—but she couldn't move. Something slammed into her temple, and a blinding pain ripped through her skull, her vision instantly blurring.

The last thing she felt was the warm, sticky flow of her own blood across her skin as her consciousness was stolen away.

29
RUNE

Silence.

Everything was full of silence.

The writing darkness, the shadowed world stretched out beneath her feet—all of it.

It wasn't a soft, blissful silence, either—no, it was the kind that came before a storm, or like the moment before a hunter leapt upon its prey.

Some would delight in it.

Some would crumble within it.

But Rune—no, she stood tall in its face.

To her, the silence was a promise.

The promise of power.

Footsteps behind her shattered her train of thought, causing her to turn. Her eyes locked with a familiar pair, a gaze so like her own that to many, they were one.

If only those people knew the truth.

"You look like you're up to something." The other girl's

voice was calm, collected—but beneath it was an undertone of warning.

"Maybe I am." Rune glanced down at her hands, adapting a nonchalant stance as she examined her fingertips. "Why should it matter to you?"

The girl sighed. "Always the immature one."

Rune scowled, turning back to the view stretched out before her. She was standing on a balcony, hundreds of feet above the sprawling stone city below. The sky—like usual—was filled with dark, ominous clouds, blocking the moon and stars from view. The only light was the faint reflection of flickering torches illuminating the cobbled streets and a soft glow from the candle behind them.

The girl stepped up beside Rune, leaning forward onto the railing. Her ash brown hair was pulled back into a messy bun, unlike Rune's, which had been left down. "It really is beautiful, isn't it."

Rune nodded. "In its own kind of way."

The girl smiled, but it didn't quite reach her eyes. "I can't believe we live here now. In the nobility district. It's so—different. Some days, I find myself angry at its elegance, and how unfair it is that the commoners' lives are so much...I don't know, lesser."

Rune shrugged. "Beauty is in the eye of the beholder. I really didn't mind our life in the commons, you know. A lot less pressure there, for sure."

"You know they're only trying to make sure we're prepared."

Rune rested her chin on her hands. "I know. But it'd be great if Mom and Dad would stop breathing down our necks.

It's as if we'll get kicked out of here if we get so much as an 'average grade' on one of Elder Senen's weird tests."

For the first time, the girl laughed. "Truth. And they're so hard, too. I can't believe this is *normal* for some people. Mom and Dad keep acting like we've been here our whole lives, but it hasn't even been a year."

Rune snorted. "Right? Did you *see* them when the Spyren family came to visit us? Bowing and scraping and kissing up to everyone, especially the heir."

The girl leaned back, her eyes shifting to the sky. "She looked about our age, too. I can't imagine the weight that's been put on her shoulders."

Rune glanced over at her. "What do you think it'll be like, someday? No one's ever seen anything like us in the past. What if we're different from the others? What if we aren't what they expected us to be?"

"We *aren't* going to be like they expected," the girl replied, turning to meet Rune's gaze. "But that's what makes us so special. We're going to change the world, you and I. I can feel it."

The scene began to blur, fading in and out as the girl's words echoed into the still night air.

I can feel it.

Darkness swept over Rune's vision, shattering the memory. The silence suddenly grew thick, almost tangible, wrapping Rune in its deep, ominous arms.

We're not like they expected.

We'll change the world, you and I.

I can feel it.

The words resounded in Rune's mind, drifting around her,

mingling with the blanket of quiet. A few stray cracks of light broke through her vision, and a new image began to form in front of her.

This time, she was looking at herself, as if through a window—and in front of her was the girl from her prior memory.

Except this time, they weren't smiling.

This time, they weren't watching the city sleep, laughing about their day.

They were fighting.

Blood ran from deep injuries, their eyes filled with anger. Instead of weapons, their hands swirled with cold, relentless energy, darkness mingling with light to create gray hues.

It was the same people, possibly two years after the memory she had just relived.

But there was nothing about this scene that felt warmly familiar.

All there was was cold.

And, behind it all—a looming silence.

The girls lunged for each other, hands outstretched, energy swirling violently in a cyclone around them. The forces collided with an earthshaking rumble, encompassing the fighters completely as they warred against one another.

Then, only moments later, the world went black as Rune was flung forcefully out of the dream.

Cold beads of sweat ran down Rune's forehead as she sat up quickly, a gasp escaping her lips. The image of the battle was still etched into her brain, as if she were actively living it instead of simply watching from afar. It hung over her like a threat, forcing unwanted questions into her mind.

Rune closed her eyes for a moment, inhaling slowly and filling her lungs with the musty air of the cave. Streams of moonlight trickled in from the doorway, illuminating the sleeping faces of her companions.

Her eyes flickered to the two contraptions made of sturdy wood that leaned against the wall—a pair of makeshift crutches Ivory had designed the day before. He had also helped gather materials for the splint Azalea had later crafted, the very same one that now cradled Rune's injured ankle.

Fresh air should clear my head a bit.

Slowly, so she wouldn't agitate her ankle, Rune supported herself against the cave wall and struggled to her feet. The leg still throbbed horribly, but she'd gotten a bit more used to it, pushing the dull ache to the back of her mind and focusing on her movement. Careful not to wake anyone, she hobbled over to where her crutches rested, having to adjust her weight awkwardly a few times before finding the right position. With a last glance at the cave, she squeezed through the crack in the stone, slipping out into the cool, crisp air that awaited her outside.

Rune instantly felt her shoulders relax as the softness of the night enveloped her, wrapping around her like a blanket. She inhaled deeply, a gust of wind filling her lungs as she made her way a bit further out from the cave.

In the distance, a long, chilling howl shattered the gentle

silence, causing a shiver to ripple down Rune's spine. Night in the Blue Biome had a notably different feel from the nights she'd spent in Green—instead of wind toying with leaves overhead, there was a faint whistle as it swept through cracks in the stone, brushing across the desolate landscape. Aside from the distant cries of animals, the whispers of the breeze, and her soft, uneven footsteps, the evenings were filled with an eerie hush—a feeling that, come to think of it, was not so different from her dream.

Her gaze shifted upwards, finding a large, flat boulder that overlooked a vast plain of stone, her mind toying with possibilities. After a moment of hesitation, she began to make her way up to it, one careful step at a time. The gentle peace of a dark sky was comforting to her, the stars seeming to ease away a small fraction of the pain with each movement. Her thoughts fell into a rhythm, her footsteps staying in time with the nonexistent beat.

Step.
Reach.
Lean.
Step.

On and on, the cycle repeated, her body quickly getting the hang of the awkward motion. Eventually, she reached the top, shifting her weight around until she could sit comfortably on the stone slab. Wind toyed with her hair, brushing it loosely into her face as her eyes traced the dark horizon. The veil—the thick, shadowy blanket in the back of her mind that shrouded her memories from view—it began to loosen slightly, allowing fragmented feelings and even an occasional thought to slip through and reenter her consciousness.

She'd done this many times before.

Many times had she sat, alone, watching as the moon traveled across a starry sky.

Many times had the clouds been there, concealing the constellations from view, yet still she had watched, her eyes open but her mind lost somewhere deep within.

She couldn't recall why, or where, or even the name of the figure who she sometimes recalled being at her side while she would linger outdoors. The girl from her dream—it could be her, and the longer she thought about it, the more the idea made sense.

A friend, perhaps—or even a sibling—but still, the blurred features remained without a name in Rune's mind.

Darkness seeped into her thoughts, and she found herself returning to the brief moment she'd experienced right before the dream ended—the image of her and the girl, fighting one another with raw hatred gleaming in their eyes. Rune shivered, wrapping her arms around herself.

In that dream, I looked like a monster.

Is that what I am?

A monster?

Suddenly, there was a clatter nearby, and Rune's head shot up, her hand going to her dagger. Skin crawling, she slowly pivoted around, scanning the terrain for the source of the noise. Her voice caught in her throat as she fished for words, an inexplicable fear gripping her tightly.

Beside her, a shadow moved, and before she could react, strong arms had wrapped around her body. A meaty hand covered her mouth before she could scream, and the rough feeling of cloth against her lips indicated a gag. She tried to struggle, but whoever had grabbed her was holding on tight, his heavy breaths sounding in her ear as she strained against his grip.

"Thought you'd said she'd be easy, with her foot like that and all."

There's at least two. Two boys—definitely both older than me.

A third boy, slightly farther away, let out a sigh. "Alright, alright. I'll knock her out."

A jolt of panic sent shock waves down Rune's spine.

I can't let them take me. The others—I can't just disappear.

The boy holding her tightened his grip as her fighting intensified, and she bit her tongue, agony flaring up in her injured leg. "Why don't we just kill her? Not like she can get away."

"We want her to tell us where the other ones are, idiot. She's not traveling alone."

Rune froze suddenly, an idea slipping into her mind. It was desperate, but it might work.

Slowly, she began to pool her concentration towards her hand, smiling slightly against the rough cloth as a familiar tingling sensation passed across her skin.

Her captor cursed. "She's trying to use her element. Hurry it up, Jett."

Rune barely had time to react before there was a dull thud, a stabbing pain tearing through her skull moments later. The last of her resolve slipped away, her consciousness following with it.

30
RUNE

A throbbing pain in her skull greeted Rune before her eyes even fluttered open. Her head pounded, and the world seemed to spin, a horrible churning feeling in her stomach making her double over. It took her a long, horrible moment for the feeling to lessen just enough that she could think, chest heaving with heavy, shallow breaths.

Her wrists were bound with rough rope, and Rune bit back a whimper, the threads digging into her skin. Pain was everywhere—every bone, every muscle, every inch of her body—she was filled with it, so much so that she could hardly function enough to get her bearings.

She was in an enclosed cave, with hardly any light—feebly, she attempted to summon a glimmer of her own, but the energy refused to answer. A sense of sluggishness had overcome her limbs, limiting her movement and slurring her vision.

"Took you long enough. Almost got too bored and took you out while you were sleeping—but that wouldn't have been nearly as fun."

The sickeningly familiar voice cut into Rune's mind, tugging at a recent memory yet failing to drag it to the surface. She squinted into the darkness, heart racing as a callused hand gripped her arm tightly. Mentally, she kicked herself for being so foolish—the unnerving nature of her dream had completely blinded her to the danger of being alone outside, especially in an injured state.

No matter what happens—this was my fault. I brought this on myself.

She hated the sinking feeling that the words created.

Suddenly, a light flooded the room, its source a tongue of fire in the palm of a tall, dark-eyed boy. Rune fought the urge to wince, her eyes flitting across the faces of her kidnappers. Her heart skipped a beat when she realized that she recognized the people who had so roughly apprehended her.

"You—I know you." Her voice was raw, but thankfully, it didn't tremble.

A girl leaned closer, auburn hair slipping into her face. "I certainly hope you do."

One of the boys gripped her shoulder, dragging her backward. "Easy Amre. She won't last long."

Amre pouted, spitting into the corner of the cave. A crawling sensation worked its way down Rune's spine, horrible thoughts flooding into her mind. *This same team has attacked us before—not once, but twice. They want us out of their way.* She swallowed hard. *And I've just handed them a victory on a silver platter.*

The boy holding the fire took a step forward, his dark, beady eyes tracing Rune's injuries with a sickening satisfaction gleaming in their depths. "Wish we had the blonde girl here. The little one with an attitude who killed Amre."

Luna. Anger boiled up inside her gut, but she bit her tongue, knowing that silence was likely the smartest course of action.

"We'll take what we can get. 'Sides, this one looks easier to crack."

"*And* she killed Rex." Amre shot a glance over her shoulder, and to Rune's horror, the green eyed boy stepped out of the shadows. The blood drained from her face as their gazes locked, a confused horror lingering in his expression.

He really doesn't know me...but he does know what I did to him. Her stomach churned, an innate feeling of wrongness sinking into her gut. *This arena...it makes us do horrible things. I did horrible things.* Even so, a tiny voice in the back of her mind continued to whisper, murmuring truths that somehow managed to console and agitate her at the same time.

He would have done the same to you.

The fire boy's eyes narrowed, and he approached Rune slowly, kneeling in front of her and holding the flame uncomfortably close to her face. "That's right...she did, didn't she. Do you realize how long it took to get Rex back? He was one of our best, and you *ruined* him. Stripped him of his memories yet again, sent him back to square one—alone, afraid, and clueless."

"Rex and I had to crawl our way back from the very beginning," Amre snarled. "Do you know what that's like? Because you're going to find out."

Rune scrambled around in her brain for something, anything to say—but her tongue remained numb and motionless in her mouth. All logic fled from her, and a new sense of panic sparked in her mind. *Stripped him of his memories. I do remember what that's like. Is that what I did?* Her heart sank. *Trying to protect myself—trying to survive—wasn't thinking— didn't think—*

She swallowed the thoughts, turmoil building up inside her. She was spiraling—fast—and she groped around for some hold on reality, anything that might be able to take her away from the voices that seemed determined to drag her down with them.

They're getting in my head.

Finally, the boy who'd first greeted her when she'd awoken stepped forward, pushing the fire boy out of the way. "Back up, Endis. I want to ask some questions."

Endis snorted. "Who died and made *you* leader, Jett?"

Jett scowled. "I don't see you volunteering. Besides, *I'm* the one who captured her."

I can't believe I let them take me.

"Oh, quit your arguing." A tall girl stepped up, roughly shoving both boys out of the way. She crouched in front of Rune and abruptly opened her fist, causing sparks of electricity to crackle across her fingertips. "Listen, kid. Here's how this is going to work. I am going to ask you a few questions, and you are going to answer as honestly and as *detailed* as I tell you to. Understood?"

Rune nodded slowly, searching for a way to buy herself time.

A cold, emotionless smile spread across the girl's lips. "Wonderful." She pressed one hand to Rune's neck, causing tiny sparks of pain to flicker across her skin. "I see the rebellion in you. Whatever you're thinking—" she gripped Rune's chin, forcing them to lock eyes— "I hope for your sake that it stays inside that brain of yours."

Rune gritted her teeth, allowing a small spark of indignation to slip into her expression. The act felt good, even if it wouldn't accomplish much. "I'm no fool."

Amusement flickered across the girl's features. "Maybe not. Tell me—where are all your *friends*? *Specifically*, the blonde girl with the fire abilities?"

Rune frowned. "You want Luna? Why?"

The girl snarled, and Rune bit back a whimper as the pain intensified. "She took something from us. Though—you might know something about that, wouldn't you?"

Instantly, the pieces set into place in Rune's mind. *The leystone. Luna stole it.* Her frown deepened. *But—they made it to Blue. That means that they had more than one.*

"Answer me!"

Rune flinched at the girl's tone, swallowing a lump in her throat and fighting to suppress the cries of agony that built up inside her chest. The pain grew worse with each passing second, and the girl seemed to be scanning Rune's face, watching for the reaction that she was determined not to give.

"You seem to be forgetting which of us is the captive in this situation." Threads of malice were laced into her voice.

"For a bunch of prisoners yourselves, you seem more concerned with putting yourselves in artificial positions of power than escaping a cell you don't want to admit you can't get out of."

The girl's reaction was instantaneous, digging her fingers into Rune's throat and shoving her roughly against the wall. Rune scrunched her eyes shut, wishing she could block out the agonizing pain that tore through her body. "Looks like you've been spending a bit too much time around *Luna*. Kid has a pretty smart mouth, doesn't she?"

"You say that like it's a bad thing."

All heads snapped towards the new voice, shock and relief warring in Rune's heart when she recognized the figure standing airily at the far side of the cave.

The girl who'd pinned Rune recoiled sharply, causing her to collapse to the ground with a groan. "*You*!"

Endis snarled, baring his fire. "Finally. Qwin's had *plenty* to say about your elemental ability—so let's see what you've got."

Luna smirked. "Bold move, hothead. But I'm afraid I brought backup."

Through the haze of agony, Rune managed to lift her head, her eyes finding five figures standing behind Luna. Her mind groped for some form of tangibility, but the adrenaline rush from the girl's torment had suddenly subsided, leaving her empty.

Jett stood, the ground rumbling as he lifted his hand slowly. "They've got an earth elemental. Wouldn't have been able to get in here if they didn't."

Ryder stepped forward, causally raising a chunk of the floor to his outstretched palm. "I have to admit, your cloaking strategy wasn't too bad." He glanced over at the tall, platinum blonde haired boy beside him, the figures hazy to Rune's muddled mind. "But Ivory can track anything."

Luna kept her gaze even, glancing around at the six hostile teens they faced. "Lucky for you, we aren't here for a fight. Let Rune go, and you live."

Jett snorted. "Bold words from the talking fireball. 'Fraid this ain't a fight you can win, though."

Rune's gaze fluttered upward, locking with the tall girl's. She looked Rune up and down for a brief moment, a smile toying with her features. "Besides, you just came to rescue her—all of you." Her smile widened. "That means she's no longer needed."

The moment the words met Rune's ears, the girl sprang forward, dragging Rune roughly to her feet and digging her fingernails into her neck. Electricity crackled across Rune's skin, stinging like a million tiny needles pressing into her all at once.

Rune cried out in pain and shock, straining against the rope that still bound her hands. A chorus of surprise, followed by rage, broke loose from Rune's friends, all of them instantly scattering to attack her captors. Electricity split the air as a bolt of lightning soared across the room, planting itself into the tall girl's chest and loosening her grip on Rune's throat. Rune let out a strangled gasp as she stumbled, shouts and muffled cries filling the air while her friends fought to get to her.

She braced herself for impact against the stone ground, but the moment never came—a hand had grabbed the back of her shirt, yanking her upright and holding her firmly. She tried to see who it was, but her head wouldn't turn, a haze of pain encompassing her completely. She wanted it—needed it—to be over, to be free of the agony—no matter what it took. Shouts reached her ears, but she didn't understand a word, flashes of light and oddly moving shadows converging on her as she wrestled herself free.

The ground rushed towards her, and she watched as another of Kaleo's lightning bolts ripped through the air, its target a short, brawny boy with a throwing knife clenched firmly in his hand. His arm was pulled back, aiming the weapon at Rune's limp form.

Panic rushed through her, and time seemed to slow, her surroundings blurring as her sight focused solely on that boy. *I can't dodge this. I can't.*

The lightning hit its mark, but it was a second too late, the knife free of the boy's fingers. With a low, horrible whistle, it streaked across the cave, embedding itself deep into her side.

A scream split the air—her scream—pain ricocheting through every bone in her body. Voices called her name, but all she saw was a distant red glow, the world blurring around her. This was nothing like being knocked out, like feeling her consciousness retreating into her mind as her body went to sleep. Nothing like it.

This time, her consciousness wasn't retreating—it was leaving. Slipping through her grasp, falling away so quickly that she couldn't have grabbed hold of it if she'd wanted to. The red glow consumed her vision, her chest falling still as thick, suffocating blackness overcame her.

Then, she died.

31
REI

When Rei tried to open her eyes, all she saw was darkness.

Her hands were bound, tied uncomfortably tight behind her back. A rough cloth was wedged between her lips, preventing her from making any sort of sound, and a similar fabric was lashed around her head, covering her face almost entirely to restrict her vision.

I'm tied to something.

A chair, maybe?

A grunt of frustration bubbled up in her throat as she tugged against her bonds, testing out the knot. Unfortunately, whoever had tied her up had known what they were doing, and the rope hardly budged.

Well—this is far from ideal.

She wasn't naive enough to believe that there would be any kind of weapon within reach, and even if there were, it wasn't like she had any way of locating it. Whoever had captured her was good—too good. Annoyingly good, in fact. Being kidnapped was no fun if your kidnappers actually had their head screwed on straight.

There you go, Rei. Keep joking. Her stomach twisted. *It's better than thinking about what a terrible situation you've once again found yourself in.*

She was saved from following that train of thought by a rough hand gripping her shoulder, squeezing just tightly enough to make her wince. After a few moments, she gave up on keeping her face stony—most of her features were covered, anyway.

I wonder if Loric's woken up yet. Her heart sank. *I hope he's safe.*

"*This* is the pipsqueak who not only managed to best Evander's *entire* party, but also get away *with the sword*?"

The obnoxious know-it-all voice came from somewhere to Rei's left, the indignation that flared up within her instantly quenching the faint flickers of pain that still lingered in the back of her skull. *Not the time for a migraine.*

The hand gripping her shoulder tightened. "Apparently. Kid put up a decent fight, I suppose. Well trained, ample combat experience. Didn't seem to know what to do against our magic, though."

Know-it-all grunted, a shuffling noise indicating movement. "She's an interesting one, that's for sure. You have any idea why the Master didn't want her dead?"

He...what?

"No. Master's got his ways of doing things—probably best that we don't question them."

"What do we do with her, then?" The know-it-all guy had come closer, practically breathing down Rei's neck. "Poor kid—bet she's scared." Not an ounce of sympathy slipped into his tone.

You wish.

The other man—the one with his hand practically drawing blood from Rei's shoulder—let out a low chuckle. "She can hear you, you know."

Unfortunately.

"Take off the blindfold and gag, Tef. I'd like to have a word with her."

The man let out a disproving snort, but obliged, and Rei felt her stomach twist in disgust as his grimy hands tore the cloth away from her skin. It only took a single inhale of the thick, musty air to cause Rei to double over coughing, her stomach heaving in protest. A dull headache spread across her temples, but she fought it off, fighting to keep herself focused.

Come on, Rei—they're practically asking to be insulted. You wouldn't deny your kidnappers of their privilege, would you?

The sheer amount of malicious snark in the thought seemed to snap her back to reality, quenching the churning inside her stomach for a brief moment. A fleeting sense of control flickered back into her mind with the words, fueling her resolve.

I may be the captive here—but there are some things that only I am in charge of. Things they can't take from me.

The source of the know-it-all voice leaned down, his deep blue eyes level with hers. "*Cas-shom,* girly."

It took Rei's muddled mind a moment to decipher the words—especially with the man's thick accent—but just like when she and Loric had spoken, the language seemed embedded into her very being.

Hello.

Still, she pretended to be confused, which only made the man's sickening smile widen. "It means hello."

"Idiot. She wields the Blade. She *knows* Jurorish." The other man—Tef—sounded particularly exasperated with his partner, a feeling Rei could relate to.

Know-it-all raised an eyebrow. "Does she? She looks a bit *confused*." Rei glared at him, wishing she could dig the sound of his oily, accented voice out of her ears.

Tef rolled his eyes, circling around and crouching in front of Rei. "Can't blame her. Probably has no idea what's going on." He stood, walking away a few paces before pausing and casting one last glance over his shoulder at Rei. "Or maybe she does. Do what you must, Sevel. Something tells me that this one doesn't crack easily."

Rei's stomach twisted, but she somehow managed to keep her face emotionless, struggling against the horror show that had decided it needed a place in her thoughts.

Tef pressed his hand to a rectangular panel in the wall, muttering something under his breath. *A runic charm.* The panel blinked blue for a moment, and there was a low rumble as a door-sized portion of the wall split in two, each half sliding apart to reveal a poorly-lit passage beyond. Rei's eyes trailed him as he exited, leaving her alone with know-it-all—or Sevel, she supposed.

Sevel turned to her, his lips twisting into an obnoxiously charismatic grin. *What a psychopath.* "Alright, kiddo. Let's make this nice and easy."

Rei made a face. "I'm going to assume that your idea of easy and mine are a bit different in this particular situation."

Somehow, his smile managed to widen, giving Rei the impression that if he smiled any more, his mouth might begin to run out of room on his annoyingly perfect face. "Such a large attitude in such a small package. How amusing."

Rei gritted her teeth. "I'm not five, you know. But you seem to be." *No sense in holding my tongue. I can't let him take that from me.*

Sevel's grin faltered slightly. "Your parents apparently didn't teach you any manners."

"Neither did yours."

The moment the words left her lips, Sevel jammed his fist into her stomach, causing her to double over coughing. Anger flooded through her, followed by waves of agony as he raised his arm once more, slower this time. *He knows I can't go anywhere.* The strike hit straight across her face, snapping her head back into the chair. A strangled grunt escaped her lips, but she bit down hard on her tongue before she could cry out, refusing to give him the satisfaction.

"No need to play tough. It'll hurt less if you drop the act."

He raised his hand, clenching his fist for a moment before opening it again. Rei hardly stifled a gasp of horror as a red glow encompassed his palm, the energy solidifying against his skin. He smiled broadly, molding it into a wicked-looking dagger.

"Now *that* is more like it."

Rei wasn't sure whether to think about the fact that he had just materialized a glowing energy knife out of thin air or that he was about to stab her with it.

He decided for her.

In a swift motion, he flicked his wrist, swiping the dagger across Rei's cheek. A sting of pain traveled in its wake, streams of warm blood trailing down her skin like crimson tears. She closed her eyes, a faint whimper slipping from between closed lips. *You've had worse, Rei. Hold on. You have to hold on.*

"Ah, the silent treatment. Many have tried it. They all cracked in the end." He leaned closer, so close that she could faintly smell an odor like rotten mint from his breath. "There is a group of individuals that have been causing us trouble for quite some time. I wonder if you've heard of them." The blade moved to her neck, pressing into her skin.

Panic surged up within her. *I thought he wasn't supposed to kill me.*

"What do you know of the Onyx, girl?"

Rei gritted her teeth. "Nothing. Never heard of them."

He lashed out once again with his dagger, dragging it across her shoulder and leaving a pain like a million needles everywhere the scarlet surface touched. She closed her eyes against his strikes, trying to shut out the reminder that this was not even close to the farthest he could go.

She'd experienced pain before, certainly...it was far from a new experience for her. But being tied to a chair, rendered helpless while an enemy slowly traced his weapon across her skin, piercing her, tearing her apart strike by strike—it was a whole new form of torture.

"I'll ask again. *What* do you *know* of the *Onyx*?"

NOTHING! Her mind screamed, but her voice refused to comply, and she found herself unable to do much besides brace herself for the blows that would certainly follow her silence. As his fist pounded bruises into her body, she noticed a strange, dull pulsing in the back of her mind, the hum filling her with a distant sense of power.

Curious, she pressed deeper into the depths of her consciousness, trying to dig up the source of the odd sensation. It eluded her, however, staying just barely out of her reach. Despite the waves of agony being hammered into her body, she was not deterred from her chase, every passing second only increasing her desire to find the source of the hum. *I'm insane. I've gone insane.*

Right now—insanity was so much better than reality.

After a long time—minutes, hours, Rei didn't know—the blows finally began to slow. She'd endured question after question, choking out the answers that her tormentor didn't want to hear. She'd been faced with names, places, phrases that she'd never heard of, things she would probably never see —things that he seemed convinced that she was involved with, no matter how many times she insisted that she knew nothing.

Sevel stepped away from her battered body, not even attempting to hide the contempt in his expression. He closed his fist abruptly around the dagger, shattering it into tiny particles of red dust. Rei watched in silence, streaks of fresh, dark blood staining her skin. Bruises covered every inch of her, and pain had slurred her headspace so much that she could hardly form a thought, her vision fading in and out.

"It would bring me no greater joy than to kill you right now," Sevel began, gripping her chin firmly and wrenching her head upward to lock her eyes with his. "But unfortunately, the

Master wishes for you to be kept alive, at least until he arrives to collect the Blade."

Rei clenched her fists. It felt good to be able to move, even if that movement was only a small gesture.

Sevel's grip tightened, causing her to wince. "I can still see the fight in your eyes. You've got grit, I suppose—but I advise you to let go of that hope. It will be torn from you soon enough."

After a few seconds of silence, he released Rei roughly, and she collapsed backwards into the chair. He stalked towards the door, opening it and sticking his head out into the hallway to shout something in an unfamiliar language. Two cloaked guards marched in, swords forged of an unfamiliar dark metal strapped to their waists.

"Take her to a holding cell," Sevel snapped. "The Master arrives tomorrow evening, so I'll have a little *chat* with her in the morning."

Rei had no time to think before the nearest soldier grabbed her wrists, the other drawing his blade and slicing cleanly through the ropes that bound her to the chair. She was dragged roughly to her feet, and it was all she could do not to cry out as her wounds resisted the motion. A vague sense of awareness informed her of the blindfold and gag being refastened around her head, and despite the instinct that told her to struggle, her muscles refused to respond.

They led her out into a hallway, and with each turn they took, the situation began to look more and more dire. She didn't need to see to know that the endless, winding hallways were practically impossible to navigate if you weren't trained—a very similar security measure to the one in the stronghold.

Things might have worked out for her there…but she knew better than to believe it would happen twice.

There really is no escape…

Her heart plummeted. *Come on, Rei. You can figure this out. You have to.*

If you don't…

She shut down the thought, refusing to let it finish.

Finally, the guards' pace slowed, and Rei felt the blindfold being lifted from her head as she was led into a room. They also removed the gag, and Rei found herself gasping for air, hating the musty stench of the room but grateful for the lack of rough cloth between her lips.

Even with her new "freedom" from her bindings, the inevitable feeling of being a captive was like ice water over her mind, the realization finally sinking in when the guards began moving towards the door. For a brief moment, her vision sharpened, adrenaline giving her a new clarity.

Her eyes found an oddly familiar charm on the belt of one of her escorting guards as he turned to leave—a small metal rectangle, no larger than her finger. The metal had runes engraved on it, and even though Rei couldn't read them, she knew exactly what they said.

The sliver was a tiny, enchanted device called a locator. When activated, it can broadcast the user's location to a person of the user's choosing—and from what Rei had read about it in one of Loric's many books, it wasn't too difficult to use.

Loric. I could contact Loric.

Before the guards could close the door, she sprang into action, lunging for the guard with the locator in a mock attack. The guard, of course, overpowered her instantly, delivering a rather harsh kick to her ribs that sent her sprawling across the stone. She inhaled quick, ragged breaths, the tiny object she now clasped in her palm providing the only consolation from the new torment that rocked her.

The last rational thought that registered in her mind was watching as the soldiers chuckled to one another, then hearing the horrible slam of metal-on-metal when they shut the door.

32

REI

Rei awoke to a migraine pounding through her skull, joining with the discordant melody of pain created by the wounds that peppered her body.

With a sigh, she forced herself to sit up, blinking a few times and taking deep breaths in an attempt to clear her blurred vision. A single thought slipped through the muddled sludge her mind had become—an instinct, something ingrained into her—and she lifted her right hand, pinching gently on the tender skin between her thumb and her forefinger. It took a long, agonizing moment, but the throbbing in her skull began to lessen, providing her with ample clarity to make sense of her situation.

I am trapped.

I was tortured.

They're going to come back for me tomorrow.

Then the Eidolon will arrive.

With each thought, a bit more of the painful haze seemed to clear, and she slowly lifted her gaze, scanning the room.

It certainly wasn't big—possibly six or seven feet across, with a similar dimension in height. The door she'd arrived through took up about half of one of the walls, and apart from a cot in the corner and a lantern made of an unfamiliar glowing metal, the cell was bare.

Her gaze traveled to the cot, and after a moment, she managed to crawl over to it, heaving herself atop it with much resistance from her weary body. It was far from the softest place she'd ever slept, but compared to the state of her existence at the moment, it felt like bliss.

She allowed her eyes to fall closed, leaning back against the wall and deciding to analyze everything in her mind. Her body was weak, but her mental strength began to return, allowing fragments of plans and unanswered questions to begin swarming around inside her head. A thin metal rectangle pressed into her palm, reminding her that not all of the torment she'd suffered was in vain.

Please let this work.

Holding it up with a shaky hand, she traced the runes, murmuring the instructions she'd memorized from the page in Loric's books. *I have to power the runes up, then—I guess I'll figure it out from there. It's just a magic device that you've never seen before in your life. Can't be too difficult.*

Pressing her thumb against the runes, she reached into her core like she'd been taught, funneling whatever tiny sparks of energy she could find there out of her finger and into the metal. The runes began to glow with a faint gold aura, the rectangle heating up against her skin to the point where she nearly recoiled in pain. She had no idea what to do, but somehow, the magic did, emitting a dull humming noise as thousands of thoughts—none of them her own—pummeled into her all at once. A tingling sensation like a million bolts of lightning spread across her, but it didn't hurt, leaving behind a trail of phantom touches that had never existed in the first place. The air thickened, and her body went rigid, vision fading in and out while her ears rang.

Then, suddenly—everything was still.

With a groan, she barely managed to stop herself from casting the metal aside, instead opting to wedge the rectangle into a gap in the cot's cracked surface. Hopefully, the guards wouldn't discover the device until her plan had worked. *Did it work? For all I know, that signal could have gone to the Eidolon himself.* She sighed, her gaze flickering to the wall by the door, where she first noticed a small niche that housed what looked to be a flask of water.

Well—I guess this situation couldn't get too much worse, anyway.

Shoving all thoughts of escape plans and whatever Sevel was planning away, she hobbled over to the nook, gripping the flask and settling back down on the cot. After examining its contents and deciding that it was, in fact, *regular* water, she lifted the rim to her lips, careful not to guzzle too much. Her parched throat cried out as she drank, even the dusty, lukewarm liquid feeling good to her dry tongue. An idea slipped into her mind once she'd finished, and she reached down, tearing a strip of somewhat clean cloth off her bloodstained tunic and dampening it with a few drops from the container.

Gingerly, she began to wipe down her body, scraping away the dirt and crusted blood that decorated her wounds. Dull, throbbing pains coursed through her, but she was used to them now, ignoring the occasional stings as she uncovered yet another cut that she didn't realize she'd gotten.

Having done what she could with the cloth, she set it at the foot of her bed, scanning her injuries and subconsciously categorizing them as she'd been trained to do years ago. Back in her home beyond the mountains, she'd been trained as a healer, serving a group of teenage exiles for a long time before they eventually became the nation's fifth clan. Those long-embedded instincts returned to her now, providing her with a list of basic treatments that would all but heal the marks.

Of course, she didn't have any of the supplies necessary for so much as a basic painkiller, but she *could* clean and dress the wounds—at least, to an extent. She reached for the thin, tattered cloth that covered the cot—not much of a blanket, but a few layers of it would serve as a decent bandage.

Rei set to work, making sure to ration the amount of water she used to lightly wet the strips of cloth before wrapping them around the deepest wounds she could see. The raw, persistent pain still gnawed at her, but a bit of the tension in her mind eased with the familiar motions, and by the time she was finished, clarity had returned to her senses.

An odd feeling washed over her suddenly, a hum surfacing in the back of her mind and weaving through her thoughts as though it were taunting her. She called to it with all the strength she could muster, and it began to draw nearer, a tingle washing through her fingertips as she felt the power grow within her stomach. It was like the spells she'd practiced with Loric, except this wasn't sourced from or channeled towards a certain object —it was its own force, a force that dwelled somewhere inside her.

"What are you?" she whispered, flexing her fingers slowly. The energy felt alive, like a creature at play, dancing around in her headspace as she lunged clumsily to capture it.

Of course, it didn't respond, but it did seem to slow a bit, allowing her to catch up. A surge of emotion flooded through her as she reached out with her mind, filling her consciousness with the dark mass that seemed to be the source of the hum.

Deja vu tugged at her senses, and a memory surfaced in her mind—her and Loric, staring off into the massive depths of the Apeiron. This energy—it had been there, too, mingling with the rivers of light and seeming to race through the infinite void.

An alignment. The word was odd to think, and even odder were the names that came with it, Loric's voice echoing in her head.

Arcana, the force of creativity and order.

And glyph...

Even as the word slipped into her thoughts, the energy inside her stirred, pulsing through her veins. A smile crept across her lips, and she lifted her hand, watching as an aura of deep maroon began to emanate faintly from her skin. *The force of chaos and strength.*

So that's what you are.

Glyph.

The glyph responded with another weak surge of energy, strengthening the glow that illuminated her outstretched palm. Tentatively, she tried pooling the energy into a single spot, causing the glow to fade as tendrils of maroon materialized faintly and curled inward towards the center of her palm. She tried calling to it, but it resisted her at first, and she was only able to manage a small wisp of the power.

Loric said that glyph was based on raw strength—which means that attempting to control it probably isn't the best approach.

As unnatural as it felt for her to simply abdicate control, she tentatively allowed herself to let go, ignoring the distant hitch of breath she got when the energy began to move outside of her commands. Slowly, but surely, she gave it more and more freedom, keeping herself focused on the cocky, indifferent attitude she preferred to don around an enemy. Memories trailed along behind the emotions, sparking threads of renewed anger and disgust towards the confinement she was in. Almost immediately, the glyph responded, ravenously consuming the feelings. She was barely able to stop the energy from exploding outwards as it quadrupled in force, a grin spreading across her features while she reined it back in.

The glyph despised being told what to do, but she continued to feed it with the chaotic memories, the power leaping eagerly on every chance it got to disorganize her mind. It wasn't being malicious—she could feel something deep within her core, an innate desire to empower everything it touched. The only power it knew was chaos.

The discordance, the unpredictability, the raw, unchecked *strength*—the longer she allowed it to linger, the more she was set free from the anxieties of her mind, her body straightening as energy rushed through it. The pain ebbed as a few scratches disappeared from the surface of her skin entirely, boosting her in a way that she'd never experienced before.

She was still hurt—still in danger, still in pain—but those feelings didn't matter nearly as much anymore, having been completely ripped from her mind. Her head was spinning, the ability to form a coherent thought leaving her, yet she functioned just fine, her instincts knowing exactly what to do.

This is what glyph does.

With each passing second, Rei's confidence grew, and she held out her hands, calling the energy to her fingertips. It responded surprisingly quickly, and she allowed it to seep out from her skin, filling the air with a faint hum. Slowly, she began to rotate her palms, and the threads of maroon energy followed along. She lightly mimicked a few of the motions she remembered Loric doing with his alignment, molding the energy into a single line.

Curious, she turned, bringing the concentrated line of energy with her. Carefully, she released her hold on the glyph, catching it with her other hand to leave her left one free. She reached out with her unoccupied arm, grabbing ahold of what was left of her blanket and holding it up in front of the glyph. Easing it forward, she flicked her right wrist lightly, directing the energy towards the cloth.

It shot forward with startling speed, shredding the fabric as it passed through and looping back to her waiting hand. An excited breath escaped her lips, and she turned, flicking the energy at the wall this time. It didn't penetrate the stone, but it did slice a long gash into the bricks, whipping back around like a boomerang.

What were you saying about no escape, Sevel?

Grinning broadly, she set to practicing, the pain from her wounds almost entirely forgotten. Hours went by, but she didn't stop, each passing moment providing yet another spark to fuel the blaze of resolve that the glyph had re-fired in Rei's heart.

Suddenly, the dull thud of footsteps reached Rei's ears. She panicked, hurriedly dissolving the arrows of energy she'd formed and tightly winding the glyph into a mental ball, shoving it down and containing it as deep within her mind as she dared.

Keep it secret. Wait for the right moment.

With a long, agonizing scrape, the door moved aside, revealing an escort of three guards in the doorway. A smile tugged at the corners of her lips, and her cocky attitude returned in an instant, likely fueled by the ball of pure chaos she had stored in her gut.

Last time, there were only two. Guess I got an upgrade.

One of the guards moved forward, two annoyingly familiar pieces of rough fabric in his hand. She kept herself as still and harmless-looking as possible while the guard fastened one cloth over her eyes and the other over her mouth, engulfing her in darkness once again.

"Where'd the kid get bandages?" The sound came from the doorway.

A scuffle, then silence.

"Look, bedsheet's all ripped up. This one's got more brains than the others."

"Shame she's gotta die. Young, strong, smart—she'd make a decent soldier."

For you? Never.

"Please, there's no chance. People like her would rather die than betray. Only the ones that crack easy are desperate enough to let themselves be recruited—that's why we have the rule in the first place."

So your commander isn't an idiot. Good to know.

"Oh, well. Hurry it up—Sevel's gonna get impatient if we don't hurry back. Wonder what she did to make him so mad."

If Rei could have chuckled, she would have. *Apparently, the man doesn't take well to stubbornness.*

The dull hum of energy in the back of her mind strengthened her resolve as they dragged her to her feet, escorting her out the door. It was all she could do to keep the smile off her face as rebellious words surfaced in her headspace, becoming an anthem for her thoughts.

By the time I'm through with this place, I promise you that Sevel will be a lot more than mad.

33

REI

Rei was blind—but that didn't mean she was helpless.

Despite the cloth obscuring her vision, she used the sounds of her guards' footsteps and the jarring motions on her body to vaguely track the turns they were making. A mental map began to form in her mind, a rough idea of where she was taking shape in her thoughts.

Right.

Three steps.

Left.

Twelve steps.

Another left.

The place was nothing short of a maze, and it nearly gave Rei a headache trying to commit the confusing path to memory —especially without being able to see just where she was.

The guards murmured to one another as they walked, making a quiet discussion amongst themselves as though they escorted a teenager to possible death all the time.

Maybe they do. Who knows how awful these people are?

"What do you think they'll do to the girl?"

Rei had tuned out most of the conversation, but her ears pricked up at the words.

The guard's companion snorted. "What they always do. I told you, newbie, don't mind it. It's better if you don't."

"Don't you care?"

"No. And you shouldn't either."

Surprisingly, no anger sparked inside Rei's gut—instead, curiosity reigned supreme, and she found herself listening intently to the guards' argument.

"They didn't even put duskcanium on her?"

Rei frowned, unfamiliar with the word. She remembered reading it a few times in passing, but it had never been interesting enough for her to linger.

"We're running low. Tef and Lyss say she's a null anyway, so we got nothing to worry about."

"Maybe, but..."

"I *said* not to worry about it. Besides, look at the kid! Ain't no one I've ever met been able to wield an alignment in an injured state like that."

Rei barely managed to stop herself from laughing. *You haven't met me, then.*

The guard on her left side shifted uncomfortably. "Don't you ever wonder if...well...if the Eidolon..."

Rei was jerked to a stop as the guard in front of her whipped around, halting the man on her left's speech before the words could even form on his tongue. "Don't you *dare* talk treason, Kothos. You'll bring the same fate she's facing upon our own heads."

Bile rose in Rei's throat. *Wonderful.*

"You two understand that she *can* hear you, right?" the guard on her right pointed out, gripping Rei's arm harder and pushing her forward. Rei winced as her body jolted with the sudden resuming of motion.

Kothos seemed uneasy at the thought, but Rei imagined that the one in the frontmost position was hardly fazed by the fact. "It's not like she'll live long enough to tell anyone about this, anyway."

That's what you think. A trace of glyph worked its way to her fingertips, remaining beneath her skin but humming lightly to remind her that it was there. Even the small gesture returned a spark of hope to her thoughts, telling her over and over that there was a hidden factor that these men did not know about.

"I feel kind of bad for her," Kothos admitted quietly.

The guard on her right snorted. "Don't. It'll be better if you ignore the prisoners. Believe me."

The group lapsed into silence for the rest of the walk, leaving Rei to her thoughts. Surprisingly, she found herself feeling a stab of sympathy for the guards—they were trapped like she was, in a different sort of way.

Focus. They're escorting you to what very well might be your death.

Eventually, the movement slowed, and she was shoved roughly into a room that she assumed to be the one she'd awoken in the day before. Rei's guards forced her into the chair, undoing her gag but leaving the blindfold intact. The air that rushed to meet her lips as the cloth fell away was almost overwhelming, and she inhaled deeply, taking in a huge gulp. Something told her that they had no intention of removing the blindfold, and she found herself struggling to keep the nonchalant smirk on her face.

I have something they don't know about.

Something they don't know about.

Phantom pains rushed through her, the feeling of dried blood meeting her fingers. *My blood. They didn't clean it.*

Something they don't know about.

Something they don't know about.

I will not submit.

Something they don't know about.

The thought was enough to awaken the energy within her, the tingles of power spreading across her skin and providing some grasp of relief amidst the horror show her mind had become.

"Welcome back, *girl*." Sevel's voice was laced with thinly-shrouded contempt, sending dual feelings of terror and annoyance piercing through Rei's gut.

"You could always ask my name, you know." Her voice trembled ever so slightly, but she kept her chin held high. *I will not let him break me. I will not let him see how much pain he has caused.*

There was a shuffle as he presumably came nearer, then a stinging pain as a dagger was lightly dragged across the top of her forearm. Her hands were no longer tied behind her back, but to the arms of the chair, making them a new target for Sevel to destroy. "Maybe I don't care what your name is."

I will not let him break me.

I have something he doesn't know about.

She bit back a whimper, forcing her tone to remain steady. "That's not my problem, then."

The blade dug in deeper to her skin, causing her to wince. Being unable to see the attacks before they came added a whole new level of unease to Rei's churning stomach, and despite her best efforts to keep them at bay, threads of fear still embedded themselves into her mind.

The glyph surged up within her in response to the fear, fueling the flame in her gut that only seemed to be growing hotter and hotter. She had no way of knowing if it was just her and Sevel alone, and the rational side of her warned her to be cautious before revealing her only hidden weapon—but that side was rapidly weakening by the moment. The glyph seemed to be eating away at all orderly thought, leaving nothing but raw strength and a sense of bone-chilling power behind.

"We're going to try something new today," Sevel snarled, drawing out each syllable. Before Rei could process the statement, a burning sensation bored into her wrist, and a gargled scream rose in her throat.

Rei's breaths were heavy and forced as the burning continued, the sickening scent of scalded flesh wafting up to her nose and causing her stomach to churn. She gritted her teeth, the desire for the pain to stop warring with the stone wall that her stubbornness had created. Somehow, not a single word slipped from her lips, despite the part of her that simply wanted to cave and give Sevel the answers he wanted—to reveal Loric, everything she knew, her link to the blade—but she didn't.

You're better than this.

The pain screamed at her in reply—so much pain, twisting her reality and making her completely numb to anything except its relentless torment. Her mind began to weaken, even the energy retreating slightly back inside her as though deterred by the awful feelings rocking her body.

NO! You can't leave me. Not now.

Not now.

"Had enough yet?" Sevel taunted, his voice worming its way into her brain and feeding the glyph. What Rei assumed was a metal rod lifted off her wrist, giving her seconds of respite before digging into the side of her arm. The agony that pulsed through her was blinding, overwhelming, and she found herself struggling to keep a hold on the intense energy that was building steadily inside her core.

What if I let it go?

Rei bit down hard on her tongue, trying anything, everything to keep her mind away from the metal as it ate away at her flesh.

No. I have to wait. If the guards come grab me, I won't be able to summon more in time.

But what if he really is alone?

If he is, how would I know?

You're not exactly in a state to fight, her mental voice decided to remind her. She inhaled sharply, a guttural cry escaping her lips as the burning sensation intensified. She tried not to imagine what her skin must look like, but the image still slipped into her mind, and the glyph bucked against her hold.

It wasn't retreating.

It was charging.

And she wasn't powerful enough to stop it.

It surged up within her, a bloodcurdling scream filling the air as energy mingled with the searing pain of Sevel's rod. She couldn't see the glyph, but she could *feel* it, bursting forth from her body and exploding outward with a volume of force unrivaled by anything she'd felt before. Sevel's agonized grunt met her ears, and she felt the soft relief of cool air as the metal rod was ripped from her arm, clattering across the stone floor.

As though compelled by an invisible force, the bonds fell away from her chafed wrists, her skin burning. The glyph slipped from her grasp, leaping at the chance to claim its freedom. Pain and power swelled in her gut as the energy took over, and another cry escaped from her parched lips, resounding around the room.

She couldn't see, yet she knew exactly where everything was.

It was a feeling she'd never experienced before, yet it was so familiar, as though she could simply *understand* her surroundings on an entirely different level.

Rei doubled over with a gut-wrenching cry, a new, horrible tug yanking on her gut. The burning sensation rocked through her, and her breathing turned shallow, as though the energy were tearing her apart from the inside out.

Then, suddenly—the agony stopped.

Moments later, the lull was filled by a massive explosion, hurling Rei's body to the stone. There was a clatter, followed by the sound of wood splintering—the chair, she realized.

She lay there for a few moments before somehow managing to lift herself to her feet, her muscles drained but the energy fueling her. Silence loomed over the room, and there was a terrifyingly noticeable lack of sound aside from her heavy, ragged breaths.

Sevel—he's gone completely silent.

A chill rippled down Rei's spine as she lifted a trembling hand to her blindfold, fumbling with the rough fabric. After a long moment of struggle, she managed to unknot it, slowly peeling it off her face.

At first, her eyes weren't quite sure what to make of the scene, adjusting to her regained ability to see after long, painful minutes without.

A mixed sense of horror and pride filled her as her surroundings slowly took shape, imprinting an image in her mind that she would never, ever be able to forget.

Sevel's broken body lay sprawled before her, a still-glowing iron rod resting a few feet from his outstretched hand. Particles of deep maroon and even hints of black swam through the air, covering the entire room with a dark, powerful haze. A few threads melted out of the wall nearest to her, slinking back to her palm as she watched, her expression numb.

Did I do this?

34
RUNE

Thick, suffocating blackness surrounded her, crushing her, pinning her down and forcing her deeper into the water that she'd somehow found herself in.

Her eyes fluttered open, the fogginess in her mind seeming to translate to her vision too. No coherent thoughts would form, and while she knew that her lungs should be burning, somehow, they weren't. The scene began to fade, dropping away as someone—or something—leaned over her, a pair of neon purple eyes meeting hers while the shadows consumed her once again.

Then, suddenly, she could feel—the wetness that had been so intoxicating before shifting to something much shallower, much softer, much more gentle. She was still in the water, but it wasn't the same, the strange eyes lingering in her mind as though they had only been a dream.

Red.

She remembered red.

A pain in her side, then the red—and then darkness.

The world solidified around her, and even though her eyes were still closed, she knew the truth.

She was awake.

She was *alive*.

A groan escaped her lips as she groped around, a cool wetness lapping against her cheeks. Her eyes fluttered open, scanning the cave she had somehow wound up in.

Rune. My name—it's Rune. The memory seemed to slip its way into her mind, a sense of surety trailing along behind. Heat wafted into the cavern through the tunnel across from her—a dry, scorching head that sucked all the life out of the land it touched.

She sat up, inhaling sharply as a stab of pain rippled through her body. Her eyes traveled downwards, scanning her outfit—a simple, short-sleeved gray tunic, a leather belt, and shorts, as well as a pair of lightweight boots. The clothing sparked a sense of deja vu in her mind, a very recent memory struggling against the thin veil of darkness in the back of her mind that kept it hidden.

Her gaze found the source of her pain, and she reached down, lifting her shirt slightly to reveal her throbbing side. A freshly-scarred wound marred the skin, the mark tinted a faint pink. Rune took a deep breath, closing her eyes for a moment and immersing herself inside her mind. She felt energy tingle in her fingertips—energy she knew, but didn't know how she knew it.

A voice began resurfacing in her mind, breaking through the frail barrier of shadow and sending shivers down her spine. The voice was deep, ethereal, strange—and it certainly didn't belong to a person. Pictures began filtering through the darkness in shattered fragments as the voice whispered words into her mind.

"Something different about you."

"Perhaps you could help me."

"Set me free."

"You shouldn't be here, Rune. So tell me—why are you?"

The voice kept going, echoing through Rune's mind. It dragged the pictures along with it, forcing image after image to the surface of her thoughts. She had heard the words before—and each fraction of the memories flooding through her consciousness acted like a lost puzzle piece, reconstructing the scene it came from.

"Why are you here, Rune?"

I don't know! Anger seeped into the thought, and it resonated around her mind.

"Yes, you do!"

Rune straightened with a gasp, her fingers flying to her temples. That time, the voice hadn't been speaking from her memory. It had said something entirely new. It had *replied* to her.

Can—can you hear me?

Silence.

Then, slowly, a sound drifted into her thoughts.

"You have to remember, Rune."

Remember what?

"Remember, Rune. You have to."

She shut her eyes tightly, slamming her thoughts against the veil that the voice seems to be originating from. Unlike she'd first assumed, there were actually two of the mental barriers—a thick, unmoving blanket of darkness sheltered behind a thin, vulnerable cloth. The cloth folded beneath her attempts to tear through it, and she could see the threads weakening with each attack.

"You can help me."

Rune gritted her teeth. *How? I don't even know who—or what—you are.*

"Yes, Rune. You do."

With a grunt, Rune funneled all the energy she could muster into her blow, aiming it at one tiny point in the veil. Upon contact, it ripped in two, memories and an overwhelming amount of information flooding towards her in a tidal wave.

Azalea.

Nyk.

Luna.

Ivory.

Ryder.

Kaleo.

I was captured.

I was killed.

I lost everything.

So why am I able to remember?

The thicker veil refused to budge, but images leaked steadily from the thin cloth, jumping at a chance to escape back to their rightful places in her mind. Moments from when she'd awoken in a cave much like this one, stranded with no recollection of anything but her name. Moments of struggle, of making new friends, of searching for a way to reveal the truth. Moments of fear, of pain, of the horror that had gripped her before a dagger took her life. They all returned in an agonizing rush of pictures and voices, finding the emotions that went with them and matching themselves up into full, complete memories.

I have to find my team.

Get to the center.

Rune struggled to her feet, wincing at the phantom pain in her side. *The place where the dagger hit me.* She swallowed hard, a new clarity washing over her. *I failed. I died. My memories—they should be gone.*

But...they aren't.

"*Something different about you.*" The voice—the hydra's voice—returned to her mind, a piece of the first memory she made in the arena.

Different. I'm different.

"*Newcomers like you are supposed to be unconscious.*"

The hydra didn't want the creator to know. That means that whatever sets me apart—it has nothing to do with this arena.

She replayed the memory of Azalea explaining the strange death phenomenon, back in the outpost. Yes, she'd been killed... but somehow, she'd managed to recover everything she had been supposed to lose.

But...why?

She pivoted in a circle, ripples of motion disrupting the water's crystalline surface. Waves of heat wafted into the cavern —no, the citadel, she remembered—from a tunnel on the far side that she assumed led up to the surface. *One thing's for sure... I'm not in Green anymore. Or Blue, for that matter.* Her gut twisted as the realization sank in—she was nowhere near her friends.

Rune was completely alone.

I have to find them.

Memories of her team drifted through her mind, driving each step as she splashed through the shallow water and headed towards the exit. *Red. I saw red when I died. Is that where I am? The Red Biome?*

She groaned. Unlike when she'd originally awoken in the arena, there was no dagger at her side. *This is going to be really difficult without weapons.*

"Hold it right there."

Rune had no time to react as the voice split the musty air of the cave, her mind deducing that the unfamiliar words belonged to a girl about her own age. She froze as cold steel pressed against the nape of her neck, the water around her feet solidifying—as though it were being controlled.

Water. That's her element.

"This doesn't need to be any harder than you make it."

Rune tried to crane her neck to get a closer look at her attacker, but the girl applied more pressure the moment she began moving. "Can I ask *why* you feel the need to kill me? One stabbing a day is already more than I'd care to experience." Despite the shiver that rippled down her spine, she had to fight to keep the grin off her lips—she could practically hear Luna beside her, speaking the words that had just left her own lips.

Her attacker's body went rigid. "You remember dying?"

Rune winced, but nodded. *I can't believe I forgot that I wasn't supposed to know.* "Unfortunately. I just need to get back to my team, okay? I really don't want to fight you."

The girl snorted, her surprise apparently gone. "And if I'd rather you not go back to your team?"

Even against the blade digging into her skin, Rune smiled. Her fingers tingled with the energy she'd been silently storing up since confrontation, her body primed for escape. *I was murdered, but I lived. My memories are still intact. And I have no intention of going down again.* "Well...then I guess you'll just have to live with it."

She flung her arms outward, a blinding flash erupting from her skin. The moment the steel lifted from her neck, Rune whipped around, ramming her shoulder into the girl's exposed chest and sending her careening into the water. Her palm was raised, already filling with another blast of light. This time, the girl managed to shield her eyes with an umber-toned hand, clutching her dagger with the other.

Rune rushed forward, lunging for the girl and pinning her dagger hand down. The girl struggled violently, and streams of water lashed at Rune's body, presumably controlled by her attacker. Blinking rapidly to clear the droplets from her eyes, she pushed against the girl, her skin glowing brightly as she emitted every ounce of light she could possibly muster.

Suddenly, the girl rolled over, a few braids slipping away from her neck. Rune's eyes immediately went to the colored rectangle drawn there, the design that marked her as one of the eight teams.

Rune froze, and the girl noticed, jumping on the opportunity. She threw Rune off, scrambling backward with her dagger raised in a defensive position and tendrils of water drifting around her palm. Slowly, Rune picked herself up, the prior hostility completely drained from her expression.

"Wait. Please."

The girl paused for a brief moment—she didn't let her guard down, but her expression shifted, and she waited just long enough for Rune to lift her soaked hair and reveal her own mark. A soft gasp escaped the girl's lips, and she straightened, lowering her weapon slowly to her side. Her deep blue eyes scanned Rune's body, examining her skeptically.

"You—you're our last member," Rune explained breathlessly. "The others—we have to find them. I know where they are."

The girl raised an eyebrow. "A complete team? That doesn't happen."

"It could," Rune argued. "Do you have a name?"

The girl rolled her eyes. "Of course I *have* one."

Rune chose to ignore the comment. "You can call me Rune, then."

The girl blinked at her. "You seriously want me to just drop everything and trust you?"

"You don't have to trust me. But if you want any chance of getting out of this arena, I'm your best bet." *I hope the others haven't traveled far. They'd probably look for me, right? And they saw me die, so they know I'm in Red. The color of those particles— they saw.*

The girl cocked her head thoughtfully. "You'd need my help, you know. The Red Biome is not a place for the faint of heart."

Rune met her gaze with steely eyes. "I wouldn't expect anything less. I mean, you just tried to kill me without even knowing my name."

The girl brushed a cobalt braid out of her face; her hair was mostly dark, but veins of striking blue ran through the twisting locks. A ghost of a smile seemed like it was trying to make its way onto her lips, but she didn't let it. "What exactly do you want me to do? Come with you?"

Rune thought for a moment. "I want to make an alliance. We're on the same team, after all—but that doesn't mean we have be friends. We just have to work together until a common goal is achieved." She met the girl's eyes, keeping her expression as neutral and business-like as possible. *She's nothing like the rest of our team. But if she can help get us out of here...*

The girl contemplated the words. "Alright. I'll help you. But cross me, and you'll regret it."

Rune nodded. She wasn't sure why the girl seemed so hesitant to trust, especially when either of their deaths would only set back their escape even further—but she certainly wasn't about to argue. *I said it myself—it's not like we have to be friends.* "What can I call you?"

"Alix." She picked herself up, sheathing her dagger and pacing through the water towards the door. "Let's get going, then. Hanging around the Citadel practically puts a massive target on your back."

Shaken, confused, and still a bit unsure exactly what had just happened, Rune turned, following Alix up through the tunnel and out into a parched, endless desert.

35
RUNE

Rune leaned closer to the flickering tongues of flame, her eyes scanning the last streaks of light on the horizon. Alix sat across from her, the firelight illuminating a golden undertone in her dark skin. Nights in the desert were uncomfortably cold, a rather stark contrast to the painfully scorching heat of the daytime.

"How long have you been here?" Rune's voice sounded awkward after the long silence.

Alix shrugged, staring at the fire. "A while. I try not to think about it."

Rune leaned back, resting against a boulder. They had traveled for the entire afternoon, moving across seemingly endless dunes of sand beneath an unforgiving sun. Finally, they'd come upon a small rock formation, jutting out from the ground and stretching upwards a good thirty feet. They'd climbed up to a ledge about midway up, building a small fire from dead underbrush and tumbleweeds.

"You weren't kidding—Red is *not* an easy biome to survive in."

The cloudless skies allowed the sun to beat down ruthlessly on the parched, reddish land, making travel a tedious ordeal. At night, however, the climate dipped sharply, plummeting into temperatures so cold Rune could see her breath cloud in front of her face.

Alix raised her head. "No. I suppose it's not too bad, though—not when I can do this." She raised her hand, wiggling her fingers ever so slightly. Small streams of water seemed to melt out of the air, drifting around her palm.

Rune's gaze traced the tiny trickles of water as she released them, allowing droplets to run down her arm. "You can just *materialize* water?"

Alix snorted. "I wish. My ability doesn't allow me to create anything new, but I can pull it from condensation in the air."

Rune made a face. "Hard to believe that there's *any* water in this air."

"Not a lot, that's for sure."

In the distance, a long, bone-chilling shriek resonated off of faraway cliffs, the sound seeming to span the entire desert. Rune's head snapped up, her heart thundering in her chest. *What is that?*

Alix chuckled. "Relax. It's miles away."

Rune shuddered. "What *is* it?"

Alix turned, examining the dry sea of sand that spread out below them. "Sandcrawler. They are *not* fun to deal with, trust me. It's basically a giant, nocturnal scorpion, and its venom is one of the most painful deaths you could experience in this place." The pearls woven into the ends of her braids clinked together as she leaned forward, closing her eyes briefly. "Hallucinations, swelling—I would go into more detail, but I doubt you'd like to know."

Not really. Rune shook her head. "I'll just—take your word for it."

Alix smirked slightly, picking up a broken tumbleweed from the pile beside her and tossing it into the hungry flames. "If you're not careful, you may end up with a firsthand experience."

Rune made a face. "Thanks for the vote of confidence." The words slipped out in a wry, dry tone, reminding her of Luna. Her heart wrenched, sadness weighing down on her like a brick.

I miss them.

The glint in Kaleo's eyes as he'd helped her up, letting her lean on him.

The cocky grin on Luna's face as she'd stared down her attackers, not an ounce of fear showing in her expression.

The soft, thoughtful gaze Azalea had often worn, staring into the distance and lost in her thoughts.

I'm going to find my way back. And then we're going to get ourselves out of this death trap.

If Alix noticed Rune's change in mood, she didn't comment on it.

For a long moment, they sat there, the only sound between them being the faint crackling of the burning underbrush that fueled the orange flames before them. Finally, Alix spoke, her voice shattering the silence like a mallet on glass.

"Do you really know where the rest of our team is?"

Rune stared into the fire. "I know where they were when I died. They saw it happen…which means they probably saw which biome I'd wake up in."

"You think they'll come find you?" There was a strange undertone to Alix's voice—a faint disbelief, a sense of longing—and other emotions that Rune couldn't recognize.

"I do." Her heart squeezed at the words. "They don't know I remember, though—so they probably won't be expecting me to try to find them."

Alix cocked her head at her. "You remember *everything*?"

Rune nodded. "Don't ask me how. When I woke up, I didn't know anything—but somehow, I knew how to find my memories again. It doesn't work on the ones I had before coming here, but at least I get to keep the few that I've managed to make."

An odd expression passed over Alix's features. "You—where do you think we should go, then?"

"I died in Blue." *That's weird to say.* "Is Red near Blue?"

"It's as far as you can get."

Oh.

Alix reached into her pocket, pulling out a leystone. "To get from Red to Blue, you either have to go through Green or through Yellow. I've got a shard for the Red Leylock—the barrier that separates Red from Yellow."

Rune nodded slowly, hating how quickly her heart latched on to the hope Alix's words brought. Nothing about this was going to be easy—but that naive, foolish part of her refused to imagine anything other than success. Clinging to hope.

Hope is all I have.

"It's getting late." The abrupt subject change startled Rune back to reality. Alix picked up another branch, this time snapping it in two before tossing it into the fire. "I'll take first watch."

Rune watched as the flames ate away at the wood, crackling noises filling the air. Exhaustion pulled at her eyelids, agreeing with Alix before the words even formed on her tongue. "Are you sure?"

Alix eyed her, a mix of distrust and fatigue filling her expression. "I'm positive." Her voice was clipped, causing Rune to recoil slightly. *She still doesn't trust me.*

Not wanting to push further, Rune stood, making her way over to a rocky crevice a little ways away from where Alix sat. She spread out her cloak, laying down with a grunt and wrapping her body in it. The stone was far from comfortable, but she simply gritted her teeth, desperately trying not to think about how sore her back would be the following morning. Forcing herself to relax, she inhaled a breath of the night air, its cool, refreshing nature filling her lungs.

Pictures surfaced in her thoughts as her mind slowed down, drifting across her consciousness like leaves in a lazily-moving river. There were images she recognized, and some that she didn't, brief flashes of recognition amidst a sea of darkness. A cool breeze brushed across her skin as her body fell still, succumbing to the inescapable force of sleep.

RUNE SAT UP WITH A JOLT, RUBBING HER TEMPLES.

Beads of sweat streamed down her face, her hands still shaking slightly from the nightmare.

Over and over again, her death had replayed in her mind, haunting every ounce of her being. Sometimes it was a knife, sometimes it was the flames, sometimes she was sinking beneath the waves while bubbles streamed from her lips—but regardless of how different the scenes seemed, they all had one thing in common:

The raw, empty feeling that had rocked her when her body hit the ground, her mind vanishing into a place beyond sleep.

She pulled her knees into her chest and buried her face in them, wanting to shut out the awful images. The memories that had plagued her so prominently before the event seemed so much less significant now, merely background noise in the constant melody of her thoughts.

Unimportant.

No longer needed.

No longer wanted.

For the first time since her awakening in the arena, not a single part of her longed for the past she didn't have. It was because of that past that she was in this situation in the first place, because of that past that she allowed herself to be caught off-guard and defenseless.

It can't happen again.

It can't.

I can't let my past consume me again.

She swallowed hard, raising her gaze to the skyline. The stars overhead were tiny flecks against the blanket of darkness, twinkling with an unsaid promise that sank deep into Rune's heart. It was at that moment that she made a new vow to herself, one that she repeated over and over until it was engraved into her very being.

I will not let my past affect the present.

I will not lose myself to the memories I don't even have.

The vow circled in her thoughts as she allowed herself to lay back against the stone once again, her eyes fluttering closed.

36

REI

Trembling, Rei knelt down, positioning her hands under Sevel's shoulders and lifting his corpse slightly off the ground. His blood was sticky on her skin as she dragged him slowly over to the closed door, her body crying out in pain and her injuries throbbing horribly.

Hand shaking, she reached down, wrapping her fingers around his wrist and lifting it to the panel. She watched through blurred vision as the panel glowed green for a brief moment, and she was barely aware of letting go of Sevel's limp body as it crumpled to the ground.

Rei took a long, slow breath, flooding her lungs with the sickly sweet air that filled the room. The faint smell of burning flesh still lingered, causing her throat to tighten. She refused to so much as glance at the metal rod as she limped out the door, leaving Sevel's body surrounded by a growing pool of blood. A shudder rocked her body as she glanced down at her red-soaked palms, a few strands of glyph leaking from her torn skin.

I just—let it loose. I let it loose, and it did exactly what I wanted—it saved me.

Normally, she would have been revolted by such a brutal sight—a past version of her might have once believed that not even the cruelest of villains deserved the deaths they caused.

She wasn't so sure what to think anymore.

She wasn't so sure she *could* think any more.

Rei dared a final glance back at Sevel's magic-torn body, immediately regretting it when her stomach heaved. His slithery, know-it-all voice still rang in her ears, sending tremors of anger down her spine—but not even the memories of all the pain he'd caused her could stop her from staring at the broken, bloody mess and thinking *I did this.*

She wasn't proud of it.

But...it had kept her alive.

And at that moment, "alive" seemed to be the only positive descriptor for the situation she was in.

Rei forced her crying muscles to move, stumbling down the hallway and leaving drips of crimson liquid in her wake. Not that she cared if she was easy to track—all she wanted was to find the Blade, to find a way out. Nothing else mattered in that moment—not her body, not the glyph, not the mass destruction she'd left behind. A dull, throbbing numbness had begun to spread over her mind, keeping her hopelessly trapped, her focus set on one thing, and one thing only.

Get as far away from here as I possibly can.

Black spots swam in her vision, and it was all she could do to clear them away, her thoughts becoming as slurred and sluggish as her movements. Still, the glyph pulsed through her veins, somehow providing the strength that fueled each painstaking step forward. She found herself falling into an agonizing rhythm of recurring torment, her motions slow but steady as she wandered aimlessly through the twisting hallways of her prison. One thought—and one thought only—played in her mind, repeating over and over again like an anthem to her aching bones.

Find a way out.

Find a way out.

Find a way out.

Find a way out.

Where she walked, how long, how far—she didn't know. Everything began to blur together in her mind, melting itself into a giant orb of tightly wound thoughts.

Suddenly, a voice broke through the haze, her head snapping up.

"Hold it, kid."

The orb of thoughts shattered.

"Where do you think you're going?"

Rei turned around slowly, vaguely aware of how she must look. Bloody, bruised, burned, beaten, a crazed look in her eye and particles of magic drifting aimlessly around her. "I'm leaving. And you are not going to try and stop me." Despite her fatigue, the words left her lips with a glyph-fueled edge, energy building up inside her fingertips. It chased away all the pain, the exhaustion, and the ability to think rationally, leaving nothing but raw instinct and power. She straightened, grateful for the relief.

"I *won't*, huh?" The guard took a threatening step closer, his hand inching towards his sword—but Rei didn't flinch. "I'm afraid that I don't take orders from children."

Rei eyed him blankly, the emotion stripped from her expression and leaving an icy, raw husk of an individual in her place. "Does the name Sevel mean anything to you?"

The response caught him off-guard, and he froze. "It does. The question is—does it mean anything to *you*?"

Rei cocked her head, a slightly insane smile flitting across her lips. "It *did*, at one point. I killed him."

The guard snorted.

"Don't believe me? See for yourself. I made myself pretty easy to follow, after all." She nodded to the trail of scarlet behind her, droplets of blood paving a violent road to the place that should have been her end. "A note of warning to you, though—not all of that is mine."

Despite the fact that he still didn't believe her, the man had begun to shrink back, unsettled by the complete lack of care in Rei's tone. His eyes flitted across her body, lingering on the worst of the burns.

"*Sevel* did this to me. Grotesque, isn't it?" She fought the urge to smile as he fished for words, an obvious look of horror creeping across his features. The pain had numbed her, robbed her of her feelings, of the things that made her a person. Her own screams still rang in her ears, a tribute to an experience that would haunt her for as long as she lived. "Don't you know what really goes on behind the walls of those rooms you guard so faithfully? What happens to each victim you escort to and from their *revolting* cells? You can't possibly tell me that you've never wondered, at least."

The guard took a hesitant step back, an array of emotion

spreading across his face. "No one knows what happens to prisoners besides Sevel and Tef. No one *wants* to know what happens. We were told they all deserve it, that when they go in, when they never come out, that it's just, that it's—" he broke off, nonsense spewing from his lips.

Rei shook her head slowly in disbelief, a bit of her prior anger returning to her. "You can't *possibly* have looked at me—a *teenage girl*—and believed the lies that I deserve whatever fate they brought on my head, can you? Is that what you thought? Is that why you stopped me?" She took a breath, her blood boiling. "Do you realize who you're working for? Do you even know his *name*?"

The man stared at her like she had just sprouted an extra head. "He is the Eidolon, the one who promises us a home in the New Oasis. Our command is to defend our city, to crush the resistance, and deliver the Blade to him." The words sounded so rehearsed, so scripted, that Rei found herself fighting the urge to laugh despite the situation.

"The Eidolon isn't a name. It's a mask. And only a coward would rule his army from behind a mask."

The man bristled, but instead of anger, fear sprang to his features. "You call the Eidolon a coward? In his own territory? Even after—after you've seen—what his followers will do to you?" His voice trembled slightly, betraying that he was still shaken by Rei's injuries.

Rei glanced down at herself, numb to the horrifying sight. "I do. If he wasn't such a coward, he would come here and handle me himself instead of making his little puppets do his work for him. I've been *dying* to talk to the man after my encounter with one of his lovely bands of thieves, you know.

Bloody wimps, sending a teenager into a stronghold that they themselves were simply too scared to enter. Guess they weren't expecting me to slit their throats with the very blade I was blackmailed into stealing."

The man's face instantly went white. "*You* were behind the deaths of Evander's squad? It was *you* who claimed the Phantom Blade?"

Rei smirked, her cocky attitude slowly returning. The glyph egged her on, giving her more and more confidence with each passing moment. "This seems to surprise you. Does it surprise you, my ignorant little friend?" *Okay, Rei, maybe calling him "little" wasn't the best idea.*

As expected, he seemed extremely enraged by Rei's airy, taunting words—but she was in no mood to celebrate another successful round of *let's-annoy-my-captors-to-the-point-where-they-want-to-stab-me*. Even with the artificial strength her magic provided, her vision still began to grow blurry, probably due to the fact that she really shouldn't be on her feet at the moment.

I need to wrap this up. "Do you happen to know where they're keeping my sword? It's quite rude to take things that aren't yours, you know. I'd certainly like to get it back." Rei cut herself off abruptly before her words could start to waver, closing her eyes for a second longer than a blink and desperately trying to clear the constant throbbing from the back of her skull.

The guard's eyes narrowed, his previous shock apparently having disappeared. "I'm afraid I can't let that happen."

Rei raised an eyebrow. "You're loyal. Such a shame that it's to the wrong side." She took a long, deep breath, summoning the glyph back to the surface as she exhaled. Her reserves were running low, she could tell—she didn't have much left in her to give. Gritting her teeth, she raised her palm, desperately hoping that she wouldn't pass out when she took the shot.

The guard laughed, drawing his sword. "I don't dissolve when pointed at, sorry. It was a good try, though. You've got a lot of guts, kid—I'll give you that, at least."

The last thing he saw was Rei's cold smile as threads of maroon energy erupted from her fingertips, engulfing him completely and dropping his body to the ground before he could even register the attack. The threads snaked back to her palm, the grin fading from her face. *At least he didn't suffer.*

A wave of lightheadedness washed over her, but she somehow stayed on her feet, fighting through the agony and turning her back on yet another life she'd brutally stolen from the world. *I had to do it. I had to.* Still, the last moment of terror lingering in the man's pale eyes when he realized what was happening burned in her brain, joining the other sickening memories.

One more to add to the collection.

She began moving again, her chest heaving with heavy breaths. There was no choice for her, taking turn after turn with the naive hope that there might be an exit waiting on the other side. Eventually, she stumbled her way into a particularly long hallway, one that was at least twice as wide as the previous ones. Thirty or forty arched openings lined the walls as far as she could see, presumably leading to various tunnels.

I must have found the main area.

The brief elation was immediately followed by fear, and she hesitated, realizing that there would likely be more guards—not to mention that she was in no state to fight. Nevertheless, she kept going, step after step, stifled cry after cry—it was all a rhythm. A painful, nightmarish rhythm, but a rhythm all the same.

A tug in her gut halted her pace, and she pivoted to the right, eyes locking on a pair of ornately carved doors that appeared to be well secured. Something drifted towards her from behind those doors—a distant call, a fleeting whisper, a feeling that made her pause and think for just long enough to recognize what that call reminded her of.

The hum that always grew in her mind when she held the Blade—this sensation was the very same.

Is it in there?

"Step away from the door."

Rei froze at the voice, immediately reaching for the glyph. Panic surged through her as her call met nothing, only a few, broken threads responding to her need. *I'm drained. My body's done—it can't do this anymore.*

"Kudos to you for making it this far—but we have a perfect record to maintain." The slow, unnerving scrape of metal against metal indicated that the guard had drawn his weapon, and a faint swish in the air paired with an icy sensation running down her spine told her that it was aimed directly at the nape of her neck.

Words formed on Rei's tongue, but her lips refused to part, fatigue crashing over her like a tidal wave. Terror set in after a moment, leaving her raw and empty as all hope drained from her body. Pain took command of every muscle she had, refusing to allow her to move.

"You've made yourself quite memorable, kid—and if it's any consolation, I'm sure that death won't be too much of a step up from what you've already experienced. Consider it a mercy, really."

He sounded so calm—so nonchalant about ending her life —and Rei would have clenched her fists if she could still feel them, her consciousness slipping away from her at a horrifying speed.

It's over.

She inhaled deeply, refusing to allow herself to think as she braced for the blow.

A shout rang out—two words, both spoken in a language that she couldn't understand. The shout was followed by a dull thud, and the nearby crackle of magic, the guard's sword deflecting off of thin air. *A charm—that was a runic charm. Someone saved me.*

The brief moment of relief caused her body to collapse, her wounds finally getting the better of her. She lay there, barely feeling it when she made contact with the stone. Blurry figures scuffled in front of her, but she was shielded somehow, a haze of silver light encompassing her while a single man warred with the guard who'd tried to kill her.

The fact that she was alive hadn't quite sunk in yet, her consciousness balancing on a strange razor's edge between life and death. It was only when her rescuer came closer, dissolving the barrier and kneeling at her side, did a rational thought finally slip through. Her lips parted, speaking the word—her voice was hardly a whisper, but the man heard it, wrapping his in his arms and gently cradling her battered body.

"Loric."

Her vision was far too blurry for her to see his face, and he clutched her tightly to his chest, a groan escaping her lips as she was lifted off the ground. One final thought broke through the haze as her mind dissolved into darkness—only two words, but they were the words that she'd been longing to hear for so, so long.

I'm safe.

37

REI

"Is she awake?"

"I don't know. Give me a second."

"Those burns were pretty bad. You sure she's alright?"

"She's fine. I'd give her some space, though. Extreme pain has the tendency to overload your brain, and after an incident like that, there might be details she doesn't remember."

Me. They're talking about me. The blurry fragments of conversation drifting around Rei's mind slowly began to click into place, and she struggled towards the surface of her consciousness, battling against the blanket of darkness that fought to pin her down.

"I'll get Sumi. The guy who brought her in, too."

"You won't have to go far. He's been hovering over my shoulder the whole time she's been here."

There was a murmured response, then one of the voices disappeared as a set of footsteps left the room.

Rei opened her eyes a crack as a gasp escaped her lips, and

she gulped in air, her body flooding with adrenaline. *Where am I? Who is that? Why...* a bright, pounding pain suddenly gushed back into her body, causing her to inhale sharply and immediately scrunch her eyes shut again. Everything was white—all around her, in her mind, in her thoughts—it was all a bright, blinding white. Suddenly, she was back home again—sitting with Ember and Cedar, laughing with her friends, staring up at a twilight sky.

"Ember—where's Ember?" Her words tripped over themselves, her numb tongue slurring them together.

A young girl fidgeted beside her, looking slightly nervous. "I—I'm sure Ember's safe. You need to take it easy, Rei. I can't have you re-agitating your wounds." Despite its slight tremor, her voice was smooth and melodic, the angelic, youthful ring to it easing a bit of the tension in Rei's shoulders.

Ember.

Why does that name sound so distant to me?

Why... She froze.

Ember's gone. He's home. He's safe.

But if he's home...then where am I?

A strangled gasp escaped her lips as everything came rushing back—her dream, her capture, being tortured, the glyph, Loric picking her up as she went unconscious...

"Loric! I need to—where is he—"

The girl placed a hand firmly on Rei's chest, pushing her back down as she tried to sit up. "Seriously, Rei! I'm a good healer, but I'm not *that* good. Loric's here. He's safe. *You're* safe."

Rei eyed the girl warily, but she begrudgingly obliged, scooting backwards and propping herself up against the wall behind the bed. They were in some kind of healing ward—cream colored walls, runic-enchanted lanterns for the lighting, and birch rafters that crisscrossed above their heads. The bed she laid on was made of a similar wood, and made up with slightly disheveled beige blankets. It was one of about ten beds total, all of them empty except for hers.

"Do your wounds hurt anymore?"

Rei thought for a moment, suddenly realizing why everything had cleared up so quickly—the pain was practically gone, reduced to nothing but a dull throb in the back of her skull. Even the migraine she'd gotten when she'd awoken didn't bother her any longer. "I—no."

"Good. The painkiller's working, then."

Rei cocked her head, a frown crossing her lips. *No remedy I know can numb pain that effectively.* "Who exactly *are* you?"

The girl turned, moving over to a wooden shelf on the far wall and rummaging around in a drawer full of yellowing sheets of parchment. "One of the healers for the Onyx. My name's Kalindra, but just Kal is fine." Her ice blue eyes scanned Rei's body, pausing for a brief moment over each bandaged wound as she murmured something under her breath.

The Onyx. That was the "organization of annoying individuals" Sevel kept questioning me about. If he doesn't like them...then I guess they'd probably be decent people to get along with.

"Rei. But—I guess you know that, don't you."

Kal nodded. "I do." She moved over to Rei's side, brushing a strand of blue hair out of her face. The long black and cobalt strands were woven into two braids that wrapped around her head, cascading down her back and framing her delicate features. She held up the parchment she'd chosen, her eyes fluttering across the page for a moment. Satisfied, she reached to the crystal basin at Rei's bedside, setting the paper down and soaking her left hand in the water.

Rei frowned as Kal shifted closer, keeping her hand submerged in the basin and using the other to unwrap the bandage around her right wrist. "What are you doing?"

Kal glanced up for a moment, offering Rei a quick smile. "It won't hurt, don't worry. I'm just going to apply another round of healing."

Rei raised an eyebrow. "Burn wounds are best treated with Thrashroot paste, and I personally use Calendula. Are you sure water will help?"

Kal nodded, setting the bandage aside and swirling her finger around a few times in the basin. "Perhaps where you come from, that is the best cure. But aquilian healing is by far one of the most effective methods for treating any extreme wound quickly." She reached up with her dry hand, tucking another loose strand of hair behind a pointed ear before lifting her palm from the water and gently placing it on the raw, reddish skin.

Rei winced at the contact, but held still, watching as Kal closed her eyes and began murmuring under her breath. The water droplets spread out across the wound, moving in an oddly unnatural way to cover the burn with a thin sheet of liquid. Kal began applying slight pressure, but no pain came with the movement, the water sinking into Rei's skin and easing the redness with each passing second. Tiny cuts knitted back together, the blisters shrank down, and the agitated, scraping feeling began to dissolve as the liquid passed across the injury. Finally, Kal pulled her hand away, taking the water with it and leaving nothing but a patch of pink skin where the burn had been only moments before.

Rei stared in shock, picking her hand up and gently rotating her palm to put a bit of strain on the newly-healed skin. To her surprise and relief, there was no pain, only a slight bit of stiffness as the skin got used to the motion. "That's—I've never seen anything like that before." One of the pages from Loric's books resurfaced in her mind…the aquili, a sub-elven race, and their odd abilities to heal using the water. *That's what Kal is. An aquili.*

Kal's eyes sparkled as she reached for a clean bandage, and Rei held still, allowing her to rewrap her wrist. "Normally, I can get it to disappear entirely—but unfortunately, I think at least some of them are going to leave scars. I'll try again later, but for now, just try to let it finish the healing process naturally. Now— let's see what we can do about some of the other injuries."

Suddenly, the door flew open, and three figures came rushing in. Loric pushed past them, hurrying to Rei's side and wrapping her in a gentle but tight embrace. When he pulled away, he was fuming, his face completely overtaken by rage.

"What in the *nine realms* were you *thinking*?" He shook Rei's shoulders, forcing her to look him in the eyes. "Going out *alone*? While I was *asleep*? You nearly *died*! Those bloody *vacillates*, torturing a girl—a *girl*—" His gaze softened as he stepped away, eyeing the bandages that covered Rei's body. "Don't you *dare* do that again."

Rei blinked at him, uncomfortably aware that everyone else was watching the exchange—but Loric didn't seem to care in the slightest. "It might be helpful if you explained exactly *who* this Eidolon guy is, and why he seems to really want me dead?"

Before Loric could speak, a short, older woman stepped up behind him, placing a hand on his arm. "You *do* deserve answers, my dear. We have a few questions that we would like to ask you as well." Her gentle, yellow-toned eyes seemed to soften Loric's fury slightly, and she turned her gaze to the young girl standing in the doorway, offering her a kind smile. "You may go, Wren. Tell the rest of the commanders that I will debrief with them later."

Wren ducked her head, glancing at Rei with wide, pale blue eyes before disappearing into the hallway.

"You as well, Kalindra—although finish whatever healing you need to do first."

Kal nodded, setting to work on Rei's wounds while the woman convinced Loric to take a seat on the bed beside hers. The woman, however, remained standing, her expression soft. "I believe introductions would be a fine place to begin. My name is Sumi—I'm one of the Onyx's leaders."

For a moment, Rei completely forgot to reply—she was too busy trying to figure out the woman's appearance. At first glance, the long, neatly styled dreadlocks, bronze toned skin, and pointed ears seemed relatively normal. What threw Rei for a loop, however, were the natural violets that seemed to sprout out of the woman's scalp right alongside her hair. *Gnomes... gnomes have natural plants in their hair.* The information surfaced in her mind before she even needed to search for it, yet another lesson she'd gleaned from hours of reading in Loric's library.

Then she remembered that she hadn't said anything. "Rei —I'm Rei." She looked away, feeling her face flush.

Sumi simply smiled. "It's a pleasure to meet you. Now,

before we explain a bit more thoroughly exactly where you are and who your captors were, I have to ask: how did you not only manage to keep yourself alive in a base that no one has ever successfully made it out of—but also faced down and *defeated* one of the Eidolon's highest ranking officers with a magic you didn't even *have* a few days ago?"

Rei stared at her. "I—got lucky?"

She could practically feel Loric's stare.

Sumi shook her head in disbelief. "No one 'gets lucky' when it comes to the Iron Heart himself. He is one of the Eidolon's top men, and has proven time and again that he is worthy of such a title."

A smirk crossed Rei's features. "The *Iron Heart*? Here I thought that it was bad enough having to be called 'Sevel' all the time."

Sumi frowned. "You know his name?"

Rei shrugged, memories of his know-it-all voice whispering threats in her ear resurfacing against her will. "He mentioned it. Seemed pretty angry with me—definitely did *not* enjoy my presence much." *Hide behind humor. Hide behind humor. Hide behind humor and the scars can't touch you.*

Beside her, Loric leaned closer, his gaze holding Rei's. "How are you holding up?" The edge in his voice had disappeared, replaced by an almost fatherlike undertone of softness.

Terrible. "I'm alright. I don't really want to talk about it."

Sumi shook her head sadly, glancing over at Loric. "It's impossible for people to be simply 'alright' after experiencing such things, Rei. The world is a broken, broken place. If we aren't careful, it will break parts of us as well—parts we cannot fix."

Rei averted her gaze. "I shouldn't be struggling this much, though—it's not like this is my first time. I was forced into an army when I was a kid, I was banished for something that wasn't my fault, I was dragged into a war against an ancient demon that my ancestors were powerless against—I'm not new to having to fight like this. I'm *not*." Her voice caught on the words, letting through a hint of the raw, fractured part of her that she always desperately tried to hide.

Sumi and Loric listened quietly, and Rei kept her eyes averted, afraid of the way they would react. The gnome simply rested her hand on Rei's shoulder, squeezing lightly. "The world will always shatter in the same way—but some people are cut by larger shards. Unfortunately, you are right in the path of the glass—and that isn't fair to you. Burdens like this should never rest on the shoulders of anyone, much less a girl of your age—but they do, and you won't be bearing them alone. Loric and I are going to explain everything to you, and then—well, then you're going to have to make a choice."

Rei swallowed hard, glancing from Loric to Sumi silently. Loric spoke first, a bit of hesitation leaking into his tone.

"Long ago, a cypher—a creature made of pure aligned energy—known as the *Saquis* began to develop abilities that had never been seen before by his kind. He misused these abilities, becoming a danger to many people, and he was sealed away, placed inside a half-mask to keep him contained. Over time, however, he began to grow stronger, his magic weakening the mask's bindings. As a safeguard, the ones who'd sealed him away forged a matching sword, severing his magic and placing it inside the vessel. By keeping the sword and mask apart—and him away from his magic—the risk he posed had been resolved."

"The mask—the Eidolon has it." Rei spoke before the words even formed as a thought, a memory resurfacing in her mind. *The man from my dream—the Eidolon—he was wearing a half-mask.*

"Yes. He does." Loric cocked his head at her, but didn't question it. "The reason he wants you dead, Rei, is because you have the Blade. It bonded to *you*. In order to take possession of it—and return the magic to the *Saquis*—he has to kill you."

Kill me. He has to kill me.

Rei closed her eyes for a second longer than a blink, allowing her mind to take in the information. "Is that why he was able to reach my dream? Because the Blade and the Mask... are bound together?"

Loric winced, but nodded. "Yes. Look, Rei—I'm sorry I wasn't able to tell you sooner. I had hoped that I'd be able to train you first, to fully prepare you before you were forced into the role—but it looks like you were never granted that luxury."

"Wait. What role? You said I was the Phantom Wielder—that people's lives were on the line—but what does that mean?" A part of her feared the answer as he opened his mouth to speak, his words slow and meticulous.

"That's why you're here, and not back at my house. Sumi—it might be best if you explain this part."

The gnome nodded. "As I said before, I am one of the leaders of the Onyx. The Onyx is a rebellion against the Eidolon and his forces, a barrier between him and full victory over the city he's currently attempting to conquer."

A shiver rippled down Rei's spine. "One of the guards mentioned the city."

"That doesn't surprise me." Sumi moved closer, taking a seat at the foot of Rei's bed. "For the longest time, our operatives scoured the world, searching for the Phantom Blade's next wielder. We are extremely lucky that Loric found you—" she glanced over at the brawny man— "even if he is technically no longer a part of our organization."

Rei frowned. "Why not?"

"I'll let him explain his reasoning to you later if he desires. The point is, we've been searching for you for many years—and we aren't the only ones. The Eidolon's power is already great, and even with some of the best fighters in the realms on our side, we haven't been able to get close to where he has made his 'base.' That city and its inhabitants are suffering, and with each passing day, the resistance grows weaker and weaker. If he managed to get his hands on the Phantom Blade, his reach will be able to extend far beyond the city. Because of that, we *need* to keep you safe."

"That's not all, is it?" Rei eyed her cooly, keeping her emotions neutral. "You want me to join you. To fight him."

Sumi didn't reply, but her expression gave it away.

"You have a choice, Rei," Loric told her firmly as she sank back, closing her eyes and letting the information sink in. "You *do*." He shot a pointed glance at Sumi, as though he expected her to argue—but she only nodded.

"*If* you decide to join us, we'd like to move you to our main location...the Oasis, in Lycrix. That's the city he's trying to take control of." Sumi's voice was level, but a bit of urgency had snuck into her tone.

"Lycrix—that's a different realm, isn't it?"

The gnome nodded.

Rei chewed her lip nervously. *A different realm. I'd be a world away from my home—literally.* Her gaze wandered down to her hands—the very hands that had woven threads of maroon energy, that had lifted Sevel's limp body, that had known what to do even when her brain hadn't. "We—" she inhaled sharply, hesitation halting her words. "When do we leave?"

Loric and Sumi simply stared at her for a long moment, but Loric spoke first, rising to his feet before kneeling down in front of Rei. "Are you sure about this? I know you agreed to stay with me, to train, but this is an entirely different situation. You *can* back out. We *can* make it work. All you need to do is say the word."

His words sounded tempting, for sure—but Rei knew she couldn't accept them. She stared at her hands, her eyes hovering over the bandages that wound so tightly around her wrists, her arms, and countless other places on her body. The bandages concealed scars, scars that had been wounds, wounds that had been pure, raw pain. But despite the pain—despite the helpless, burning desire to tell Loric and Sumi she couldn't do this, to run as far away from these people and this universe as she could —there was a part of her that still longed for this world.

Going back to her home—if that was even possible—would be safer, yes, at least in the short term. But—that would mean being alright with returning to a life hiding amongst lies, keeping her head down and pretending that none of this had ever happened. This world—this vast, incredible universe—was full of truth. Truth about her friends, about her own world's existence, and about the experiences she'd had that were very, very real. Maybe there would be more pain. Maybe there would be more fear. Even so—she wanted to know more.

She wanted to *be* more.

If she went home now, she'd never know the person that she was now faced with the chance to become.

And if there's one thing I've always hated, it's questions that never got answered.

She raised her gaze, clenching her fists tightly. *I can't believe I'm about to say this. Sorry Ember, Cedar—guess it's gonna be a little bit longer before I can come back home.* "This is my world now, and I've been given this power to help me fight for it. I'm in."

38
RUNE

Endless dunes of sand stretched out before them, the cloudless sky above being extremely unhelpful in providing any protection against the relentless sun. Rune reached for the leather flask she'd attached to her side, taking only as big of a sip as she dared. Alix had mentioned that there was a small oasis about halfway to the highlands—a massive range of mesas that spanned the border between Red and Yellow—but she had also warned against running out of water too quickly.

"Have you always been here in Red?"

Up ahead, Alix's pace fell out of rhythm for a moment. "I— I'm not sure." Her voice was slightly pinched, and she avoided Rune's gaze, two tells that a past version of her had learned to identify. "I don't remember ever leaving this place."

She's lying. But why?

"You said you had a red leyshard?" Rune tried, struggling to keep the undertones of suspicion from creeping into her voice.

She was certain that Alix was lying, but as to her reasoning, Rune couldn't even try to guess.

Alix nodded absentmindedly. "I got it off the body of some idiot who thought I'd be an easy target. He thought very, very wrong."

Rune reached up to wipe the beads of sweat off her brow, Alix's words sending a shiver down her spine despite the scalding temperatures. Normally, she considered herself to be fairly adept at reading people, but Alix—there was something off about her. The way she kept herself guarded, always thought before she spoke, and even the sheer level of distrust that radiated off her made Rune uncomfortable in a way she couldn't quite put her finger on.

A memory pushed against the veil, filling Rune with disconnected feelings from a past she still couldn't recall. She didn't realize she'd stopped moving until Alix turned around, calling her name.

The kind of person Alix is—I've been around others like her. People who acted like her, who hid things in the same way.

At least...a past version of me has.

As they walked, Rune felt her body beginning to grow fatigued beneath the heat of the sun, but the enticing pull of the mystery surrounding Alix kept her mind busy and, for the most part, distracted. Alix had given her no reason not to trust her, at least so far—it almost seemed like *she* was the one struggling to trust *Rune*.

Then, out of the corner of her eye, Rune noticed a massive figure looming out of the sands. She paused, her abrupt stop causing Alix to circle around back to her side.

"Something wrong?"

Rune hesitated, nodding towards the odd lump in the landscape.

Frowning, Alix moved closer, and as they neared the location of interest, the mysterious object began to take shape.

Bones jutted out from the sand, forming the broken rib cage of a creature much too large for Rune's comfort. The remains of what seemed to be a scaly barbed tail lay at one end, and rough patches of decaying, reptilian skin still clung to the exposed white spokes.

"What is it?" Rune approached the corpse, barely comforted by the fact that it was clearly long dead.

Alix knelt down, lightly brushing one of the largest ribs with her fingertips. "Sandcrawler. A very, very dead one. It's been laying here for weeks, probably...months, even." She stood back up, brushing herself off and staring at the half-buried remains.

"A sandcrawler? Like the screech we heard last night?"

Alix nodded. "They tend to be nocturnal," she assured Rune, practically reading her thoughts. "Their scale covering retains too much heat for them to be comfortable when the sun's out."

Rune frowned slightly, her eyes still skimming over the dead creature. Her gut twisted slightly as her gaze fell atop what was left of the creature's barbed stinger—despite being long-decayed, it was still larger than her head, its oily black color stripped away by days of uninterrupted exposure to the sun.

"We should keep going." Alix turned, and with Rune in tow, resumed the trek towards the plateau. Casting one last uneasy glance at the corpse, Rune set her eyes on the mountains ahead, tracing the skyline with her gaze as each step carried them closer to the reddish peaks.

"Have you ever seen a Sandcrawler? Alive?" A bit of Rune's nervousness seeped into her tone.

Alix started to shake her head, then stopped. "Once. From a distance. I've never actually encountered one directly, though."

This time, the odd, pinched feeling wasn't packed into the words, giving them a ring of truth. Rune fought the urge to smile as she made a mental note, proud of herself for the deduction. Falling into the old habit felt entirely natural, bringing with it a sense of calm despite the tense environment around her. Something deep in the back of her mind tugged at her consciousness, the veil weakening for only a moment.

With a start, she realized why she had so easily been able to detect Alix's lie.

There was someone she'd known before—someone who lied in the exact same way.

Rune trailed behind Alix, her pace unfaltering, but her mind wandered down a completely different path that she made up as she went. The inescapable feeling of familiarity followed her everywhere, serving as an infinite, unshakable reminder of the frustrating darkness she faced where her memories should have been.

I know someone, she repeated, trying to shake the memories free.

Someone who lies just like her.

Who?

The word was a silent plea, one directed at both nothing and everything. A message to herself, an idea that somehow *she* could reach deep inside her very core and cough up the memory.

She was tired of not understanding.

Tired of puzzles, of games her own mind played on her.

Tired of not knowing who she was.

Tired of having the pieces but being unable to see the true picture.

Ahead, Alix's pace slowed, and Rune shook her head rapidly, attempting to clear the anger that was beginning to brew in her stomach. They rounded the crest of a dune, and Rune nearly cried out in relief when her eyes found the unrealistically blue surface of a small, rippling pond. Trees with long, featherlike fronds and rough, tiled bark loomed over the pool, casting the only shade Rune had seen since that morning. The splash of color against the dull, redwashed landscape was welcome to her weary eyes, and her throat cried out for the clear, sweet water sheltered between the dunes.

The girls circled around to the edge of the pool, kneeling beneath the shade of the largest tree. Rune leaned forward, allowing her fingers to brush the water's surface and leaving small ripples anywhere her skin came into contact with the liquid. It wasn't cold by any means, but compared to the dry, scorching grains of sand that surrounded them, it felt like an arctic plunge.

Reaching down, she fumbled with the clasp of her water flask for a moment before submerging it in the pond. Beside her, Alix reached out, streams of water splitting off from the rest of the pool and hovering airily around her palm. Her skin glowed in the sunlight as she gently directed the streams towards her open flask, lowering them in with a half-smile.

Rune frowned, an idea suddenly hitting her. "Why didn't you just pull water out of the air and fill the flasks? Why stop here?"

Alix shrugged, flipping her flask closed. "I could...but usually, I try not to. The humidity here is absolutely terrible, meaning that the water in the air is usually mixed in with a bunch of dust and stuff." She flicked her wrist, materializing a few drops to showcase her point. Unlike the mostly translucent liquid of the oasis, the water in the air was tinted with a dusty haze that made it appear less than appealing. "Normally I just rely on the oases, but if I have to, I'll use my ability." She closed her fist quickly, letting the water dissolve into mist.

"Makes sense, I guess." Rune lifted her full flask to her lips, a warm feeling of contentment washing over her as the slightly sweet liquid flowed down her parched throat. She allowed herself to drink her fill, topping off the vessel before securing the cap and refastening it to her hip.

Alix rose, brushing the sand off of her clothing as she directed her gaze to the east. For a moment, she stood there, brow furrowed and eyes narrowed towards the horizon...until suddenly, her body went rigid, pointed ears perked. Rune's heart instantly doubled in pace, and she slowly rose to her feet.

"Alix...?"

A low, ground-shaking rumble answered before the girl could, throwing Rune off-balance. Alix turned to her, and for the first time, there was a flicker of pure fear deep within the girl's navy eyes. Only a single word left her lips, but it was the only one that Rune needed to hear.

"Run."

39
RUNE

Rune's heart thundered in her chest as she took off, unsure of exactly where she was headed. The rumbling intensified, and panic wormed its way into her gut, urging her on. A familiar rush of terror and adrenaline pumped through her veins, taking over her system and completely overwriting any prior fatigue she'd been feeling.

"Get to the cliffs!" Alix shouted from a few feet ahead, her words slightly slurred by the chaotic rush around them. "It can't follow us there!"

"*It!?*" Rune screamed over the noise. "What is *it!?*"

If Alix replied, Rune didn't hear her.

The sand directly behind them erupted, a thunderous roar splitting the air. Rune dared a glance backwards, instantly regretting it as the image of their pursuer was forever branded into her brain.

"It" was probably the most terrifying thing that Rune had ever seen.

Its body was long and limbless, giving it an appearance like a massive serpent. Like a serpent, it was covered with scales, but unlike the thin and fragile-looking material Rune was used to, each individual plate was the size of a small shield and looked practically impenetrable. Of course, two eyes didn't seem to be nearly enough for the desert monstrosity—so it had settled on four, jet black pairs instead. Rows of ridge-like "fins" ran along its back and sides, and to complete the nightmarish look, a massive, gaping mouth filled with rows of tiny, interlocking teeth was held open *very* wide as it slammed back into the sand.

"*ALIX!!* WHAT *IS* THAT?!"

Alix's reply was scattered, but there were two words that found their way to Rune's ears as her feet pounded across the plain, mentally engraving themselves alongside the image of the monstrosity that pursued them.

Dune worm.

It slipped in and out of the sand as it chased its prey, the combination of the ground rumbling and the creature's roars creating a discordant melody in Rune's ears. Ahead, Alix's pace continued to quicken with each stride, and Rune found herself struggling slightly to keep up.

Realms, she's quick.

The expression came out of nowhere, resurfacing in Rune's thoughts for a brief moment before burying itself back down. She shook her head in an attempt to clear her mind, forcing herself to focus on nothing but her pounding footsteps against the cracked ground. The sand dunes had become smaller and scarcer, slowly melting into a ground made of packed red earth.

Not stone...but getting closer.

Rune pushed her aching body as much as she could, her speed boosted by adrenaline and desperation. Each tremor in the earth, each guttural cry, each snarl from their pursuer—it sent a new thread of terror into her heart, winding together, creating a knot inside her stomach. She fished around in her mind, searching for some kind of logic to grasp for.

"*Alix*!" Rune screamed, forcing herself to be heard over the noise. She fought the urge to look back at the monster, not willing to risk even a few precious seconds. "There's no way we're outrunning it!"

Alix cast a quick glance over her shoulder, locking gazes with Rune for no longer than a brief moment. "Keep going! It can't tunnel through stone!"

Sure enough, as they neared the fractured plateaus in the distance, she noticed the creature's pace finally beginning to slow ever so slightly—but slightly was enough for them to pull farther ahead. Even so, it kept itself effortlessly in the race, and while it *was* losing ground, that ground certainly wasn't much. The threads of panic solidified completely, the fleeting realization she'd been desperately trying to avoid setting itself in stone inside Rune's mind.

It's too fast. We aren't going to make it.

Grains of red sand whipped into Rune's face, pelting her skin and making her eyes burn as if they were on fire. She raised one arm, attempting in vain to shield herself as the wind picked up around them, hindering their vision. The world dissolved around Rune, fading into a blurry mass of roars and dust.

Suddenly, a particularly powerful tremor erupted right beneath Rune, destabilizing her footing and causing her to stumble forward. The motion cost her greatly, she dared a peek over her shoulder, her chest tightening when she realized that the scale-covered worm had almost closed the gap between them entirely.

"RUNE!"

Alix's cry tore through the clamor that had become Rune's mind, flying straight like an arrow shot from a powerful bow. It landed right in the center of her thoughts, snapping her attention back to the task and sharpening her senses.

"YOU HAVE TO MOVE!"

Her mind didn't know what to do, but her body did, and Rune flung herself left as the creature reared up behind her, its unhinged jaws closing on the air where she had stood only moments before. She scrambled to her feet, using the brief moment of respite while the creature circled back around to take off running in a new direction.

It's at least two hundred feet long, if I had to guess—but massive creatures like that usually aren't very nimble. Combine that with the tougher soil, and it should take it a decent amount of time to pivot and chase me.

About a hundred feet away, Alix had unstrapped her bow from her back, standing tall with an arrow nocked and an unbelievably calm expression plastered across her regal features. She leaned into the shot, unflinching as the worm burst out of the ground and redirected its attention to her. It gathered speed with its approach, but she held the weapon perfectly steady, the only motion in her body being the rhythmic rising and falling of her shoulders with each breath.

You have to do something. The thought entered Rune's mind, but her body refused to move, knowing that there was simply nothing to be done. She was too far away, forced to do nothing but watch as the gap between the girl and the monster closed rapidly.

Alix, move!

The worm continued gaining, cracks forming in the ground as its head rose from the surface and its body trailed along beneath.

Alix...

Rune held her breath as the creature began to unhinge its jaw, wishing she could tear her eyes away. It reared back, its face only a few feet away from Alix's arrow.

With a cold smile, Alix let it fly.

Time seemed to slow as the arrow hurtled into the air, the bowstring snapping backwards into Alix's arm guard with a *twang*. Before the creature could show so much as a single row of teeth, the head of the arrow embedded itself deep into one of the creature's eyes with a sickening squelch, digging so deep that the fletching nearly disappeared.

The worm recoiled, letting out a strangled roar that sent chills rippling down Rune's spine. Alix gave it no time to recover from the blow, and in only seconds, she had nocked a second arrow, releasing it straight into one of the seven remaining eyes.

Screeching, the monstrosity reared back, giving Alix the opportunity to rush towards Rune's position. The quaking in the ground intensified as the creature slammed its head down, writhing on the ground and trying to knock the arrows free.

"We have to move," Alix hissed, shooting Rune a glance.

Don't need to tell me twice.

They took off running, the ground trembling under their feet like it had a mind of its own. Rune struggled to maintain her balance, gritting her teeth and pressing forward against the sharp particles of dust whipping up around them. Sweat streamed down her face, her lungs heaved, her muscles screamed, and her throat cried out for water—but adrenaline somehow kept her going, pushing her on far past the point when her body should have fallen still.

Her vision began to go blurry, her chest burning as the breath was slowly drained from her body. The sun sapped everything she had, heat gripping her with an iron fist and crushing her within its grasp.

Keep going.

Keep going.

Keep going.

She gritted her teeth. *Keep going, idiot, or you're going to die again.*

The worm broke out of the cracked soil once more, and something inside of Rune stirred, a strange and distant energy pulling at her mind. Time slowed to a crawl, the unrecognizable power awaking in her gut and pushing upwards, responding to a call she didn't even realize she'd sent out.

The sun was still beating down—her muscles were still screaming for relief—her lungs were still devoid of oxygen—but none of that seemed to matter anymore, an odd clarity passing over her. A jolt rippled down her spine, heightening her dulled senses and replenishing her strength when she needed it most.

She dared a glance over her shoulder at Alix, who was just a few steps behind. Alix, too, had begun to grow fatigued, but the girl's body was set firmly, her pace unwavering despite the agony in her eyes.

Suddenly, the ground below them heaved again, causing a

positively ridiculous idea to spark inside Rune's mind. Her pace slowed, and she turned, catching Alix's attention.

"Can we kill it?"

Alix just stared. "Are you insane?" They dodged another attack, the surety in Rune's gaze only increasing.

We can. We have to.

A plan took root in her mind as she nodded, watching the ground buckle around them. It was crazy, she knew that—but a crazy idea sounded much more appealing than waiting for the creature to land a strike.

I need to draw it to the surface again.

Beside her, Alix's hand was already moving to her quiver, her eyes tracing the mound of soil that circled around them. She cast Rune a quick sidelong glance as she raised her bow, but Rune wasn't looking, crouching down and placing her hand on the hilt of her dagger.

Come and get me.

The shifting in the ground lessened as the creature pivoted its head to leap out again, and Rune took the chance, charging towards the lump of soil before her brain could talk her out of it. With a flying leap, she managed to get herself above it just as the worm surfaced. Her feet found the gritty scales of its head, and she stumbled on impact, barely managing to catch herself on a nearby fin.

The creature bucked instantly, intent on dislodging its uninvited rider. Below, Alix fired a shot, the arrow finding a small break between the scales of the creature's neck and causing it to thrash even harder. Rune clung to the creature's head for dear life, panicking as it prepared to reenter the ground.

"Keep shooting it!" she shouted, heart thundering in her ears. "It has to stay up!"

Alix's reply was lost to the wind, but the arrows kept coming, each shot enraging the worm even more. Rune's arms began to ache from the strain of holding on, but she kept climbing towards the crown of its head, the thought of losing her memories again fueling her aching body.

Death may not be the end here...but there are worse fates than losing my life.

I will not let my team down again.

Somehow, Rune managed to free her left hand as she neared her target, mounting the top of the creature's head and reaching for her dagger. Her fingers probed across the thick layers of scales, searching desperately for the right place to strike.

I've only got one shot.

Suddenly, an arrow landed uncomfortably close to where Rune was perched, sticking fast in a patch of tender skin that barely peeked out from between the scales. The creature reared, all thoughts of tunneling down apparently lost from its mind— if it had one.

There's my chance.

Her fingers found the skin, and she raised her dagger, hoping beyond hope that the last scraps of strength she had left would be enough.

With all the power she could muster, she brought the weapon down hard, embedding the blade deep into the monster's head.

An agonizing screech sounded as it buckled beneath the strike, dislodging Rune from its back. She tucked in midair, landing on her feet and rolling out of the fall to distribute the impact and hopefully avoid injury. The ground shook as the worm's body hit it, cobalt blood dripping from its wounds as the life slipped from its eyes.

Alix moved to her side, grinning despite the obvious exhaustion in her features. "I suppose that's one way to handle the situation."

Rune cracked a smile, casting a glance over her shoulder at the monster's body. "I...I don't think I'm getting that dagger back."

Alix chuckled and reached down, unclipping one of the four blades attached to her belt. "Take this one. And try not to lose it, please."

Rune offered her a nod of thanks. "I'll try my best."

40

REI

A sigh escaped Rei's lips as her eyelids fluttered open, the achingly familiar world disappearing from her mind.

I dreamed of home. Again.

She swallowed hard, tears threatening to spill over. It had been just over a month since she'd last seen Ember, Cedar, and her friends back in Akaidia—but it felt like years. *I miss them. I really miss them.*

With a sigh, she forced herself to sit up, resting her back against the wall. Thankfully, Kal's magic healing abilities had done their job perfectly—the stabbing pains had been replaced by nothing but a dull, aching stiffness. Even so, many of the wounds had ended up scarring, leaving behind permanent reminders of an experience she could never erase.

Her eyes found her hand, and she curled her fingers inward, trying to remember what it was like to stroke Ember's scales or brush her fingers through Cedar's fur. A cry bubbled up in her throat, her chest tightening.

They're safe. I'm keeping them safe by being here, by fighting to keep these evils away from Akaidia's borders.

I will go home someday.

I will.

A knock on the door broke her train of thought, and she turned, a smile creeping across her lips as her gaze found Loric's. His expression was neutral, but his eyes gleamed, the tiny sign of affection enough to warm her heart.

"Sleep well?"

She nodded. "What time is it?"

"Almost midday."

"I slept *that* long?"

Loric cracked a half smile. "You needed it." His gaze wandered to her nightstand. "Do you think you're up to walking?"

Rei thought for a moment before nodding. "I should be. I'd like to know where I'm going before I just waltz out of here in my pajamas, though."

Loric barked a laugh. "I left an outfit by your bed—one of your favorites from home. You can get changed, then come meet me outside." Without another word, he closed the door.

Okay. Grunting, she rolled over, grabbing the pile of folded fabric off her nightstand. A curtain was set up to wrap all the way around her bed, and she pulled it shut, grateful for the privacy. Loric was right, the outfit was one of her favorites—a cropped lavender compression top, a complex leather belt to store a variety of materials and weapons, fingerless gloves, baggy pants made of lightweight fabric, and a pair of training sandals. *He remembers. He remembers what I like.*

Satisfied with the fit, she quickly pulled up the covers of her bed, making her way over to the door and tugging it open. Loric offered her a nod, turning and heading down the hallway without so much as a word. Rei hurried to keep up, casting a quick glance around at the polished marble flooring and tiled stone walls.

"Where are we going?"

"To meet some people," he replied briefly, his pace not slowing once.

How helpful. "Will Sumi be there?"

"Yes."

They rounded a corner, emerging into a large, square room with a rather sizable table in the center. Five of the sixteen seats were filled, four of them with people Rei didn't know. *Sumi...a blonde woman...a man, he looks pretty young...Wren, the girl who was with Sumi and Loric yesterday...and a boy who looks a lot like her.*

Sumi smiled as they came in, her expression being the only warm one of the group. "I'm glad you're feeling better, Rei."

"Me too." Rei winced, hoping she didn't sound too hostile. The blonde woman was eyeing her strangely, and she found herself making a face in return.

"Why don't we begin with introductions," Sumi tried, glancing at the group. She had a grandmotherly air to her, the kind that softened the tension in the room as she spoke. "Some of you know Loric, and this is his student, Rei. This is Commander Arla—one of my fellow leaders—Flyn, our head spy, and Wren and Wylder, two of our younger operatives."

Rei nodded politely, glancing around at the table. "How many of you are there? Total?"

"We number at just over two hundred," Flyn responded, his

voice smooth and emotionless. He was young—only about five or six years older than Rei, if she had to guess—but his vocal control was absolutely flawless. His light brown hair was pulled back into a neat man bun, and a thin beard framed his jawline. Every inch of him appeared guarded and professional, from the way he sat to the calm glint in his brown eyes. *No wonder he's head spy.*

Arla cocked her head at Rei, her cerulean eyes seeming to dig into Rei's very being. "Kal's told me of the injuries you suffered, and the way you seemed to handle things. You're quite resilient for a fifteen-year-old."

"Sixteen," Rei corrected. "And thank you."

"Her combat abilities are also rather exceptional," Loric added. Rei fought the urge to stare at him—he'd never praised her so blatantly. Never.

Arla cracked a smile. "I'd love to see for myself sometime."

"Arla is our head of combat," Sumi explained, glancing from Rei to the blonde commander. "While you will still be training with Loric, she will most likely be overseeing many of your lessons."

Rei barely managed to stop herself from frowning, examining the woman more thoroughly. Based on her narrow frame, fragile features, and flawlessly styled hair, she had to admit, "head of combat" was not the title Rei was expecting. However, there was a subtle glint in her eye that made Rei think twice about her assumption—the type of look that implied she was not one to be judged by appearance alone.

I think I'm going to like her.

Navy streaks intermingled with strands of the woman's blonde hair, which, paired with her pointed ears and blue eyes, made Rei assume that she was aquilian—a sub-elven race that thrived in the water. *Like Kal.*

"I look forward to it."

Arla met her gaze, and Rei spent a solid ten seconds trying to decide if she was smiling at her or judging her. *Yep. Definitely going to like her.*

"I'm sure that this is a big adjustment for you, Rei," Sumi told her, holding her gaze gently. "I want you to know that we are *all* here to help you. You may be the Blade's wielder, but that does not mean you are the sole proprietor in the fight against the Eidolon's forces."

Rei nodded slowly, swallowing a stubborn lump in her throat. *Rei, focus.* "Thank you." *Ew, why is my voice so shaky?*

The gnome smiled, rising to her feet. "No—thank *you*. It is an honor to welcome someone with courage like yours to the Onyx." She shuffled around, not giving Rei a chance to respond. "Now—as much as I'd like to let you get to know one another a bit better, I'm afraid that we need to leave for the Oasis soon or we'll be pushing up against curfew. Rei, your things are already at the base—Loric sent them with another of our operatives this morning. You've rifted before, I assume?"

Rei felt her cheeks grow warm. "Yes—I think so."

"Why wouldn't she have?" The boy who looked like Wren —Wylder—spoke up, cocking his head at her.

"Rei isn't...from here. I'll let her tell you later...to be completely honest, I'd love to hear the story from her own lips myself."

Loric must have told her. Rei nodded again, glancing at her mentor.

Wylder's gaze lingered on her for a long moment before he

turned back to Sumi, watching as she pulled a pair of stones out of her pocket. The stones were similar to the one she'd seen Loric use, back when he'd taken her to the Apeiron for the first time. *Alistones, he called them.*

"Rifting is a method of travel where you pass through the Apeiron as a way to expedite your journey," Loric explained softly, leaning closer so he could whisper in her ear. "Since the laws of time and distance don't apply to the Apeiron, people will use portals called rifts to enter it for a brief period of time, then exit in an entirely different location. It is the only way to cross between realms, and it's also commonly used to span great distances in only a matter of seconds."

Rei couldn't help but grin. *That is the coolest thing I've ever heard.* "How do you know where to exit, though?"

Loric smiled. "With those." He gestured to a small, circular silver disc that Wren was holding. The disc had another, smaller golden circle set into the center, and indented designs covered the entire coin. "It's called an annex chip. Each one is coded to a particular annex—or landing place—and by throwing one into a rift, you link that rift to the annex you want to arrive at."

"How does that even work?"

Loric smirked, crossing his arms. "Magic."

"Are you sure we want to rift to *this* annex, though?" Wren's voice was silvery, a reflection of her youthful features. *She can't be any older than thirteen, surely.* "The gateway is guarded pretty heavily to restrict outbound traffic—how do we know they haven't done the same to the annex?"

Sumi thought for a moment, her features engulfed in perfect calm. "We don't. But that's the only public annex in the city, and the only other nearby locations are outside the gates. We certainly couldn't get through those, not with Rei's sword."

Wren glanced towards Rei, the blood suddenly draining from her face. "What about her eyes?"

Sumi turned, sighing as her gaze locked with Rei's. "I forgot about that. We can't pass her off as a human or a normal jurori, the kedori wouldn't be known, faerin certainly wouldn't work, and her ears would stop her from posing as any of the other species..." she trailed off, murmuring to herself.

Rei made a face. "What do my eyes have to do with this?"

"They're purple. All normal jurori have dark eyes—and I've never seen a human with such a vivid eye color before. You would instantly be flagged down, especially since purple is a color linked rather heavily to phantom magic."

"She could borrow my cloak." All eyes turned towards Kal, who was now standing in the doorway. "If she keeps the hood up, she'd probably be fine."

Rei thanked the girl as she slipped off the long, navy cloth that decorated her shoulders, handing it over.

"We'll cover for you, don't worry." Kal smiled as Arla stepped closer, placing a hand on the girl's shoulder and squeezing gently.

"We should probably get going." Arla glanced down, smiling at Kal. *They must be related somehow.* "Can't risk being on the streets during evening patrols."

Patrols?

Sumi nodded, placing the two stones she'd been holding on the ground side-by-side. Both were shaped with four points, and constructed with opposing color schemes. One was black, veined with gold, and the other was white, shot through with streaks of silver. In the center of both was a diamond, energy swirling in the gems' milky depths.

Rei took a step back, watching intently as Sumi brushed the diamonds together. Within an instant, both stones began to glow, releasing threads of energy—arcana and glyph—that wound together in the air before them. The rift took shape, but the colors were slightly faded, appearing like faint mist instead of the vivid composition Rei remembered from her time with Loric. Before she could comment, however, Wren stepped forward, tossing the annex chip into the mist and watching as the threads swallowed it completely.

Upon contact with the disc, the portal seemed to erupt with life, its colors solidifying and forming a writhing mass of green and gray tones. Sumi reached out her hand, lightly brushing the threads. "Wren and I will go last to make sure that everyone gets through safely. It *is* a temp gate, so I want everyone with a partner—" her gaze traveled to Rei— "regardless of your experience rifting. Wait on the other side until we're all through."

Rei swallowed hard, her eyes following Kal and Arla as they disappeared through the portal first. Wylder and Flyn trailed behind, and Loric stepped up beside Rei, his lips curling into a reassuring smile as he offered her his arm. She placed her arm atop his after a moment's hesitation, taking a deep breath to steady her nerves. *You're with Loric. Loric won't let anything happen to you.*

Stomach churning, she closed her eyes tightly, allowing herself to be led forward through and into the tangle of energy.

41
REI

This time, she was able to better brace herself for the odd sensations that pummeled her, her body being tugged in all directions yet somehow going in none at all. Instead of aimless floating, however, it felt like she had a destination, the energies around her knitting themselves together to pull her into a current that led wherever they wanted to go. Loric kept a firm grip on her hand, keeping her soundly within the funnel of energy as a bright, blinding light began to consume her vision.

With a gasp and a final, heaving tug, Rei was ejected from the rift to find herself stumbling across a large, circular platform.

Loric grabbed her shoulders before she could trip, her stomach churning at the sudden lack of motion. She blinked a few times to clear the haze from her eyes, head spinning. Somehow, she managed to thank her mentor as he gently led her down a short flight of steps that bordered the platform, taking long, slow breaths to regain her balance.

"It gets easier, don't worry. The first time's always a bit rough."

Rei allowed herself to believe him as they joined with the rest of their group, and she turned around, her eyes tracing the dome-shaped room they were in.

The platform they'd arrived on—the annex—was made of an unfamiliar, translucent stone, and swirls of energy drifting beneath it created the illusion of a seemingly endless void of fog. Above the platform hung a massive crystal orb, filled with the same mist.

"Pretty interesting place, isn't it?" Flyn stepped up beside Rei, gesturing at the marbled walls. "Annexes hold a tremendous amount of aligned energy, making them easy to lock onto from inside the Apeiron."

Before she could comment, the air around them suddenly went cold, her hair standing straight up as a low hum began buzzing around the area. Her eyes stayed locked on the center of the platform where the air had begun to thicken, distorting the colors around it and emitting a faint, pulsing light.

Suddenly, the hazy pillar shattered, fragments of light erupting from where two figures now stood. Wren and Sumi moved to join the rest of the group, entirely unfazed by the threads of aligned energy that lingered around them. Rei found that she was unable to do anything but stare, mentally begging her racing heart to calm down.

People appearing out of thin air—hurling myself into an alternate dimension and traveling across space and time in mere seconds—I don't think I'll ever get used to this.

Sumi offered Rei a smile as she passed, leading the group down a wide hallway. Right before they reached the exit—a pair of stained glass doors joined together with obsidian trims—a guard stepped out from an alcove in the wall, examining them with a weary eye. He reached for the bulging notebook at his side, turning to one of the last pages and brandishing a thin, pointed rod.

It's a writing tool—an enchanted one. She couldn't help but grin. *So cool.*

"State your information." His tone was flat, consumed with boredom.

Sumi stared him down, a slight smile on her lips. "Eight from Ekal, Akareldia, returning home. Six residents and two guests."

The guard made a few notes on his paper, glancing up once to count the group. His gaze lingered on Rei the longest, and she resisted the urge to pull her hood down further, pleading that he wouldn't notice her eyes.

If he did, he didn't comment.

The guard reached into his pocket, pulling out a palm-size slab of obsidian with a milky crystal set into the center. "Present identification—residents first."

Rei felt the blood drain from her face, but Loric squeezed her shoulder gently, leaning in to whisper something in her ear. "When it's your turn, place your finger on the gem and channel magic into it like you do when casting a rune."

Before she could ask for an explanation, the guard turned his attention to her, and she found herself moving forward and pressing her fingertip lightly into the crystal.

The moment she released the magic, she felt the gem buzz ever so slightly beneath her fingertip, flashing black as she stepped away. The guard nodded to her, jotting something down in his book.

"Alright. Remember, a regularly scheduled curfew is in effect today, meaning that all citizens discovered outside an hour past sundown will be brought in for temporary containment and questioning. Enjoy your day."

Geez. I may have never been to a real city before, but I don't think there are supposed to be rules like that.

He stepped aside, watching them with an apathetic expression as he pressed his palm to a panel on the wall. The doors slid apart, and Sumi led them through, emerging into the open streets of the city.

The first impression Rei had of the Oasis was the sheer chaos that radiated from each sun-scorched brick.

Buildings piled on top of buildings, creating a seemingly endless maze of civilization. Splashes of color from vibrant fabrics and faded tent covers filled the crowded streets, and the air was a clamor of vendors advertising their wares. A wide concoction of smells drifted through Rei's nostrils, filling her nose with scents of fresh baked bread, lavish spices, and the musty odors of people. She stood there, overwhelmed by the sudden mass of information pouring through her from every sense her body possessed.

"Is every city this...big?" She leaned in towards Loric, taking comfort in the shadow of his bulky frame. "You could fit every person in Akaidia in here."

He chuckled. "The Oasis is one of the more sizable civilizations, certainly...but it's not the largest."

I can't believe how many people there are.

Her gaze drifted upward, and she instantly did a double take, everything else forgotten.

"Why—why is the sun *blue*?"

Instead of the faintly yellow orb she was used to, the sun she saw now was a fiery ball of cobalt rays, the already stifling air around her seeming to increase in temperature the longer she looked at it.

Loric's lips curled into an amused smile. "Since every realm exists in a very different location across the universe—some even in an entirely different time period—the natural environments can differ rather extremely. The sky you know in Akareldia is not the same as the one you see here."

Rei blinked at the bizarre sun one last time before she lowered her gaze, red creeping across her cheeks. "Sorry. I probably sound like an idiot."

Sumi, who had been walking beside them, shook her head immediately. "You simply don't know. A lack of education does not equal a lack of intelligence. Come—we have a ways to go."

Rei followed the gnome silently, careful to stay in the center of their group and keep her hood up despite the beads of sweat forming on her face. She was extremely grateful for the cloak's thin, moisture wicking fabric—a material Kal had mentioned to be designed for the intense climate of the city.

And here I thought the Darklands was hot.

They wound through street after street, pushing their way through endless crowds of people and climbing three flights of stairs only to descend four more. The whole place was nothing more than a maze, and with each turn, Rei found a new respect for Sumi blossoming in her chest. The fact that anyone could remember how to find their way around in a place like this was simply absurd to her village-raised mind.

As they moved, she struck up conversation with the Onyx members, asking countless questions about the realms and their culture. According to Flyn, the obsidian panel the guard had used at the annex was called an Alignment Identification Device, or AID. AIDs were used universally to identify the magic of a particular individual, serving as a way to ensure that a person was who they claimed to be.

"What did Sumi mean earlier? When she said you weren't from here?"

Rei jumped—she hadn't noticed Wren come up beside her. The girl cocked her head curiously, her ash brown hair braided into neat cornrows that fell around her pointed ears. Between her youthful complexion, freckled features, and big eyes, Wren wasn't exactly the most intimidating figure—but the fact that she was a member of an underground rebellion was enough to make Rei think twice about her true strength.

"I—it's a really long story."

Wren shrugged. "Tell it. I don't mind." Rei noticed a few of the other Onyx members around them glancing over in her direction, their interest obviously piqued.

Guess it couldn't hurt. "You ever heard of the kedori?"

"In stories. But...even if they did exist, they went extinct, like, two thousand years ago." Wylder was the one who spoke, sticking close to his sister's side. His dirty blonde hair was styled loosely, left in a mass of curls on the top of his head. "Didn't they?"

"That's what you were told." Rei felt a smile creep across her features at the expression shifts around her, realization instantly dawning on their faces. "Let me tell you what *really* happened."

For the first time since she'd first arrived in the realms, *she* was the one with the information, telling people about something they'd never heard of before. It felt really good—at last, something she understood, that she didn't have to ask questions about or look like a fool for not knowing. Flyn cocked his head at her as she explained the way each bonded creature had an ability, one that was brought out when united with their owner.

"So the legends are true...bond magic does exist." His tone held a note of innate curiosity, and even a bit of a challenge, as though he were questioning the truth of Rei's words.

She didn't flinch. "If that's what you call it. I grew up thinking it was a normal trait in a human...though now I know that we weren't even human at all."

He frowned. "Almost two millennia is a very long time to live being entirely oblivious to the world beyond your borders."

"I don't know exactly *why* we never realized, or how no one ever so much as glanced at the Horizon's Teeth. It might have been a part of the initial magic, stripping us of any curiosity that may have ruined the facade the elves created. All I know is that I'm here now...and that I don't intend to let the rest of my people live a lie any longer."

Flyn's lips curled into a thin smile. "You're an honorable girl, Rei. I admire that."

Ahead, Sumi stopped, halting the group in front of a slightly run-down building. It stood four stories tall, and a sign over the door read '*The Smokeflower Inn.*'

"We're here."

THIS PLACE IS SO COOL.

The innkeeper had instantly recognized Sumi, handing her a room key without any further questioning. Room 108—the room the key belonged to—was actually the location of a hidden ladder, one that led down to a series of passages beneath the city.

This is just like the books, the ones that I used to read back in Wolf Clan about corrupted cities and brave rebellions living beneath them. Those stories…I'm living them now.

Rei trailed behind Sumi as she led them into a massive room, with a circular table in the center taking up at least a quarter of the floor space. Overhead, a massive silver dome decorated the ceiling, run through with veins of onyx. The symbolism forced a smile onto Rei's lips.

Around them, the rest of the group spread out—Arla and Kal headed down a hallway on their left, Wren and Wylder slipped out a door to their right, and when Rei glanced around, she realized that Flyn had disappeared altogether. Even Loric left, following behind the twins and offering a reassuring nod to Rei.

Rei, however, couldn't tear her eyes away from the central table.

She moved over to it, circling it a few times. A thin coating of mist covered the smooth surface, colored fog piling on top of itself to form a three-dimensional image that looked startlingly realistic. Frowning, she leaned closer, examining the image.

The fog had formed into the shape of a circle—sectioned

off into four quadrants with different colored lines separating each one. In the center was a much smaller, white circle, bordered equally by each of the four sections. The one in the upper left was green, the one to its right blue, the one below blue was yellow, and the one to yellow's left was red. The green section was filled with trees, and had a few markings here and there in a language Rei couldn't read. The blue one had mountains, the yellow one was populated by thick, jungle-looking foliage, and the red was just a long stretch of land with a range of mesas in the east.

"Sumi—what is this?"

The gnome glanced up, moving over to Rei's side and gently tracing a finger over the fog's surface. "This visual was included in an intercepted message from a few weeks ago. It contained a variety of blueprints for something that had been referred to as a sort of arena, so we held onto them in case that matter became more important. One of our commanding members—Marko, who is an expert in outside connections— was intrigued, and has been investigating it. So far, however, I don't believe he's had much luck."

"On the contrary—" a new voice proclaimed, and Rei turned as a tall, middle aged man stepped through the door. "One of my scouts *just* returned to me with a new lead regarding that very topic."

Sumi smiled. "Do enlighten us, then."

The man returned her smile, approaching the table and placing his hand right in the center of the mist. "The arena isn't just a plan—it's currently active," he began, his dark eyes skimming over the map. "There are sixty-four 'contestants' inside, and as far as we know, none of them have any desire to be there.

We've been unable to locate the alleged mastermind behind this operation, but we *have* learned what he or she calls it.

"What you see before you is a strange, horrifying project that traps innocent people and forces them to fight for an unknown purpose. We would call it cruelty—but its creators refer to it as the Compass."

42
RUNE

A breath of crisp, slightly singed air filtered through Rune's nostrils as she inhaled deeply, allowing her lungs to swell with the night breeze. Her eyes wandered to the sky, where the dull notes of dusk were beginning to consume the vibrant colors the sunset had painted across the horizon.

She and Alix had chosen a sheltered location beneath a rocky outcropping to spend the night, building a fire and cooking a rabbit that Alix had found and killed. Glancing over at her companion, Rune felt a strange sense of deja vu wash over her, the feeling carried into her mind alongside memories from the night before. Alix had worn that exact same expression earlier—a forced peace, a desire for calm yet an unwillingness to release her guard.

Words slipped onto Rune's tongue, but she held them back, unsure if she wanted to let them free. Her thoughts warred about whether or not to confront Alix about her lies, and since they seemed so irrelevant, a large part of her hesitated at the idea

—but a small, meager voice in the back of her mind urged her to find out the truth.

"There's something I should probably tell you." Alix's voice was soft, laced with hesitation.

Rune glanced up instantly, her thoughts silenced. "There... is?"

Alix nodded, her eyes finding the graying sky. "Yes. A story."

A frown crept across Rune's features. "Does it have anything to do with why you're always so suspicious of me? *And* why you feel the need to lie about things that don't even matter?"

Alix winced. "It does." She tilted her head, meeting Rune's gaze for a moment. "Sorry, I—I didn't realize that you—I'm usually a pretty good liar." It was the first time since they'd met that she let a bit of raw emotion creep into her tone, masked by a layer of uncertainty.

She's really uncomfortable. "I have a thing for reading people, I guess."

Alix returned her attention to the sky, laying back and allowing her head to rest against the boulder behind her. "I'm sorry if I've been so reserved. I *want* to trust you, I really do. But I have trouble with...people. Always have, I guess, even if I don't remember it—and since I got switched, it's only gotten worse."

Rune's brow furrowed. "Switched? What do you mean by switched?"

"Switched teams. I wasn't originally purple—my first team was yellow. They—" she took a deep breath, closing her eyes for a second longer than a blink. "They killed me. Normally, people don't kill their own teammate—but if you do, that teammate gets removed from the arena altogether, and is switched with whoever is next to die. Since purple didn't have a complete team at the time, they simply exchanged me with a new capture, sending me down to compete with a group that might actually think I was worth working with."

Rune's head swirled with information. *Kill your own teammate. Switch with someone new. What kind of people would do that?* Her hands clenched into fists. A thousand different questions bubbled up in her mind, toppling over one another in a race to be voiced. One question, however, stuck out much more boldly than the others, slowly consuming her headspace. "How do you remember?"

Alix hesitated. "Because...I tricked it. I tricked the reset."

Rune blinked at her. "The...reset?"

Alix nodded. "The creators of this place—they're the reason our memories are gone, the reason we can come back from death itself, and the reason we have all these powers." She opened her palm, allowing a dusty stream of water to trickle across her skin. "It's all a lie, Rune. Every part of it. They stop us from remembering so that *they* can stay in control, so they can make us believe that we're all the same. You and I—we're clearly different. Well, we should be."

She gestured to her ears, which were pointed—and then to Rune's round ones. Her eyes also trailed to Rune's wrists, where bracelet-shaped birthmarks were branded onto her skin —but Alix's own were noticeably bare.

"We are different," she repeated. "At least, we were, in the world beyond this place. But here—we're the same. Stripped of any power we once had. Stripped of our past. Stripped of everything that makes us who we are. Forced into a place of blood, betrayal, and endless striving to complete a task that very well might not be possible."

Rune frowned. "You don't think there's a way out."

"I mean, of course I *hope* there is—but I can't be sure. I—I met him. The creator. I don't have many memories from the time I spent outside, but I do remember a brief part from the switch, where I was being kept in a building that I think may have been underground. This man came into my cell—he had a mask on, and everything was blurry, but I don't think I'll ever be able to forget what he said.

"'*Where does this one come from again?*'" She paused, obvious resentment for the masked man creeping across her features. "He said it like I was nothing more than an object. Another subject of his little test, my worth reduced to a number on some page." Her fingers curled into fists. "And the reply—I remember that too. The only fragment of my past—of my life before this *wretched* place—that I have. Someone was beside me, and even though I couldn't see her, I will never forget her voice. '*Atiula,*' she told him. '*One of the few aquili we could get our hands on.*'"

Rune clenched her teeth. *These people are monsters—real monsters.* "An aquili? That's what they called you?"

"And Atiula...that's where I'm from." She sat up, gazing into the amber flames.

"So you remember everything? From before your reset?"

Alix nodded. "To be completely honest with you—that's why I gave you a chance in the first place. It wasn't because we were on the same team, though that did help a little—it was because you remembered. You remembered what happened to you. In that moment, I had wondered if you were like me—if you had found a way to trick the reset." She tilted her head, examining Rune. "But you didn't, did you. You found a way to keep your memories—yet you have no recollection of the reset process itself."

Rune hesitated. *Should I mention the hydra?* "Nothing about what you're describing sounds familiar to me, anyway. I have no idea how it happened, but it's like a veil was created during the reset—just like the one that guards my memories, but weaker somehow. When I first awoke, I didn't have my memories—but I found a way to break through that veil. I've even been using the same techniques to make some progress on the main one...but I haven't had a whole lot of luck so far."

Alix raised an eyebrow. "You mentioned the veil before. What is it?"

Rune frowned. "You don't feel it? It's like a wall in my mind, but the one that hid my memories from the reset was really thin, and it didn't take a whole lot to bring it down. The main one—I can feel my memories on the other side, but I can't reach them, if that makes sense. Rarely, I've had one slip through, but without the context, it's usually pretty unhelpful. When I'm asleep, though..." she trailed off, but Alix's expression urged her to keep going.

"Sometimes, when I dream, it's almost like a few of my memories have returned...showing up in my sleep, reminding me of a past that I'm not totally sure I ever lived." She wrapped her arms around herself, hating how hopeless the words sounded.

Alix glanced down at her hands. "What you're saying makes sense...but I've never experienced anything like that before. I can't even feel them there." A strange emotion filled her eyes as she looked up, meeting Rune's gaze. "They *are* there, though? Those memories—they aren't all the way gone?"

Rune felt a warm smile creeping across her lips, a bit of the new hope Alix was experiencing finding its way into her heart, too. "They're still there. And we will get them back."

Alix thought for a moment. "I suppose we'll just have to find a way out of here, then."

Rune tilted her head. "I thought you said you didn't believe there was an escape?"

Alix shrugged. "I don't. But I'm choosing to hope that there is. I'm *also* choosing to trust you." She raised her gaze, the sheer amount of sincerity in her eyes filling Rune with no doubt that those words did not leave her lips often. "And...I'm going to do my best to let you trust me."

Rune's smile widened. "I do trust you—and I definitely don't believe in betraying someone's trust in me."

Alix nodded slowly, a mirror of Rune's smile slowly but surely consuming her features as well. Determination sparked in Rune's stomach, refueling the dying flicker of hope that had somehow survived through the ordeals she'd experienced over the past few days.

"We're going to find a way out," Rune assured her, just as much for her own benefit as for Alix's. "We will escape this place—whether that escape be through an existing exit or one we have to create ourselves."

Shadows danced behind her eyelids as she slept, filling her mind with a sea of familiar images. The memories swept past her before she could look at them, however, caught up in a rapid of chaotic sensations. There were so many emotions—they wrapped around her tightly, binding her, strangling her as she resisted their hold.

Fury.

Terror.

Regret.

Joy.

And—the worst of them all, lingering beneath everything like a hunter waiting to leap upon its prey—a dull, aching numbness, the knowledge that the darkness she'd been battling for so long had finally claimed its victory. It was a darkness that had been buried beneath a veil of shadows, hiding away in her mind, but now, it had broken free, stretching its wings and preparing to return to battle.

No.

You can't do this.

But I can.

The thought was nothing more than a whisper, but it was a dangerous one, creeping across her senses and taking a chokehold on her mind. It was her voice—but not her voice—that spoke, the pain lingering deep within the phantom Rune's tone sickeningly familiar to her.

You're not in control here. You're not.

Are you sure?

Back then—in those memories—that may have been your life. But this is mine.

Ours.

No. It's mine. You have no power over me.

A laugh, then silence, a cold, creeping sensation settling over her.

You can't do this without me.

In that instant, Rune felt her mental voice merge with the other girl's, combining into one, confusing tone.

*We are **one**.*

A scream burst forth from her lips—whether it was real or not, she couldn't quite tell—and she wrestled against the darkness, watching as it slithered back behind the veil. The realization it left behind was not shaken as easily, however, lingering in Rune's mind as she drifted off into an even deeper sleep.

That veil—it keeps me from my memories, yes.

But it also keeps me from a life that I'm not sure I want to go back to.

43

RUNE

Despite the fact that the sun had barely emerged from the horizon, the air around them was still heating up at a terrifying speed, beads of sweat beginning to form on Rune's brow. Her feet scuffed against the ground, fingers trailing along the rough grains of the sandstone walls that bordered them on either side. Up ahead, Alix's eyes flickered quickly across the landscape, and she kept slowing down, muttering things under her breath. Rune let her be, mapping out the mesas as they traveled to pass the time.

Suddenly, the girl's pace faltered, and Rune stepped up beside her with concern decorating her features.

"Something wrong?"

Alix shook her head. "It's just—strange. I could have sworn there were only two passages here." She gestured to the three breaks in the rock ahead of them, each one heading in a completely opposite direction. The mesas had started off with wide, obvious passages, but as they got about an hour into their travel, the walkways had become much narrower and more mazelike.

A frown crossed Rune's lips. "Do you know which way?"

Alix took a hesitant step towards the left passage, examining it closely. "Roughly. We need to head east—and preferably, a bit north, since there's a wide open plain near the southern border that's usually camped by a bunch of bloodthirsty vacillates."

The last word slipped in one of Rune's ears and out the other, confusing her mind but not her gut. She debated questioning it, but was glad she didn't, fighting the urge to chuckle as the meaning returned to her. *An insult. Not a very nice one, either.*

She glanced back and forth between the three directions, going over possible routes in her mind. It didn't help much—since she'd never been in the area before—but it did calm her down a bit, allowing her to concentrate.

"I mean—technically, any of them could lead anywhere," Rune speculated aloud. An idea slipped into her mind as her eyes traced the cliff that towered above them. *I wish Ryder were here, with his earth abilities. Or Ivory, with his air.*

Alix seemed to be thinking along similar lines, since she glanced over at Rune and examined her closely. "Remind me again what your element is?"

"Light. Not super helpful."

Alix sighed. "Mine's not too useful either. We'll probably just have to guess." They both winced at the thought.

Rune glanced around, a nagging tug in the back of her mind catching her attention as her gaze found the path on the far right. Each time she blinked, a faint flash seemed to bore into her skull, and the more she focused on it, the brighter it became.

She hesitated, an idea beginning to form in her mind. *Maybe I was wrong about the light. Maybe it could help.*

She allowed her eyes to fall closed, raising her hand tentatively. Her focus shifted to the hum in the back of her mind, the one that she felt whenever she used her ability, and took a deep breath as waves of warmth rippled across her skin. Slowly, the darkness beyond her eyelids began to brighten, shifting into a strange, black and white map that spanned across her vision. A smile crept over her lips as it solidified, and suddenly, she could see her surroundings perfectly...despite the fact that her eyes were still scrunched shut. Hesitantly, she began shifting her focus, moving her mind's eye forward and tracing the grayscale tunnels.

The light. I can see everything it's hitting. Her gut began to tighten as she moved further and further along the passages, but she ignored it, her thoughts documenting every twist and turn. The harder she pushed her concentration, the more her body began to strain, a pounding headache working its way through her temples. A grunt of exertion escaped her lips, and her stomach tightened, stabbing pains rocking through her. Still, she kept going, following each passage to the point where her head began to spin and the image grew blurry.

Suddenly, her strength buckled, causing her to fall to one knee with a gasp. The energy instantly dissipated, her concentration shattered.

Alix knelt beside her, their eyes meeting. "Are you alright? You're shaking."

Rune glanced down at her trembling hands. "I'm fine. Pushed myself a bit hard, is all." She thanked Alix as the girl helped her to her feet, pivoting around and pointing to the tunnel on the far left. "We should go that way. The center and right passages merge after a little while, and as far as I can tell, they head south."

Alix raised an eyebrow in surprise. "How do you know?"

"The light. I—it's kinda hard to explain, but I found a way to sense where it hit the rocks." A half smile found its way onto her lips.

Alix glanced down at her fingers, a few wisps of liquid making their way across her palms for a brief moment. "Huh. That's actually pretty smart." She nodded at the tunnel, motioning for Rune to lead. "Go on. You probably know the area better than I do, now."

Tentatively, Rune headed into the valley, instantly grateful that she wasn't claustrophobic as the walls began growing closer and closer together. Thankfully, it widened out a bit just as it was beginning to restrict her movement, and she found herself letting out a breath of relief that she hadn't even noticed she was holding.

They took turn after turn, and eventually, she lost track, relying on the vague sense of familiarity that followed her from her exploration of the mental projection. Trails of light began to accumulate around her fingertips, a side effect of the concentration she was beginning to build up.

Curious, she shifted her focus a bit more, tightening the threads of light and enhancing her mental field of view. While her vision blurred, the mental map expanded, sharpening in clarity as much as it could while Rune's eyes were still open. Suddenly, a hand gripped her shoulder, yanking her to a stop and shattering her concentration. Alix kept her grip on Rune's arm firm until her vision cleared, revealing that she'd been inches from walking straight into one of the cliffs.

"Thank you," she murmured, pink spreading across her cheeks. "Sorry—I was using the light thing to look at the paths ahead."

Alix stepped back with a chuckle. "Maybe you should stop moving before you try that," she warned. "How far can you see?"

Rune let her eyes fall closed, the gesture halving the amount of energy she needed to exert for the mental projection to become clear. "We don't have too much longer before the valley ends," she noted aloud, retracting her focus and opening her eyes. "Something's stopping me from looking much past that. It's a short stretch of open plain, then—nothing."

Instead of looking concerned, a grin spread across Alix's features. "Your power is probably being blocked by the leylock. It means we're almost there."

The words both encouraged and worried Rune, and she found her mind shuffling through memories of her previous companions—her friends. Were they heading towards Yellow, too? Did they know where she was? Were all of them still there? A chill traced her spine as a horrible realization hit her. *What if one of them...didn't make it?*

She shook the thought away almost as soon as it entered her mind. *They're alright. I know they are.* A smile toyed with her lips as the memories of all the conflicts they'd fought their way out of worked their way across her consciousness. *They can fend for themselves. You were the one who got yourself killed.*

Ahead, the valley widened suddenly, the mesas breaking off and forming into a wide bubble of space. Rune's smile broadened as her eyes found the massive energy barrier on the far side, a scarlet sheen rippling across its translucent surface. She turned to Alix, opening her mouth to voice her excitement—but froze when she noticed how rigid the girl's body was. Nervously, Rune turned, following Alix's petrified gaze to a strange creature perched on a rock ledge just above them.

The second her mind registered the hulking, scorpion-like monster, it lunged for them, and Rune barely managed to knock Alix out of the way as its tail barb—which was probably poisonous—embedded into the ground right in front of their feet.

Rune glanced up into the creature's beady eyes, her hand fumbling for her dagger. "Alix—please don't tell me that's what I think it is."

Beside her, Alix unclipped her bow from a strap on her back, free hand hovering above the quiver at her side. Her lips parted to form a word—the last word that registered in Rune's mind as the creature raised its tail to strike.

"Sandcrawler."

44
RUNE

By some miracle, Rune's muscles sprang into action before her brain could, moving her out of the way of another deadly strike from the creature.

The massive barb at the end of its tail sent shards of sandstone flying as it slammed into the cliff face, separating Rune from Alix. The brief moment of decision as the scorpion debated which one of them would be its first target allowed the girls to create space, and Alix nocked an arrow while the creature reeled on Rune.

Frantically, her mind began analyzing the situation, recalling everything that Alix had mentioned about sandcrawlers. *Something's not right.* "Aren't these things nocturnal?" Her voice was tight with panic, her gut wrenching as she dove to the left to dodge another assault.

"They're supposed to be!" Came Alix's reply, followed by the sound of a bowstring being drawn back. "I've never seen one in broad daylight like this!"

Well—that's just wonderful, Rune thought ruefully, turning to face the monster. Around them, the wind began to pick up, sending stray grains of sand whipping into Rune's skin. She raised her free arm, hoping to shield her eyes from the dust, but the gesture didn't do much.

A bone chilling screech was the only warning Rune had of the monster's next attack, and she sidestepped away from where she figured it would go, a shiver rippling down her spine. Thankfully, she was right, the strike finding nothing but sand. Taking the brief opening she had while the creature's tail was stuck, she rushed in towards her opponent, ducking down to slide right beneath it. Reaching up, she dragged her dagger across the massive scorpion's exposed underbelly, leaving a long trail of cobalt blood in her wake.

Somehow, Alix's shout of warning managed to find Rune's ears before another bloodcurdling cry sounded. She pivoted around, flinging her body out of the way of the sandcrawler's massive pincers right before they could close on her. This time, she fumbled on the landing, scrambling out of the sloppy roll and wasting precious seconds as the monster set its sights on her.

Suddenly, there was a dull *twang*, and the scorpion reared back with a snarl as an arrow wedged itself right between two of the terga on its back. Almost immediately, Alix had another nocked, releasing the bowstring before the creature could even register the attack.

Recovering from her mild startle, Rune frantically scanned her surroundings, clumping everything into a neat mental analysis of the immediate area. It was something she knew she'd done before, and something she somehow knew how to do— but of course, she had no idea how the habit had been made.

For the first time, however, she found that the annoyance of the gaps in her memory didn't strike her at first. *I don't care how I have this skill. I'm just glad I do.*

Using the hastily gathered information, Rune directed her next dodge towards the cliff face, positioning herself in such a place that the rocks would provide multiple escape routes and a decent amount of shade. *Scorpions don't have good eyesight. They can distinguish light from dark better than many other animals, and of course they track movement, but if I'm still and disguised among a bunch of similarly-shaped rocks...*

Her thought was cut off by the scorpion whipping toward her, its tail slamming into the rocks inches from her head. Despite every instinct in her body screaming for her to move, she held herself still, tracking the creature's movements and bracing herself to dodge at the last second if needed.

Another crash sent a splash of ice cold blood pumping through her veins, and the effect was completed by the shower of rocks raining down on her from where the sandcrawler's tail had stuck above. She dared a quick glance in Alix's direction, watching as the girl leveled out the arrow. A frustrated look on her face told Rune that there wasn't an opening...and as the creature decided to give up on the tail and try to grab Rune with its pincers, she set her mind to finding a way to get Alix a clear shot.

Running a few quick mental calculations under her breath, she shifted to the left, using large, sporadic motions to catch the monster's attention. It fell for the bait a bit quicker than Rune had anticipated, and she gritted her teeth against the stab of pain that ran through her body when it managed to drag the tip of its claw along her side.

Taking deep, ragged breaths and urging herself *not* to look down at the wound right above her hip, she pivoted around, staring the scorpion down. She likely wouldn't be fast enough to dodge the next attack this time, not at this distance—and from the way the scorpion seemed to be taking its time to approach her, it knew that. What it *didn't* seem to know, however, was that she had just lined it up perfectly for a shot from Alix—its entire right side angled at the ideal position for an arrow or two to break past the hard surface protecting it.

Based on the calculated smile spreading across Alix's features, she'd noticed.

Two dull thuds, one after the other, ensued almost at once, causing the creature to rear back with a cry of pain—exposing its belly. Alix fired one more arrow directly into the soft underside, piercing—hopefully—something important. The scorpion doubled over, but it didn't take a genius to realize that it was only stunned for a few moments, the thought forcing Rune's muscles into action as she bolted towards the Leylock.

Footsteps behind her indicated that Alix was right on her tail, but it was only seconds before an agonized hiss let them know that the sandcrawler had recovered from its temporary shock. Rune dared a glance over her shoulder, her blood running cold when she realized just how close the monster was getting to Alix.

She won't be able to dodge in time.

Going against every instinct she had, she forced herself to come to a stop, redirecting her motion back towards her companion. Alix opened her mouth to shout at her, to ask what she was doing—but Rune didn't hear her, her focus on the scorpion raising its tail behind her. Her lips formed the warning, but her tongue refused to let it go, knowing it would be no use.

I just have to get there first.

Right as the attack came down towards Alix's back, Rune lunged, tackling the girl and knocking her out of the way of the strike. A line of stings like a thousand needles instantly erupted from her arm, which had been grazed by the tail briefly on the way by. A strangled scream erupted from Rune's lips, pain consuming every muscle in her body. She collapsed to the ground as Alix rolled to her feet, instantly nocking an arrow and firing it straight into the creature's exposed neck.

The venom began to sink into her skin as the creature reared back, its jaws unhinging and a guttural hiss of pain forming on its arachnid tongue. Rune lay there on the sand, her vision blurring and her consciousness slipping away like a river from a breached dam.

She watched as Alix raised her hands, a small jet of water materializing out of thin air and shooting into the scorpion's wide open mouth. As soon as the creature's front legs hit the ground, Alix flung her hands apart with a cry, her eyes filled with raw, adrenaline-fueled power. The jet of water inside the creature's mouth exploded outward as her arms separated, shattering its skull completely. The scorpion collapsed instantly, its blood staining the soil blue.

Black veins began to form along Rune's arm as the venom set in, spreading far quicker than the rational part of her knew to be safe. That rationality was fading away by the second, however, leaving only bright, blinding agony in its wake.

Someone leaned over her, whispering—no, she was

shouting—a name that she knew, but that the venom told her she didn't.

"RUNE!"

"*RUNE!*"

Rune. That's my name. Isn't it?

The girl knelt beside her, shaking her shoulders violently, but Rune didn't feel a thing, her body numbed to everything except the pain. That venom was her master now, filling her, eating her alive from the inside out. She wanted to struggle, but she couldn't, forced to lay there, defenseless, as the toxic liquid imbued itself into her blood.

The girl—Alix, that was Alix—slipped her arms underneath Rune's shoulders, struggling to lift her off the ground. Fragmented groans slipped from Rune's lips as Alix awkwardly shouldered her weight, somehow managing to help her to her feet.

She didn't know how long they moved, only that they did, Alix taking it one slow, agonizing step at a time and Rune struggling to keep herself conscious. It helped a bit that Alix was at least a few inches taller than Rune was, allowing her a bit more leverage against Rune's limp figure. Even so, guilt bubbled up in Rune's stomach as the girl stumbled slightly with each motion, her wiry frame having a difficult time supporting Rune's body.

I wish I could help.

Wish I could move.

Wish I could be rid of the pain...

Spots swam in Rune's vision, and even as she tried to keep herself awake, her mind seemed to have other ideas. A soft, distant ringing in her ears drowned out any external noise, the sights and sounds trapping Rune inside her own mind and leaving her to drown in a mental haze of torment. Her veins burned as the venom spread, whimpers of pain rolling off her tongue and her muscles constantly spasming, trying anything at all to stop the poison.

Stopping that venom—it was all that mattered.

She writhed in pain, her stomach heaving in a futile attempt to eject the venom from her veins. The world was gone now, all that was left was pain—pain that she could be rid of if only the venom would leave her be. Her body hit the ground again, more lightly this time, and there was a strange, distant hum that some part of Rune's mind recognized. A tingling sensation spread across her skin, a thought tugging at her, nagging at her fading consciousness. The thought refused to form, however, leaving her in a dull state of disconnection as a familiar voice began to whisper in her ear.

Suddenly, a new pair of strong arms gripped her limp body, lifting her with relative ease. They began moving again, and she rummaged around in her mind, searching for information about the blurred face above her—a name, one she knew, but couldn't remember.

She couldn't remember anything right now.

Who she was, where she was—it didn't matter anymore.

All that mattered was the venom.

A scream—her scream—split the air again as the arms carried her through the strange barrier, the pulsing agony in her body becoming almost too much to bear. A rush of humidity hit her face, followed by a blast of cool, musty air as the arms took her down—down to a place of shadows and stone walls.

She was laid on the ground, becoming vaguely aware of something soft pressing against her nose. A sickly sweet smell filled her nostrils, and for a brief moment the blackness in her vision cleared away, allowing her to lock onto a pair of familiar pair of eyes before the darkness rushed back to suffocate her.

Right before she slipped into unconsciousness, however, a single coherent thought slipped through the haze, imprinting itself in her mind as she was surrounded by the darkness.

Azalea.

45
REI

A flicker of dull, throbbing pain was the first to meet Rei when she opened her eyes—except the pain wasn't her own.

Images surged past her as though carried in a raging rapid, memories of a life that she'd never lived spilling over and ingraining into her brain. She couldn't make sense of anything, but they bombarded her all the same, filling her mind with a sea of scattered thoughts and faded colors.

The scene blurred around her, fading in and out. An image solidified in front of her, the shadowed figure of a familiar girl appearing from the mental river. Her lips parted, forming words —but Rei was whisked away before they reached her ears.

When her mental vision cleared again, she was standing in the corner of a clearing lit by rays of a morning sun, watching five figures chat around a fire. The green-eyed girl Rei had seen in her past dreams was there, watching as the others conversed just quietly enough that Rei couldn't quite make out what they were saying.

Curious, Rei moved closer, approaching the group. They paid her no mind, none of them seeming to notice the purple-eyed figure obviously eavesdropping on their conversation.

This is just like the other dreams. I can see them, but they can't see me.

A blonde girl leaned back, her eyes locked on a red-haired boy who had asked her a question a few moments before. "Long as I can remember," she told him airily. "Which isn't a whole lot, I guess, but it sure feels like it. I met him right outside the Green Citadel, shortly after I awoke."

"*Green* Citadel?" The green eyed girl was the one speaking this time, a frown playing with her features.

"Oh, yeah—sorry, forgot you're a newbie." The blonde girl cocked a grin at the annoyance in her companion's expression. "The arena's divided into four sections—called biomes—and each biome's labeled with a color."

The girl kept talking, but Rei stopped listening, her mind stuck playing the line on repeat. *The arena is divided into four sections, each labeled with a color.* A gasp escaped her lips after the third or fourth repetition, realizing why the words had felt so familiar to her. The blood drained from her face as another image slipped into her thoughts—the fog map Marko had proudly displayed to her and Sumi.

Four sections, each labeled with a color.

Marko called it an arena.

She glanced up, circling around so she could see the strange, green eyed girl again. There was something about her—something Rei couldn't quite put her finger on. *I guess I'm not going crazy, then. You aren't just a figment of my imagination.*

You're real.

She pivoted around, examining the group. Marko's voice joined with the anthem of realization her thoughts had become, cementing her theories.

"Its creators refer to it as the Compass."

With a final glance back at the girl, Rei turned away, unsure of where she was headed. Memories of past dreams, visions of that very girl portrayed in many different forms. An innocent victim, a ruthless soldier, a lost girl, trapped within a game she never wanted to play.

I know where you are.

And I'm going to find you.

REI SAT UP IN HER BED, CHEST HEAVING. HER MIND raced with the barrage of revelations she'd experienced, the dream remaining branded in her mind.

Unmistakable.

Powerful.

Something far, far beyond a normal nighttime vision.

Careful not to wake Wren or Kal—who shared the dorm-like room where she slept—Rei cast aside her sheets, pressing her palm to the panel on the wall and slipping out the door as soundlessly as she could manage.

I need to move. I need to clear my head.

Despite not being able to see the sky, something inside Rei told her that it was likely around midnight, meaning that she would hopefully be the only one awake. A smile toyed with her lips as she wandered through the dark halls, finding comfort in the soft, gentle silence of the shadow that enveloped her. It wasn't the brutal, terrifying darkness she had grown used to in the past few days—this darkness was sweet and nurturing, blacking out the harmful sights and wrapping her in a thick embrace.

Rei felt the glyph stir inside her as she moved, staying obediently dormant yet warming her gut just enough to remind her that it was there. A few threads of it slipped into her thoughts, adding a mildly chaotic tinge to the already confusing mess of information she had been forced to take in.

Breathe. One thing at a time.

She focused on her footsteps as she moved, wandering aimlessly through endless corridors. Despite the fact that the place was practically a maze, she felt no fear of losing her way, keeping her attention trained on clearing her mind and walking herself through what was happening. It was a technique that she didn't use often, since she was generally able to sort through information quickly and easily to clear the way for all her random, spontaneous imaginings—but this time was different. For the first time, she found herself lost in a labyrinth of new ideas and questions, the vast sea of truths mixed with a few stray droplets of lies overpowering her chaotic processing abilities.

Pausing for a moment, she inhaled deeply, backing up in her mind to when she had first crossed the Horizon's Teeth. It had only been just over a month since then, but it felt like years, her mind still spinning from the fact that the realms were even real —despite the fact that she'd been living in them all this time.

What do I know?

She closed her eyes, rearranging the events of the past few weeks into a mental timeline that she could slowly work through. The process felt unnaturally orderly to her, but it forced her mind to focus, which she had to admit *did* help a lot with the overwhelming confusion.

To start, I know the realms are real. I know my father was originally from here, that he was a jurori, and that he was prob-ably on the run from the same people who kidnapped me...twice.

I am an interracial hybrid—and my entire race has been deluded into thinking that they are human when they...aren't. We were trapped in our own world, surrounded by a magical border and convinced that there was nothing beyond.

Yeah...that's not messed up at all.

I "found" a sword that gave me magic and turned my eyes purple. Loric trained me to use it, but I still got captured by the people who really don't like me...or the fact that I'm the Blade's wielder. He rescued me, and now the Onyx needs my help to beat up those jerks and their leader, the Eidolon—who has possession of a mask that grants him powers like mine.

The Onyx is a rebellion working to free the Oasis, a city in Lycrix—one of the nine realms, and arguably the hottest. The realms are linked together by the Apeiron, a dimension that spans across time and space—it's a little weird, but definitely cool.

Rei had resumed walking as she rearranged her thoughts, listing each life-changing revelation in an un-Rei-like orderly fashion. While the method was still entirely alien to her, it did seem to be working, and she found a smile creeping across her lips as she faced the final mental pile of information—the green eyed girl.

I've never met her before...but I know where she is. She's not the only one, either...she, and so many others, are stuck there.

Sixty-four, Marko said. Sixty four innocent people, trapped in a deadly game they never wanted to play.

But...I could help them win.

Rei froze as the thought ended, realizing that she'd accidentally wandered into a very familiar dome-shaped room. In the center was the table that had projected the fog image the day before, filling Rei with a renewed curiosity. At the moment, the table was completely plain, but Rei still felt drawn to it in a way she couldn't explain.

"Looking for something?"

Rei scrambled back from the table with a yelp, frantically searching her body for some kind of weapon. She felt red seep into her cheeks when she realized it was only Sumi, a hint of fatigue lingering in her eyes.

"Apologies. I had no intention to scare you." The gnome stepped to Rei's side, one of her long braids slipping into her face.

Rei let out a long exhale, clutching her chest as she re-sheathed her sword. "Guess I'm just jumpy."

Sumi glanced down at the blank table. "I don't blame you. Especially with your past experiences."

Rei winced, frantically fishing through her mind for a subject change. "What are you doing up so late? Or early?"

A half smile spread across the gnome's grandmotherly features. "I suppose I could ask you the same, could I not?"

"I had a—a dream. Needed to take a walk, to clear my head."

The gnome nodded. "I do that often. Why come here, though? You seemed interested in the Achlys."

Rei ran her fingers along the glassy surface of the table,

marveling at the thin, misty atmosphere that coated the exterior in a pale sheen. "Is that what this is called?"

"It is." Sumi lightly brushed the rows of runes that ran around the edge of the table with a delicate hand, her eyes as milky as the layer of fog drifting around the Achlys. "It is a very advanced enchanted object—one used universally to project interactive, three dimensional maps using special fog. If I turn it on..." She leaned closer, murmuring a strange word in a songlike language.

Suddenly, the Achlys sprang to life, swirls of mist spiraling across the iridescent surface. Rei leaned closer, examining the map of the Compass once more with a new perspective. The blonde girl's words kept coming back to her as her eyes scanned the fog, cementing the idea in her mind even further with each passing second. Her gaze lingered on the green quarter of the circle the longest, her thoughts enveloping her.

Green Citadel.
Green Citadel.
Green.
Split into four sections—biomes—each labeled with a color.
Green.

Rei stepped back, mind spinning. "She's there. No—*they're* there."

It took a moment for her to remember that she wasn't alone.

Sumi frowned, puzzled. "Who? Do you know something about the arena?"

Rei hesitated. "I might...you'll think I'm crazy, though."

The gnome held her gaze, her eyes filled with nothing but a calm curiosity. "I have spent over two hundred years walking these realms, Rei. I have heard many, many crazy things in that time. I doubt that this will faze me much."

Deciding to ignore the fact that Sumi was over two centuries old, Rei allowed the words she had been holding back since she'd awoken to fall off her tongue, spilling everything about the green eyed girl, the dreams, and the theory that the girl was trapped inside the Compass.

When she'd finished, Sumi remained silent for a few long, agonizing moments, processing the information. "You're absolutely certain?"

Rei nodded, not trusting her voice.

The gnome frowned, a pensive look crossing her features as she leaned forward to examine the projection more closely. "You want to find her."

"Yes. I can't explain why—I just do. She's important, I know she is."

Sumi nodded. "You don't have to explain, Rei. They say that being bonded to the Phantom Blade comes with strange responsibilities, sometimes placing the bearer in situations that cannot be rationally explained. This seems to be one of those situations."

Rei bit her lip nervously. "What do we do about it?"

Sumi glanced up, meeting her eyes. "We listen to what your gut is telling you. Chances are, those feelings are far from coincidental." The gnome thought for a moment. "Actually—Marko was just filling me in last night on a report one of his scouts had sent in just yesterday evening. That report included evidence for the location of the arena."

A shiver of excitement or fear—Rei couldn't tell which— rippled down her spine. "Where is it?"

"A realm called Orako," Sumi continued. "That realm contains only four islands, all of which are well populated—but there was a fifth, once. It was said to have been destroyed thousands of years ago, but—we have evidence that it may still be out there. If it is, it would certainly make the perfect place for an operation such as the Compass seems to be."

Rei took a deep breath, not wanting to get ahead of herself. "Could I—could I go there?"

Sumi hesitated. "It would be risky—not to mention that it would take our focus away from our goal. *However—*" she continued before Rei could protest— "I am not against it. I trust your instincts, Rei, and I also believe that the Compass holds information that might be invaluable to us—if it didn't, we wouldn't be investigating it. I may be able to put together a small team of operatives to accompany you on a short scouting trip to where the fifth island is rumored to be."

A giddy grin slowly spread across Rei's face, the combined promise of answers and adventure creating an irresistible sense of excitement. Her infectious smile spread to Sumi, who let out a soft chuckle at the raw elation in Rei's expression.

"Right now, though—I will escort you back to your dorm. We can discuss this matter with the rest of the commanders in the morning."

The grin remained plastered on Rei's face as Sumi led her through the hallways, both traveling in a content silence. *I'm coming to find you,* Rei thought, part of her imagining that the green eyed girl could hear her. *Just hold on until I get there.*

46

REI

"And you're proposing that we do...what, exactly?"

Rei glanced around the circular wooden table at the five people she sat with, pushing away any stray nerves that tried to hinder her thoughts. Sumi had arranged for a meeting with the commanders that morning, and of course, Loric had insisted on sitting in and listening to the conversation. "The girl—the one I told you about—she's *in* the Compass. I know for a fact that she's important, even I'm not quite sure how yet—which is why I want permission to try and find her. I know it's dangerous, but I really feel like it's a risk I need to take."

"We," Sumi corrected softly, making Rei pause to glance over at her.

"We?"

"A risk *we* must take," the gnome repeated. "You are a part of our order now, Rei. Being the wielder of the Phantom Blade, your choices *will* impact the rest of us—and I'm not saying that as a bad thing," she added hurriedly before Rei could respond, "but I simply want to make sure you know. Any risk you take, we take right along with you. Willingly."

Rei nodded slowly, her chest tightening slightly at the thought of her crazy ideas affecting this whole order of people she hardly knew. If she was wrong...she shook her head vigorously, refusing to go down that path. Her eyes flickered to Loric, who stayed silent, offering a brief nod of support. *I'm not wrong. This girl is important, and she's in the Compass. We have to go get her. I don't know why I feel this way, but I know it's the right thing to do.*

"If we were to allow you to do this, there is no chance we would ask you to go alone. You would need people to go with you—and there *have* to be adults." Marko was the one speaking this time, and Rei got the vibe that he and Sumi were the ones who did most of the talking for the Onyx's leaders. The only one Rei hadn't met before—a tall, pointy eared man with neatly braided cornrows and deep, bronzed skin hadn't said a word through the whole meeting, instead opting to watch Rei with a pair of intense gray eyes.

"I would go with her," Arla offered, cocking her head at Rei and examining her. "There seem to be enough unknowns in this idea that there is a high possibility of encountering conflict. What better way to ensure her safety than to send the head of combat for our operation?"

Come to think of it, Rei had never seen any of the Onyx members actually fight—but a part of her suddenly wanted to.

The quiet commander, who happened to be sitting on Arla's right, turned to her with a slightly concerned expression. "Is it really a good idea to send one of our top operatives on a mission filled with variables?"

Arla glanced from him to Rei. "If we're going by that logic, then she shouldn't go either, being bonded to the only thing that keeps us from utter annihilation by the Eidolon and all. If I'm being honest with you, though—I feel like the kid's got a point to this. We've known that this arena was going to be something worth keeping an eye on since we first heard rumors that it might exist. She knows what she's talking about. I think we should listen to her."

A warm, bubbly feeling blossomed in Rei's stomach at Arla's blunt support, followed by a newfound respect for the woman. A permanent scar of pain lingered within the woman's striking cerulean eyes, but the raw strength and determination showed that she had embraced the wound, allowing it to fuel her.

It would probably be pretty awesome to fight at her side.

The man still looked slightly uneasy, something in his expression hinting that the hesitation went deeper than simply being worried about the Onyx as a whole. "You have a good point. I'll agree to it—but only if there are at least five of you total. I will not allow you to be left vulnerable, especially in a relatively unguarded realm."

Arla thought for a moment. "I don't remember Orako being too bad. Lycrix was always the unruly one."

The man shrugged. "Still. Be careful."

Arla sighed, shaking her head. "When am I not? Actually —" she corrected at the man's expression— "let's leave that as a rhetorical question. What do you think, Rei? Five people enough?"

"Yes. Um. Five is perfect." She blinked a few times, her

words tumbling over one another in a rush to be allowed off her tongue. "Do I get to pick who goes?"

Arla shrugged. "You're stuck with me, sweetheart. As for the others, I'm sure you'd get a say."

"At least one of them has to be an adult, though," the man beside Arla interjected, casting her a hilariously stern glance. "I don't trust you on your own with a group of teenagers."

The expression Arla shot him in response was so sarcastically innocent, Rei found even Sumi fighting back laughter. "I'm there for their protection, Castor. We don't know what we could find, and if we end up in a position where we can get this mystery girl into our custody, there's a good chance that we won't be able to get her out of there without a fight."

"I will be joining you as well." Loric spoke up from the side, glancing pointedly in Rei's direction. "That's non-negotiable."

No one argued.

Rei leaned back in her chair, scanning the faces of the four commanders. Sumi was supportive, as was Arla. Castor seemed hesitant, but reluctantly agreed. Marko, however—Rei couldn't tell what was going on behind his dark eyes. He had voiced a tentative support earlier, but since, he had done nothing but watch Rei's face as the others debated. Sumi seemed to have noticed the same thing, turning towards him.

"Marko? Do you wish to share any thoughts?"

He exhaled deeply, tilting his head ever so slightly as though deep in thought. "I am not against it. Need I remind you that my scouts were the ones to discover this arena's existence in the first place? No, of course I would not oppose a further expedition—I will, however, nominate Flyn to accompany you. He is extremely vigilant, and one of my best operatives. Hopefully he would be able to identify trouble before it identifies you."

Arla rested her chin on her hand. "It would be Flyn, Rei, Loric and I—and one other?"

"Well, what if..." Rei trailed off as all eyes turned to her. "I know this would technically bring our group up to six, but what if Wren and her brother came? Wylder, right? I don't know—it would just be kinda nice to have a few younger people with me. From what I've seen, they seem pretty skilled for their age, too."

Sumi nodded before any of the others could say anything. "Of course. Wren and Wylder would do well on this mission— and it would serve as a perfect opportunity for them to hone their skills outside of the training areas and the cities they're used to."

Arla stood. "I'll find Flyn and the twins. They'll have to agree, of course, before we finalize any of this."

A hint of red seeped into Rei's cheeks. "Yes. Of course."

Sumi shot Rei an encouraging glance. "Bring them back here, if you will. We'll treat this like any other scouting mission that Marko runs—with systematic caution."

Arla shot a quick glance in Rei's direction, offering a smile with an unreadable message written into it. Rei returned it with a slightly nervous grin of her own, watching as the woman gracefully swept out of the room. The moment she was gone, Marko leaned in towards Castor, casting him a knowing glance.

"You really do need to stop being so protective of her, you know. She probably thinks it's hilarious now, but I wouldn't push your luck."

Castor's face went red. "I'm just trying to look out for the organization. Putting one of the commanding members in possible danger is usually not a decision most leaders would make."

Marko snorted, and even Sumi seemed to be hiding a smile—making Rei wonder just what was going on between Arla and Castor. *I mean...maybe...NOPE! I do not need to be caught up in this right now.*

Castor stood, his face still a shade of bright fuchsia. "I'll leave you two to handle the details of this mission," he informed them hurriedly. "Now if you'll excuse me, I have other matters to attend to at the moment."

Marko chuckled as he strode out the door, murmuring something that sounded like *"sure you do"* under his breath. Rei got the idea that the two of them were quite close friends.

Not much conversation was made until Arla returned, Flyn, Wren, and Wylder in tow. They took a seat, hints of confusion lingering in the expressions of the three newcomers. Sumi waited until they were all settled and silent before speaking, her tone sturdy and commanding.

"Rei has presented us with a proposal for an investigation into the Compass, and we have decided to grant her request. You three were nominated to accompany her and Arla to Orako, where you will be tasked with finding the truth about the arena's existence."

Rei fidgeted uncomfortably as Sumi repeated the details of the mission, her mind still on the green-eyed girl. She couldn't shake the odd feeling that even though they had never met, they should already know one another—a feeling that left bundles of nerves in her stomach.

Wren glanced from Sumi to Rei. "That's not all, is it. You

wouldn't send a commander with us if there wasn't something else."

Sumi hesitated. "There is something. There's—a girl. One that Rei is certain is currently trapped inside the Compass. We have the feeling that she could be important, so if you get the opportunity—we want you to bring her back here."

Wren leaned back in her chair, processing the information. Both Wylder and Flyn remained silent, contemplating. One by one, they slowly began to nod, agreeing to the mission.

"This is unlike any procedure we've done before," Sumi continued, leaning forward and holding each person's gaze for a brief moment. "This means you must approach it with extreme caution. I will have a temporary annex set up here in the event of an emergency or for if you do actually manage to perform the rescue. You will follow standard protocol, and be given a maximum of one week to complete this quest. If you are not here by sunset of the seventh day, we will assume that something is severely wrong. Do you understand?"

All nodded except for Marko, who simply watched intently, and Loric, who's eyes were on Rei.

"What if we find something, and need more time?" Rei couldn't stop the question from falling off her lips, a slight blush coloring her face.

"One of you will return here to notify us of the change," Sumi told her calmly. "Those are the rules every scout follows when sent on a mission, and I expect each of you to honor them." The gnome stood, sending bubbles of excitement surging through Rei's veins. The dream surfaced once again in her mind, and Rei felt a smile creep across her lips.

I'm coming to find you.

"Given that this seems to be time sensitive, I will arrange for you to depart at dawn. Any questions?"

"Can we talk?"

Rei glanced up, her eyes finding Loric's. He stood in the doorway of her dorm, a neutral expression written across his gruff features. "Something wrong?"

Loric stepped into the room, taking a seat beside her on her bed. Wren and Kal were out training, meaning that it was just her and her mentor. "I just want to make sure that you're really sure about this."

Rei thought for a moment. "You mean the rescue."

He nodded.

She glanced down, her eyes finding the open journal on her lap. Lines of scrawled text—written in the native kedorian tongue, so Loric probably couldn't read them—spanned the page, describing as many of her dreams about the green-eyed girl as she could recall. "I'm sure."

Loric's eyes followed hers, scanning the pages. "Who is this girl you spoke of, anyway? You never mentioned having dreams like those before."

Hints of red seeped into Rei's cheeks. "I—I'm sorry for not telling you. If it helps, I just thought it was some weird trick my imagination was playing on me...it wasn't until last night that I actually realized that she was *real.*"

"And...you're sure she is?"

"Yes." Not even the slight undertones of doubt in Loric's

words could shake her resolve. *I know what I saw.* "Hopefully, finding her will give me some answers as to why she keeps showing up in my dreams."

Loric nodded thoughtfully, rising to his feet. "I'll be with you every step of the way. I trust your judgment, Rei. I do."

But... Rei's thoughts added the word he neglected to, her mind searching for the reason of his doubt. "You still aren't sure about this, are you." She said it like a statement, but the questioning challenge in the words wasn't very well masked.

"I'm not," he admitted. "But I will do my best to support—and *protect*—you, regardless of your decisions."

Her heart warmed slightly at the words, despite his doubt. "Thank you. Really."

His face was stony as he nodded again, but she could have sworn that his eyes were smiling at her. "Always."

Then, he was gone, leaving her alone with her thoughts.

47

RUNE

Rough, musty air filled Rune's nostrils, pressing in on her as her consciousness slowly began to return. Her eyes fluttered open as a pained groan escaped her lips, her body tingling from head to toe with feelings both foreign and familiar to her slurred senses. Black dots swam in her vision, her heartbeat thundering a rhythm like frantic footfalls in her chest. There were people around her, people she knew—but rational thought eluded her, retreating back into the dark, muddled slush her mind had become.

Breathe.

Remember who you are.

Remember why you're here.

A pair of concerned pale eyes were the first she locked onto as she forced herself to focus, the room around her slowly taking shape. A word formed on her tongue, rolling off her lips and connecting in her mind even before the memory could surface.

"Azalea."

The girl nodded, her lips curling into a slight smile. "You were unconscious for almost a whole day, Rune. I was starting to wonder if I hadn't been able to get all the venom out of your system."

Rune tried to return the smile, but the dull, throbbing pain refused to let her lips do much more than tilt upwards slightly at the corners. "I'm alright." The words were both for Azalea's benefit and her own. She turned to Alix with a grimace. "You really weren't kidding about the whole excruciating death thing."

Alix was sitting beside her, looking extremely uncomfortable with the number of people crowded into the cave. "No. I don't joke often."

"You should try it sometime," Luna piped up from the other side of the cave. "It's quite fun."

Alix pursed her lips. "I think I'll pass."

Rune glanced from Alix to her friends, realizing just how tense the meeting must have been. "Are you all introduced?"

Alix glanced around the room. "Not really. We've been focused on keeping you from dying again."

Rune winced. "Well—uh—this is Alix." Alix shot her a look, but Rune pretended not to see it. "Alix, this is Azalea, Nyk, Ivory, Ryder, Luna and Kaleo."

Azalea glanced from Rune to Alix. "How'd you two meet?"

"She found me almost as soon as I woke up," Rune explained, deciding to leave out the part where they'd tried to kill each other. Judging by Alix's expression, she was thinking along the same lines. "I convinced her to help me find you guys. Since she only had a red shard, we decided to come this way."

"You remembered us? How?" This time, it was Kaleo speaking, and Rune had to crane her neck to see him. He was sitting behind Azalea, his eyes locked on Rune.

"I—don't know." She debated whether or not to tell them about the veil, but decided that it might be too complicated of a conversation to repeat. "But I'm really glad I do."

Her eyes traveled to Alix, remembering the conversation they'd had the other night. Alix likely knew more than anyone, but she also had her reasons for keeping the information secret —something Rune respected.

"How did you find us?" Rune winced—it was such an obvious subject change, but for Alix's sake she wanted to take the conversation away from memories for the moment.

"Ivory was the one who saw you get knocked out by those guys," Nyk began. "He tracked the team to the cave, where we..." he trailed off, realizing he was talking about Rune dying.

"We knew you'd end up in Red," Luna continued, standing up and moving closer to where Rune lay propped up against the cave wall. "So...we found a team with a yellow shard, and after a bit of convincing, we ended up with it."

Ivory snorted. "That's what you'd call it? *Convincing*?"

Luna shot him a dirty look. "*Anyway*, we headed towards Yellow, since we figured it'd be easier than backtracking towards Green. We didn't have a red shard, so when we reached the Leylock, we were pretty much stuck...until that one stumbled across the border, a half-conscious Rune leaning on her." She nodded at Alix.

"I am lucky that you were there," Alix admitted. "I wouldn't have been able to carry Rune much farther, and even if I could have given her the care she needed, I doubt I would have been fast enough."

Kaleo shifted around, sitting up. "I'm just glad Ryder saw you two. I wouldn't have been able to grab Rune quick enough if he hadn't."

Ivory adjusted slightly, casting a wary glance in Alix's direction. "I think we should address the more pressing matter," he noted, murmuring something under his breath. "We have a complete team. That means we can open the Nexus."

A jolt of excitement flared up inside Rune's stomach at the thought. Escape suddenly seemed so much closer—no longer an idea, but a tangible object she could reach out and almost touch. This was what they'd been fighting for, what they had striven towards despite everything that happened.

The image of the hydra resurfaced in Rune's mind once again, its voice filling her thoughts. *"The only way out is through. Destroy it. Destroy it all. Then you'll see. Then we'll all see."*

"I take it your element is water, then?"

Azalea's voice shattered Rune's train of thought, snapping her back to reality. Alix nodded, opening her palm and watching a thin stream of liquid flow down her wrist. A faint expression of surprise flitted across her face for a moment, making Azalea frown.

"Is there a problem?"

Alix shook her head. "The air in Yellow is just so much more humid than in Red. I'm not used to being able to draw this much moisture this quickly."

Luna watched, cocking her head slightly. "You better not try to stop me from burning stuff."

Alix blinked at her. "That depends on what you're burning."

Ivory smirked at Luna. "Finally, an ally."

The expression on Alix's face was a bit skeptical, but she didn't argue.

"Where exactly is the Nexus?" Rune felt a bit embarrassed at having to ask the question. "Or rather, how are we going to get there?"

"The Nexus is in the exact center of the arena," Azalea explained, her attention on a small bundle of herbs in her satchel. "From where we are—it's probably north of us? We might want to travel a bit deeper into Yellow before we head up there, though, just so that we don't run into unwanted trouble at the Leylock."

"How long will that take?"

Azalea thought for a moment. "Not long. A day, maybe—if that."

"Oh, wait..." Nyk piped up suddenly, standing up and carrying something over to where Rune sat. Her face lit up as he handed the object to her, a grin crossing her features as she examined the sword she'd traded for back at the outpost.

"I really missed this in Red," she told him, watching as his lips slowly began to mirror her smile. "Thank you." She turned to Alix, reaching to the dagger at her side. "Do you need this back?"

Alix shook her head. "Nah, keep it. I have plenty."

Luna cocked her head at her. "You don't use a sword?"

"I prefer not to engage in close-ranged combat anyway, but if I must, daggers are my first resort." She paused to glance down, unsheathing one of the knives attached to her hip and flourishing it airily. "They're quicker, and I can throw them if I want to—though that's also what these are for." She unclipped her thin outer layer, pulling it aside to reveal rows of throwing knives stashed on the inside of the fabric.

Luna grinned. "You know what, you might actually be pretty fun."

Alix didn't seem to know how to respond, so she simply ignored the comment, resheathing her dagger and clipping her outer layer back together.

Rune glanced around at her friends' faces, trying to read their expressions. Her gaze lingered on Kaleo's the longest—he was watching her, and offered a smile when their eyes met.

"When should we leave? For the Nexus," she clarified as all eyes turned to her.

"You are in no shape to move right now," Kaleo told her, which Rune did have to admit was not inaccurate. He turned to Azalea, concern written on his features. "How soon will she be on her feet—safely?"

Azalea leaned closer, lightly pressing a hand to Rune's forehead. "Her fever's gone down, which is good—and the venom should be out of her system. Maybe tomorrow morning? That gives her the rest of the day and a good night of sleep to flush anything I missed out of her system."

Rune straightened, ignoring the starbursts of pain that flared up from the wound above her hip. A quick glance down told her that Azalea had bandaged it, and the lack of blood staining the cloth indicated that it couldn't be *too* deep...but it still didn't feel great. She gritted her teeth, pulling her knees into her chest and resting her chin on top of them. "What time is it?"

Ivory stood, moving a little ways towards the entrance and

poking his head out. "Early afternoon. You've got a little while before sunset."

Azalea nodded, glancing down and rummaging through her satchel again. "I'll stay here and do my best to get Rune feeling a bit more comfortable. If a few of you could hunt, that would be amazing—we have to feed eight now, remember."

A pang of guilt rippled through her as she looked down at her bandaged wounds, another reminder of the fact that she was holding her team back. *I didn't let the past command me this time, though.*

I won't let it command me ever again.

Rune's attention was diverted to the abundance of strange plants Azalea laid on the stone, reaching for a wooden bowl that she had set aside. A pestle rested against it, which the girl then used to thoroughly grind the herbs into a chalky powder that emanated an earthy aroma.

Satisfied, she leaned back, reaching for her water flask and filling the bowl halfway with liquid. The water shifted quickly to a murky green color, and she stirred it with a long utensil before stopping and extending the bowl to Rune.

Rune begrudgingly accepted it, examining the water. "I have to drink all of it?"

Azalea nodded firmly. "I mixed a few mild painkillers in there with the medicine, just for good measure. I figured it would make you more comfortable."

Rune guzzled the medicine, wincing as the liquid trickled down her throat. She was unable to fight the grimace that wormed its way across her face at the unpleasant taste, but the pain did ease after a moment. Azalea's smile was somewhere between satisfaction and amusement, but she didn't comment on Rune's reaction, simply reaching out to take the bowl from her when she had finished.

"You should try to rest," the girl instructed her, helping Rune adjust to a more comfortable position. She wadded a few of the colder weather cloaks into something of a pillow, handing it to Rune. "Minimal movement is best for now, and sleep is even better—the medicine needs time to circulate through your system."

Even if Rune had wanted to argue, she found that her eyelids had suddenly become like weights, pulled to the ground by an unseen force. Realization hit her, and a drowsy smile crossed her lips. "You...you put sedatives in it, didn't you."

Azalea shrugged unapologetically. "I doubted you'd have gotten a good rest without at least a bit of help. Don't fight it, Rune. It's going to win anyway."

Begrudgingly, Rune allowed herself to relax, sleep coming for her at an unnatural pace.

The last thought she had was of the hydra's words, ringing in her mind once again like an anthem. *The only way out is through. Destroy it. Destroy it all. Then you'll see.*

"Then we'll all see."

48

RUNE

The Yellow Biome was a jungle.

Literally.

Massive, overgrown trees were everywhere, their leaves creating layer upon layer of thick canopies above their heads. Vibrant foliage covered every inch of the ground, so much so that Kaleo was forced to cut paths through many of the plants with his sword.

"I still think it would be easier to just burn our way through," Luna argued, sparking a tongue of flame on her palm and pointing to the unrelenting barriers of huge bushes, flowers, and rather horrifying looking plants that Rune definitely never wanted to touch.

Ivory shot her a look, which she gleefully ignored, proceeding to toss the ball of fire from hand to hand.

"Come on. You can't say it wouldn't be super nice to just like—HA—" she mimed tossing the ball at the plants— "and watch everything in our way *BURN.*"

Ivory sighed. "Not all of us are fireproof, Luna."

Luna groaned dramatically. "Well that's not *my* problem, is it?"

Ahead, Kaleo stopped moving, his gaze traveling upwards towards the interlocking branches forming a net above them. Luna frowned at him, opening her mouth to protest the delay, but he cut her off.

"Actually—I think I might have just found an easier way to travel—*without* burning anything." He pointed upwards, and at first, all Rune saw were the spiderweb of tree limbs that formed a massive net. After a moment, however, what Kaleo was suggesting registered in her mind, her eyes locking on exactly what he was seeing.

Right in between the branch layer and the canopy, there was a string of nearly invisible bridges, constructed in a web from tree to tree. A grin slowly spread across her face, mirrored by her friends as they, too, recognized the bridges.

"How exactly do you plan to get up there?" Luna tilted her head sideways, regarding the bridges with a rather annoyed expression on her face.

Kaleo shot her a grin, moving over towards the nearest tree. "You guys can climb, right?"

Ivory snorted. "If you think I'm gonna climb all the way up there, you're crazy." He raised his hand, a breeze picking up around him as he closed his eyes in concentration. With a sharp exhale, he flung his arm towards the ground as if throwing something. Instantly, he was rocketed upwards, grabbing onto a branch and swinging himself onto it with ease.

Luna rolled her eyes. "Show off."

He smirked. "You're just jealous. Perks of being the air wielder for our group, huh?"

Kaleo shrugged. "Suit yourselves. " He backed up, taking a running leap and barely managing to wrap his fingers around the bottom limb of the tree. With a grunt, he pulled himself up, scanning the branches around him.

Rune hesitated, glancing around at the remaining five people who were still on the ground with her. Azalea's eyes were on Nyk, who seemed to be contemplating something, Alix stood in the corner watching, Ryder was on one knee with both hands on the ground and his eyes closed, and Luna was busy shooting Ivory a death stare.

After a moment, Nyk's face lit up, and he turned to the rest of the group with a huge grin. "I don't know how to get myself up there...but I think I can help one of you."

Azalea glanced around, nodding to him when the rest of them stayed silent. "You can try it with me."

Rune's eyes traced the trees as the others worked out their own solutions to the problem, her mind mapping the branches in an attempt to decide on the most effective method for climbing.

That was when she noticed it—and was barely able to stop herself from laughing.

A few paces away was a ladder, hidden behind a patch of foliage and dangling against a tree trunk. Judging by Alix's faintly amused expression, it appeared that she had discovered it as well.

The girl shot Rune a grin, nodding towards the ladder. Rune wove through the undergrowth, staring up at the huge, not exactly stable-looking web of planks and rope. A quick glance over her shoulder at the clearing told her that her absence hadn't yet been noticed, each of her friends occupied with their own methods of problem solving.

Alix chuckled quietly as she passed Rune, reaching up and grabbing the third rung. "Work smarter, not harder, I guess." Tugging a few times to make sure it was sturdy, she hoisted herself up, scaling the incline at a rather impressive speed for such an unstable contraption.

Rune waited a moment until Alix was nearly at the top, then reached up and placed her foot on the bottom rung. At first, she struggled to get her balance on the already trembling structure, but after a moment, she was able to find a comfortable rhythm. She and Alix ascended much quicker than the rest of the group, passing through a convenient break in the middle layer of branches with relative ease. As they rose in elevation, Rune felt her pace slow, her mind echoing a continuous chant of *don't you dare let go.*

Finally, she reached the top, carefully making her way over to where Alix stood at the edge of the platform.

Alix cracked a smile, leaning back against a nearby tree. "They're still trying to get through the understory layer."

Sure enough, Rune leaned over the side as far as she dared, unable to fight back the smile that came as she watched Ivory and Kaleo hack their way through the thick branches and mass of leaves. The bridges themselves were constructed right beneath the canopy layer, so as to provide decent coverage from the sunlight while also keeping them suspended far off the ground.

When Kaleo's hand finally grasped onto the platform, Alix shot Rune a grin, and they leaned over the side to help him up. He did an immediate double take, and likely would have fallen if not for Alix and Rune's combined grip strength. A stunned expression spread across his face as he found his footing on the platform, gaping at them like they had suddenly grown two heads.

"How?"

Alix nodded at the ladder. "A little shaky, but not the worst climb I've ever done. Definitely better than wrestling my way through those branches." The playful triumph in her eyes reflected an array of emotions, feelings that she was still hesitant to let out.

Alix wants to trust them, too. I know she does.

It took a few minutes, but eventually, their entire team was safely up onto the bridges. Ivory pivoted around, muttering something to himself as he examined the spiderwebbing pathways ahead of them. After a pause, he gestured towards a bridge that veered off to their right, heading in a similar direction to where they'd been traveling before.

"That looks like our best bet. Any objections?" He shot Luna a pointed look, but she stayed silent.

The group began moving again, traversing across the uncomfortably narrow platforms. Massive trees hemmed them in on all sides, their interlocking branches occasionally dipping low enough that Rune had to duck beneath them. She stuck as close to Kaleo as she dared, watching her feet to make sure she didn't accidentally step off the narrow lane of planks.

By the time the first sliver of a white energy barrier could be seen through the trees, the sun had already disappeared beneath the horizon, leaving only a darkening gray sky and a few dying traces of red in its wake. Rune channeled a bit of her focus into the last fragments of light she could pull from the air, pooling them into her palm and floating the glowing orb that resulted above her head to illuminate the area.

Suddenly, Azalea froze, her body going rigid. "Stop. We're not alone."

As soon as the words left her lips, the snap of a bowstring shattered the silence of the still air,

In an instant, Alix had an arrow nocked, and the rest of the group drew their weapons. Rune flung her arms wide, spreading the light out and illuminating eight silhouetted figures hiding in the nearby branches.

Azalea scowled. "You again?"

A boy stepped forward, fury in his gaze. Rune's chest constricted, phantom pains in her side sending jolts like lightning through her body. The wound was nothing more than a scar—the dagger gone from her body—but the person who'd thrown it was standing only twenty feet from her, another knife in his hand as he prepared to repeat the experience.

She recognized the others too—people she'd fought, and even—her heart skipped a beat as her eyes met a pair of sickeningly familiar dark green ones.

The boy I killed.

He's here.

His whole team is here.

She glanced over her shoulder, her gaze finding the white surface of the barrier that surrounded the Nexus...and all the pieces instantly clicked into place.

They want out, just like we do.

But...I thought only one team could escape.

Jett examined the group, drawing his sword slowly. "Looks like you got yourself a complete team."

At the far end of the line Rune's friends had formed, Alix stood, a stricken expression on her face. A horrified sense of recognition was written all through her eyes, and with a start, Rune realized why.

Yellow was the team that betrayed her...and they think she doesn't remember them.

The woman with a lightning element leaned over, nodding at Alix and whispering something in Jett's ear. Rune balled her fists, her fear of heights completely forgotten.

"I suppose you had the same idea we did," Jett continued, gesturing to the Nexus. A maniacal grin slowly spread across his features, and he flourished his weapon, raising it to point it directly at Rune.

"Such a shame that your journey ends here."

49
REI

Rei glanced around warily at the curved marble walls of the room, her eyes trained on the circle of elevated floor in the very center. Gold bordered the perimeter of the glass platform, and a void of infinite power swirled beneath it, maroon and sky colored magic twisting and winding around each other in small, intricate threads.

According to Sumi, the Oasis was extremely strict about rifting, meaning that the use of a temporary gateway to exit the city was explicitly prohibited. Instead, they had traveled to one of three rifting stations, documenting their magic once again on one of the AIDs and stating their destination. It was now their turn to use one of the portal rooms, which Loric had informed her would provide a much more stable gateway and an overall better experience.

I hope he's right...

Wren reached into her pocket, pulling out a small disc—an Annex chip. She held it up to the sluggishly-moving gateway of swirling energies, tossing it through with a flick of her fingers and watching as the portal sprang to life. Behind them, Arla had her arms wrapped around Kal, whispering something in her ear before gently pulling away. Kal waved to Rei and Wren, stepping away from the rifting platform.

Rei turned to Wren, who offered her a smile, stepping aside to let Rei be the first one through the gateway. "You're the head of our mission. Lead on."

Steeling any nerves that lingered from her previous rifting experience, Rei approached the gateway, taking a deep breath before pushing herself into the swirling mass of energies. The threads instantly grabbed onto her, dragging her down and into the strange tunnel once again. This time, she managed to keep herself from falling upon exiting the gateway, awkwardly scrambling to move out of the way for the rest of the group.

Proud of herself for not feeling nearly as nauseous that time, Rei stepped down from the wide open platform, glancing around at the village. It was incredibly different from anywhere she'd been so far in the nine realms, and a smile slowly spread across her face at the powerful atmosphere.

Wooden, slightly misshapen buildings lined the tiled brick streets, their peaked roofs made of mossy shingles. The air was filled with a faint aroma of saltwater, a scent Rei hadn't encountered in months. People bustled about, paying them no mind as they hurried to their destinations. A group of young men—hardly twenty—brushed past them, struggling with a massive fish-filled net. One of the boys noticed Rei watching them as they passed, and he ducked his head respectfully, gray eyes meeting hers for but a moment before he turned back to his comrades.

No AIDs or pushy guards this time...just wide open space.

Arla practically materialized beside Rei, nearly giving her a heart attack. "Did you have a plan from here, or are you just winging it?"

Rei flushed. "Uh..."

Arla chuckled. "Me too, kid. I'll have to apologize to Sumi later for being a bit of a bad influence." She looked over her shoulder, shooting a glance at Flyn. "Didn't you say you've been here before?"

He nodded. "I've been to Adon-Bedrel many times, and its sister islands as well."

Arla cocked her head at him. "I didn't realize that the Orakon Islands were named in Aquilish."

"Yes, they are. And the central island you're referring to is known as Adon-Telrel—it is nothing more than a myth to the locals, however. It'll take some convincing to find a boat to take you there."

Arla frowned. "The Isle of the Titan? That sounds a bit ominous."

Flyn glanced around, his gaze lingering the longest on a sign hung above a shop across the road. The sign was written in runes that Rei couldn't translate, but there was a line of finer text underneath that seemed familiar to her eye. "It's an old legend. Some said that the island was inhabited by a titan—a mythical cypher that possesses incredible power," he explained for Rei's benefit. "The Phantom was actually a titan, once—one with the ability to manipulate time. It grew too strong, and the blade and mask were forged to keep it in check. The mask to contain it...and the blade to command it."

Rei glanced over her shoulder at Loric, who stood at the edge of the group and watched with a neutral expression. When she met his eyes, however, his lips cracked the faintest bit, a ghost of a smile finding its way beneath his evenly trimmed beard.

"If we need someone to take us to the island, one of the deep-water fishing crews is our best bet." Her mentor spoke up, stepping forward and regarding them all stonily. "I hear they're some of the toughest sailors out there."

Flyn chuckled. "And the most likely to do something if it's for the right price."

Wren shot a quick glance at Wylder, reaching into the satchel that dangled at her side. "In that case—I brought a few of these." She pulled out a handful of milky, opalescent pearls, holding them out for the whole group to see. As they rolled around in her palm, Rei realized that they were actually subtly changing color, shifting from shades of white and gray to muted tones of blue.

Flyn inspected the orbs, a smile tugging at his lips. "Mirage Pearls—brilliant. May I?"

Wren nodded, carefully passing the pearls over to him.

"They're a rare variety of pearl, and often used as trade currency among fishermen," Loric explained softly, leaning just close enough to whisper in Rei's ear. She thanked him, her face reddening.

I hate how little I know about the world.

"Yes, these will be perfect." Flyn handed the pearls back to Wren, who pocketed them. "Now we just need to find someone willing to take us."

For the next few hours, they traveled slowly through the village, asking vendor after vendor for assistance. Many people were baffled by the request, calling them crazy—and there were even a few occasions when Arla had to argue rather heatedly with a man in a tongue Rei was unable to understand.

Arla shot a glare over her shoulder at the widely-built blue haired fisherman they'd just approached, motioning for the group to leave him. "*Not* the kind of person you want to be talking to. Realms, who knew there were so many *vacillates* in Orako."

Flyn shot her a look. "Arla, there are kids running around. Is the language necessary?"

Arla did a quick once-over of the crowd. "Necessary? No. Hilarious? Yes." Something strange lingered in her eyes as the words left her lips, and she paused for a moment, the cockiness fading from her features.

That look in her eye—she's remembering something.
Or...someone.

Rei swallowed hard. *All these people—they've been through so much. It's just like Loric told me, back when I first came here: "Thousands of people have been waiting for that sword to choose its next wielder. For them—it's a matter of life or death."*

How many of them have already lost their lives fighting a battle that should have been mine?

She forced herself to look up, creating a distraction from the awful thought. Her eyes skimmed across the town, lingering on a large group of people wrestling with a variety of glittery decorations. Leaning closer to Loric, she nodded at the people, shooting him a questioning glance. "What are they getting ready for?"

Loric shrugged. "Cyrostice festival, most likely. The first days in each season are some of the few holidays shared by all the realms."

Rei frowned, doing a double-take. "It's almost winter? Already?"

He chuckled. "Yes. It is."

Her frown deepened, and she glanced down at her three-quarter sleeve tunic made of mid-weight fabric. "How come it's not cold, though?"

"Orako's climate tends to air on the milder side throughout the year," he explained. "Lycrix is always sweltering, and Akareldia gets colder the closer to the arctic strip you are. It's a line straight through the middle of the realm," he added at her confused expression. "The north and south poles are the hottest, and the closer you get to the midpoint between the two, the cooler the climate becomes."

Before Rei could form another question, the cobbled streets beneath her feet became mossy, weathered wood planks, diverting their attention once again to the task at hand. After a short chat, they decided to split up, covering more ground but still staying within eyesight of one another. Rei headed towards the right, her eyes scanning the thin crowd for someone who looked like they might be willing to listen to an outlandish request from a strange teenager.

Unfortunately, all of them looked at least mildly sensible.

Suddenly, a tingle ran down her spine, body going rigid with the uncanny feeling that she was being watched. She turned, her shoulders relaxing ever so slightly when her eyes met the pale brown ones of a young girl—hardly older than seven. A faint frown crossed her features, and she approached the girl. She smiled sheepishly as Rei approached, a cute blush coloring her cheeks.

"Sorry, miss. I didn't mean to bother you—but you're really pretty."

A smile spread across Rei's lips as she knelt down, examining the girl. Her ears were pointed, sticking out amidst a sea of messily braided curls. A deep tan covered her skin, and patches of silver scales adorned her nose and cheeks, glittering in the sun like jeweled freckles.

"What's your name?" Rei cocked her head slightly, a warm bubbly feeling filling her stomach as the girl let out a nervous giggle.

"I'm Andi." She tilted her head sideways to match Rei, another adorable laugh escaping her lips.

Rei chuckled. "That's a beautiful name."

Andi blushed. "Thank you, miss."

"I'm Rei." She extended her hand, gently shaking the little girl's. Andi's contagious grin spread from ear to ear as she stood up from where she sat on a pile of netting and rope, glancing around the crowd excitedly. Her eyes lit up as she seemed to find who she was looking for, jumping up and down and waving rather dramatically.

"*Tahvoik*!! I made a friend!! I made a friend!!"

Rei startled slightly at the harsh, breathy sound that erupted from the girl's mouth, taking a moment to register it as a different language. After a moment, a man came over to them, one who resembled Andi in an unmistakable way. He was about Rei's height, but his heavyset build and chiseled features still made him an imposing figure.

"You did, did you?" Andi giggled as he picked her up, hoisting her onto his broad shoulders. "What's your friend's name, sweetheart?"

"This is Rei!! She's really pretty, see?"

Andi's father—which is what Rei assumed the man to be—flipped the girl around a few times, causing a stream of giggles to burst from her lips. He offered Rei a smile that was a combination of grateful and apologetic, setting Andi back down on the pile of netting. "I hope my daughter isn't bothering you. She has a tendency to stare at people, and I've had many strangers come up to me and complain that it makes them uncomfortable."

Rei smiled at Andi. "She's not bothering me...just caught me off guard a little, that's all. In my experience, a stranger staring at you isn't a great sign." Her eyes wandered to the netting, then to the string of fishhooks and other tackle attached to the man's belt. "You...you don't happen to be a fisherman by any chance, are you?"

The man nodded, a gleam of pride in his eye. "I am. My vessel is one of the largest in the area."

Rei thought for a moment. "I'm here with a group of—friends—and we were looking for someone who might be willing to take us to a rather difficult location. We'd compensate you handsomely for your trouble, I promise."

He examined her expression for a moment, searching for a clue in her gaze. "Where exactly is this 'difficult location?'"

"A friend of ours has recently gathered a large amount of reliable evidence to prove that the lost island—the one you call Adon-Telrel—" Rei let out a breath, relieved that she'd been able to remember its name— "exists. We don't have a ship of our own, or the experience to sail it...but we do have an idea of where the island could be."

A frown spread across the man's lips. "Adon-Telrel...many

youths have gone to find it, but none have ever returned successful...and a few never returned at all. I mean no offense by this, but...I'm afraid that the word of a teenager isn't enough to convince me to endanger my crew. I am truly sorry, Rei—and I wish you and your friends the best of luck."

Just as he began to turn away, Rei heard footsteps approaching behind her. "Orrin of Itruli, heart of Adon-Bedrel...with whom do you stand?"

The man froze at Arla's words, turning slowly to face them. Andi and Rei, completely clueless about the exchange, glanced back and forth at the two adults.

"With whom do you stand?" Arla repeated, holding his gaze evenly.

"I stand with those who resist the masquerade," he recited slowly, his gaze flickering to Rei. "Who am I joined by?"

"Arla, Commander of combative operations," Arla replied smoothly, her lips twitching slightly at the instant expression change in the man's face. "And our newest member, Rei of Akareldia...the wielder of the *Saquis Mal*."

Silence.

Rei fidgeted slightly, her fingers twitching towards where the Blade was concealed beneath her indigo cloak. Orrin's amber eyes instantly latched onto Rei, his features consumed with an unashamed shock. Slowly, he ducked his head, averting his eyes in a gesture of respect.

"My apologies. I had no idea who you were."

Rei blinked—his mannerism had just changed in a matter of seconds. Sure, he'd been respectful before, but he'd still seemed doubtful of her. But now...

Is this really the power I hold? This man—who I assume is a member of the Onyx, judging by the weird mantra he exchanged with Arla—a simple introduction was enough for him to suddenly begin treating me like royalty.

"I—don't apologize, really. It's perfectly fine."

Orrin nodded, tilting his head at her slightly. "I don't mean to be rude, but...I had heard that your eyes would be purple? Or was that a quirk that only takes effect when the wielder holds the Blade?"

The raw awe in his tone—the willingness to listen, to believe whatever it was she wanted to tell him—it was overwhelming, and at first, Rei had no idea what to say. Thankfully, Arla had her back.

"Rei's mentor created a veiling device to conceal her true eye color," the woman explained, glancing over at the star-shaped pendant resting against Rei's neck—the enchanted object. "Given that she is still in training, we wanted to take extra precaution, allowing her to keep her head down in public for the time being."

One of the main problems Sumi had wrestled with the night before was Rei's eyes, so Loric had volunteered to craft her the necklace, staying up until dawn to perfect the rune. From what Rei had read, a veiling charm—even one as small as this—was one of the most difficult runic spells to perform, taking hours of uninterrupted focus.

Orrin nodded. "Of course. Rei...I assume that your desire to visit Adon-Telrel has something to do with your role?"

"The Onyx has business there, yes." Arla responded for her. "I completely understand if you don't want to endanger your crew, but it would truly mean a lot if you were to take us."

Orrin nodded slowly, glancing down at his daughter. "In that case...my crew and I are ready when you are."

50

REI

First came the pounding pellets of rain, hammering down on the layered wooden planks that served as both the ship's deck and the roof over Rei's head.

Then came the thunder.

Rei's eyes flew open as the ship heaved, rocked by vicious waves battering it from all sides. She frantically sat up in the hammock she'd been sleeping in, scanning the room by light of a single suspended lantern that swung wildly in wide, erratic movements.

One by one, the heads of her companions poked up also, glancing around in confusion. Above deck, frantic shouts rang out, reaching Rei's ears below. She couldn't decipher most of the words, but a few said in a mixed tongue stuck out to her, ringing in her ears and putting ridiculous ideas in her mind.

"WE DON'T HAVE ENOUGH MANPOWER FOR BOTH AT ONCE!"

"WHAT DO WE DO?"

"ALL MEN TO THE PORT SIDE! SUPPORT THE MAST!"

Rei sighed, knowing it would be no use to shoot the idea down before it formed. Before she knew it, her feet were on the ground, her legs trembling as she struggled to get her balance on the steeply tilting floor. She reached for the Blade, making sure that it was securely fastened to her back before continuing. It wasn't that she thought she needed a weapon, but simply being able to feel its presence, to have its energy urging her on...it strengthened her resolve, giving her the courage she needed to defy any rational thought trying to stop her.

You are an inexperienced teenager. What do you have to offer a ship full of trained sailors? Still, she made her way over to the door, her fingers finding the handle.

"Where are you going?" Wren's voice was still slurred slightly with sleep. She, Rei, and Arla had been placed into a cabin together, and the boys were somewhere on the opposite end of the ship.

"I can't just pretend to sleep through something like this," Rei told her. "They need help."

"There's not a lot we can do," Wren pointed out, voicing Rei's earlier thoughts. Arla was stirring now, and Rei didn't feel like convincing the woman that her idea was anything less than completely outlandish.

She glanced down at her hands, remembering the massive surges of physical strength that had coursed through her when she'd first discovered the glyph. *Before—in Akaidia—I wouldn't have been able to help. Now, though—now that I know who I am, now that I know of the power I possess—maybe I'm not completely useless.* Closing her eyes, she held out her hand, experimental threads of glyphic energy faintly revealing themselves and twining around her fingertips. "Maybe not. I'm going to try, though."

With that, she flung open the door, scrambling up the steps that led to the main deck. Sheets of rain poured down around her, restricting her vision and making the already heaving wood dangerously slippery. She fought for her footing, panicked cries and desperate commands from the crew members ringing in her ears. The Blade pushed against her back, her fingertips reaching up to brush its handle for a brief moment. A tingle ran across her skin, her courage restored.

I can help them.

She closed her eyes, reaching deep within her for the hint of glyph that she knew to be there. It reared up almost instantly, but she kept it down, determined to stay in control. *You are going to do as I tell you,* she commanded mentally, pooling all her focus to the tiny threads. *You empower me...but you do not hold authority over me.*

This wasn't like the Eidolon's base, where she didn't have to fear it wreaking havoc...if she let it loose now, she would destroy the ship, bringing everyone down with it.

Come on, Rei. Concentrate.

It took all her strength to keep the glyph from running wild, but her body immediately straightened, a hint of red rimming her vision as her muscles were filled with a new energy. She rushed over to where a group of men were struggling to hold a bundle of rope steady, trying to fold the sail in. Grabbing hold of the end of the rope, she planted her feet, glyph coursing through her blood. A few of the crew members shot confused glances back at her, shock filling their expressions when they realized who was helping them hold it steady.

"I got this one!" Rei shouted over the thunder. Bolts of lightning split the sky, illuminating the tumultuous oceans that seemed to hold a cold, hungry desire in their navy depths. "Seriously, I'll hold it here! Go!"

They looked like they wanted to argue, but another clap of thunder solidified their answer, one by one releasing their hold until Rei was left alone to keep the sail from tearing itself off the mainmast entirely. A man rushed over to her, shouting something in the gruff language that most of the crew members seemed to speak. She ignored him, shaking her head a few times and hoping he realized that she couldn't understand the foreign language.

Her arms began to ache, but she simply gritted her teeth, forcing more and more glyph into her body as her muscles grew weary. The air around her became thick with waves of maroon that emanated off her skin, a residue of the powerful magic she was channeling.

I will not let go.

With her having taken over holding the line steady, much of the crew was freed up for other tasks, and the ship began to stabilize slightly with the combined workforce spreading out across the decks. The storm seemed determined to keep the upper hand, however, and a bolt of lightning struck far too close to the ship for comfort, illuminating a massive wave heading straight towards them on the port side—right where Rei was standing.

Panic gripped her, and she tried to open her mouth, to warn the crew, but her words were carried off by the wind. All she could do was watch as the wave reared over the deck, prepared to crash down on top of her—but it never did. Each individual droplet was halted, frozen midair as though someone had pressed pause on time itself.

A familiar whoop of triumph rose above the sound of the storm, a grin spreading across Rei's lips as she noticed Arla stationed beneath the wave. The woman's lithe figure was the only thing standing between the wave and the ship, her arms outstretched and her brow furrowed in concentration. With a cry, she jerked both hands sideways, folding the wave in on itself and redirecting it away from the hull.

She stepped back, chuckling. "Realms, it's been a while since I've used that power." Her gaze lifted to where Rei stood, nodding at her. "Using glyph to boost your strength—brilliant move, sweetheart. You and I will get along quite well."

Rei tried her best to smile, but her body was beginning to buckle under the strain, her face twisted into discomfort. Arla began to head towards her, but a pair of powerful hands got there first, relieving a good chunk of the effort from Rei's aching muscles.

Loric's glyph joined with Rei's to create a maroon haze around them, mentor and student holding the line steady while chaos reigned about them. Arla offered a nod in their direction, rushing over to where Orrin was stationed. They talked for a few moments, and Arla gestured towards the stairwell, where Wren and Wylder stood. Flyn was right behind them, eyeing the crew with his signature blank expression. Orrin seemed hesitant, but he agreed to whatever Arla suggested, hurrying over to the twins and relaying the instructions.

Arla rushed back to Rei's side, nodding at Loric. "I've got

her. The crew could use help securing the rigging over on the starboard side."

He returned her nod, gently squeezing Rei's shoulder reassuringly before passing his section of the rope over to the woman and joining the crew on the opposite end of the ship. Now that his hulking form was replaced by Arla's, Rei braced herself, expecting the rope to jerk against her—but to her surprise, it was exactly the opposite.

She cast a glance over her shoulder, her jaw dropping when she saw what Arla had done. The woman had taken the same glyphic technique Rei was using and elevated it to a whole new level, controlling four different coils of magic threads and using them like extra arms to grip the rope.

"How?"

Arla grinned at the awe in Rei's expression. "I've got decades more practice at this than you, sweetheart. You'll get there."

Rei made a face, turning back around as the ship heaved dramatically. "Decades? You only look, like, twenty-five?"

Arla snorted. "Try forty five—forty-six, actually, but who's counting?"

Rei thought for a moment, her brain needing time to register the information. *Oh, wait...* "Because you're aquilian, right?"

"Exactly. The sub-elven races stop physically aging a few years after we reach our fully grown state, meaning that the way I look now is the same way I'll look when I'm a few centuries old...if I somehow manage to make it that far, anyway." She paused with a chuckle. "Interesting choice of conversation to be having in a situation like this."

A hint of red seeped into Rei's cheeks, her voice straining slightly from the struggle of keeping the glyph under control for so long. "I—yeah, sorry." Her eyes wandered to where Orrin led the twins, a grunt escaping her lips as the boat lurched suddenly. She leaned back further, tightening her hold on the rope.

"There they go." Arla's tone portrayed a hint of fatigue, but her body remained strong.

Rei watched as first Wren, then Wylder, began scaling one of the shrouds that connected to the foremast, the very shroud that Loric was currently assisting to secure. "Did you volunteer them to climb up there? In this weather?"

"I advised the captain to let them. They're young, nimble, and have experience with high places...especially in unstable conditions. They'll be twice as quick as any of the crew could have been...most dwarves simply aren't built for agility stunts."

Dwarves. I was right. She made a mental note of the unique features she'd observed, matching them to what she remembered of Loric's books. *Pointed ears. Broad shoulders. Patches of dragon scales that happen to be fireproof. Realms, this is going to take some getting used to.* A smile crossed her features when she realized that the word had worked its way into her thoughts without her noticing. *Guess Arla's rubbed off on me a bit.*

A shout of triumph from the crew announced that the twins had made it up successfully, setting to work repairing and fastening the tattered sails. Her throat tightened as she watched them work, balanced precariously on the mast...but the crew down below held the twins' foothold steady, Loric among them.

He won't let them fall.

Suddenly, Arla shifted behind Rei, cursing under her

breath. "There's another wave coming—they're going to need my help. Do you think you can hold this on your own for a moment?"

Not seeing any other options, Rei nodded, instantly regretting it as the full weight of the load was suddenly returned to her. She gritted her teeth, forcing herself to stand her ground and channeling more magic towards her muscles. Arla hurried to the bow, raising her arms and deflecting the oncoming tidal waves out of the way of the ship.

Rei didn't know just how much longer she managed to hold on...it could have been minutes, hours, days, even, and it wouldn't have mattered. At some point, Arla returned, but Rei was practically oblivious to her presence, black spots dancing in the corners of her vision as her physical and magical strength finally began to buckle. She barely noticed when her hands released the twisted cords, vision blurring as her body crumpled against the deck. A pair of strong, familiar arms lifted her up with ease, carrying her half conscious figure down a flight of stairs and into her room.

Loric leaned over her, gently laying her down atop something soft and whispering in her ear. She never got to hear the words, the world fading away into darkness around her.

REI AWOKE ON A PILE OF BLANKETS, HER BODY aching from head to toe. Loric was gone, but Arla sat on a wooden stool by her side, a ghost of a smile decorating her fragile features. "Welcome back. Feel alright?"

Rei sat up groggily, rubbing her temples in an attempt to make the headache stop. "What happened?"

"Magical overload. You exerted so much energy that your body simply couldn't keep up anymore...so it stopped trying. Glyph in particular can be rather draining, especially without formal training. I'm impressed you held up that long." Arla took a sip of the drink she was holding, a faintly floral scent drifting through the salty air as steam wafted from the cup.

"Where are we?" Judging by Arla's lack of concern and the gentle rocking of the ship, they'd made it through the storm— but as to where it had spit them out, Rei had no idea.

Arla's smile widened, and she stood, extending a hand to help Rei to her feet. "Why don't you see for yourself?"

She led Rei out the door of the cabin and up the stairs, the wood beneath their feet still slick from the night's downpour. Rei closed her eyes, a grin spreading across her face as she allowed the early morning sun to sink into her skin. The air was filled with the sweet, musty smell that always lingered after a storm, giving the atmosphere a fresh feel to it as it filled Rei's lungs.

She moved over to the bow, butterflies fluttering up in her stomach as her gaze fell upon the rapidly nearing shoreline of a massive island shrouded in a faint aura of mist. Salty spray splattered her face, and she leaned over the side, straining to get a better look at their destination.

Her body went rigid as the island took shape, a strange new sight coming into focus.

Covering the island was an impossibly massive, daunting structure—a dome, one that wasn't made of normal, physical material.

It was made of energy.

Pure, crackling silver energy.

That dome...that's it. It has to be.

They had reached Adon-Telrel, the island that shouldn't exist...and the location of the Compass.

51
RUNE

Rune whipped her sword out of its sheath, gripping the handle like it was her lifeline as the yellow team closed in on them. A girl leapt at her, and she stood her ground, flashing an orb of light directly into her attacker's eyes. The brief moment of hesitation that ensued was all Rune needed, slipping around the side and jamming the butt of her sword in between the girl's shoulder blades to send her sprawling.

A flicker of movement off to her right caught her gaze, and she turned, flashing another ray of light towards a boy who seemed to think he'd be able to sneak up on Alix from behind. Alix whipped around, elbowing the boy in the stomach before whipping out a dagger with a ferocious speed and delivering a barely-blocked strike.

"Rune!"

Kaleo's voice broke through Rune's consciousness, alerting her to the danger on either side. She backed as far away from them as she dared, bracing her weapon and glancing back and forth between the two attackers.

They lunged, but she was ready, leaping forward and throwing herself right between them. Her feet tried to find the other side of the platform, but her momentum was too great, sending her careening over the edge. Somehow, she managed to catch herself on a particularly thick branch, struggling to hang on as the limb swayed under her weight.

Please don't break.

Please don't break.

Please don't—

The thoughts were cut off by the sound of a bowstring, instinct forcing her muscles to move before her mind could talk her out of it. She let go of the branch just before the arrow slammed into the wood above her, sending splinters raining down on her head as her feet found a lower limb.

Rune swallowed hard, anxiety worming its way into her thoughts as she quickly scanned the area. *Right...now what?* The maze of branches surrounding her greatly limited her mobility, especially since very few of them looked sturdy enough to support her weight.

She could see the bridges—they were about ten feet above her, the wood planks dominated by bolts of lightning and fire and who knew what else. Her eyes skipped across the figures she could see, tracking their movements.

Only six from my team...never mind, Kaleo's over there. But where's yellow's last member?

With impeccable timing, a lithe girl leapt from the platform, finding her footing on a branch a few feet away from Rune. The sharp clang of metal as their weapons met joined with the thundering rhythm of Rune's heartbeat in her ears, clearing her senses.

The adrenaline-fueled clarity was like a bucket of ice water over her head, and she let out a grunt, slipping under the girl's attack. Rune kept her back against the tree trunk as her opponent closed in, using the rough bark as a stabilizer to help her keep her footing while her eyes remained on her enemy. A snap of her fingers was all it took to blind the girl with another flare, and Rune took advantage of the opportunity, chancing a flying leap to a nearby branch to create space.

The girl turned, a scowl decorating her narrow features. Spots of light danced across her fingertips, illuminating her heartless gray eyes. *She's their light elemental. Like me.*

"You're quick for a little thing." She cocked a smile, strands of raven hair slipping into her face.

Rune bristled. *We're the same size.* She hardened her gaze, an indignant determination filling her. *This is a fight. You can do a fight.*

The gray-eyed girl lunged for Rune once again, but she was ready, swiveling to the side and dodging the strike. Instantly, she retaliated with a counter-blow, knocking the girl off-balance and sending her into the trunk of the tree. Her muscles moved without her telling them to, a distant, fleeting instinct taking over as she delivered a flurry of attacks, each one just barely parried or blocked.

Suddenly, her opponent's movements slowed, her hand twitching ever so slightly. Rune knew exactly what she was doing, lowering her weapon and flinging out her hand to quell the burst of light erupting from the girl's skin. *Two can play that game, you know.*

Taking advantage of the girl's brief confusion, Rune rushed in, ramming her shoulder into the girl's chest and sending her hurtling off the branch. Her own balance swayed as the girl fell, somehow managing to catch herself on a limb about fifteen feet below where Rune stood.

Rune clutched at the tree trunk, her heart hammering. *That was close.* She cast a glance at where the girl was still struggling to pull herself up, eyes filled with pain but expression consumed by rage. Quickly, Rune fixed her gaze onto the platform, running quick mental calculations of the distance. *It's gonna be close.*

Her fingers guided her weapon back into its sheath, and she backed up towards the trunk, taking a few deep breaths to clear the faint blur from her vision.

I don't have much of a choice.

Steeling her nerves, she forced her muscles into action before she could talk herself out of it, taking a flying leap towards the bridge.

For a moment, she hung in the air, momentum carrying her right through a pocket between the branches. A moment of panic washed over her when she realized she'd undershot the jump, her arms rapidly flailing around until her fingers found something to hold onto and clung to it for dear life. She gritted her teeth as her body slammed into the side of a tree trunk, the bark scratching a tapestry of marks into her skin.

Before she could take the time to think through what to do next, a pair of hands reached out from what seemed to be thin air, gripping Rune's wrists and helping pull her up onto the branch. Green eyes locked with teal for a brief moment, and she shot Kaleo a grin of thanks, clambering up and onto the bridge with him not far behind.

Kaleo stayed at her side as she rose to her feet, and she

scanned the chaos, counting off the people she saw. As far as she could tell, the yellow team hadn't suffered any casualties, but thankfully, neither had they...wait.

Four.

Five.

Kaleo, six.

Seven, including me...

Rune's heart plummeted.

They were missing someone.

She rushed forward, a new panic completely nullifying any of her prior fears. "Luna!! Where's Luna!" One by one, her friends' expressions changed as her words reached them, a sense of dread settling over Rune with each passing second.

Before any of them could react, however, there was a deafening crash, the battle halting as a nearby kapok tree burst into flames. Two of its neighboring trees were immediately engulfed with the bloodthirsty blaze, the fire illuminating the shocked faces of their opponents. A triumphant "HA!! SERVES YOU RIGHT!!" rang out from somewhere within the arson, and Rune found her previous horrified expression shifting into a grin.

Nyk snorted a laugh, his lips mirroring Rune's smile. "Found her."

Luna vaulted herself gracefully back onto the bridges, casting a rather proud glance over her shoulder at the destruction she'd caused. "We better get out of here. This whole place 'bouta come down."

Ivory jammed the butt of his sword into his distracted attacker's neck, dislodging his grip and providing an opening. He sliced his weapon neatly across the boy's neck without hesitation, watching grimly as his opponent's body was reduced to blue smoke. "I'll have to float us down. The fire's too quick— we won't have time to climb." He shot a pointed glance at Luna, who only grinned. "A little warning before you start a forest fire would be nice, you know."

She shrugged, entirely unfazed.

Ivory rolled his eyes, motioning for the group to join him at the edge of the platform before the rest of the yellow team could close in on them. Rune shot a glance out over the edge, her stomach doing a slight flip at the sight of the dizzying drop below them.

"There's a lot of branches in the way," Nyk pointed out, glancing over at Ivory nervously. "I'm not sure we'll all be able to fit through there."

Luna's grin widened, and she stretched her arms out dramatically, tongues of flame rippling across her skin. "That can be amended."

Ivory raised an eyebrow. "Preferably using a method that will *not* burn as alive?"

"If you say so."

Comforting.

Ivory shot her one last skeptical look for good measure, casting nervous glances around him. "Alright. When I say so— we all need to jump."

Rune swallowed hard, her gaze finding the faces of each of her friends. Each and every one of them was battered, bloody, and bruised—but the same flicker of determination lingered within all of their eyes.

Just a little longer.

We're almost there.

At Ivory's command, she forced herself to step off the edge of the platform, her stomach leaping into her throat as gravity instantly reached up to claim its prey. The ground rushed towards Rune at an impossible speed, tongues of flame erupting around them and tearing through any unfortunate growth that happened to be in their way. Miraculously, Luna managed to keep it controlled, stopping the hungry element from reaching their group.

Right as they were about to hit the forest floor, there was a rush of air in her ears, followed by a dramatic jerking motion as her body was forced to a stop. The wall of air released, dropping them all to the ground in a heap.

She slowly stood, casting wary glances at the ceiling of vermillion flame that ate away at the canopy above. A slight twinge rippled through her, reminding her of the seven people they left behind.

It's all a part of the game.

Kill, or they'll kill you first.

Even so, the words didn't sit right with her.

Luna's voice shattered her train of thought, providing a very welcome distraction. "We need to hurry, before some of these trees start coming down altogether. I can get us to the Nexus safely, I promise—but you have to stay close."

"Don't you think it was a little much to set the *whole* place on fire?" Alix glanced down at her hands. "I can't use my ability anymore. There's no water in the air—none."

Luna winced. "I didn't realize it would catch this quick," she admitted. "Come on, we have to go."

Leaving no time for arguing, she rushed forward, the fire parting before her as if repelled by an invisible force. Rune felt a refreshing clarity surge back into her thoughts as her mind flushed out the crippling panic, pace quickening.

A jolt of excitement washed over her, filing her veins as the barrier separating them from the Nexus grew steadily closer. Smoke closed in on her, choking her, suffocating her—but she didn't care, her focus fixed solely on the barrier ahead.

We did it.

We're almost there.

We're almost free.

The barrier looked like any other leylock, but the energy rippling across it was white, a powerful, pulsing aura emanating from the surface. Rune's heart skipped a beat, and she stepped closer, hand instinctively raising to meet the barrier.

The moment her skin made contact with the wall of energy, the mark on her neck began to burn, an innate instinct telling her not to flinch away. Slowly, a faint purple glow began to spark from where her palm met the barrier's surface, strengthening as each of her friends neared. One by one, they placed their hands beside hers, the same light emanating from both their palms and their marks.

Finally, Nyk rested his hand against the energy, wincing slightly. The light instantly doubled in brightness, nearly blinding Rune. She shut her eyes tightly against the purple gleam, barely noticing as her hand began to sink deeper and deeper into the wall. Then, with a sound like thunder, the barrier liquified beneath their touch, Rune's eyes shooting open as her body was dragged through the wall by an invisible force. Darkness pressed in on her, and it felt like all the breath had been sucked out of her body, the strange sensation of sleeping with her eyes wide open filling her as she passed through the leylock.

A gulp of crisp, slightly sweet air filled her lungs before the darkness cleared from her vision, feeling like pure bliss after the thick, intoxicating smoke. Her form lay sprawled on the ground beside her friends—her teammates—and she dug her fingers into the unnaturally soft grass, her mind finally forming the words she'd been waiting to hear for so long.

We made it.

52

RUNE

Fluffy, impossibly green grass brushed against Rune's skin as she rose to her feet, pivoting in a circle to get a good look at the Nexus. Her first observation was just how calm and quiet it was—walking the line between tranquil and haunting. Her second was that the leylock—or any of the leylocks that she should have seen—simply weren't there. They were laying in the middle of a wide-open field, with no sign of the arena anywhere around them.

"Woah." Luna stood slowly, a trickle of blood running down the side of her face. She certainly wasn't the only one wounded—most of their group was extremely banged up, slashes and bruises decorating their skin. "It's so..."

"Peaceful," Azalea finished. Her eyes were fixed ahead, set on the steep hill in the center of the Nexus—the only break in the plain for miles, as far as Rune could tell.

The hill was taken up by a huge structure, made of smooth white stone and polished to perfection. Elegant, sweeping arches spanned between elaborately carved pillars, and veins of gold spiderwebbed across the whole building. Gilded doors were set into the walls, and a long, steep staircase scaled the hill in front of them. The staircase was bordered by bubbling fountains placed at even intervals, the faint smell of seawater mingling with the slightly sweet aromas of the grass.

After all this time—all the battles, the unforgiving environments, the death—is this really where it leads?

This strange, ghost-like paradise...is this really what waits at the center of such evil?

"I mean—I don't know about you guys, but I think I know where we're supposed to go from here." Luna stepped forward, casting a glance over her shoulder at the rest of the group.

Ivory moved to her side, hesitantly holding his hand out. A frown crossed his features, and he balled his hand into a fist, his brow furrowing in concentration as his frown deepened. "That's odd. My power isn't responding."

Luna glanced over at him, her gray eyes filling with the same nervous curiosity as his when she tried to summon a tongue of flame. "Neither is mine. I guess they don't work here." Her nonchalant tone faded with the words, a hint of unease slipping into her voice.

Briefly, Rune extended her own hand, searching deep within her for the familiar hum of energy that came with the light. After a moment, however, she withdrew her concentration, having felt nothing where she knew something should have been. *I wonder why. Is it because we're finished fighting?* A strange, unshakable feeling of doubt in the back of her mind warned her to stay on her guard, despite the seemingly gentle nature of the Nexus.

There's something more to this place...something past the elaborate temples and perfect grass.

I can feel it.

Silently, the group began to move forward, making their way towards the bottom of the huge staircase.

"What do you think we'll find?"

Rune jumped at Kaleo's voice—she hadn't seen him approach. "Where? In there?"

He nodded, opening his mouth to say something else when a realization surfaced in her mind. She froze, realizing just why the whole place had felt *off* to her—her eyes drifting upwards.

The sky.

"Rune?" Kaleo tilted his head at her. "What's wrong?"

"The sky." She echoed her own thought, unable to tear her gaze away. "Wasn't it dusk?"

Kaleo frowned, his own eyes traveling up with hers. Rune knew the moment the thought hit him, his face shifting to a mix of shock and confusion. "I thought—I could have sworn it was." Around them, the rest of their friends began to notice as well, a ripple of uncertainty washing over them.

"It's...sunrise." Azalea cocked her head, examining the sky as though she had never seen it before. "But...how?"

The memory of the strange sleeping feeling that had engulfed Rune as she passed through the barrier surfaced in her mind once again, making her wonder if there was more to it than she'd thought. *The sleeping feeling...the darkness...could it be...* She frowned, hoping she wouldn't sound crazy. "When we entered the leylock—did anyone else experience a weird sensation? Like you were asleep, but your eyes were wide open?"

Ivory thought for a moment. "Come to think of it—yeah.

That does sound familiar." He raised his head, realization shining in his eyes as he suddenly understood. "You think that time—sped up somehow?"

Rune winced—it did seem like a bit of a reach. "Whoever put us here already has the ability to wipe our memories, give us strange powers, and even revive us when we die. I think it's safe to say that bending time—even if only for a few hours—isn't exactly out of the realm of possibility."

"You do have a point," Azalea remarked, shooting a quick glance up at the remainder of the stairs they had left to climb. "Though that does make you wonder exactly what we're going to find when we get inside that building."

By the time they reached the top, a deep sense of unease had wormed its way into her stomach, the memories ringing in her mind like a warning. Azalea lifted her hand, her palm lightly brushing the door's surface. At the simple touch, it swung out of the way silently, revealing a massive inner chamber open to the sky.

Rune hesitantly stepped inside the room, spinning in a slow circle and making a mental map of the whole place. There were four doors, each one identical to the others and evenly spaced apart. All of them had swung open as they entered, revealing three other staircases leading down the opposite sides of the hill. Embedded above each door was a massive, colored gemstone— one red, one green, one blue, and one yellow. Rune inhaled sharply.

The biomes.

Each door represents a biome.

The center of the floor was taken up by a huge mural, one that Rune realized was actually shaped like a giant compass.

Each point was colored to match one of the four biomes, but the circle in the middle was white, which Rune assumed was meant to represent the Nexus. Early morning sunlight refracted off of the colored glass shards used to create the mural, casting polychromatic rays around the room. Curious, Rune knelt down on the center of the design, lightly running her fingers across the smooth surface.

Around her, her friends poked around at the various plants and sparse gilded furnishings that decorated the walls. Murmurs of confusion and frustration filled the air as they searched, but found nothing, the temple turning from the gateway to freedom into nothing more than a dead end.

"I don't get it." Ryder's voice was filled with obvious annoyance, but his usual confident air was lined with undertones of a raw, vulnerable emotion. "This is the place. It *has* to be the place."

Azalea stepped forward, her features becoming a battleground as discouragement and determination warred against one another. "There's something we're missing...there must be. Maybe whatever will get us out of here is something that needs to be manually activated...like a hidden switch, or a lever, or...I don't know. *Something.*" Her voice cracked on the word, revealing a hint of the desperation buried beneath the surface.

The group lapsed into a rhythm of low chatter and frantic searching, but Rune found herself zoning out, her focus set on where her fingertips met the glass. Each passing second only fueled the rising unease inside her, her gaze fixed on her hand yet her eyes looking beyond.

"You aren't supposed to be here. So tell me—why are you?"

"I am nothing more than a power source for the great horror you will soon need to face."

"I was imprisoned here by the same person who now imprisons you."

"You must find your way through. Set me free."

"You know who I am."

Rune clenched her fists. *We're missing something. Something big.*

"There is power in your blood."

The thought illuminated something within her, and she frowned, a sudden feeling of urgency causing her head to snap up. An energy—a new, yet familiar energy—stirred within her gut, responding to the warning. Scrambling to her feet, she glanced around, every inch of her alert.

"Rune—what's going on? Did you find something?" The hope in Nyk's voice was threaded with desperation, digging into Rune's heart...but she didn't have time to think, her mind suddenly moving at a million miles per hour.

The energy within her shifted once again, sharpening the strange sense of danger that had gripped her so tightly. Her body went rigid, her senses enhanced. Suddenly, she was aware of anything and everything that happened around her, right down to the heartbeats of each of her companions.

The response formed on her lips before she could even think through its meaning, the words coming from somewhere deep within her that knew before her mind even came to the conclusion.

"The Nexus isn't an escape."

"What?" Alix whipped towards her, but Rune didn't flinch, her voice slurred with energy.

"It's not an escape. It's a trap."

The moment the words left her tongue, all four sets of doors slammed closed with a deafening crash, causing everyone except Rune to startle. They reached for their weapons, backing in towards the center and forming a circle around Rune...but still, she remained motionless, her eyes traveling down to the white glass circle beneath her feet. An odd, alien feeling began to fill the air, the dull hum of raw power ringing in Rune's ears as a tingling sensation swept across her body.

The atmosphere around them seemed to thicken, and a low, unnatural growl split the silence, snapping Rune's attention to a massive creature crawling out of the shadows. Its entire body radiated with strength, wisps of maroon smoke drifting around its monstrous form as it watched them with a pair of beady red eyes. It only took a quick glance around to realize that their entire group was now surrounded by strange creatures, each one covered with layers of the strange maroon force. The monsters roughly resembled a variety of animals—hulking scorpions, bears, and oversized wolves, all of them moving in a chilling unison.

The powerful feeling in Rune's gut strengthened with each step the creatures took, ringing in her ears and chasing away any hint of fear that tried to penetrate her guard. Her hands remained limp at her sides, her weapons untouched. A single thought broke through, the hydra's words once again resounding around her consciousness. Even as the creatures lunged, the thought held strong, her eyes fluttering closed and a feeling of perfect peace spreading across her body.

"There is power in your blood."

"The kind of power that no one will ever be able to take from you."

53
RUNE

Time slowed as the creatures landed right in front of their group, the energy she'd felt so strongly rising up within her and consuming her mind. It was vaguely similar to the power she'd channeled when she commanded the light, but this was so much stronger, a real, tangible force that could not be stopped or taken. It swirled within her—order and chaos, power and control—working in harmony, forcing itself to the surface. A faint glow caught her eye—it was coming from her wrists, where the elaborate bracelet-looking birthmarks on her skin had begun to gleam with an otherworldly light.

She raised her gaze to meet the nearest monster's, waiting for the familiar chill of panic to ripple down her spine—but it never did. Oddly enough, no fear set into Rune's body, even as her friends flinched away with their weapons braced. She'd seen these creatures before. Even if she didn't remember where, she knew them. That knowledge gave her power—the power to control her strength, to wield it, to bend it to her will.

Everything was in balance.

A perfect, effortless balance.

A grin slowly spread across her face as the creatures paused their approach, each one rearing back to prepare a barrage of strikes. The energy within her surged upward with a jolt, the veil thinning for a brief moment and allowing a single memory to slip through.

Power is useless without mind to control it—yet mind is useless without power to back it.

The words were the final missing piece to the puzzle, allowing the energy to find its place in the natural workings of Rune's being. She and the power were one, like a soldier and his blade. Two parts, seemingly disconnected, but working as a single unit.

Rune closed her eyes, chaotic energy and its orderly counterpart seeping from her outstretched fingertips. Threads of maroon—emanating pure strength—battered at her mental barriers, begging to be unleashed. The calmer, more controlling force held it back, keeping Rune's consciousness in a state of perfect harmony. They seemed to obey an unsaid code, one that Rune couldn't consciously interpret yet understood perfectly.

A riddle.

A puzzle.

A cipher.

A cry escaped her lips as her eyes flew open, and she flung her arms out wide, her body engulfed with raging threads of crimson and pale blue. They wound themselves together, weaving into a powerful force and ripping through the monsters.

The creatures fought back against the magic, and Rune found herself slowly balling her hands into fists, beads of sweat streaming down her face as the strain of holding back the brutal attacks from this many enemies weighing down on her. A scream built in her throat, slipping off her tongue and fueling another outburst of the strange strength. Her vision blurred, but the energy only increased in magnitude, heightening her awareness. She couldn't see, but she *knew*—not even the smallest of movements went unnoticed.

No longer did she feel weak or helpless, an inexperienced girl dragging her team down with her.

No longer did she struggle to keep herself alive, to keep herself from setting them back any further than she already had.

This was her power.

This was her place.

This battle was one she could win.

Her friends were there, circled around her, impervious to the intense magic radiating from Rune's body. Regardless of the extra toll it took on her to keep the power from harming them, her determination to keep them safe made up for any failing strength. Maroon waves ripped at the monsters' similarly-colored flesh, kept in check by the streams of pale blue that had formed a shield-like bubble around Rune and her team.

Attack and defense.

Push and pull.

Again, the mantra circled back into Rune's mind, the words clear despite the haze surrounding the rest of the memory.

Power is useless without mind to control it.

Mind is useless without power to back it.

They are opposites.

But neither is strong without the other.

A dull, pulsing light began to glimmer beyond her eyelids,

calling to her—but she resisted it, continuing to push her body harder as energy flooded out of her. Everything around her was reduced to a blur of color and sound, but still the power streaming from her fingers grew steadily stronger, pushing the monsters back. She became suddenly aware of a new barrier in her mind, one that she could reach out and touch—and maybe even destroy.

There was more power on the other side.

More strength.

Part of her hungered for it, longed to push past it and see just how formidable she could be.

Something stopped her, though—a warning, a memory. It warded her away from the barrier, refusing to allow her to touch it no matter how much she wanted to.

I've broken that barrier before.

A flood of emotions crashed over her, filling her for a brief second. Screams, a bloodstained battlefield, the innate feeling of helplessness as hundreds of lives were ripped away. Ringing through it all was a single word, one she had thought herself not too long ago.

Monster.

With a cry, she withdrew the energy right as she was about to brush the barrier, refusing to allow herself to cross that line again. As the energy subsided, another voice rang in her thoughts, one that her heart knew even though her mind didn't.

"Power is what shapes people, Rune. It can strengthen them, boosting them to new heights. It can also be their ruin. Power creates nations, inspires change, and enthrones kings...but it can destroy a civilization just as easily as it can build one."

Rune didn't know she had fallen until her body hit the ground, her ears ringing. Energy drained from her as the monsters exploded into mist, tendrils of maroon smoke seeping back into the ground. She forced herself to sit up, her eyes finding Kaleo's. His expression held undertones of worry, but there was a deeper emotion hidden underneath, lingering in his gaze as he knelt by her side.

Fear.

Is he...afraid of me?

For a moment, she was tempted to shove the energy back down inside her where it had come from, to turn her back on it and the fear it caused—but a strange pulsing in the back of her mind forced her to keep herself open to it, a dull hum in the air registering on her mental radar.

There's something else here.

Something we can't see.

Rising to her feet, she slowly lifted her head, opening her mind to the tiny hints of magical energy drifting through the air. She inhaled sharply as a new memory suddenly wormed its way into her thoughts, puzzle pieces falling into place.

Rune pivoted in a circle, glancing at each of her friends. Some were flat-out stunned, some looked a bit shaken, and a few were eyeing her warily. *They're safe. You kept them safe.* "I think I can get us out of here...but I'm going to need you to trust me."

They glanced at each other, a shared unease passing between them. Finally, Nyk spoke, his voice soft yet filled with undertones of a firm confidence Rune had never heard from him before.

"We do."

She nodded, taking a step back and inhaling slowly. Aware that all eyes were now on her, Rune lifted her hand slowly, extending her consciousness to the invisible threads lingering in the air around them. This time, she wasn't pulling the magic from within herself—the magic was already there, ready to be commanded, to be bent to her will. It convened right above the center of the glass compass, and she stood tall, pooling it all in front of her.

Despite the deep, instinctive knowledge that she'd performed this same trick before, the veil kept the full memory from her, and she was forced to rely simply on muscle memory to complete the task. The whole time, the idea of freedom reigned supreme in her thoughts, keeping her focused.

Slowly but surely, the energies began to materialize before her, forming into a swirling mass. *A gateway.* She focused hard, but something still remained in her way, a roadblock before their method of escape was truly active. It seemed to speak to her, searching for something, a piece of information she didn't quite know how to give it.

Where?

Where?

Where?

Rune gritted her teeth. *Anywhere,* she told it. *Anywhere but here. Take us out. TAKE US OUT!* The final thought seemed to have much more force behind it, and the image of an unfamiliar beach surfaced in Rune's mind, put there by something else.

A thought that didn't belong to her.

"There, Rune. Go there."

The hydra. It was helping her. She focused on the image, allowing it to feed her, to fuel her. With a grunt, she projected the image as best she could onto the swirling doorway of energies, a grin spreading across her features as the gateway spurred into motion, the sluggish movement and distant sheen gone from its glassy surface. She turned to her friends, her face twisting into a strained reflection of the toll the action was taking on her body.

"Go through. Now!!"

One by one, they rushed forward, throwing themselves blindly into the gateway. A strangled cry slipped off her tongue as her gut twisted, her body finally having enough. *I can't hold it...I can't get through...*

Suddenly, there was a rush of relief, like a burden had been lifted off her shoulders. The hydra's voice echoed in her mind once again, this time sounding just as exhausted as she felt.

"I can hold it...for a moment. My bindings prevent me from doing any more—I'm sorry."

A slight smile crossed her lips. *Thank you.*

For everything.

"Hurry, Rune."

Gritting her teeth, she launched herself into the portal, the hydra's final, parting words ringing in her ears as her body was sucked away to a dimension she knew but simply couldn't remember.

"I knew you could do it."

A sensation like a thousand needles washed over her as she passed through an unseen barrier, but somehow, it didn't hurt, her consciousness beginning to slip away slowly from the strain. She was flying, then falling, then spinning, then floating—there was no up or down, no right or left, only a void of empty space and the invisible force that dragged her limp form along with it.

Finally, her eyes managed to lock onto something tangible—a light, one that grew increasingly brighter as she drew near. A brief rush of pressure from all sides squeezed her for a moment, then suddenly, the world took shape again, her body ejected out onto the soft sands of a beach.

A breath of thick, salty air filled her lungs when she inhaled, spitting out a mouthful of sand. The glowing faded from the swirls adorning her wrists, the marks returning to nothing more than that—marks. She rolled over, all strength draining from her body at even the simple motion. Her eyes were open, but her vision blurred in and out, her thoughts slurring.

Did...we do it?

The triumph that should have been there was not, however, and even as she tried to sit up, to find her friends, her body refused to respond. She lay there, sprawled on the gritty ground, the faint rhythmic thud of footsteps registering in the back of her mind.

Just as the world faded to black, someone leaned over her, a pair of vibrant purple eyes looking down into her green ones. Rune didn't care who the person was, didn't care where she was, didn't care what was going to happen—only one thing mattered, and it rang in her mind even as her mind lost the ability to think it.

We did it.

I'm—free.

54
REI

The moment Rei's feet touched down on the scattered grains of sand making up the shoreline of Adon-Telrel, she knew that there was something inherently *off* about the island. And not just because of the massive energy barrier in the center serving as a protection mechanism for a twisted operation—there was something else in the air, sending Rei's body into a state of natural unease.

"What a weird place." Arla's words echoed Rei's exact thoughts, and she found herself glancing around at the rest of her group, the feeling of disquiet only strengthening inside her when she noticed that the rest of them seemed to be experiencing the same. Loric, of course, stayed silent, but his hand did subtly move to cover his sword.

Wylder stepped to the lead for a brief moment, squinting into the distance. "The beach is long. Like—really long." He shot a glance at his sister, who was also scanning the horizon.

"We should get moving, then. If we want to find any information on that—" Arla gestured to the massive cliff face separating them from the energy dome— "we're going to need to find a way in first."

Flyn turned to Orrin, who had escorted them onshore. He ducked his head respectfully, offering the captain a smile. "You've done us a great favor. I give you our thanks." Reaching into his bag, he pulled out a satchel full of the rare mirage pearls, holding them out. "A token of our appreciation. Please accept—we have no use for them."

For a moment, Orrin was too shocked to move. He gripped Flyn's hand, shaking it firmly. "I wish you luck on your journey. And as for you, Phantom Wielder—" Rei straightened as his gaze found her. "You truly have the spirit of a fighter. I believe in you—we all do."

Andi poked her head out from behind her father's back with a goofy grin, saving Rei from figuring out how to respond. "Bye bye, Rei!"

Orrin chuckled, scooping her up playfully. "Come on, Andia."

Andi scowled, but no matter how much anger she mustered, she still looked adorable. "*Andi*," she corrected sternly.

Orrin couldn't help but laugh again, casting a final glance over his shoulder at the group before helping his daughter into the small boat they'd rowed to the shore. "Well then, *Andi*. We'd better hurry back, before your mother thinks I got us into trouble again."

Rei found herself smiling as the captain rowed away, and she turned, glancing around at her companions. "Where should we look first?"

Arla raised her gaze, staring down the beach at where

Wylder and Wren had been examining moments before. "I suppose we just start walking. Unless anyone has any better ideas?"

No one did.

The sun rose higher in the sky as they moved, the last dying bands of pastel color just barely beginning to fade from the horizon. Her boots left prints in the soft grains, her eyes flickering across the alien landscape. This beach reminded her of home—of trips she'd taken to Hawk Clan's shores, of hours spent sitting near the cliff's edge, watching the waters below— the memories flooded back one by one, consuming her mind as she walked.

Those memories were why she was here.

Why she was fighting.

They'd shaped her, built her, torn her down and created a masterpiece from the wreckage.

A smile crossed her lips, her thoughts following trails of old, happy scenes from the days spent in the woods, chasing the sunsets and hiding with friends. There were days of training, of laughter, of community...good and bad, painful or not...she let them all pass through her, reinforcing her resolve.

Her smile widened, and she glanced up, her eyes finding the barrier.

The smile faded.

A strange feeling had settled into Rei's stomach, refusing to leave her. The very peak of the barrier had begun to glow just a bit brighter, a haze settling over it. The air around her thickened slightly, only causing her frown to deepen, watching as another wave of energy crackled across the barrier's surface. It was difficult to see with the cliff face in the way, but she could have sworn that it had blinked out of sight for a brief moment, like it had been turned off...or like something had gotten through.

Maybe it did.

Suddenly, a flash of light up ahead caught her eye, and she paused, causing the rest of her group to slow to a halt and glance at her in confusion.

"What—" Flyn cut himself off as his gaze traveled where Rei's eyes were trained up ahead, realization spreading across his face. One by one, the others' expressions shifted to mirror his, and Rei hesitantly took a step closer, squinting at the odd disturbance in the air.

At first glance, it appeared to be nothing, but the longer she looked at it, the stranger it felt. It was like the atmosphere in that one particular area was thickening on its own, slowly forming into a tangible object rather than an invisible gas.

Just as Rei was beginning to notice wispy tendrils of maroon and periwinkle smoke materializing around the anomaly, Wren inhaled sharply, understanding dawning in her eyes.

"It's...a rift. A rift...on the *arriving* end."

Loric turned to her. "That's impossible. There's no annex —which would mean it would have to be a free rift. No one has *ever* performed one successfully."

Wren's response was soft, but firm, her eyes flickering from Loric to the rift. "I know it's just a theory, but—what else would you call that?"

No one could seem to find a reply.

Arla stepped forward. "If it is—somehow—a free rift, then we have to be cautious. We are in hostile territory, and have no way of knowing who might be coming through that gateway."

Rei frowned, glancing at Loric. "A theory? But when you took me to the Apeiron, we didn't land on an annex."

"We didn't need to. Traveling to the Apeiron is different—the portal simply spits you out exactly where you are in the real world, but within the dimension. A free rift is a *theoretical* concept where two people—each with an opposite alignment—would be able to create and activate a working rift on their own, setting the location in their minds instead of locking on to a physical waypoint. Like I said before, no one's ever done it."

Apparently, someone might have. She reached up slowly, grasping the Blade's handle and drawing it out of its sheath. Power flooded through her blood, her eyes taking on a violet sheen. Silently, they stood there, hands on their weapons and attention trained on the gateway.

After only moments, it sprang to life, familiar energies swirling around one another in a faintly green mass. The air began to hum, a faint feeling of being pushed on from all sides washing over Rei briefly as a figure was forced from within the energies.

The group stiffened—then instantly relaxed, confused.

It was a girl, about Rei's age—and she was practically unconscious, her eyes closed and her body caked with blood. The white flowers in her hair and her pointed ears marked her as a gnome, just like Sumi.

Before any of them could form so much as a word, more figures fell out of the gateway, all of them in similar or even worse states than the first girl. A few glanced up at where Rei and her companions stood, and one of them even looked ready to fight, but his wounds got the better of him, his body going limp against the sand. Rei felt a stab of pity ripple through her as she examined the teenagers, most of them already blacked out...but, thankfully, none seemed to be dead.

What happened to them?

Who would do such a thing?

Suddenly, the gateway sputtered, its energies beginning to fade. Right as it was about to disappear entirely, one final girl was spat out onto the beach, her form radiating exhaustion from every bone. A spark of recognition immediately set into Rei's mind, and she found herself sheathing the Blade, rushing forward towards the teenagers despite a flurry of protests from her group—Loric especially.

It's her.

The green-eyed girl.

She's real.

She approached the girl, watching as she rolled over to her back, her eyes filled with a distant pain. Rei leaned over her, kneeling at her side. They locked eyes for only a moment, a spark of mutual recognition passing between them before the girl's eyes fluttered closed, her body falling still.

Rei turned to Wren, who had followed right behind her. "We have to get them to the Oasis. They need medical attention, all of them."

Wren hesitated.

"It's her, Wren. The girl we came here for." Rei gestured to the green-eyed girl, her ash brown hair caked with sand and blood. "We can't just leave them here."

Wren contemplated for a moment before reaching into the bag at her side, rummaging around. "We'll get them the attention they need, don't worry. I hadn't expected there to be eight —but I think I might have enough." Before Rei could ask what of, Wren pulled out a metal band made of a strange material, its surface swirling with faint purple and blue hints that shifted to catch the light in an odd way. The girl knelt down, taking a boy's arm and gently locking the band into place right above his elbow.

Rei leaned forward, stopping Wren before she could pull another band from the bag. "What are you doing? They're on our side."

"Let her, Rei," Loric commanded gently. "It's not going to hurt them. They *are* strangers, though—and as much as we all trust your judgment, none of us—including you—have ever met these people before. We don't know what they could be capable of..." he paused, and Rei could tell he was thinking of the rift— "and it's better to be safe than sorry."

Rei stepped back, biting her lip nervously. "What is it?"

"Duskcanium. When in contact with a person, it restricts that person from using their alignment or other forms of natural magic. We will remove the bands after we get a chance to speak with them, I promise...it's just a precaution to keep them from freaking out when they first wake up." Arla knelt down beside the green-eyed girl, examining her wounds carefully. "This is her? The girl you kept seeing?"

Rei nodded.

A frown crossed Arla's features. "Odd. My guess was that she was an elf, using a mind ability to somehow communicate with you through dreams—but it appears that I was wrong. She's faerin—the birthmarks on her wrists are unique to her race."

I read about those marks in one of Loric's books...every faerin has a unique set, and they glow whenever they use magic.

Across from them, Wren stood, having finished attaching armbands to the whole group. "It appears that all of them are different race. There's one of each—besides the kedori." She raised her gaze, glancing at Rei. "It's strange. I doubt they met by accident—someone placed them together on purpose. Four boys, four girls, all different races—it's too perfect to be natural. They're a team."

"A team of what purpose?" Flyn stepped forward, his brow furrowing as his eyes fell on one of the teenagers' necks. "They're marked. Look."

Sure enough, each of the teenagers had a purple rectangle etched into their neck.

Wylder let out a breath. "We should take them to Sumi. She'll probably be able to figure out more than we can."

"Kal, too," Arla added. "They need a healer, and quickly." She shot a glance at Wren. "You have the temp gate?"

Wren nodded, pulling out two alistones—one arcanic, one glyphic—and an annex chip. "Yep. The chip's coded to Sumi's annex, so no need to worry about the guards."

"How are we going to get them all there safely, though?" Wylder piped up, glancing warily at the group. "Aren't temporary annexes *super* unstable?"

Arla sighed, murmuring something under her breath that Rei didn't really think she should repeat. "They are. That might be an issue."

Loric stepped forward. "Wren, Wylder, Flyn, and Rei—you each take one. Arla and I can handle the rest of them."

He reached for the green-eyed girl first, lifting her and an auburn haired boy into his arms without exerting too much effort. Rei knelt down, slipping her arm under the shoulders of a tall, white-haired boy and awkwardly pulling him to his feet. She allowed a bit of the glyph swirling in her stomach to seep into her arms, helping her support the boy's weight. *I probably shouldn't have picked one of the two people who are taller than me.*

Wren placed the alistones on the ground and tossed her annex chip into the gateway. The rift sprang to life, and Rei glanced over at the unconscious figure slumped against her, a faint smile crossing her features.

You're safe now.

I promise.

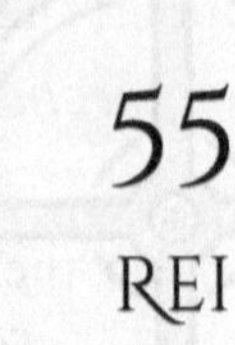

55

REI

Rifting had always been a bit of an intense experience... but having to hold onto an unconscious boy who was at least six inches taller than Rei herself brought it to an entirely new level.

The swirling tunnel of energy tossed them around, sensations pummeling Rei's body from all sides. Somehow, she managed to keep her grip on the boy, inviting more of the glyph to seep into her muscles and strengthen her. After a few moments, the vortex ended, releasing them onto the floor in the very same room where the Achyls was located.

Well—not the floor.

They had landed on a platform, one that looked to be a little unstable. Its glass surface was smaller than the other annexes she'd rifted to, but it contained the same energy, tendrils of arcana and glyph swirling beneath their feet. Rei groaned as they hit the ground, using her body to cushion the impact for the boy. He didn't stir, his pale features marred by splotches of blood and massive bruises.

Wait...

I know this boy.

He was there, in the dream...so was the blonde girl, the boy Loric's carrying, and the gnome.

The realization sank in as she lay there, her body too drained to do much of anything else. *They were all trapped. And —somehow—they found a way to escape.*

Suddenly, Marko was there, lifting the boy and extending his hand to Rei, helping her up. Frantic footsteps sounded from the halls as Castor, Sumi, and Kal rushed into the room, their faces consumed with a combination of fear and worry as the blood-covered group appeared on the stone platform.

"Is everyone here?" Sumi's voice was clipped, the words coming out in a much harsher and more urgent tone than Rei had ever heard from her before.

"Everyone's—safe," Arla panted, gently setting down the two girls she'd been carrying. Castor hurried to her side, making sure she was alright before taking the girls into his own arms.

"None of our group suffered any wounds," Flyn added, still breathing hard. "Whatever battle these children were caught up in, they managed to escape it before we found them."

Sumi nodded, but she still looked agitated, leaning closer to examine the injuries of the gnomish girl. "They need help, and quickly. To the infirmary, now. Kal, prepare your supplies— especially sleepflowers. I want them kept under until their wounds heal. Wren..." she raised her gaze to where the young girl stood. "I need you to find Enya, and bring her to the conference room."

Wren nodded, hurrying off into the halls.

The rest of the group spurred into action quickly. Sumi

poked her head out into the hallway, calling for a young man with sand-colored hair and a heavyset dwarf to come help transport the rest of the rescued youth. Despite the aches consuming her body, Rei rallied her strength, determined to see all eight to safety. She took the green-eyed girl from Loric, sliding her arm under hers and following the group down through the winding passages.

A surge of deja vu washed over her as she entered the healing ward, realizing just how similar it was to the one back in the base she'd first found herself in—except this one was at least four times the size, with twelve beds lining each wall and a door at the end that probably led to a storage room of some kind.

Marko set down the white haired boy on a bed near the door, immediately turning to help Rei with the girl she carried. Rei sagged in relief as the weight was lifted from her shoulders, watching as he gently set the girl down, rushing to help Kal grab medicine from the back.

Sumi cast a worried glance at Rei and Arla, the ones who appeared the most exhausted of the group. "You two should rest. They'll all be in good hands, I assure you." Her gaze rose, and she nodded to the sandy-haired man and his friend, offering them a smile of thanks. Flyn and Wylder had left, but Loric hesitated for a moment, pausing to meet Rei's gaze for a moment before ducking out the door.

Rei hesitated. "I can rest here. I just—I don't know. I don't want to leave them yet."

"I understand," Sumi assured her, leading her over to the bed beside the green eyed girl's. "*Rest*, though. I'm going to speak with one of my officers, figure out what to do next."

As she exited the room, Castor turned to Arla, shooting her a pointed glance. "I *will* stay here and tie you down if I must. Sumi said to rest."

Arla seemed to contemplate the seriousness of his words for a brief moment, finally caving when he stepped towards her mock threateningly. "Alright. But a *brief* break. I have a lot to do."

Castor sighed. "It can wait. You took a massive toll on your body, using that much glyph. You know that."

Arla made a face, but begrudgingly agreed, moving over to an open bed and allowing herself to collapse back onto the single pillow. "Realms, just when I thought that carrying two people—people *my size*—was hard enough...try rifting with them. Through a *temp gate,* I might add."

Castor chuckled, sitting on the bed beside hers. "Maybe you shouldn't try to drag eight unconscious bodies home with you next time."

Arla shot him a pointed look. "And do what instead? Leave them?"

Kal cast a hilariously accusing glance over her shoulder at Castor as she passed, her arms full of herbs and bandages. "I'll have you know that she does *not* find that kind of second-hand worrying attractive." She wrinkled her nose, keeping her voice to a whisper that was just loud enough for Rei to hear. "But hey, what do I know."

Rei found herself stifling a giggle, especially since both Arla's and Castor's faces went bright red the moment the words left Kal's lips.

"Kal, we've talked about this. Castor's just looking out for me." Arla's voice was ever so slightly pinched as she spoke, however, making her statement not nearly as believable. "Which —I do wish he would relax now and then—but still."

Kal shrugged. "Whatever you say. Telling Castor to stop being protective of you is like asking him to stop breathing, though."

Castor said nothing, another wave of scarlet consuming his dark features.

An innocently devious spread across the girl's lips as both commanders glared at her, their eyes shooting daggers towards Kal's figure. She pretended not to notice, setting to work dressing the wounds of the eight unconscious teenagers while humming an unrecognizable tune under her breath.

"I suppose it would be best to gather your thoughts on this first, hm?"

Rei jumped, pressing a hand to her chest as Marko practically melted out of the shadows. She had completely forgotten that the man was there, but judging by the amused expression on his face and the side glances he kept sending at Castor and Arla, he had been there the whole time.

"My opinion on—what exactly? Do you mean them?" She nodded at the teenagers.

Marko nodded, taking a seat at the foot of her bed. Rei shifted around into a position where her legs were crossed—she didn't need to lay down to rest. "Convincing Arla, Loric, and Flyn to transport eight unconscious strangers directly back to our base—even with duskcanium bonds—is not an easy task. I'm curious as to what made you so adamant for their rescue."

Rei pondered for a moment, fishing for words inside her still-muddled brain. "I—just had a feeling. A feeling I couldn't shake." Red seeped into her cheeks. "It sounds kinda pathetic, I know. Hear me out, though? I mean, I've been seeing that very girl—and even a few of her companions—in my dreams recently, and now, she's laying there in front of me. But...I never met her. I'd never met any of them before. I didn't even know that their species *existed* until a month ago." She paused, exhaling slowly. "It was just too perfect to be a coincidence. I couldn't ignore it. Like I told you when I asked for permission to even go on this mission, she's important. We just don't know how yet."

Marko listened intently, reaching up to stroke his beard thoughtfully when she'd finished. "Don't forget that you may have just secured us valuable inside information about the Compass, Rei. These people were clearly part of an experiment of some kind. When they wake, I would love to speak with each, to find out a bit more about their unique situations."

"I guess so." She glanced down at her hands. "Is it bad that I'm a little nervous to talk to them?"

"Not at all." He stood, nodding at her firmly. "You did well. Regardless of who this strange girl turns out to be, we will finally have access to a way to fill many of the gaps in our knowledge about this operation. Who knows? Maybe we might be able to shut it down." He winked at her as he turned to leave, casting one last glance over his shoulder at Rei. "I'd recommend heading back to your dorm. You look like you could use a nap."

A sigh escaped her lips...but he wasn't wrong.

Rei's eyelids had begun to grow heavy, her body completely drained from all the energy she had exerted. Standing up, she thanked Kal for her help, offering a timid wave to Arla and Castor before she followed after Marko. Right as she reached the doorway, however, her gaze found the green-eyed girl's unconscious form one last time, a strange, uncertain feeling settling in her gut.

That feeling stayed with her for each step down the long hallways, making her wonder just what secrets this girl she'd rescued could be guarding.

56
RUNE

The first thing Rune saw when her eyelids fluttered open was a pair of brown eyes staring down at her.

She startled, scrambling backwards. Something cold pressed into her arm, and she glanced down, her eyes locking on a metal band right above her elbow. The band reminded her of something—she knew that metal.

Duskcanium.

Panic began to flood through her, but she felt a hand grasp her shoulder firmly, snapping her out of the haze. The man's face was calm, and void of any emotion—but his eyes reflected a deeper concern. His brown hair was tied back into a neat man bun, though a few stray strands still lay free in front of his face.

"Easy. You've been unconscious for two days."

Rune paled. *Two days?* "Who are you? Why did you put this on me?" She nodded at the armband, fighting the urge to tug at it.

"It's nothing more than a precaution, I assure you. We intend you no harm."

Rune bristled. "Are you the people behind the arena?"

The man shook his head vigorously. "We have no idea who's behind the arena. Six of our operatives were sent to investigate it, and found you and your friends unconscious on the beach. They brought you back here, and our healer tended to your wounds. You lot looked like you'd been in quite the situation."

"So my friends are alright?"

"They're perfectly fine. You were the last to wake."

She thought for a minute, her head still a bit fuzzy. This man seemed to be genuine—and he hadn't given her any reason not to trust him just yet. A frown crossed her features as she struggled to recall what had happened.

The Nexus.

The monsters.

The portal.

Purple eyes leaning over me.

She raised her gaze to meet the man's, cocking her head slightly. "One of your operatives has purple eyes?"

The man seemed slightly surprised by the question, but nodded. "Yes. Rei. She was in the group that rescued you."

Rei.

Images from her dreams flooded through her thoughts, matching themselves up to the name. The purple-eyed teenager, training early in the morning because she couldn't sleep. A girl who'd haunted her at night, appearing in her mind even though they'd never met.

"Who are you?"

Her words...the first words Rune had ever heard her speak.

Words that felt like they may have been directed at Rune herself.

Her name is Rei.

Rune shifted uncomfortably, glancing at the man. "Who exactly are you?"

For the first time, a smile tugged at the corner of the man's lips. "My name is Flyn. I was also with the party who rescued you and your friends. All we'd like is information—if you are willing to provide it, that is. We'll let you go free as soon as you've recovered...unless you'd prefer to stay."

Rune thought for a moment. "Information about what?"

"The Compass. The arena you were in. We were investigating it, wondering if it had something to do with the Eidolon."

Rune blinked at him. Compass—that's actually a fitting name. I didn't realize it had one."

Flyn's brow furrowed. "What do you know?"

"There were a lot of us in there...divided into teams of eight by a color on our necks." Absently, she reached up, feeling where the purple rectangle was etched onto her own skin. "Everyone had a power. Each team had one person with each power, and the goal was to find the rest of your team to open the way to the Nexus." She paused, hesitating as the memory of the Hydra surfaced again in her thoughts. "I—there was this creature. It had seven heads, and it could—talk to me. At least, it could when I died."

Flyn did a double take. "Died?"

Rune winced. "When you die in the arena, you wake up in a citadel with your memories wiped again. I don't know how it works, but it happened to me."

Flyn frowned, stroking his chin thoughtfully. "And...of the free rift?"

Rune blinked at him. "The what?"

"The free rift. The portal you and your friends fell through. What of that?"

Rune blinked, forcing the memory to resurface. His words felt accurate, but also distorted in her thoughts somehow, the memories still blocked by the veil. "I don't know. I don't know what it was, or how I did it..." she paused, looking away. "The people who put us in there—who built it—they took our memories."

But I will get them back.

"They...did." Flyn's frown deepened. "Well—you're safe now, and we will do everything in our power to help you recover what was stolen. I suppose I should take you to the commanders, then—perhaps Sumi or Marko will know more than I. Here..." he reached into his pocket, pulling out a small black disc. "If I remove your band, will you promise not to use any magic?"

Magic. Like the power I used against the monsters...that was magic. Rune nodded in agreement, holding her arm out. He pressed the disc to the band, and with a click, a line appeared in the middle, separating the metal and allowing it to clatter to the ground.

A gasp escaped Rune's lips as a rush of power flooded her, her mind snapping into action. She leaned over, panting hard and choking back the energy that had surged up so eagerly. "Thank you," she whispered as Flyn reached down to help steady her.

He smiled. "Taking duskcanium off is always a bit intense. My apologies, I should have warned you." Rising to his feet, he moved over to the door of the small room, pressing his palm against a panel on the wall and watching as the door moved out of the way. "Sorry—I realize I never got your name."

"Rune. My name is Rune." She stood, returning his smile.

Flyn led her down a network of winding hallways, taking so many turns that Rune was beginning to wonder how anyone found their way around this place. Finally, they emerged into a massive, dome-shaped room, with a circular table in the center projecting an image that immediately sent alarm bells blaring in her mind.

She ignored the four figures standing around the table, pacing forward and fingering the colored mist forming the projection. "This is the arena."

A slightly older woman nodded, her pale eyes seeming to bore into Rune. The purple flowers in her braided hair sent a spark of deja vu rippling down Rune's spine as a realization slipped its way into her head.

She's a gnome.

Startled at the thought, Rune leaned back, contemplating the word. It fit, but she had no idea where it had come from, fragments of memories that hadn't been there before suddenly slotting themselves into empty spaces in her mind. With a start, she realized why.

The veil.

It was still there, but it was thinner somehow, tiny gaps and tears allowing images from her past to seep through. Her heart quickened as she reached out her consciousness, pushing against the shadowy surface in her thoughts.

Are you alright?"

Rune's head snapped up, and she jumped, startled. "Yes.

Sorry. I was just—I don't know." Her cheeks went pink. "I thought I might have gotten some of my memories back, is all."

The gnome frowned. "Your memories?"

Rune nodded. "My mind was empty when I woke up for the first time. All I knew was my name."

The gnome thought for a moment. "Curious. None of you had your memories?"

Rune shook her head. "No." Flyn's words from earlier slipped back into her mind, bringing with them a thread of confusion. "You didn't talk to them? I thought Flyn said I woke up last."

"You did." This time, the speaker was a blonde woman, watching Rune carefully as she reached up to brush one of a few navy strands of hair out of her face. Despite her fragile features, her vibrant eyes were filled with steely determination that demanded respect. "We wanted to speak with you, though —since you were the one we went to Orako for in the first place."

Me? Why me? "I—what?" Rune's face was filled with plain confusion, her thoughts whirling.

"We went for you," the woman repeated. "To rescue you. Rei had been seeing you in her dreams, and was extremely adamant that we find out who you are."

Rune paled. "She saw me, too? Do you know why?"

"We—we'd been hoping that you would be able to tell us," the woman admitted, her tone shifting.

The gnome cast a glance over at the blonde woman, and something unseen passed between them. When she turned back to Rune, her expression had softened, and Rune found herself relaxing slightly. "I do apologize. We had assumed that you'd know a bit more—we didn't mean to overwhelm you. Why don't we begin with introductions?"

Rune nodded, swallowing the nerves that had decided to bunch up inside her stomach for some strange reason. "My name is Rune."

The gnome smiled at her. "I'm Sumi. Arla—" she gestured to the blonde woman— "helped rescue you, and Marko's the one who discovered the Compass in the first place." She nodded at a gruff-looking man sitting across from Rune.

"My name is Castor," added a pointy-eared man sitting to Rune's left. He extended a dark hand to her, his gray eyes glinting with an underlying kindness as she shook it. "I'm very glad you and your friends are alright. You were in quite a state when you arrived." His eyes flickered briefly to Arla. "What happened?"

Rune swallowed hard, allowing the brutal memories to slip back into her mind. "The Nexus. We found the Nexus...the escape point," she added at the abundance of confused stares she was receiving. "But it was a trick. The moment we were inside, these creatures appeared—their bodies covered in a weird energy coating. Glyph." She paused as the word slipped off her lips, yet another memory that had found its way through the veil.

The alignments.

Arcanic and glyphic.

Those creatures—they were cyphers—physical embodiments of aligned energy.

A giddy feeling washed over her as the information returned, clicking into place as though it had been there all along. "The creatures were cyphers. They attacked us, and I..."

she trailed off, realizing that she actually had no idea what she had done. "I don't know. It's kinda fuzzy, but I remember a mix of energies, the creatures dissolving, and then I made the gateway. It spit us out on the beach, I saw the purple eyes—Rei's eyes, I guess—and then nothing."

Arla leaned forward. "Hold on. Did you say *you* created a gateway? By *yourself*?"

Rune nodded—hesitantly at first, then with a bit more surety as her mind was able to register more details of the Nexus battle. "Yes. I did."

Sumi made a face. "That—that can't be. Not unless..." her head snapped up, and she turned to Flyn, her gaze overcome with intensity. "The orb. I'd like to test her alignment, please."

Flyn ducked his head in acknowledgement, hurrying over to a random portion of the wall and whispering something under his breath. To Rune's shock, he reached his hand straight through the wall, pulling out a milky orb that swirled with a fog of dark and light energies. He carefully carried it back over to the table, and as Rune watched, the fog inside the orb began to thin, revealing a tangled mass of white threads and a few black ones drifting around the knot.

It was arcana and glyph...but unlike the maroon and periwinkle shades she was used to, the grayscale colors gave off an aura of pure power, their strength amplified through the colorless threads.

Sumi nodded at her encouragingly as he reached out, offering the orb to Rune. Gingerly, she took it, wincing at the frigid temperature of the glassy surface.

As soon as it left Flyn's hands, the fog returned, shrouding the energy threads. After a moment, however, it began to clear once again, and Rune felt something small tug at her gut when the mist finally cleared completely—resulting in a ripple of simultaneous gasps from everyone in the room. Rune, utterly confused, glanced down at the ball, her brow furrowing.

The threads weren't white, like Flyn's.

They weren't black, either.

They were all one color, knotted into a tight, unmistakable mass in the center of the orb.

Arla was the first to speak, her voice consumed with pure awe—and even a little bit of fear.

"It's...gray?"

57
RUNE

ray.

Rune leaned back on the bed, her eyes tracing the textured ceiling above her head. All she could think about was the orb, and just how shocked the council had been when her alignment showed up as gray. Frustratingly, no matter how hard she pushed at the veil, attempting to glean even a bit of information about her alignment—it eluded her, leaving her stuck.

I'm arcanic, or I'm glyphic.
That's how it is.
How everything is.
So why did it show up gray?
Why didn't it work?

With a groan, she rolled over, glancing at the door. After the test, Flyn had hurriedly escorted her back to the room she'd awoken in, assuring her that he would return shortly. It had been at least twenty minutes by now, and Rune found herself debating as to whether or not she would try to get the door open. It was undoubtedly locked, but the duskcanium armband was gone, and the energy swirling inside her seemed more than happy to help.

They saved your life, Rune.

Sighing at the logical voice, she closed her eyes, turning her attention to the veil. It seemed to be slowly growing weaker, but it still held on tight to most of the memories, keeping them away from her no matter how hard she tried to reclaim them.

Show me something. Anything.

Nothing.

Fighting back a groan, she focused on the memories she *had* regained, playing over them as many times in her mind as she could. The species—she remembered the species, yes. And the alignments—at least, roughly. She glanced down at her wrists, her eyes finding the bracelet-like birthmarks that adorned her skin. The memory of those very marks glowing faintly as she fought off the monsters slipped into her mind, lingering in her thoughts.

I remember the species.

I know the species.

If I remember the species, then—what species am I?

The word resisted her as she searched for it, hiding away while she called to it with a burning desire to know. *What am I?* She repeated, frustration building as it still eluded her grasp. *I know who I am. I know what I am.* Still, the term ran from her, tucking itself away between the folds of the veil where she could not yet reach.

She sighed, leaning back on the cot. All adrenaline had faded from her body, leaving a strange, confused mess of emotion where memories should have been. The thoughts she'd managed to keep at bay during her time in the arena returned now in full force, surrounding her with *what-ifs* and *what nows.*

A sob rocked her body, and she pulled her knees in tightly, resting her chin on top of them and closing her eyes against the tears that left tiny wet trails down her face. Emotions crashed over her, overwhelming her and leaving her stranded with nothing but feelings and no memories to calm them.

In the arena, everything had been about survival, about finding their way to the Nexus. Of course she had been eager to learn more about herself, but the thought was always second to staying alive, to fighting their way through to freedom.

Now she had that freedom. Except...it was nothing like she'd hoped it would be. The Nexus had been a trap, and if it hadn't been for the strange energy inside her, she and her friends would have been reset once again—or maybe even killed for good. They'd made it out, but fifty-six other innocent people still remained inside, trapped with no hope of escape. The hydra was there, the creature who had saved their lives and helped them break free. And she was completely and utterly helpless to save them, forced to let the awful operation continue while she hid away.

I don't even know where I am.

Rune curled into a ball, wishing that the awful thoughts would leave her mind—but they stuck fast, dragging her down like a pit of quicksand. Even the people who'd captured her— who'd killed her—they didn't deserve to be stuck in the Compass, oblivious to the fact that they were nothing more than pawns.

Players in a game that simply can't be won.
Not unless you change the game.

Rune's head snapped up, startled by the thought. It had come from a tiny voice buried deep in the back of her mind, but the words held a new, startling strength to them.

Change the game.

She was alone now, in a place that she didn't recognize. She was afraid, she was exhausted, and she had no idea who she truly was. But the game wasn't over yet. It wouldn't be over until someone won.

What if I'm a monster? What if I really am not a good person?

Change the game.

What if...

My past doesn't define me, especially when I can't remember it.

Change the game.

Change the game.

Change the game.

Rune inhaled deeply, the slightly musty air filling her lungs. She might be a villain. She might be a hero. She might be a nobody. Regardless of whatever identity hid behind the thin veil of shadow—it didn't matter.

I can set this right.

I was a victim of something far larger than I'm sure I can even imagine, but now, I have the chance to put an end to the villain who trapped me.

I am free.

Lost, wounded, afraid—but free.

I can change the game.

And someday, somehow—maybe I can even win it.

A knock on the door startled her out of her thoughts, snapping her forcefully back to reality. She watched as the panel slid away, revealing Flyn's stationary figure. Mentally begging that her eyes were no longer red, she rose to her feet, obliging as he motioned wordlessly for her to follow him.

Once again, Flyn led the way through endless winding corridors, but a strange feeling of unease still crept through Rune's mind as they walked. He hardly even cast a glance back at her, let alone speaking to her, her mind catching on to the odd behavior. Despite the fact that she wanted to trust him, something deep within her still warned her to keep her guard up, a bit of the energy she'd wielded against the cyphers bubbling up inside her stomach.

Finally, they reached a closed door vastly different from the rest. Where the others were made out of pure onyx with gold veins, this one was constructed from a vibrant purple gemstone, gleaming with faint adornments of silver. Flyn turned to her, his face unreadable.

"Rune—can I see your arm, please?"

Rune hesitated. "Why?"

Before she could react, Flyn reached forward, gripping her forearm tightly and pulling out the band he'd removed from her earlier. Smoothly, he latched the ends together just above her elbow, using his other hand to grip her shoulder tightly as she moved to resist him. Panic surged through her as the faint hum of energy disappeared from her mind completely, rendering her helpless.

"I'm not trying to hurt you, Rune. It's just to be safe."

Rune glared at him. "You're taking my magic—*again*?"

Is this because of the orb?

Because it was gray?

Flyn met her gaze, a hint of remorse flickering in his brown eyes. "The commanders were a bit concerned about your alignment—and they opted for the safer approach until we know for sure that we can trust you. As much as I hate restricting anyone's magic—especially a young girl's—I was left with no choice. I promise, no harm will come to you as long as you're in our care."

Rune held his gaze for a long moment, deciding against fighting back. She was unarmed, and despite the fact that this man had just taken away her only defense, a small part of her reminded her that he had, in fact, made good on his promise so far.

Flyn pressed his hand to a panel on the wall to make it slowly slide out of the way, nodding for her to step inside. The door shut behind her with an ominous slam, leaving her alone inside the dimly lit room.

She blinked a few times, her eyes adjusting to the faint glow. The room was a circle, with a low marble roof and sparse furnishings. As far as she could tell, the only sources of light were the gleaming veins of purple that spiderwebbed through the walls, creating a strange atmosphere. The floor beneath her feet was a large slab of smooth black stone, polished to the point where she could see the reflections of the strange violet crystals in its opaque surface.

A slight scuffle behind her made her body go rigid, and she whipped around, her hand angled to strike whoever was attempting to sneak up on her. There was a dull thud as the strike was barely intercepted by the newcomer, stopped inches from the girl's face.

"Easy. I'm sorry I startled you."

Rune took a step back, regarding the figure warily—but the moment her eyes locked with the other girl's, her body went rigid.

They were purple.

Bright, unmistakable purple.

It was *her*. The girl she'd been seeing all along in her dreams, the one she'd never met but somehow always knew.

"Rei."

Rei nodded, taking a slow step towards Rune and holding up her hands to show she was unarmed. She was only about Rune's age—maybe a year or two older, with her blonde hair tied back in a slightly unruly half-up half-down style.

Just how Rune had remembered her.

"It's a pleasure to finally meet you, Rune."

58

RUNE

"So...where *are* we, exactly?" Rune trailed behind Rei as they walked through the surprisingly empty hallways, her eyes flickering to the sword at the girl's side. Upon discovering that Flyn had reapplied Rune's binding, the purple-eyed girl had adamantly insisted he remove it, leaving Rune's arm bare despite the man's protests.

That sword—I feel like I've seen it somewhere before.

"The Oasis, a city in Lycrix." They rounded a corner, and Rei reached up, pressing her hand against a panel on the wall. The door slid aside, and they stepped into an amply-sized library, where shelves lined three walls and a massive window completely took up the fourth.

Woah.

Rune paced over to the window, her eyes widening as she looked out over the massive, sprawling city that stretched below. Buildings upon buildings spanned almost as far as the eye could see, with a strip of distant desert lining the horizon. Overhead, a cobalt sun beat down on the metropolis, the heat so stifling that Rune could practically feel it through the glass.

Rei grinned as she joined Rune, looking out at the Oasis. "It's pretty epic, right? The base is pretty much just one big underground complex, so this is the only window in the whole place. Loric told me it was actually enchanted to look like a regular wall on the other side."

"Wow." Rune turned to look at Rei, examining her closely. "If you don't mind me asking, though—who are you guys? I don't remember a whole lot about the Lycrixian government, but I'm pretty sure they don't hide out in a base under the city."

"That's because we aren't the government. Actually, we're trying to overthrow it." Rei led Rune over to a table near the window, motioning for her to sit down. "There's this really evil tyrant ruling the city right now. He calls himself the Eidolon, and he's been hunting me down ever since I came to the realms."

"Hunting you? Why?"

"Because of this." Rei unsheathed the sword Rune had noticed earlier, laying it on the table in front of them. It was a long, oddly-shaped blade forged of flawless obsidian—a strange material to make a weapon out of—with veins of gleaming purple crystal running through it. The whole sword seemed to be alive, pulsing with pure energy.

Energy Rune recognized.

"Can I see it for a second?"

Rei hesitated, her fingertips tightening on the weapon's hilt. "Why?"

"I feel like I've seen it somewhere before."

The girl frowned. "You remember this sword?"

Rune nodded. "I think so. Can I see it?"

Begrudgingly, Rei handed it over, her lavender eyes closely tracking Rune's movements as she adjusted the weapon. It pulsed beneath her fingertips, sending jolts of power rippling through her body—but an underlying feeling of discontent lingered beneath the energy, an innate knowledge of disconnection that had blossomed the moment Rei had removed her hand.

"I don't think the sword likes me very much," Rune remarked, setting it down on the table and examining it more closely. "I have definitely seen it somewhere before, though. I remember that energy. I remember..." she froze, images suddenly flashing across her mind.

Soldiers with pointed ears, presenting Rune with a blade forged of flawless obsidian and pulsing with purple energy.

The sword being lowered into a stone in the ground, hidden deep within a fortress and surrounded by hundreds of guards.

Magic threads spun by Rune's own hands, binding the sword to the stone and sealing it tightly.

No man could draw it.

No man could steal it.

No man could abuse its power.

It would be up to the sword to choose its next wielder.

Rune slowly raised her gaze, the information slotting itself into her memory as though it had never left. "I...remember."

"You remember the sword?"

Rune nodded slowly. "I was the one who sealed it."

Instantly, recognition exploded across Rei's features, her eyes consumed by a sheen of memory. "*You* sealed it?"

"You found it in a fortress, right? An elven fortress, buried deep within a mountain?"

"Yes—I did. I—" she broke off, her eyes tracing the intricate veins of the weapon as though she'd never seen it before in her life. "That's why I'm here in the first place. That fortress..."

"The *Hadoch Aril Immula*," Rune breathed softly, the name falling off her lips effortlessly. "The Fortress of a Thousand Passages." She met Rei's gaze, watching the strange tumult deep within the girl's eyes. Feelings were at war inside Rei, Rune could see it—excitement, disbelief, and even a distant look of longing...of homesickness.

This girl has had to fight for much of her life.

She looks only a year or two older than me...but I can tell she's been through a lot.

"If you sealed the sword away...does that mean you know who the guards were?" There were many layers to Rei's question, her tone interwoven with complex emotion.

"Not really. It was more of an alliance situation, I think—they wanted my help, so I did what they asked." Rune turned her head, her gaze trailing across the room and over to the window. "There's one thing I remember very distinctly, though. The seal was not a part of the stone—I cast the seal on the sword itself. My magic was sort of like an internal barrier, an unnatural energy within the sword that built up inside it over time and kept the sword's own power pinned down. But that means that the moment the seal was broken..."

"The magic would have basically exploded," Rei finished. The girls locked eyes again, a sudden realization passing between them.

"*That* must be why we saw each other in our dreams!" Rune jumped to her feet, too excited to stay seated. Memories had begun flowing back to her, thoughts and teachings imbued into her when she was young returning in a rush of color. "When the magic exploded, some of it must have accidentally latched onto you. That magic would have created a connection back to me...which is why we kept seeing each other's memories when we were asleep!"

Rei rose to her feet, pacing around the room. "If you're right...and that's why..." She stopped, turning to look at Rune again. "Could you undo the link, then? Just to see if it would work?"

Taking a deep breath, Rune reached out towards Rei, opening her mind to the energy. The energy's call was fainter this time, but as she extended her consciousness, she could begin to feel a faint pull from Rei, a distant hum of magic that didn't belong. A smile worked its way across her lips, and she extended her fingertips towards the energy, pulling back towards her. It was reluctant to come at first, but then it seemed to recognize her touch, a faint wisp of maroon and periwinkle magic materializing in front of Rei. It looked just like any other aligned magic—yet it felt so different.

It wasn't just any magic.

It was Rune's magic.

It was a part of her.

Rune closed her hand, dissolving the threads. Rei watched, a pensive expression passing over her features. "I don't feel any different...did it work?"

"I think so." Rune glanced down at her hands, her gaze lingering there for a moment. "That magic was stuck inside you. I could feel it pulling towards me, wanting to get to me—but it was trapped. All I had to do was set it free."

"That was kinda crazy," Rei admitted, making Rune frown and look up. "I mean, Arla told me about the whole mixed alignment thing...but I didn't really believe it until now."

Rune smiled sheepishly. "I—yeah."

"I mean—it's only been like a month since I learned what the alignments were. Loric seemed shocked, though—so I guess what you have is pretty uncommon?"

Only a month...how?

"What do you mean, *only a month*?"

Rei winced slightly. "I'm not from the realms—at least not the parts of them you know of. It's a really long story."

"Where *are* you from, then?" Rune tried to imagine a place outside the realms, but given the current gaps in her memory, that proved to be a rather difficult task.

"Akaidia. It's—yeah. It's a long story."

"Oh." Rune glanced over at a stretch of wall where some of the bookshelves had been cut away, revealing nine intricate maps lined up in a grid.

The nine realms.

My home is somewhere on those maps.

Rei seemed to notice where she was looking, walking over towards the maps. "Do you want to try and find your home? Do you remember where you're from?"

Rune glanced down again at the bracelet-birthmarks on her wrists. *Faerin. They're faerin marks.* She thought for a moment before responding, the veil in the back of her mind standing like a massive, imposing wall between her and those maps.

Do I want to find my home again?

Do I want to return to whatever life I had before?

But where would I go if I didn't?

The magic inside her gut began to stir, returning again to her fingertips. That magic was so familiar to her, the center of hundreds, thousands of memories that were still buried beyond the veil. It was her weapon. Her tool. A part of her that could never truly be taken away.

There is more to this power than I remember.

"I want to remember why I have this magic in the first place," Rune answered softly. "It's important...but not just to me." She pointed to the sword. "Somehow, that sword—and its other half—are connected to my magic, and not just because I was the one to seal it in that stone. There's something else. Something I used to know, or something I may have been on the verge of finding out."

Rei was silent for a long moment after that, glancing down at the weapon and then over at the wall of maps. "The Blade's other half...do you mean the Mask?"

"Maybe. All I know is that its magic feels incomplete."

"How do you know?"

"I don't know." Rune looked away. "I just...do."

"So...you can tell that the Blade's magic is incomplete—and you can feel some weird connection to it—but you don't remember anything about how you know that or what your magic might be?"

"Uh...yeah." Red seeped into Rune's cheeks. "Stolen memories can be kinda inconvenient."

"What do we do, then? I'm already connected to the Eidolon...but if this weapon is somehow connected to your magic, too, then maybe having you here could help us defeat him." She looked up at Rune, her expression an unreadable tempest of feeling. "What now?"

"We get Rune's memories back, of course."

Both Rune and Rei immediately whipped around towards the door, Rune's face lighting up when she realized who had spoken. Eight familiar figures stood in the doorway, with a slightly bewildered-looking Arla standing behind them.

"Sounds like we have a couple things to figure out, yeah?" Luna paced forward, patting Rune on the shoulder a bit harder than she really needed to.

"Don't you guys want to go home? To get your own memories back?" Rune looked around at her friends—the people she'd fought with, laughed with, and even died with. It had only been a few weeks, but they'd been through so much that it felt like they'd been together for an eternity.

The team exchanged a glance, and Ivory stepped forward, glancing from Rune to Rei.

"I don't think we *can* go home, at least not yet. We may have escaped, but there's still fifty-six people trapped in that arena—and so many questions we don't have answers for. I don't know about you, but I don't think I'll be able to just go back to my life and pretend like nothing happened." Everyone else nodded in agreement, not a single shred of doubt in any of their expressions.

"Plus, we have to pummel the dude who put us in there in the first place," Luna remarked with a grin. "*And* whatever moron is running this city. Like, seriously—what kind of tyrant has to regulate *fire*? I am *so* offended right now."

Arla stepped into the room, clearly amused by Luna. "I can promise that the Onyx is going to do everything in its power to help you...and to help the rest of the prisoners inside that arena. We do not expect anything in return, but if you did choose to fight alongside us, it would mean a lot."

Rune nodded slowly, glancing from the blonde woman to her friends. They'd fought so hard for freedom—but even though they had it now, it seemed like that fight wasn't over just yet. They could try to run from it, to return to whatever lives they may have led before and pretend that it never happened— but it did happen. It was real. And it would continue to be there whether they wanted it to or not, a very real threat to a world that was so much bigger than any of them might have ever imagined.

Nine teenagers, all from complete opposite ends of the universe.

They were different races, different ages, stolen from completely different lives.

But this game—no matter how strange and twisted—had brought them all together. *And I don't intend to just go on living like it never happened.*

"Alright, then." A grin slowly spread across Rune's face. "Sounds like we have a lot of work to do."

EPILOGUE
NAYA

Lime green wings beat at the air, holding the dragon and its riders aloft. A panther's paw pressed into Naya's back, strengthening her resolve. Her fingers were closed tightly around a small obsidian compass, the purple gem in its center gleaming with an ethereal tint.

Almost there.

"Ember, is this where you and Rei crossed the border?"

Ember let out a high-pitched chirp, which Naya assumed was a yes.

Her grip on the stone tightened—a wayfinder, Rei's letter had called it—as a sharp, tingly sensation began to set into her stomach, waves of needles rippling across her skin. The atmosphere around her had shifted from the common hues she knew so well, fogging with a strange lavender haze. Naya blinked rapidly, pushing forward and hoping that the scattered theories she'd created were correct.

Another world, Rei said.

A place beyond the peaks.

I want to see it.

I want to know.

The gem in the center of the wayfinder was glowing now, twice as brightly as the faint glint before. It pulsed with an ethereal purple gleam—a shade that almost perfectly matched the color tinting the sky.

Suddenly, the tingling grew sharper, causing Naya to wince. Ember slowed his pace, the air around them growing foggier and foggier until it was nearly impossible for Naya to see so much as ten feet in front of her. A strange feeling wormed its way into Naya's gut, the only things keeping her from full-on panic being the gentle press of Astral's paw into her back and the knowledge that Rei had done this before—and lived to tell the tale.

I can do this.

I can do this.

Just as it became almost too much to bear, there was a rush of energy, pressure pounding on her ears and sandwiching her from all directions. It felt like a bowstring being released, every muscle in Naya's body letting go of the unnatural tension she'd built up.

Hot air rushed into Naya's face as a sound like thunder ripped through the air, causing Ember to slow and hover above the mountains.

But...were they even the mountains anymore?

The temperature wasn't unbearably hot, just enough to be a bit uncomfortable. Ahead of them stretched a land of vast plains, patches of forest, and scattered signs of civilization as far as the eye could see. There was barely a cloud in sight when her gaze traveled upwards, landing on a flawless blue sky.

One thing was for sure: she was not in Akaidia anymore.

Naya brushed a strand of shoulder-length brown hair out of her eyes, reaching up to readjust her ponytail for probably the eight or ninth time that flight. Her hazel eyes traced the landscape, making notes in her mind. *There's so many towns. So many people...*

She nudged Ember's neck, directing him towards the ground. The dragon's talons found a patch of flat soil on the midpoint of the cliff they'd emerged over, providing a perfect vantage point of the breathtaking scenery. A smile found its way across her lips as her feet met the ground, and she knelt down, gently stroking the ebony fur of Astral's neck.

"We made it. Rei was right." She chuckled softly, glancing down at the panther's aquatic eyes. Faint traces of light rippled across her fur—a side effect of her ability as an emitter.

Rei's wolf, Cedar, had also decided to tag along with Naya, her golden fur rippling in the wind as she, too, slid down Ember's wing. The wolf shook herself off, letting out a low whine and padding towards where Naya stood beside Astral.

"We'll see her again," Naya whispered, crouching down to meet the female's striking viridian eyes. "Rei made a promise. She doesn't break promises."

"Rei sounds like a *lovely* girl."

Naya scrambled to her feet, whipping around in a circle in a search for the voice. The words seemed to rub her in just the wrong way, slithering into her ears and snaking down her spine like a bucket of ice being dumped over her head. "Who's there?"

A chuckle. "Dear girl...I didn't frighten you, did I?"

Naya's hand moved to her dagger, her body rigid. "Come out."

"I suppose it can be a bit scary, being approached by a complete stranger in such a new environment. I was much like you once, darling. Youthful, alone...adventurous, yet afraid of the dangers that awaited me..." a tall, lithe woman practically melted out of the shadows, her cold emerald eyes boring into Naya's very being. Everything about her was poised, elegant, and reserved—her immaculate black hair, her pale, delicate skin, pointed ears, and the emotionless expression she wore that only added to Naya's unease.

This is not a woman I want to mess with.

But what does she want with me?

As though reading Naya's mind, the woman's thin lips curled into an almost taunting smile. "I realize how new you may be to this world, Naya. But I'm afraid that I'm going to have to—" she stopped, her eyes trailing to the wayfinder in Naya's hand—and then to the wall of lavender looming behind them. Her smile widened. "So *that's* how you did it."

Naya's eyes widened, her mind skipping over the fact that this creep had just addressed her by name and focusing more on the fact that her sights were now set on the wayfinder.

If we can't get out...maybe she can't get in.

I can't let her put everyone in danger.

The woman moved instantly, her fingers filling with a pale blue light as she sent a beam flying straight towards Naya's head. Millions of thoughts raced through her mind, but instinct was quicker than them all, her hand flying up to block the attack with the only thing she had...the four-pronged compass.

It shattered instantaneously, shards of obsidian exploding

outward and leaving marks on every spectator. Even with traces of scarlet running down her face, the woman was completely unfazed, stalking towards them with a hauntingly perfect stride.

Naya whipped towards Cedar and Astral, shooing them towards Ember. "Run!! Get out of here!"

Cedar obeyed, but Astral refused to leave Naya's side, baring her teeth as waves of light rippled across her fur. Naya swallowed hard, slowly drawing her dagger as the woman neared. *I wasn't expecting trouble...and that blast...that power... I've never seen anything like it...never....never....*

Her mind went into a spiral, her stomach twisting with each step the woman took. Something told her to run, but she was rooted to the spot, stuck fast. The woman barely so much as spared a glance at the animals, her eyes locked solely on Naya's trembling figure.

I don't know why this woman instills so much fear...why my body won't listen to me...

"So many strange things have been happening in this world lately," the woman mused, her eyes glinting with a sickening enjoyment. "So many disturbances in the alignments, so many uproars in the balance. I don't suppose you might know a thing or two about those changes, would you?"

Naya barely had time to register the words before her mind simply went blank, her consciousness wrenched from her body by a blow that had never even been dealt. She hit the ground, the faint sound of frantic wingbeats reaching her ears before the world was plunged into darkness.

ACKNOWLEDGMENTS

After nearly two years of work, you'd think I'd find something better to say about this moment than simply "wow." Unfortunately, I don't think that's going to happen.

There are just so many people I need to thank for helping me make it to this point, people that are probably staring at this page and still maybe hoping that I'll add another chapter. Truthfully, I am sorry. I promise it'll make sense someday :). Annoyingly vague endings aside, I do have a lot of people that deserve recognition for everything they've done for me.

First and foremost, thank you to my parents, who listened to my crazy ideas and put up with a sleep-deprived teenager as she tried to juggle high school, athletics, and book-writing. (Sorry about the late-night sessions... I really was trying to be quiet, promise). I am forever indebted to you for all the love and support you've shown me throughout this process.

An immense amount of gratitude to my incredible beta readers, including Megan Schreck and Mrs. Cantu. Thank you for being some of the first people besides myself to lay eyes on this story, and for putting up with all its craziness as I worked to refine it into the best book it could be. Grayblood: Compass simply wouldn't be the same without all your amazing feedback.

To Ellie, Ava, and Hayley, for listening to my late night plotting rants and providing much-needed inspiration as I attempt to outline a nine-book series. Thank you to Jackson, for listening to my "big words" and letting me ramble about things for far longer than I should. And, of course, thank you to Abbey, since Rei wouldn't exist without you.

To my amazing youth group, for all your enthusiasm and prayers as I shared book updates. Wednesday nights are always looked forward to :)

Thank you to my classmates and friends at school for your endless support and encouragement—and to my friends at my taekwondo school, for continually asking if the book is done yet.

To my grandparents and extended family, for all your incredible support and advice despite the distance between us. I would not have been able to wade through this process yet again without all the help you've been able to lend me.

A special shout out as well to my instagram audience—y'all are simply amazing :). Thank you so much for the encouraging comments and overall excitement you've shown for this book.

And the greatest thanks must go to God, for gifting me with the ability to create these stories and placing so many incredible people and opportunities in my life.

I hope this book was as enjoyable of a journey to you as it was to me, and that you'll choose to join me as I continue navigating this strange and magnificent process called writing. These characters are just as much yours as they are mine, and I cannot wait to see where they take the story next :).

ILTARAN TERMS

"Slang"

Vacillate - A derogatory term, essentially meaning "useless" or "weak"

By the Realms/Realms - Exclamatory expression

Realms (Mentioned in the Book)

Akareldia - Location of Akaidia, hiding place of the Phantom Blade

Lycrix - Desert realm, location of the Oasis

Orako - Location of the Compass

Magic (Mentioned in the book)

Arcana - Aligned force of logic and order

Glyph - Aligned force of strength and chaos

Runes - A method of magic that can be cast onto objects to alter them in some way, whether temporarily or permanently

Alistone - A vessel that contains a concentrated version of one of the two alignments, usually used when rifting

AID - A device used internationally to identify people by their magic

High Races

Elves - A pointy-eared high race with four different types of natural magic. Capital is in Akareldia.

Humans - A round-eared race scattered throughout the realms. No natural magic, but an extremely high magical capacity and generally more powerful alignments.

Kinetlings - A sub-elven race with natural magic based around the elements. Their eyes change color to show which elemental form they're currently in. If they aren't actively using their magic, their eyes are gray.

Aquili - A sub-elven aquatic race with natural streaks of blue somewhere in their hair. Can breathe underwater, and there are is a variety of possible natural magic they can possess.

Faerin - A sub-human race with unique birthmarks around their wrists that glow when they use magic. Shadow-like natural magic.

Jurori - A sub-human race that lives for exactly a century. They have a diamond on the back of their necks that fills in as they get closer to death. Naturally adept runic mages.

Kedori - A sub-human race that has been confined to Akaidia since the Centennial War. Natural bond magic.

Gnomes - A pointy-eared race with natural flowers or leaves growing somewhere in their hair. Persuasion, plant, and healing magic is all possible.

Dwarves - A pointy-eared race with patches of fireproof dragon scales somewhere on their body. Natural earth and/or fire magic, can see in the dark.

ABOUT THE AUTHOR

Samantha Raymer is a teenage author from north Texas who loves puzzles, dragons, and excruciating plot twists. She self-published her first book at the age of twelve, marking her entrance into the writing world. Now she works to expand her universe of stories, and is always ready to reach higher with each new book released. When she's not working on her latest project, preventing her two adorable puppies from eating her laptop, or doing homework, she's at her taekwondo school, training.

For news and to see more books by this author, you can visit saraymer.com or check her out on instagram: @saraymer.author

'Tis a most foreboding rhyme
A story told, long lost to time
Of mind and power, a line does fade
The balance tilts, a choice is made

And so it has begun...